Seconds to Act

STEPHANIE FLYNN

Small Fish Publishing
USA

First edition
Cover design by Stephanie Flynn
ISBN eBook: 9781952372018
ISBN paperback: 9781952372452
ISBN hardcover: 9781952372186
ISBN large print edition: 9781952372100

Special Note

Time travel is real.
For a few short hours, you will be transported to 1852
and back again.
Enjoy the ride.

Chapter 1
Present Day, Green Bay, Wisconsin

"YOUR ROCK SMASHES MY scissors," April McCall said dryly from losing this round of her favorite argument-breaking game of rock, paper, scissors. Behind the high reception desk at Animal Care of Wisconsin, her knees touched her co-worker Becca's as they played in rolling office chairs. Someone was about to get some fresh air. April was itching to get out of her brother's stuffy clinic.

"I win," Becca announced with a broad grin.

April exaggerated a sigh. "You did, so the loser gets the mail, and that's me."

Becca scoffed playfully. "Winner chooses who gets the mail and the winner says: I'll get it." Becca leaned forward and the chair creaked. She paused in motion as if deciding whether the effort was worth it. Becca was happily married and very close to the due date with her first child.

April laughed and teased. "How about we race for it?"

Becca's face pinched as if she'd gotten kicked again, and she leaned back. She belly-laughed, shaking her enormous swell. Her hands protectively covered it and smoothed the fresh wrinkles in her scrub top. "Go then. With only a few weeks left, my knees aren't in the mood."

April dashed around the vast reception desk and through the pair of double glass doors. Getting the mail wasn't that exciting, but fresh air on a sunny May morning in Wisconsin was worth it. She pulled in a deep breath and rubbed her upper arms. Her lungs appreciated the cool breeze even if her insides shrank from the icy chill. She strolled across the near empty parking lot and pulled down the back door of the mailbox. Bills and more bills. Sometimes April worried about Mathew's finances, but she trusted her big brother to keep everything together. April closed the mailbox door and turned on her heels.

Fastened to a corner of the converted log cabin's exterior was a pitted and dented steel plaque engraved with 1841, and she was glad when Mathew had remodeled, he hadn't removed the original address plate.

An animal control van sped into the parking lot and rolled up to the clinic's side door. April released a deep sigh. It would be another one of those days. She jogged back inside and tossed the stack of bills on Mathew's office desk. She returned to her seat next to Becca and lifted her steaming cup of coffee to her lips. Her eyes caught on the outdated granny-style wallpaper. Mathew'd had a tight budget for the remodel, so something had to give.

"Loser," Becca mumbled.

April's snort almost caused her coffee to declare open warfare on her nasal passages. She set the cup down. "Someone's grumpy about winning."

Becca cracked a smile and shifted her weight on the chair while typing away at her computer.

The phone rang and Becca answered it at the same time the next customer on the schedule stepped inside, so April scooted around the desk to help the elderly lady with the heavy door. "Welcome to Animal Care of Wisconsin, Mrs. Tanner."

"Oh, thank you, dear. Captain here needs to see Dr. McCall for a tummy ache."

April returned to the computer and clicked a few buttons to begin checking her in. "I see that here in his file. Have Captain step onto the scale." The little Pekingese hopped in circles while his owner attempted to sweet-talk him into position.

After a whole painful minute, April lifted the little dog onto the platform herself. "Ten pounds. I'll update his record. Please have a seat and the doctor will be right with you."

The Pekingese hopped off the doggy scale and shuffled alongside Mrs. Tanner, nails ticking across the hardwood. April returned to her seat and sipped her slightly less-steamy coffee, grateful for the warmth thawing her chilled insides. She glanced at the fireplace she'd whitewashed from its previous red brick and silently demanded it heat the cabin. Mathew always said no because it was a fire hazard. Something else about insurance, too.

The sharp scent of antiseptic blew aside the rustic headiness. She started the countdown in her head—three, two, one—and the door to the operating room opened as if by telekinesis. April shook her head and smiled. Mathew, clinic veterinarian and big brother, poked his masked head out and said, "I need an assistant STAT, please."

April spun in her chair to Becca, wishing to play rock, paper, scissors again, but with Becca's condition, April volunteered again. "I'll take this case."

"Thanks. I owe you one." Becca rubbed her swollen belly.

"That's what you said yesterday and the day before, and the day before that, and..." April trailed off with a wink.

"How about donuts? A peace offering."

"Accepted."

Becca shook her head with a grin and tapped away on her smartphone, probably making a reminder note.

April covered her clothes with a paper gown, which she tied behind her neck, slipped on paper shoe liners, and covered her head in a blue surgical hairnet. She stuck her hands under the stainless steel commercial sink faucet and stepped on the foot pedals to turn the water on. "What do we have today, Matty?" she called over her shoulder while vigorously scrubbing soap all over her hands and forearms. The bright sterile lights reflected on the shiny stainless, and behind her, Mathew lined up instruments on a tray.

"Bring him here," Mathew said.

The animal control worker unloaded a leaking, matted mutt onto the table with care.

April hated being in here, because it meant poor animals were in distress and blood was involved, but she helped her big brother anyway.

On the operating table was today's emergency case, a twenty-pound dog so messy April couldn't determine its breed. Its tail thumped around even though it was bleeding and had to be in severe pain. Her stomach roiled while her heart broke. As Mathew held the mask of isoflurane to its face, its whimpers and tail movements petered out. Poor thing had spirit.

April released a few deep breaths to steady her hands and shaved the fur around the bleeding sites. Mathew intubated the mangled dog.

"Can you do this, meatball?" Mathew asked her, using a nickname from childhood, one of few pleasant memories they shared.

Her hands shook, cutting sloppy lines in the fur as she watched the blood pump in rhythm to its heartbeat. "What happened to this poor pup?"

"Stray, hit by a car. The driver called it in. Can you get those cuts sutured? I'll work on this large gash here."

"Thanks, Doc!" The animal control lady yelled while leaving.

Mathew nodded in acknowledgement, and she closed the access door behind her.

Blood rolled down the fur and dripped onto the table. A flashback to blood speckled all over the kitchen knotted April's stomach—no, not right now. She blocked the images and exhaled a deep breath to center herself. April swabbed the site with Betadine. Her shaky hands threaded the needle and nylon in and out of the split skin. The sooner she accomplished the task, the sooner it would be over.

April had sutured animal wounds many times, and ever since her mother's accident, her stomach twisted while her head floated at the sight of blood. Which would she succumb to first today? At this point the jury was out, but from experience—her stomach, which would force her to rush to the utility waste bin where her last meal would return to say 'hello'. Not something she wanted to think about right now. Being a surgeon was not in her future, or a veterinarian. That eliminated two distinct career options but left twelve thousand more to pick from. Some progress was better than none.

Mathew snipped off a line of thread and began a new one. "Head or stomach today?"

April chuckled through the paper mask. He knew her too well. "Just the stomach so far."

"Great. Don't need you cracking your head on the tile. Insurance really frowns upon that. If you need to take a break and vomit, can you wait until after this little pup's blood is no longer pumping out?"

April groaned. "You're not helping."

Mathew laughed. "Lighten up, kid. Hey, Artstreet is coming up soon. Planning on going this year?"

"I don't know if I like art anymore," April hedged. She'd long since abandoned her drawing pencils.

Her brother made a noise of disbelief. "I think you should be a vendor this year. Whip up a few portraits and make me proud."

April narrowed her eyes at him. "You never hung any of my portraits at your apartment."

"I can't put holes in the walls," he countered.

"You don't *own* any of my portraits," April pressed.

"Got me there." Mathew tied off his suture line, snipped it free, and threaded a new piece of nylon through the tiny needle hole.

"Tell you what—make one for me, and I promise to hang it. Security deposit or not."

"Art isn't exactly a high-paying career," she said, still not ready to pick up the pencils yet.

"That's why they call it a hobby."

April frowned. "You're so annoying sometimes."

Her brother laughed. "I know this isn't the career you planned, but I am truly grateful you're here."

"I couldn't let Becca do it. The smell alone would trigger her morning sickness." April snipped her line and started a new one. The poor pup had so many lacerations.

"That's not what I meant," Mathew said and paused. "You need to let it go, meatball. You couldn't control Mom's or Dad's actions, and you survived. I'm proud of you. But now you need to look out for yourself."

April scoffed. "I know what Mom and Dad did, and I didn't come back here for a pep talk." Mathew believed she was only working here to help him out, and he was right. But she couldn't abandon her brother, her only family. Sure, her parents still breathed. Mom had moved across the country and decided the McCalls were strangers. Dad had drunk himself into assisted living. They were dead to April.

"Hey," he said, capturing her eyes. April paused her suturing. "Thank you for your help. I know how much you struggle. Can you promise me one thing?"

She waited for him to continue.

"If you ever find something that truly makes you happy, will you just do it? Ignore what everyone else thinks. Use this." He pressed a gloved pinkie finger against the paper gown over her heart. "Not this." He pointed at her temple.

She unwound a length of thread and resumed the sutures. That was terrible advice. Her lack of career path was because she was thinking with her head, but if she made all her choices with her heart as Mathew suggested, then she would've been a starving artist. How was that any better? Bills didn't pay themselves. At least not yet.

Unless he wasn't talking about careers. Did Mathew know something she didn't about her boyfriend? Levi seemed fine when she texted him this morning. He didn't mention anything out of the ordinary.

April squinted at Mathew in annoyance and piled on the sarcasm. "That's great advice. From this moment, I'll ignore what everyone else thinks, Matty." April would leave her brother when she was ready, and fat chance it would ever happen.

Mathew finished stitching the nicked artery and started closing the protective layer.

April began scooping her needle and thread through the final laceration.

"I don't mean for you to ignore what I say. Kid, I'm only looking out for your best interests. You must know that by now."

Her pride refused to admit he was right, and anger flashed through her veins. "I don't want to hear your opinions on my life. Stop treating me like a child."

Mathew brought the staple gun to the skin to finish closing the gash on the mutt's throat. April leaned over and pressed the halves of the skin together for him. Mathew stapled a series of metal bars like a zipper across the dog's flesh with loud cah-thunk cah-thunks.

"I'm giving you advice whether you want to hear it or not." His sharp voice and bold blue eyes pierced her. He was always supportive and helpful, but she'd rejected his pushing. "You can be such a brat sometimes. Do you hear yourself? I want you to be happy, to be selfish for once, and you blow me off like I'm..." he trailed off.

She dared him to finish the sentence. "Say it."

"Like I'm Mom." He blew out a frustrated breath, puffing out his paper mask.

April's vision blurred with tears. She predicted what he would say, but she hadn't braced herself for how much it hurt. "I didn't mean..." she trailed off, not trusting her voice to stay steady.

Her stomach twisted with a sharp spike.

April hurried to snip the last suture free of the needle. She dropped it on the tray, and rushed to the trash bin where she balled up her protective covering and tossed it away. She pushed through the door and dashed straight into the bathroom, ignoring Becca and the patients, and grabbed a fistful of tissues.

Chapter 2
1852, Bridgeport, Wisconsin

At Stanton's Spirits, the best and only bar in this growing settlement town along the swift and broad Fox River, Sam Hartley dismounted his horse and pushed through the heavy door. Normally, Lloyd Stanton, owner and sole employee, propped the door open during the summer months to be more inviting, but the drought this year caused dust to form a sticky haze over the town, and Lloyd wanted to minimize the cleaning. The darkness left the interior dim and suffocating, just like his reason for being here today. Once this bar was his favorite social place, and Lloyd his best friend, but now...

Sam's weight creaked the wooden floors, and he flexed his calloused hands—remnants of a beloved skill he no longer had the freedom to enjoy. His own word choice paused his thoughts. Freedom... Something so precious he'd taken it for granted, and now it was gone. That was why he'd come to Stanton's Spirits this morning.

Lloyd had decorated the walls with black and white photographs of the town and a few abstract paintings by Hannah Smith, the schoolteacher. Sam admired her use of color, but he didn't have the patience for a gentle dabbling of a brush. He preferred a much more physical medium for art.

Unlit candles decorated small round tables, and the overhead gas lamp fixtures hung a wee too low for Sam's comfort. It reminded him of the cramped quarters when he was a lad in Ireland. He didn't remember much of his homeland, but the anxiety of tight quarters would always follow him around. That was why he insisted on a large home with spacious land here in America. Mam and Da dismissed his input, but the family still built exactly what Sam needed.

And now it was up to Sam to do whatever necessary to keep it, even if he hated it. But his unfortunate circumstances didn't need to sully his friend's day. Lloyd cleaned a mug in his hands behind the bar. His lips pressed together, and his strong back stiffened. Sam hated Mondays. He was sure Lloyd did too.

Sam hooked his thumbs into the belt loops of his trousers and put on a smile to make this a wee bit more tolerable. Typically, there weren't any customers this early in the day, which was when Sam preferred to make his collections. The less the public saw, the better.

As the only customer, Sam chose the prime seat at the bar, directly in front of Lloyd. The slightly elder bar owner and Sam shared a similar history of struggle before settling in Bridgeport, Wisconsin. Lloyd was from one of the southern states where Lloyd, too, grappled with freedom. Clearly having succeeded, the quiet man never said much about it, and he didn't have the intonation of the south either. Sam sensed Lloyd tried hard to fit in, just like Sam suppressed his own accent. When the Hartleys had first arrived, schoolchildren teased Sam, so he used his fists to set them straight and keep his little sister Sarah safe. But their words stuck with him.

"Good day, Lloyd. How's your Monday going?" Sam asked, digging deep for that casual friendliness to set Lloyd at ease.

Lloyd replaced a glass and picked up another one. "It's Monday, Sam. Same as always, especially now that you're here."

"Oh, come on. You love seeing me. This face right here is what you waited all weekend for." Sam grinned, tilting his head.

Lloyd's composure cracked, and he shook his head with a chuckle.

"That's what I needed," Sam said. "Now just because this Monday is the same as the last, doesn't mean we'll be doing this forever. I will put an end to Gabriel Grignon."

"That is what you said last week," Lloyd said with a half-smile and continued cleaning the mug.

"Seven businesses, seven owners, nineteen hundred citizens, all under the rule of one man and his band of miscreants. Why can't almost two thousand men, women, and children just say, 'No more'? What will be necessary for them to step out from under his rule, to stand up for their freedom? I tell you"—Sam paused and leaned closer as if sharing a secret—"as soon as I figure it out."

"How am I supposed to take you seriously when you're a mirror of your little sister?" Lloyd smiled at the mug in his hands, perhaps not meaning to speak at all.

"What about Sarah?" Sam asked, dropping his levity at once.

Lloyd started at her name. "I only meant, why don't you end the tyranny yourself? Why haven't you stopped doing Grignon's bidding? You're young, strong, and a well-respected man of this town. And yet, here you are."

Sam couldn't read Lloyd's dark features, beyond the disappointment of Sam's errand. "The last time I took a stand against him and his mercenaries..." Sam trailed off, suppressing the nightmare of his wife. His stomach curdled, and he fought the emotion from clogging his throat. "You know what happened to Isabel. Who would he choose next? I tell you. If I refuse Grignon again, he will go after Sarah. I can't be responsible for anyone else becoming a statement for my insubordination. Especially not my sister."

Lloyd reached under the bar and brought up a thick envelope and dropped it on the surface. "This week's payment as ordered."

Sam stared at it with disgust, not wanting to touch dirty money.

Lloyd settled a heavy glass on the scratched and dinged wood bar in front of him—a tall mug of beer. "On the house."

Sam finished off the heady brew with four generous swallows and set the glass back down. "Thanks, man. I owe you one."

"Listen," Lloyd said. "If you're ever serious about getting something started around here, count me in."

The front door swung wide, bathing the dim quarters in daylight.

"Good morning, gents." Jaime Perez and his unmistakable tinny voice joined their small party.

Sam spun on the stool and smiled. "Dashing today as usual, Jaime. How are things going for you?"

The short man with black curly hair poking out from under his hat strolled up to the bar. His face was smooth with a life of ease. Jaime hadn't dealt with struggle like he and Lloyd had, and one could assume some of Jaime's character was from lack of building it. But Sam wasn't jealous of his brother-in-law. He and Jaime remained good friends even after Grignon got his hands on Jaime's sister, Isabel. Jaime Perez, after spinning out of control for a while processing his grief, didn't blame Sam for what happened to her. Sam appreciated that maturity in the younger man, and they'd only grown closer because of it.

Jaime reached out and grasped Sam's hand and clapped backs with him. "Did you hear about farmer Joseph?"

Lloyd leaned forward against the bar. "Word hasn't reached us. What happened?"

Jaime lit up with the town gossip. "At Common Square last night, they left him hanging only long enough to get the job done. Ross cut the body down, and everyone kept it quiet."

Lloyd frowned. "What did Joseph do?"

Jaime shrugged. "Lots of speculation, no confirmation."

Sam didn't ask. He knew enough. Farmer Joseph must've been dodging toll payment on his way to the market in Astor, the town across the Fox River. Grignon's men must've caught him during the night trying to sneak across the bridge. "That's a bloody shame," Sam said.

"Joseph's widow is understandably distraught," Jaime explained. "So Marisol brought her a loaf of bread."

"Your sister is a kind woman," Sam said and caught Jaime's eyes flashing to the envelope on the bar. Time to finish his day's work. Sam thanked Lloyd for the drink, tucked the envelope into his breast pocket, and nodded to Jaime. "I must be going. Good day."

Sam pushed through the door and cherished the summer sun's heat warming his face. He was grateful for the beer, because he would need it to survive the day. Sam mounted his horse and with a quick jab, sent the beast trotting north to the dreaded estate of Gabriel Grignon.

Chapter 3
Present Day, Green Bay, Wisconsin

APRIL BLEW HER NOSE and tossed the tissue into the trash. She didn't want to be reminded of their parents. She didn't want to be told she was wasting her life working for her brother, but there was nothing else she fathomed doing until she knew he would be okay. Mathew was all she had.

Light tapping on the door interrupted her temporary reprieve from judgment. That would be Becca. "April? Levi is here." She used a soothing voice, almost apologetic.

Crap.

Checking the bathroom mirror, April's face was a mess. She yanked another tissue, blotted her eyes, sniffled, and snorted. She couldn't leave Becca stranded at the desk for too long, but now she had Levi to deal with. She plastered a fake smile on her face and stepped out to see her boyfriend.

Levi wore his usual black suit. The tie flavor of the day—mustard. He held a bouquet of spring flowers in pinks, purples, and whites in his hands. The big smile on his boyishly good-looking face was comforting. "These are for you," he said, handing her the scented mix.

April set the heavy vase down by her keyboard and buried her nose for a deep whiff. "These are beautiful. Thank you."

"And this here is for tomorrow night." He slid a white envelope on the counter toward her.

"What's this?" April opened it with curious fingers, while Levi waited for her reaction. She wasn't sure what to expect, since there wasn't any holiday or gift-giving occasion coming up. She slid the papers free. Tickets to a gig at the local casino wasn't what she expected. She read aloud, "Purely Plaid."

Levi's favorite local country band. She would rather get a root canal than listen to country music. And making her see a live gig she couldn't escape—she would welcome an infected root canal with open arms. At least she'd get a day of eating soft junk foods and watching television.

"Tomorrow night is a little short notice, no?" Her clear disappointment didn't falter Levi's grin.

"I'll pick you up just before." Not a question, just a statement.

"But Levi," she protested. "We saw Purely Plaid last month. Are they playing new music?"

"You'll be able to sing along this time."

There was logic in that—disappointing logic. "But—"

"Hey, no 'buts'. It's going to be fun. I promise you a night you'll never forget."

April pressed her lips thin. How could she escape a miserable repeat of Purely Plaid? By not hearing it at all. An idea struck and April grinned. "Levi, can I bring—?"

"No," Levi cut her off with a light tone as if an adult refused a child candy for dinner. "Whatever it is, the answer is no. Trust me."

Headphones. Earmuffs. Ear plugs. None of those things would offend anyone, but the night would be tolerable for her. If a silly gig made him happy, she would go. Besides, she did trust him to make it a memorable night, and relationships were about compromise. "Okay, but can we go to Artstreet next week?"

Levi scratched his chin. "I'll think about it, but it's not likely to happen."

She bit her tongue before asking why. It was just one quiet afternoon.

A gown-free Mathew came out of the surgical suite and fist-bumped with Levi. "How's it going, man?"

"I just brought her the tickets." Levi's grin was back in position.

"Really?" Mathew smiled and winked at April. Did he know about Levi subjecting her to torture? She wouldn't be surprised. April was grateful Becca didn't pile on too. Perhaps she should set a few things straight before she ran herself ragged making everyone happy.

Tomorrow. Yeah, tomorrow would be a better time.

"You kids have a great night," Mathew said. April frowned at being called a kid. She was twenty-five years old and only four years younger than her brother.

Levi leaned over and gave her a peck on the lips. "I have to get back to work." He dashed out the door, charged with excitement.

Levi didn't ask about her messy face, the dirty tissue in her hand, or how she was feeling. He was busy though. Pleasantly predictable, but always busy. April turned to her brother. "I'm glad you like Levi. He's looking for a date. You want to see Purely Plaid tomorrow?"

Mathew laughed. "Not a chance. Country's not my thing. Besides, the show sold out weeks ago. You'll love it."

Levi'd had the tickets for weeks! He should've asked her. Why did everyone assume they knew what she liked more than she did? It was infuriating.

Becca called the next patient, and Mathew walked ahead to the exam room, holding the door open for two elderly females, a woman in desperate need of a haircut and her Yorkshire terrier.

April sighed and plopped onto her chair. She gave the flowers the evil-eye, waiting for them to recoil in shame. They didn't. April muttered an angry curse under her breath and inhaled the exotic scent again.

"That sounded like a tough case in there," Becca said.

"Yeah. It really was." April absently stared out the window at the parking lot, where Levi had just left.

"Is the pup going to make it?" Becca asked.

How did April end up miserably working for her ungrateful brother while dating a guy who didn't know her at all? Replaying her past decisions, trying to find the source of her current life, April didn't hear Becca's question.

"Levi seems great," Becca said, prodding. Her co-worker offered her the tissue box.

April returned to reality and snapped one out. On paper, he was great. "He checks all the boxes." After a beat, she asked, "Do you like Purely Plaid?"

Becca laughed. "I'd rather have appendicitis." April understood that sentiment. "Now, if Levi offers you Garth Brooks tickets, shoot me a text. I'm your woman. But that ticket is yours. Sorry."

April had a strange knot in the center of her stomach, and this one had nothing to do with the scruffy dog's blood. Purely Plaid was her least favorite band with its twangy ridiculousness and riffs that never ended, but in the grand scheme of life, a couple-hour show wasn't a big deal. Of course she'd go, but she'd track down flesh colored ear plugs that Levi wouldn't see, and she'd don her favorite perma-smile that Levi would misinterpret.

Something wasn't sitting right this time though. Regardless of how long her brother knew about the tickets, something about Mathew's reaction to a dull concert seemed off.

AFTER WORK, APRIL DROVE the short mile home in her compact car. Yeah, it was overkill for her pitiful commute, but many drivers in Green Bay didn't respect pedestrians and especially not bicyclists. Public busing was slow, and April wasn't big on patience.

April parked in one of two empty spots on the pale concrete driveway. She rented a two-bedroom Victorian house with her roommate Kiko Takai in the historic district. She never saw much of the college student this past year, but April liked the woman enough to renew their lease a second year, if Kiko was sticking around after graduation.

April walked up the porch steps. The front door was unlocked as usual, and April stepped inside. They shared a couch and a television that was hardly ever on. The walls were plain rental white, and she had a beat-up table in the kitchen with a pair of chairs tucked under it. She crossed the living room and poked her head around. "Kiko?"

No answer. Shocker. Kiko was always busy with her research project. She was set to graduate with a master's degree in a couple weeks, and April wasn't sure if she was jealous or not. But she wondered if failing to finish college was such a great idea now.

'You'll be twenty-six someday either way; you might as well have a degree when you get there!' her brother always told her. She'd majored in many things over the years and nothing stuck. After finally paying off her student loans a few months ago, April didn't want to go back down that road without a solid plan. For now, she'd work for her brother and save. For what? She wasn't sure, but when she figured it out, she'd be ready to take that leap.

April entered her bedroom, a place that used to be a room of inspiration. She dropped her purse on the bed and inspected her framed portrait drawings hanging on the walls. She drew everyone from photographs, since her memory wasn't good enough to render the correct proportions otherwise. She only had space for a dozen to hang. Even Kiko was up there—her broad, high cheekbones, beautiful eyes, and lips pulled into a smile. Her long raven hair hung loose around her shoulders.

A lingering cloud shadowed all April's portraits. Especially one, the largest one—her mom and dad. She drew them happy, smiling, and embraced in a hug. She used two unrelated photos to render this portrait because as far as she knew, they had never posed together like this. She assumed they had for their wedding photos, but she'd never seen them.

April drew Mathew by himself, his gaze focused off to the side and creases of a frown on his forehead. She didn't understand why she drew him unhappy, since he was always so cheery in photographs. Perhaps she saw what he hid from everyone. When they were younger, Mathew attempted to rescue her from Dad's belt twice. Mathew'd said he didn't regret it, but his time in the hospital wracked her with guilt.

A few nights per week she would sit at her artist's desk and hold the pencil over her ivory drawing paper, and none of the photographs she had collected seemed worthy of permanence. The joy to create just ended...about the time Levi came into her life. Perhaps she was just too busy with him to focus on her craft. She had a photo of Levi sitting on her nightstand, right next to her beat up copy of The Count of Monte Cristo. Her boyfriend was smiling, teeth showing in a big boyish grin. It never struck her before now that she should draw him, and that bothered her.

Since April had nothing more important to do at the moment, she sat at the desk and pressed the pencil tip to the paper. Her arm jerked. A dark line severed the paper. She stared at it as if it weren't her hand that did it. She moved the pencil back to the starting point again and made another streak. And then another. She scribbled across the paper, tearing lines through it. When it fell apart and scraps landed on the floor, she finally stopped.

She remembered why. April's heart thundered in her chest.

Levi had made a comment, just a small insignificant remark, about how drawings were a waste of time when photographs were faster. And stupidly, she'd agreed. Now she wished she hadn't.

April dropped the pencil on the desktop and sat down on her fluffy unmade bed. She lifted the photo of Levi. The nerdy cute guy she'd been seeing for several months, an accountant with an affinity for country music.

They were so very different.

April did have a semester of accounting under her belt, because Levi suggested it would be a great fit for her. She didn't hate it or anything, but either her brain just didn't spark with excitement, or she was afraid of becoming like Levi—dark boring suits, extended work hours, long meetings. Taxes—she shivered. She preferred more fluidity to her day, but not the blood sort of fluid either.

Maybe her problem was that she and Levi hadn't come up with a hobby to share. They spent all their time doing what he wanted and never what she wanted. Okay, so he let her pick the restaurant sometimes. Did that count?

Becca liked him. Kiko seemed supportive. Her roommate never rooted for him the way her brother did, but Mathew understood her the best, so she trusted his judgment. And Mathew thought highly of Levi. What if April wasn't trying hard enough to like his interests?

April set the frame down and picked up the torn pieces of paper. She crumpled them and released them into the trash. She stared at her wasted artist's paper in disappointment.

Chapter 4

1852, Bridgeport, Wisconsin

Sam tied his trusty mount to the post outside Porter's General Store, ready for his next collection. A familiar voice nearby felt like a fist to the gut, and Sam quickly slipped to the side of the wooden building out of sight. Gabriel Grignon and his men approached, and with a fresh image of Isabel on his mind, Sam didn't trust himself in front of his dangerous boss.

"You've got three days to get it done," Grignon said to his men. His French accent grated like rusty horseshoes on rocks. "I want him arrested and brought to the jail. He's a big man, so if all of you have to do it, so be it. When the townsfolk question you, spread the story I gave you, and if they interfere, they join him as accomplices. Understood?"

Mumbles reached Sam's ears.

Grignon continued, "His legs will dangle free at Common Square by the end of the week."

They planned on hanging someone again. Sam sucked in a breath, and his fists squeezed until his knuckles whitened with rage. He needed to find out who the next victim was and get out of here unseen.

"What of his place then?" one of the twins, Dennis, asked. The differences between the twins were minor. Both were calm fortresses of muscle without souls, but Dennis had a nasty scar from brow to cheek. The voice sent Sam back to his wife suffering in her last moments, and he would never shake the image away.

"Do we leave the bar empty or must we guard it until your declaration speech?"

Sam's fists tightened again, and his pulse throbbed at his temples. The only bar in town was Lloyd's. They planned to hang his best friend and steal his bar. Sam spun and pounded the building with his fist, unleashing months of pent up fury. At the rate Grignon quietly slaughtered people in this town, soon no one would remain but slaves and his mercenaries.

"Monsieur Sam!" Grignon said with a fake warm welcome.

Sam wasn't afraid of much in life, but Grignon made his blood curdle. Gooseflesh rose on his forearms. He reluctantly faced the man himself. Grignon was shorter than him by almost a full head. His clothes were exquisite and custom fit, and his full beard was more pepper than salt, but it was his French accent and tiny round spectacles that made him want to punch the guy in the nose. The four bodyguards—Dennis and Daniel Durand, Rob Bertrand, and Joe Pool—each armed with dirks and brand-new Colt revolvers, gave him instant self-control.

"What a lovely surprise," Grignon continued. He pressed the bridge of his spectacles higher up his nose, and his friendliness slipped from his voice. "I was just detailing my next move in this town, and unfortunately for you, I believe you heard too much."

"I heard nothing, sir," Sam countered.

Grignon glanced at Sam's fists and smiled. "Silly boy, I don't believe you."

Sam could take out two bodyguards himself with his bare hands, possibly three with his knife. He'd learned after Isabel that four men were beyond his abilities. Especially four that were armed to the hilt, plus the weaselly Grignon himself. Sam stood no chance and hoped whatever punishment the Frenchman planned would end swiftly. He could bear the pain and humiliation. Nothing could top what he'd already survived. Sam dropped his eyes to Grignon's shiny black boots and waited.

The boots shifted position, and Sam looked up with confusion. All five men were leaving. That was it? It was never that easy. Assuming he'd blocked out the entire incident, Sam's fingers touched his cheek, but he didn't find any tenderness or excessive heat. He pressed the rest of his face. Same results.

Grignon hadn't punished him.

Sam's stomach twisted in fear of what was to follow. He wished his parents were around to help. They made everything seem so easy. Somehow, Sam was going to stop Gabriel Grignon once and for all and free this town of his cruelty, even if it cost him his own life.

Chapter 5
Present Day, Green Bay, Wisconsin

THE NEXT AFTERNOON APRIL arrived home and found Kiko eyeballs-deep in her senior project with wires, gears, and random plastic boxes spread all over the living room. She wrote notes in a thick book as she worked on her doodads. What did any of this have to do with a psychology degree? Perhaps everything, but Kiko never spent much time at home, so April really had no idea. She picked up a thingy with wires sticking out, inspected it, and placed it back on the coffee table. It didn't look like anything of use to her. Kiko was weird and super smart.

Her roommate clicked away on a laptop keyboard. "Hey," she called out from behind clear safety glasses, "Can I ask a favor?"

"Sure." April wanted to spend some time alone to mull over her Levi problems, but she wouldn't turn down anyone who needed help, and maybe Kiko could give her some pointers. April dropped her purse on the couch and plopped her rear next to it. "What do you need?"

"My project is due in three weeks. I need one person to experiment on and report what happens—the dream study I told you about. Think you can give it a shot for me tonight?" Kiko asked.

"No problem." She didn't mind if Kiko wanted to put her weird thingies on her head while she slept. Then it hit her, that dreadful date. "Wait, I have tickets to a concert tonight with Levi."

"Purely Plaid again?" she asked.

"Rain check?"

"I'll still be up when you get back; we can do it then." Kiko opened the tackle box, selected a gear-like round doodad, and closed the box. Her other hand gripped wire strippers and yanked the coating off the end of a short wire. "Are you enrolling in classes this summer or the fall? It's not too late."

April heaved her tired bones up off the couch and shuffled to the kitchen. "Tuition is so expensive, and I've already tried enough majors. I can't start over without total confidence in what I want to do for the rest of my life." She slathered peanut butter and jelly on opposing slices of bread. "And right now, I've only crossed off a few options. Besides, Matty needs me, and I need the paycheck, you know?"

Kiko paused from her project, looked up at her and said, "No, I really don't."

"Yeah, yeah. Must be nice. I see the equipment you've got, the clothes you wear, the car in the driveway. That stuff isn't cheap, and since you haven't worked all school year, where's your half of the rent coming from?" April chowed down on her sandwich and stepped to her bedroom.

Kiko didn't respond.

"Enough said."

"It's not like that at all," Kiko said with no offense.

"I'm sorry. I didn't mean to assume anything. I'm just a little frustrated at this whole concert thing," April said from her bedroom.

"Come here. Talk to me," Kiko said.

After slipping into an AC/DC T-shirt and torn skinny jeans, April stuffed her feet into high heeled booties and placed her cowboy hat on her head, the one Levi had bought for her. She sat back on the couch next to Kiko.

Her roommate tapped the hat's brim. "This really doesn't suit you at all."

"Can I admit something?" April asked.

"Anything."

"I hate country music. Levi insists on dragging me to these gigs, but it isn't fun to me. When I try to suggest anything else, he dismisses me. I mean, everyone has their quirks, and he's definitely predictable, but he has a stable job…" As April thought of his good points, it felt like checking off a list of boxes and nothing more. She should've felt more when talking about him, right?

"A fancy car, and a big house too," Kiko added and smiled.

"But sometimes it's like he doesn't see me. Does that make sense? Maybe I'm just ungrateful."

"Are you going to break up with him?" Kiko asked.

"No," she said without hesitating. April never considered the possibility. They'd had six good months together, and bad taste in music wasn't a good enough reason to break up. But what about his inability to choose something she wanted to do? To blame him for that, she would have to stand her ground first. Her parents hadn't even broken up after alcoholism and abuse. Oh wait, they had, but it had taken over two decades. Was that the bar April had set for herself?

"Do you love him?" Kiko asked.

April finished her last bite of sandwich and licked her fingers. She and Levi hadn't exchanged the big L-word yet. Was it weird it took so long? They had fun, they shared stories, and laughed. He really was great, but she didn't think she loved him. She would know if she did, right?

"I'm not sure." April shrugged.

"Sometimes love comes slowly or sometimes not at all."

"Have you ever been in love?"

Kiko leaned back against the lumpy couch cushions with a goofy grin on her face. As if the memories rolled through her mind, the smile faded away. "Yeah, once."

"What happened?" April leaned back so their faces were close.

"I guess it just wasn't meant to be." Kiko sighed, and her eyes glassed over.

April reached out and squeezed Kiko's hand. She didn't want to push if her roommate wasn't comfortable. "How long would you wait until you knew for sure?"

Kiko blinked rapidly, recomposing herself. "I can only give anecdotal evidence, but for what it's worth, I've seen love at first sight. I've also seen where it takes weeks. In reality, when they are the one, capitalized The One, it's obvious within a couple months at most. Quicker if you survive big hurdles together, like adrenaline-infused danger or a challenging family situation, and you work well as a team. Compromise and communicate for the best chance at success."

Compromise. That magic word.

"You're younger than me and yet give better advice than my mom ever did. You'll make a great therapist. Maybe I should go back to college."

"Marriage and family counselor, not that it matters," Kiko corrected. "But you should do whatever makes you happy. That's the most important thing in life."

April rolled her eyes. "Now you sound like Matty."

"Great minds think alike." Kiko laughed.

"Yeah, yeah. Just don't tell him that."

The last thing she needed was her over-protective know-it-all big brother to grow a big head too. Then his nagging snippets of worry and advice would get worse. And she didn't want to find out how much more paranoid he could get. Kiko reaffirmed what she'd suspected—April needed to compromise and be patient.

Chapter 6
Present Day, Green Bay, Wisconsin

All dressed up and ready to go, April sat on the couch, nervously deciding how she was going to explain to Levi after the concert that she didn't want to go anymore. A quick text seemed cold and likely to spur many more texts her fingers couldn't keep up with. Kiko worked on her project gizmos. How she could focus so intently this late at night baffled April.

The doorbell rang, and Kiko leaped from her project and let Levi inside. He wore khakis and a plaid button up with cowboy boots. His cowboy hat caused his black hair to stick out around his ears, and his brown eyes were swirling with excitement. Admittedly, he looked a little ridiculous, just like her. Their joint ridiculousness eased her anxiety.

"There's my girl. All set?" he asked.

April stood up, hooked her purse on her arm, and gave Levi a peck on the lips.

"Wait," he said, backing her up to arm's reach and giving her a once-over. "You can't wear that shirt."

April looked down at her AC/DC shirt. "Why not? I wore this last time."

"I figured you didn't know better. You do now. Don't you have some plaid or a denim jacket? Even a plain white or black T-shirt would be better."

"Nope. None of those."

Brian Johnson, lead singer of the greatest band on Earth, was the only man capable of blocking Purely Plaid from her ear drums...and earplugs. This was about survival.

"You two have a great time," Kiko said, glaring at April as they walked out, almost as if Kiko was sending her a secret message.

Levi sighed in defeat, and they climbed into his hybrid car for the drive to the west side of the city to the casino. He prattled about his band more than usual and then touched on the weather a few times. He seemed nervous about something, a little extra focused on his own world.

"How's the CPA exam coming along?" April asked, knowing Levi studied for hours each day and talked about that test like it was a rite of passage only the elite could manage. And he wanted to be one of them.

Levi smiled. "I think I'm ready. Auditing and Attestation is coming up in a few weeks. After I see how that goes, I'll register for another part, probably Regulation. I want to pass the hardest ones first."

His perseverance impressed April. With her track record, she didn't believe she was destined to go that far in any career field. Especially not accounting. "Sounds like a plan."

"We just finished the rush of tax season," he said, perking up. "Quarterly taxes are next, so I compiled all the clients' statements. Today I found something truly exciting."

"What's that?" April asked lightly. She didn't believe any sentence with the word 'exciting' referring to accounting could be true, but he was cute when he talked shop.

"Fields and Smith had depreciation they missed last fiscal period on new sandblasting equipment, which resulted in a net operating loss for last year, and I amended their taxes."

"Um, that's great." April didn't know what that meant, but she was sure Levi would tell her. With one semester of introductory accounting on her transcript, she understood debits and credits, balancing the balance sheet, and memorizing formulas, which she promptly forgot after the semester ended.

"Net operating losses carry over. I reduced their tax bill for this fiscal year. Boom!" He slapped the steering wheel.

April laughed at his enthusiasm. "I had some excitement myself yesterday."

"Oh! Did you hear Alex is sick?"

April stared blankly. The name didn't ring a bell.

Levi continued, "Hopefully he can make it through the night. Can't play without a drummer." He chuckled and his fingers drummed the wheel. "Poor guy. Next year they're dropping a new album, and I can't wait. Will you go with me to their first show?"

April inhaled a deep breath and balled her hands, swallowing a hasty retort. Relationships were about give and take. Communicate and compromise, Kiko had said. But this conversation needed to wait until after the concert. So, she gave him a white lie. "Sure. Sounds great."

Levi grinned and patted her knee.

They parked on the outskirts of the full lot. The evening air was chilly for early May, and April rubbed her arms and walked alongside her boyfriend. He held the front door open for her, and her senses were immediately assaulted. Bells chimed, lights flashed, and music impaled her just like the noise of Purely Plaid did. One man shouted with glee in the distance over a loud rattling of coins. A few people lined up at the ATM.

As they walked by, cards and chips were flipping and clacking at the tables. It smelled like rotisserie chicken and fresh baked dough. Way yummier than peanut butter and jelly. Her stomach growled.

April and Levi found their way to the showroom, and it was thin. They must've been early, because Levi wasn't the only crazy pants to love Purely Plaid. Levi and April sat in their folding metal chairs right next to the center aisle, and Levi fidgeted. Dozens of people filtered in and scattered throughout the audience, staring at their bright phone screens. He leaned over, gave her a kiss on the forehead, and April smiled. He captured her hand and his sweaty palms squished against hers. Something was not right with him tonight.

"Are you okay?" she asked.

His gaze flicked to her and the room lights blacked out. April dug in her purse and stuffed the earplugs in her canals. The velvet drapes screeched on their tracks as they opened, and a pair of spotlights revealed the band. The crowd cheered, now almost a full house. April estimated over six hundred people attended. The lead singer calmed everyone down and played through all the favorites. At the end of the show it was hot, everyone was wired, and the band was sweaty. April's nerves were strung out. The earplugs only lowered the decibels. She popped them out so she wouldn't get caught.

The lead singer quieted everyone down again and said, "I've got something that needs saying before we play the last song of the evening."

Back in they went.

One spotlight landed on Levi and he stood. Her boyfriend looked like an angel with a halo of white glowing around him.

"Levi," she whispered, "what's going on?"

The crowd spun to watch Levi, and a sinking pit grew in her stomach. As his shaky hand reached into his front pants pocket, she placed a hand over her mouth to stop herself from vomiting. Levi's lips pulled into a grin. He must've thought she was in shock from happiness. He held her hand and pulled her to standing, and then he kneeled down on one knee.

The crowd cheered. April's legs turned to jelly, and her stomach quivered. The lead singer calmed the audience down again. Levi was so not serious right now. This couldn't be happening. She scanned for the nearest exit and nearest garbage can, unsure which to prioritize. The spotlight shifted to bathe her in the blinding light too.

Levi opened the box. It was a single stone, square-cut diamond in a platinum setting. Under the spotlights it sparkled as if it were still in the jeweler's case. If she had to guess, it was a full carat, and it was simply breathtaking.

"April Elizabeth McCall, I love you more than I can even describe. I cannot imagine my future without you in it. I cannot imagine not seeing your smile every day for the next fifty years. Will you marry me?" His voice cracked. The crowd moaned in sentimental approval and waited.

April's gaze flickered around the room. The darkened faces were impossible to distinguish, but every pair of eyes drilled into her face like carpenter ants chewing through wood.

The seconds ticked by in an exaggerated slow motion. She wanted a hole in the floor to open up and swallow her. The only nightmare worse than this was when she dreamed she was giving a speech in school while naked—and that wasn't reality. Her palms were sweating, so she rubbed them on her torn jeans. She had to say something. Levi not only proposed, but he used the L-word. Publicly. All in one go. She didn't even know if she loved him. This was not a time for a white lie. "I can't do this now. Levi, please," she whispered. "Can we talk?"

Her boyfriend blinked. After her answer processed, he closed the box, and his genuine smile faded to a fake smile for the audience. He stood. Awkward murmurs danced around the room. April's head spun, threatening to test the casino's insurance policy.

The lead singer's voice jolted everyone. "Ah, how about the encore folks? We've got 'Lonely in Waiting' for you. Tune it up boys." The spotlights left Levi and April, and the guitar riff started. The pairs of eyes shifted to the stage, and one by one the cheers came back.

"We should go," he said and grasped her arm, dragging her up the center aisle. He brought her straight to the exit and out to the parking lot without another word. His grip hurt, and finally he released her. Levi walked with a purpose toward the car. April tried to keep pace in her heeled booties, and when she joined him in the car, they sat in silence.

"I'm sorry, Levi. You caught me off guard, and all those people..." April trailed off, not knowing what to say that wouldn't make the situation worse.

The car's interior was dimly lit by the yellow parking lot lights. He stared out the windshield, and there was pain in his profile. They'd never argued or disagreed before.

"No, I'm sorry," he said. "I shouldn't have put you on the spot like that. We hadn't even talked about it yet. But what I said is true." He turned to face her. "Will you marry me?" He slipped the box out of his pocket again and reopened it.

"What?" April said in shock. "Levi, I can't give you an answer right now. We never discussed our future, kids, where we'll live, any of that. I don't...I don't know."

"Let's hash it out here. No better time, right?" He paused. "So, kids—that'll be four, where to live—my house for now, but I plan to move back to Orlando where my family lives. I mean, the college here is great, but the winters, not so much. I just need enough experience for the next pay bump. I can add another car too. How about his and hers BMWs? What else?"

April's mouth gaped open like a fish out of water. Orlando, Florida, where the mosquitoes were the size of cats? And four kids? April's mind flashed to pushing four babies out, diapers, and vomit. She couldn't leave her brother. He was her only family, the only one who understood her. But what was the alternative—lose Levi forever and be alone again? She'd spent enough years alone. Six months they'd been together and not once had this conversation come up, and now he sprung a mapped-out future on her?

Buried anger popped out in a sharp tone. "I need to think about these things. I didn't even know you wanted to move to Orlando, and four kids? Wow. Can I have some time to think about it?"

Levi's face dropped. She didn't mean to, but she'd hurt him again.

"Sure," he grumbled. "How long do you need, a day? Sleep on it, and I'll drop by in the morning."

April wanted to open the car door and run, but that wasn't logical. It wasn't safe to dash around alone at night. Especially in the cool spring air, wearing a thin T-shirt and jeans. Never mind her impractical high heeled booties. No matter how afraid she was to speak up for herself, she was furious Levi continued to dismiss her opinions. But she still had self-preservation from years of practice. "Take me home Levi, okay?"

What was she going to tell him?

Chapter 7
1852, Bridgeport, Wisconsin

With saddle bags full after a horrific morning, Sam dismounted in front of his and Sarah's home, the cabin he and his father built, log by log. 'Build with your hands only what you would be proud of,' his father had told him. The man had worked hard and had the hands to prove it. Sam had a prideful amount of callouses himself, but he could no longer follow his father's philosophy. Sam collected his purchases off his horse and brought them inside.

Sarah Hartley fixed lunch while singing. Fresh cut flowers rested on the kitchen counter and on the dinner table. His seventeen-year-old sister had to grow up fast, but she made this cabin a home, filling the walls with love—just like Mam used to. Some days, like today, he missed his mam. It made him feel weak not to have control of his world. Everyone he cared about was at risk, and he had no guarantee he'd wake up alive tomorrow.

Like Isabel. Sam's gaze shifted to the front of the fireplace where Isabel's vacant stare had cast straight at him. The guilt tore into him all over again. He was so glad Sarah had washed away all the stains on the wood planks. Sam avoided the photos lining the mantle for his heart's sake.

Sarah finally noticed he'd returned. She stopped, assessed him, and frowned. She cleaned her hands and approached him. "What happened, my dearest brother? You look like you've seen death."

Sam dropped onto a chair at the table and rubbed his face. If he told her, she'd do something rash.

Sarah filled a glass of water and sat across from him at the table. She pushed it toward him. "Have a drink. By the unfortunate odor overpowering my flowers, you've been by Lloyd's. How is he?"

'He's great,' Sam wanted to say. 'He's fantastic, healthy as an ox.' But next week, not so much. Grignon's words repeated in his head, 'His legs will dangle free at Common Square by the end of the week.'

"Silence is never good news. How much have you drank this morning?"

Sam shook his head. "It's not that."

"I'm making sandwiches. Hungry?"

Sam had zero appetite, but he needed to try, so she didn't worry. "Starved."

Sarah brought a plate over for him, and he reached for it.

"Tut, tut, tut," she chided. "Wash up, please."

Sam didn't see the point of washing hands before eating when his friend would die soon, and there was nothing he could do about it. He washed to appease her, not in the mood to bicker, and he took a generous bite. His stomach surprised him.

"If something were to happen to me," Sam said between bites, "can you promise me you'll seek Jonathan Arris?"

Across the river, the farmer on the outskirts of the neighboring settlement town was expecting her, a deal their parents had made before their passing.

Sarah recoiled. "What are you talking about? Nothing's happening to anybody. Not on my watch." The stubborn woman folded her arms across her chest in defiance. She got that from their father.

Sam had shielded her from the dangers of their town, and now she wouldn't take him seriously. Perhaps he was wrong about not being able to do anything. A promise after he was gone would be too late. To keep her safe, he had to send her away now.

"Sarah, please," Sam said. "It's only a few weeks before your eighteenth year of birth, but Arris would accept you earlier. Send word ahead, mount up with everything of value and just go. I'll arrange an escort to see that you make the journey safely across the bridge." Grignon's bridge.

"Nonsense. I'll not leave unless forced. This is my home."

"Mam and Da already made the arrangement. We can't break it. We don't have the funds to pay off the contract."

Sarah's shoulders hunched in defeat, mulling over the predicament. Then she lit up. "Can I choose the escort?"

Sam chewed another bite and said, "As long as the other party is amiable, sure. Who do you want?"

"Oh, I don't know," she said. "Ross...or how about Lloyd? He's strong enough. Safe."

At the sound of his friend's name, Sam's body chilled. He would graciously send his friend to protect his sister, but Lloyd wouldn't be around in another week. Sam might be around less than that just for overhearing. Maybe that was the perfect idea to keep them both safe. "I promise to do my best." If he could get the stubborn Lloyd to agree, and now Sam needed to work out his troubles in the only way he knew how. Sam picked up the last few bites of sandwich and tore it up.

"All right then." Sarah collected their empty plates and brought them over to wash.

Sam tossed the last few bites of his sandwich out the back door, and marched to the barn. He threw open the heavy doors. Bright daylight flooded his workshop. All his tools rested were he'd left them and remained just as dusty since his last visit.

Wrought iron and steel works hung all over the walls like night watchmen for the large forge in the center. His anvil sat next to a table of implements. The thought of firing up the coals to a deep glowing orange had brought no sense of joy since Isabel's death.

He searched for one particular piece and retrieved it off the wall. He wiped off the dust with strokes of his thumb, satisfied with the craftsmanship. It was several pounds of black rods twisting like a ballet dancer. Sam would never admit that to his sister. She would have his hide over it.

Inspired by his wife, Sam had made this piece for her, but Isabel thought it was a gaudy old thing with no use. She didn't understand all his hours spent hammering away at the metal. Only when he made horseshoes for commission did she approve.

Several months past since Isabel had died, right in front of the fireplace. She hadn't deserved that end. Sam wanted to make things right by stopping Grignon, but after sending Lloyd and Sarah away, what could one man do against his band of mercenaries, his power and influence?

Sam placed the dancing piece on the table near the door so it would be the first thing he saw upon returning. Even if Isabel didn't like it, he did. Sam collected his trusty ax and left the barn as he found it, a collection of happiness better soon forgotten.

Under the infinite blistering sun, Sam lined up a log on top of the stump to put his anxious energy to good use. They didn't need any more wood at the moment, but there was no such thing as extra when the winter winds and snow blew in from the north.

The ax soared down at the unsuspecting log and speared straight through it in a single swing. The split hunks tumbled over. His hands steadied as pride in his productive work eased his anxiety.

Without a doubt, Lloyd would honor him in protecting his sister, but Sam didn't want to burden his best friend. Lloyd had to keep the bar running for his livelihood. It was half a day's journey west to the Arris farm in Astor, and the whole trip could stretch into a week. Sam knew firsthand what happened when a Bridgeport business owner didn't have the funds for his weekly payment.

This once, Sam could scrounge up the funds somehow to meet the shortage. If he could protect his friend and keep his sister safe, there was nothing he wouldn't do.

The back door to the house opened, and Sam lifted his head to see what the matter was. Sarah peered out.

"What is it?" he asked.

She shook her head and closed the door. Sarah always spied on him. She worried just as Mam used to, and he hated that.

Sam lined up another log and continued swinging the ax until his strength drained away.

He needed to convince Lloyd to flee, an impossible task.

Under the cover of darkness, Sam walked to the bar, keeping to the shadows. He found Lloyd's private door leading upstairs and knocked.

After several rounds, shuffling reached Sam's ears, and the door opened.

"Sam?" Lloyd asked groggily. "Bar's closed. What brings you here at this hour?"

"Can I come inside?"

"Of course, of course," Lloyd said, shifting aside.

Sam brushed past his friend and turned. "I know how this is going to sound, but I need you to hear me out."

"This sounds like bad news. Sit down."

Sam couldn't. He had too much energy. "I overheard a conversation, and you need to prepare yourself."

Lloyd perked up. "What's this about?"

"Grignon and his men intend to hang you and steal your bar."

A long pause filled the air.

Lloyd laughed. "Are you mad? How much have you drank tonight?"

"I am sober and serious. You need to pack up and leave before they come for you."

Lloyd folded his arms across his thick chest. "They can pull my bar out from under my dead body."

"That's what they intend to do. I can't lose you too, Lloyd. Please go. Come back after Grignon has been taken care of."

"This is my entire livelihood, Sam. I can't just walk away from it. Besides, how am I supposed to make that weekly payment if I have no income?"

"You won't be making it if you're dead."

"I've already left my home because of old white folk telling me what they own. I'm not doing it again. And if they come around, they'll get a shotgun to the face."

Sam sighed. He'd figured his warning would fall on deaf ears. "Please, Lloyd. For me, will you go?"

"I'm not leaving, but I'll stand by you and fight."

Hopefully it wouldn't come down to that, but Sam was grateful for the support.

Chapter 8
Present Day, Green Bay, Wisconsin

WHEN LEVI DROPPED HER off, April left the car without looking back. She went inside, locked the front door, tipped back against it, and sagged until her butt rested on the floor. She had approximately ten hours to give Levi an answer that would determine the course of the rest of her life. April flung her cowboy hat toward her bedroom door and smoothed her long hair.

Kiko paused from packing away her project supplies. She appeared fresh as if she hadn't spent the last several hours working on it. The woman was an Energizer Bunny.

"How was your night?" Kiko asked.

April stretched her legs in front of her with no intention of getting up. "I don't know. I can't decide if it was the worst night ever or the best."

"That's quite a range," Kiko said with a chuckle. She collected a fun size bag of chips from the kitchen and sat on the floor beside her. Kiko offered April the open bag.

Since she and Levi hadn't eaten before the concert or afterward, her stomach rumbled. She wouldn't have accepted a meal with him after that, anyway. April picked out a nacho. "Levi proposed."

"And that's good or bad?"

"I don't even know if I love him. Since he 'checks all my boxes' can love come later, or am I in love and I'm just broken?"

"Love shouldn't be this difficult. If you have to fight to have it, it's easy to give up, but if it's easy to love, you'll fight to keep it. Do you see a difference?" Kiko asked.

"How do you know which one you have?" April didn't have much experience with men. She'd had two not-so-serious boyfriends—one in high school that lasted three months, and one in college for four months—before Levi, and they both freaked when they saw her scars. At least Levi accepted her as she was.

"Picture yourself with him years from now. Thinking of places you've gone, things you've seen, the curtains you've picked out, and the pet you'll have, do you feel warm and fuzzy?"

"When Levi visited me at work, I buzzed with warmth, because his presence made me feel important, that I was worthy of his time, and it was amazing. Although, this morning he had terrible timing."

"That's a start."

April's stomach was unsettled—hungry or terrified, she wasn't sure whether to hurl up her butterflies or cram them in the face with nachos. She was too nervous to picture anything. "But isn't it kind of fast? I mean, six months. Most people have a jar of pickles older than that." April took another chip. "Maybe it's that thing everyone talks about—cold feet? Or does that only apply after accepting the proposal?"

Kiko lifted off the floor and tossed a full bag to April as if she'd read her mind. Even Kiko knew her better than Levi. "If it makes you feel any better, I'm sure the soy sauce in our fridge expired two years ago."

"Exactly," April said sharply as if that proved a point. "Soy sauce is older than my relationship with Levi."

"Then the question is: What do you want?" Now Kiko sounded like Mathew again, but for some reason, April was less annoyed.

April cracked into the new bag and savored a fresh nacho. She'd never clearly expressed what she wanted from their relationship. Rejecting Levi without giving him a fair chance, wasn't, well, fair.

A spine-rattling knock on the door cut off her worries. April stood up from the hard floor. Her rear end tingled with newfound blood flow. She had almost been used to that tingle.

Kiko stood up next to her, and April, the taller of the two, checked the peep hole. It was late for surprise visitors.

Mathew?

The clinic would be closed now, but Mathew never left before nine P.M. with paperwork and morning prep. Or at least, that was what he always told her.

April opened the door for him, and he barreled right past her and spun. He was far too energetic this late. Something must be wrong.

"So, how was the concert?" Mathew asked.

Her big brother never came over and asked about one of her dates before, which meant Mathew knew about the proposal before she did. Should she be flattered Levi asked permission or annoyed Mathew knew first and didn't warn her? "I don't want to talk about it."

Mathew's excitement slipped from his face. He scratched the back of his head and walked to the fridge. "Kiko," he said over his shoulder. "Beer?"

"No, thank you."

He came back with two bottles and handed one to April. He dropped on the couch and asked, "That bad, huh?"

"I have until morning to answer him." April sat next to her brother and cracked open the bottle. The scent of hops calmed her.

"He's a nice guy," Mathew said.

April bristled. "Yes, he's nice. Is nice enough to marry someone? Little Ms. Lewis next door is super nice. She'll feed you muffins until you drop and then wrap you in a cozy blanket right where you lie. Is nice really enough to marry someone?"

Mathew held up his hands in surrender. "Whoa, I got it. You're right. I just..." He exhaled a deep breath. "I just want to see you happy. That's all."

Kiko made haste in retreating to her bedroom. April wanted to follow. Instead, April threw his privacy invasion back at him. Right now, annoyed was winning over flattered. "If you're so concerned with happiness, then why are you still single? Huh? Maybe you should put more effort into your own personal life and stay out of mine."

Mathew didn't hide his irritation. "I'm trying to be financially responsible by clearing my six-figures in student loans before I begin a relationship. I don't want to burden anyone else with my baggage. You of all people should be able to understand that."

April guzzled half her beer. Mathew followed suit. They both stared each other down as if daring the other to stop drinking first. She swore it was not a race. April remembered the stack of bills in the mail that she'd tossed on his desk. His struggles were worse than she thought. She finished the bottle and picked at the label. "Sorry."

"It's fine," he said and patted her knee. Mathew stood and carried his empty to the recycle bin and then waited by the door. "Call you tomorrow? Or how about you call me after you figure this all out?"

"I'll call you."

He nodded and left, closing the door behind him.

Kiko inched back into the living room. "You okay?" she asked.

A lump of guilt nagged at her for assuming the loftiness of Kiko's background. It wasn't even any of her business. April just wanted to hand out sorries like candies right now. 'You get a sorry and you get a sorry. Sorries for everyone!'

"I'm sorry for that comment earlier about the rent. I just hate how stressful that big bill is, how little is left over, and Ramen noodles. Don't get me wrong, those noodles are awesome, but more than a dozen times a week? Not so much."

Kiko smiled. "How about a little reprieve from the day? I can take your mind off this whole Levi thing for a while. What do you say?"

April shrugged. "Sounds better than dwelling on it. Every moment that ticks by, the stress of the decision gets heavier. I mean, he's not exactly patient."

"He gave you a deadline," Kiko said.

April side-eyed her. Sometimes her roommate was creepy good at guessing things. "He did."

"Then, no time to waste." Kiko pointed at the couch. "Stretch out comfortably. My dream project will feel hyperrealistic. Time isn't the same in your head as it is here in reality. Like I'd said, my project is due in three weeks, but I need time to assess and report the findings."

April sunk into the fluffy couch and crossed her bootied ankles. She knitted her fingers together over her stomach and closed her eyes, trying to clear her mind.

Kiko folded over her laptop and typed for a moment. "One last thing," Kiko said. "There's a mission involved for the research portion. This is important too."

April opened her eyes to pay attention.

"You need to find Sam Hartley, and you need to prevent his arrest tonight, otherwise two good men will die. Understand?"

April's face scrunched in amused confusion.

Kiko shrugged. "It's a quantitative measurement."

As if that made perfect sense and explained everything. Only Kiko could think up something so specific, but maybe the computer was preprogramed with the simulation. Why not a simpler test, like pluck a daisy from a field? That was her level. Instead, she had to channel her inner Bond. Jane Bond. Only in her dreams. "Okay, boss. It's your project."

Kiko smiled. "Perfect."

April closed her eyes and her body tingled like thousands of spiders crawling over her skin. She opened them in alarm and her vision rippled like a stone tossed into a pond. Her heart rate increased in a panic. "Kiko? Is this norm—" Her voice cut off as all the air left the room in a vacuum. The last thing April saw was complete blackness.

Chapter 9

1852 Bridgeport, Wisconsin

WHEN APRIL BLINKED AWAY the darkness, the ceiling had vanished. She squinted at the bright blue sky dotted with popcorn clouds. Her hands went to the couch to lift herself up, when she touched grass. The hell?

April climbed to her feet and swiped dirt off her jeans and shook out her hair. Somehow she'd dropped into a field of tall grasses. Several blocks to the northwest, or what would be blocks if she were in the city, were a few buildings, the equivalent of a rustic village. Oh, right. Kiko's dream simulation. She wasn't kidding when she said it would feel hyperrealistic.

Alright, the mission was to prevent Sam Hartley's arrest. It would help if she knew what he looked like or where to find him, but the dirt road into town was a good place to start.

April fished her way through the grasses and walked along the road, careful where she placed her ankle bootied steps. These shoes were totally not appropriate for this rugged dream world, but this couldn't take long. An hour, at most? And when she was done, April was getting a drink and a long night's rest.

The thunder of horse hooves behind her made April hop off the road. The large beast trotted past her and shifted to a stop. The rider wore a hand-stitched black leather vest over a red, long sleeve tunic. A round straw hat on his head shadowed a jagged scar over his forehead and cheek. A sheathed shotgun leaned against the saddle, and his boots had brutal spurs jutting from the heels. He looked menacing, but his expression was kind.

Kiko sure had a vivid imagination for this dream world.

"Good day, miss," he said. "By golly, where did you get those clothes?"

April looked down at herself. Clearly not where he got his. "The store," she said simply.

His head tilted with confusion. "I'm Dennis Durand. I'd be pleased to offer you a ride. It's a long walk to town from here, and you must be exhausted." She couldn't place his light accent. Where did Kiko program this guy to be from?

In reality, April would decline and keep to herself, aware of stranger danger since kindergarten, but this wasn't reality, so April moved closer and took the hand that lowered. Having never been on a horse before, she eyed the animal with distrust. The horse snorted, and April startled.

"Is the horse safe?"

"Safer than you walking all by yourself dressed like that."

Errr, okay. Dennis Durand lifted her up onto the saddle behind him, and the horse shifted. April wrapped her arms around the man and squeezed, suddenly regretting this decision. Her fingers found hard lumps of hidden weaponry. With a shiver, she adjusted her hands higher until certain she touched the softness of his body.

Dennis Durand spurred the horse into action.

With her legs, April squeezed the shifting muscles between her thighs, trying to keep herself on the beast. It was much harder than it looked. To distract herself from an impending spinal cord injury, she absorbed her temporary surroundings as they trotted by. A brick clothing shop with mannequins in a picture window wore lacy, fluffy dresses that reminded her of a historical western movie—from what little she knew of them. April wasn't a fan, but judging by this level of detail, Kiko loved this stuff.

Next was a feed mill. The telegram office was plain, just a small door and a sign. There was a general store with a lot of foot traffic. The women were dressed like the mannequin—long heavy gowns and lacy bonnets carrying baskets as they strolled between the stores. Next was a bar—presumably—by the name of Stanton's Spirits, and a few men were talking and drinking outside it, wearing suits and hats. Other people traveled on horses. One man drove a cargo wagon north full of hay and pulled by a line of four horses. He looked dirty and sweaty but with a good physique.

A new building was under construction, a skeleton of boards and logs rising from the earth. The scent of heavenly food reached her nose, and she inhaled deeply. Rich grease and meat. Max's must be a restaurant. Oh, and Bridgeport Chemist, an old drugstore. It was like cruising through a Hollywood set. Did Kiko take a trip to California for research as part of her class? That must've been why Kiko was always gone—months of research leading up to this project. April wouldn't fail her roommate.

April's thighs trembled with the effort of staying topside, and her dreaded butterflies returned as Dennis Durand steered them away from the epicenter of town north on the dirt road. "Didn't we just pass the town?" she asked over his shoulder.

He didn't answer.

The dirt road rose up a hill, and horses pulling a carriage approached from the other side. Her rider signaled the coachman to stop. The horses nickered with the disruption of their routine, and her rider dismounted. April's hands planted on the horse's backbone for balance while her stomach somersaulted. He was leaving her alone on this thing. The muscular beast between her legs shifted its weight, and no one controlled it. Unsure of her ability to get off this thing safely by herself, April hoped the horse would forget she was on it.

The scarred rider made quick talk with a hidden passenger of the carriage and returned, offering her a hand down and a gentle smile.

April dismounted eagerly, and he led her to the open carriage door. "Go on," Dennis insisted.

April stepped up inside, ducking with the short ceiling, and sat on a narrow seat. Across from her was a lean man with mostly gray hair and a full beard. He had a lined face with round glasses and a fine cut suit, but it was his expression while he took in her appearance that had her shifting uncomfortably.

"How do you do, mademoiselle? My name is Gabriel Grignon, and I'm the town banker." He pronounced it 'green yawn,' and that was French. She remembered that much from high school. His last name sounded familiar. Kiko must've picked it up from somewhere around the city.

Uncertain of her purpose in the carriage, she said, "The rider, Dennis, offered me a ride to town, but we passed it when he brought me to you instead."

Grignon nodded his head, and the carriage jerked forward, slowly rolling back toward town where she'd just come from, and April relaxed.

"What is your name, mademoiselle?"

"April McCall," she supplied, while picking at her fingernails.

"Mademoiselle April then. We shall arrive shortly. Where are you from? I have to declare your choice of clothing is...peculiar."

Why did these dream people care about her clothes so much? His seriousness and stern features brought her nerves back. April didn't remember having so many feelings during her dreams, but since she didn't want to fail Kiko's simulation, April said vaguely, "I'm from the city."

"Right. The city always was ahead of its time. Some might say it's too ahead of anything. Everyone always trying to stand out, to be unique in the hustle and bustle. That's not for me, as you can see. I prefer things quieter. Safer."

April relaxed again, sensing this Grignon wasn't going to give her trouble.

"Still, I dare offer you advice." His pleasant tone reduced just slightly. "While in this town, do attire yourself appropriately."

Fine, Kiko, point taken. To complete her mission, she had to fit in just a little, or catch more friction trying to succeed.

The carriage came to a stop, and the coachman opened the small door. April looked to Grignon for a clue what he expected her to do, but he simply smiled and nodded. April stepped out, finding herself on town soil.

Grignon followed her out, but he entered a building on the other side of the street. With him away from her, April rushed into Stanton's Spirits to get out of the sun and away from the Frenchman.

Chapter 10

After stacking logs until he'd made up his mind on what to do with the information he'd heard, Sam pushed into Stanton's Spirits. Customers filtered into the bar as the afternoon rolled into early evening. Later it would be packed after a long day's hard labor in the sun.

For now, Ross played the piano, and people spun around dancing on and between tables, with beer sloshing out of their mugs. Many more were milling about. Mr. Jenkins slapped a fellow drunkard for groping him. The offender simply laughed, and Mr. Jenkins hugged his shoulders, laughing right along with him. To the general public, this was a normal day in Bridgeport.

Sam headed straight to the bar and carved out a space to reach Lloyd. Over the noise of the customers, and Lloyd pouring drinks with a smile on his oblivious face, Sam held up a hand for Lloyd's attention.

Finally Lloyd came over, and Sam gestured for him to lean close. Sam used a cupped hand to whisper into Lloyd's ear, "Meet me at the far end of the bar. We need to talk privately."

Lloyd's smile slid away, and he nodded.

Sam fished through the crowd, and Lloyd met him at the end of the bar, within eyesight of the front door and the back storage room.

"What's going on, Sam? The place is hopping, and you look like someone kicked the snot out of you," Lloyd said. "Do I need to ban another customer for a week?"

"I have a favor to ask you. Tomorrow, can you take—?" Sam paused when he realized the bar turned dead silent. Was he too late already? Sam assessed the distance to the storage room's back exit. How much of a head start would Lloyd get if Sam stayed to fight Grignon's mercenaries?

Lloyd tapped him on the shoulder, and Sam turned around to see the beginning of the end.

Instead, a shocking woman stood in the doorway in the most outrageous clothing, something he'd never seen before. She must've been a whore from Chicago. He couldn't think of any other explanation, and how she traveled all the way up here was unimaginable. Sam already had his hands full with Grignon and his men. Sam didn't need a whore spoiling his town too.

But he couldn't peel his eyes away from her. Long, dark brown hair, stick straight, hung over her shoulders and glistened in the lamp light. Her bright eyes were round, and she had the pinkest lips he'd ever seen. Her long legs were wrapped tight with a torn material that if he had to guess was some perversion of denim. Without a proper dress, she looked almost naked! Sam's eyes were drawn to her curious tunic. The lettering made no sense. A–C–D–C, he read, confused. The letters were out of order and missing a B. Something else about her kept drawing his attention. The boots at her feet were the most bizarre thing. They only reached her ankles. Where was the rest of them?

Her witch-like power extended to everyone in the room as they all stared. A mug fell on the floor with a thump, but still the staring continued.

"I'm...I'm looking for Sam Hartley," she said in the most intoxicating voice he'd ever heard. He froze. Why him?

The whole room turned to look at Sam. His cheeks burned, and his pulse jumped. What did this outlandish whore need with him?

Wait. Was this Grignon's next trick? Had he hired some city gunslinger to do him in? Sam wouldn't fight a girl, and Grignon knew that. With a second quick assessment, she didn't appear to have any weapons on her. If so, where on earth could she hide them in that outfit? That meant she was bait for the assassin.

Sam couldn't be too careful right now. He touched around his belt for any weapons at his disposal, but he came up empty. Perhaps he could distract her long enough for Lloyd to escape, capture Sarah, and ride off to Jonathan Arris's estate.

But Sarah hadn't packed, and Sam hadn't told Lloyd the plan.

The last thing he needed right now was an assassin's bait or a city whore to distract him. And distracting she was. She smiled and walked right up to him.

Chapter 11

APRIL HAD ENTERED THE bar for refuge from the Frenchman, uncertain how to find Sam Hartley. When her booties clanked on the wood planks, the crowd slowly quieted and stared at her, filling her stomach with heavy dread and reminding her of Levi's nightmare proposal.

This was a simulation.

Kiko's graduate project.

This time the attention wasn't a bad thing, since it led her straight to the man she needed to find. Kiko hadn't warned her that Sam Hartley was a gorgeous, ruggedly handsome gunslinger cowboy. How did Kiko know to program this simulation with exactly the kind of man April would dream Sam Hartley to be? All the faces in the bar twisted with confusion and disapproval, and Sam wasn't any different.

April's cheeks heated. He was broad shouldered, built like the man knew his way around a gym. He had shoulder-length wavy brown hair, a deep five o'clock shadow along a square jaw, and those captivating blueish-green eyes the color of sea glass. His clothing matched everyone else's: dark brown trousers, a black vest, and a brown button up, but his sleeves were rolled to his elbows, exposing thick forearms.

Yummy.

And he gazed right back at her. April walked up to him, focusing on not tripping over her own two feet, and trying to ignore all the heads following her movements. The heat of her face spread throughout her chest and to the tips of her toes—some from embarrassment, and some, the more exciting part, was from Sam's gaze.

She held out her hand in greeting, "Hi, everyone here pegged you as Sam. I'm April McCall. It's nice to meet you." He glanced at her hand with squinted eyes. She added, "I don't bite."

Reluctantly, his hand enveloped hers. Touching his rough skin made her flush again and sparks ignited under her skin. The corners of her lips lifted, and her knees wobbled. This dream-perfect man made her come apart by a simple touch.

Reality sucked compared to this.

Sam's grip was loose, as if he hadn't shaken a hand before.

"What the hell is she wearing?" someone nearby whispered.

"I have no idea," another person responded.

Seriously, these judgy people were getting annoying. Why did Kiko have to include that part? April liked her outfit. It was cute, and Grignon could stuff it.

"I don't know about you, but I could use a drink." April lowered herself on the closest stool, and slowly the noise of the bar returned. After walking through a field and riding on the back of a horse through a hot summer's dusty town, her dry throat needed a drink.

April reached in her tight pocket and withdrew a twenty-dollar bill. Sliding it on the counter, she asked the bartender, "Cold beer please, whatever's on tap is cool by me."

The black man cleaning a mug glanced at her twenty and back. "That's not good here."

"What do you mean? My money's as good as yours." April found the first bug in the simulation. At the worst time, too.

Sam sat next to her. His intoxicating scent, a rugged mix of pine and leather, fluttered her heart. His large hand touched the twenty and slid it back toward her. He dropped a coin on the counter and said, "Give her a tapper, Lloyd."

April's chest fluttered at his deep, slightly lilted voice. He had a lovely accent—just a hint of Irish, and the pleasant surprise caught her off-guard. Her butterflies danced with excitement, and she wanted to slap herself in the forehead, but that would just gather more attention and delay her objective. Sam was only her dream, crafted by a super nerd. Of course, he was perfect. When April returned to report on her mission, she and Kiko could laugh about how well Kiko knew her.

Lloyd the bartender finished wiping out the mug, and he filled it from the tap. He placed it in front of her without a coaster and then took the coin. There was very little head, and she liked it—more room in the mug for beer.

"Thank you," she said to Lloyd. She downed the whole mug of beer, ignoring that it was warm, and keenly aware Sam watched her. When she finished, she set the empty down and said to Sam, "Was that a dime?"

Sam said, "Look, Miss April McCall, I'm happy to help you quench your thirst, but I don't want anything to do with whatever you're here for. I would appreciate if you leave me alone."

April ignored his dismissal. She had a mission to fulfill. She didn't know how or when he was supposed to get arrested, but the longer she distracted him, the less likely that was to happen. "I insist you let me repay your kindness."

Sam stood, but a loud shout from the back corner of the crowd turned his attention. April lifted off the stool to see. A fight broke out, and within moments the whole bar was yelling, swinging, and crashing all over the place. A chair flew and knocked a drunk moron into April, shoving her against the bar's edge with a rib-bruising crash, and he splashed warm beer all over her clothes. Her face pinched with the sudden sharp pain.

Sam grabbed the idiot and tossed him back into the crowd.

"Let's get out of here before you're turned into mashed mutton," he said to her, grasping her upper arm with his thick fingers and leading the way out.

A heavy glass mug soared through the air and hit Sam on the back of the head. He toppled over, pulling April down, and she landed on his chest. April blushed while lying nose to nose on the most handsome unconscious stranger she'd ever seen. She beat back the desire to stroke his short-trimmed whiskers to find out if they were bristly or soft, but she inhaled his scent with no shame.

The drunken crowd cheered and hooted at the sight.

Lloyd leaned over the bar with brows furrowed in concern. "Is Sam all right?"

"He's breathing. I think he's just knocked out."

The front door opened wide, and a man in a primitive police uniform stepped inside. Ice cold fear slid through her gut. This angry-looking officer was not here for a beer. She tugged on Sam's arm and tapped him on the cheek. The whiskers were soft. That wasn't important right now, focus!

"Sam. Sam, wake up. We have to go now."

From the back of the room a tinny voice shouted, "He's there, officer, on the ground! Get his little whore too!"

Oh no.

April's stomach twisted. She was about to fail. She pulled with all her might and propped Sam up to a seated position. He leaned back against the bar, and his unfocused eyes opened.

"Sam, we have to get out of here now."

He didn't respond.

"Sam?"

The officer pushed his way closer.

"Sam, can you hear me? We have to go now."

April could step away and watch Sam get arrested, where two good men would die, or she could delay the officer. Knowing herself, she'd be able to buy about thirty seconds before getting herself arrested too.

Was there a reset button here?

Sam had been kind and accepting, while Grignon had been insulting. She just couldn't leave him like this. Plus, she didn't want Kiko to get a bad grade.

April tapped at his cheeks again, checking over her shoulder as the officer, who dodged flying mugs and drunken bodies, weaved his way through the crowd toward her.

With all the chaos around them, the officer clearly targeted Sam. What did Sam do?

Chapter 12

THE FIRST THING SAM noticed was a throbbing head and a sore neck from leaning forward. Eyes pinched shut with pain, he shifted to touch the wound, but surprise at iron shackles on his wrists stopped him, and that was when the bouncing ride tipped him to the side. How did he end up inside a police wagon? He didn't need to see through the bars behind him to know they were headed south out of town, toward the jail. Grignon had wanted his hide since he'd overheard the Frenchman's plans for Lloyd, and there was nothing to stop the bastard now. He sighed, resigned to his fate.

Sam tipped his head up to rest against the iron bars blocking the window, and when they hit a bump, his bruised skull woke up with a spark of pain. April McCall sat across from him, likewise shackled. Sam raised his eyebrows. If she was Grignon's accomplice—the bait for his assassin—she had no business in here. Which meant her being a whore from Chicago had to be the most likely assumption. Regardless of what the next few hours would bring, curiosity had him asking, "Why were you looking for me?"

April leaned forward into his face, studying him strangely. "Does your head hurt? Are you seeing double?" She lifted three fingers on one hand. "How many fingers do you see?"

But even a whore from Chicago still wore a dress, usually with extra skin exposed at her bosom. April's trousers were torn like she'd fought a bear, but there were no marks on her skin. Through the revealing gaps in the fabric, her smooth upper thigh peeked through. Sam cast his gaze away out of respect. "Who are you?"

"You don't seem surprised about being arrested. I suppose that's part of the program. Kiko didn't tell me, so what did you do?"

April didn't act like a whore either. She hadn't thrown herself at him. She hadn't asked him what he wanted. If neither of his assumptions were true, he was completely baffled. The way she spoke, and the things she said were so foreign to him. He didn't understand most of it. Since his life would end shortly, there was no reason not to tell her the truth. She appeared doomed to his same fate, and he could use some entertainment.

"I tried to impress a man. Turns out he was the wrong man. You?"

"I'm helping with a research project," she answered and tilted her head at him. "I'm curious what your programmed response is."

Sam laughed. "You are the strangest person I've ever met. Research? You don't look like a physician."

This time she laughed. It was a sweet feminine sound, bringing a spot of cheer to an otherwise melancholy day.

"Veterinary assistant, actually. I work for my brother. He's the veterinarian, the man in charge. I've majored in nursing, teaching, and business, but so far, I haven't found my place in the world yet. So until then, the vet clinic is my nine-to-five."

He understood 'brother', and 'place in the world', and figured he could cross whore from Chicago off his list, leaving him completely baffled. The pungent scent of horse filled the wagon, the only thing that made sense right now. "Where did you say you're from?"

"The real world, and from the likes of things in here, the future."

If she'd escaped a women's institution for her mad ravings, that still didn't explain her attire. "Pardon?"

"I don't know how this works either. I'm not a nerd like my roommate, but I was on a couch in my house, and after some weird sensations, I woke up in a field of grass back that way." She lifted her shackled arms and pointed north. "I'm not sure if there's a malfunction in the program, but I don't think I'm supposed to be in here with you. Come to think of it, Kiko didn't put her weird thingies on my head, so how did I end up in her dream program? Whatever technology she's using is really scary. The detail in here is incredible. I would never have thought to buy a beer with a dime that looked super old. And you"—April blushed—"I tried to wake you after that mug hit you in the head, and you feel real to me. These shackles are cold and heavy. That Grignon guy gave me the creeps. In a dream, the most abstract bizarre things imaginable are perfectly normal. Something about this isn't normal."

Out of her confusing ramblings that Sam couldn't begin to reply to, one name jumped out at him. "You know Grignon?"

"I met him. He gave me a ride to town after one of his friends gave me a ride through town. That's probably another glitch."

"That's all he did?" Sam asked with a raised brow, trying to ferret out her real relationship with the murderous tyrant. Lloyd was unaware of his precarious situation, and Sarah was undefended and oblivious to the danger right in front of her. Anything he could discover about that bastard, the better the odds of surviving this mess.

April squinted at him. "Well, he told me I had to dress better."

Sam sighed. That wasn't useful information, but it confirmed her story. "That's him all right." As he held April's bright blue gaze, she vanished in a blink as if she'd never existed. What kind of witchery was this?

Sam exclaimed in surprise and scooted back as far as his shackles allowed. How had she escaped? He peered through the iron bars of the wagon, but she wasn't out there.

He reached back and touched the injury on his head. He must've been hit harder than he'd thought. Skeptically, he placed a shackled hand over the spot where she sat, expecting to confirm his suspicions.

The seat was warm.

Chapter 13
Present Day, Green Bay, Wisconsin

APRIL BLINKED, A SUDDEN chill skirting across her skin. The police wagon vanished, but her arms remained shackled, and humid darkness and working streetlights surrounded her. She sat on a patch of cold grass in a familiar residential neighborhood. Vehicles with headlights drove by, and one had bass thumping in the trunk. So, she'd been pulled from the Matrix, but how did she end up here?

Why were her arms still shackled?

Was this some dream-within-a-dream—another glitch? April was not volunteering to be anyone's Guinea pig ever again.

If Sam's world badgered her about her perfectly cute outfit, this world was going to say something about these shackles. April gripped the wide rusty cuff and tried to slide her hand through it, but all she did was hurt herself. The shackles weren't loose enough.

What now? After her embarrassment from Levi's public proposal, and the unfortunate, but admittedly useful, allure from Stanton's Spirits, April didn't want to find out what kind of attention she'd get this time. She used her fingers to tuck the chain under her sticky T-shirt and hooked her thumbs into her belt loops to hold the chain snug and rattle-free. She walked back home with only the sounds of her booties snapping and crunching the dusty pebbles on the concrete sidewalk.

Her front door was unlocked, and she walked inside, closing it behind her in relief. Kiko's laptop sat on the coffee table. Grateful for the bathroom, she washed the dirt from her hands and face and for a flash of a second, wondered if she'd find another of herself in here. Nah, Kiko made this world too, but at least it was clean, familiar, and had running water.

April sat heavily on her couch. How was she going to get these chains off? A locksmith wouldn't carry an antique skeleton key for these. And she'd have to explain where they came from. Dirt caked her torn skinny jeans, beer stains crusted her favorite AC/DC T-shirt, and her hair was frizzy and sticky with beer from the chaos at the bar. How would he react? Who would he call? This was all a mess.

Kiko came out from her bedroom.

April was relieved to see a familiar face, but she had so many questions. "Where am I?"

"You're back home. We need to talk."

No kidding. "So this is the real world? I'm not in the simulation anymore?"

"I've operated like this for many years. Usually, the match figures out exactly what they need to do to change history and find their happily ever after. Sometimes they accept the truth, other times it's a struggle. I wasn't sure which way you'd lean, so that's why I fed you a story." Kiko looked down at her hands.

"Story?"

"I'm not a student. I'm an agent of Chaos. I signed on the dotted line, and I have to keep going until my term is up someday. My job is to match people who otherwise would never meet, most notably, through time."

April stood. "Are you kidding me right now? The simulation is a lie, and you're telling me that the Sam I just met was real? That I traveled through time to meet him?"

"That's correct."

April scoffed. "And here I gave you credit for the incredible detail in the simulation."

Kiko didn't answer.

Sam was real. April had suspected the simulation was a little too good to be true. "I failed the mission or whatever that was. How did I get back here?"

"I pulled you. I can create a tunnel through time to push and pull as needed, but I have limits. I can only send one person across the threshold, there and back again, and since modern people tend to adjust to the past easier than the reverse, I need you to complete the mission, because Sam Hartley is destined for greater things."

The words processed but didn't make sense. "If he existed over a hundred years ago, how is he destined for anything? He's already dead." Picturing that handsome face, that youthful, sexy man dead before his time hurt more than she'd expected.

"Time is not so linear as that," Kiko said.

With time at her fingers, April thought of the first thing she would do. "Can I kill Hitler?"

"You wouldn't get within a hundred feet of him."

Good point. "I need a beer." April went straight to the fridge and cracked a bottle cap. Cold hops slid down her throat. Her nerdy roommate turned out to be...inhuman? April didn't know whether to be in awe or terrified, and she hated that confusion. Kiko was her friend. She trusted her, or she used to. April chugged the entire beer—one hand on the bottle, the other raised at the end of the short chain. How uncomfortable and humiliating to be shackled like this.

What if Levi saw? Levi... She had to give her boyfriend her answer, and she hadn't even thought about it. This was the worst time to drop an existential crisis in her lap. April set the empty in the recycle bin and turned to her roommate. "Why now? If you can play with time, why not yesterday? Why not last year before we signed the lease? Why not four years ago before I wasted time on two prior boyfriends and a lot of tuition?" Wait a minute. April slowed her angry roll. Kiko only asked her to prevent Sam from getting arrested to save two men's lives. It wasn't like April had to stay there. She added, "Actually, none of that matters, but I'm curious. Why me?"

"April, you needed to hear something very important from someone you care about before you could leave. I also needed you to trust me."

"After all that time to prepare me for this—which by the way, wasn't very good—why did you return me so soon? Sam and I could've escaped. But since I'm here...he didn't. He was executed, wasn't he?"

Kiko nodded solemnly.

"Is there anything you can do now?"

Kiko said simply, "No."

The guy was a stranger, but April couldn't stomach his death on her hands. "Is there anything I can do?"

Her roommate smiled. "That's the right question."

April's cell phone rang. Levi's name popped up on the caller ID, and her stomach flipped. She didn't have an answer for him, and she hadn't even thought of him, but now she remembered Kiko had said time wasn't the same from one side to the other. "How long was I gone?"

"It's only been fifteen minutes."

"Fifteen minutes? And Levi's calling me already?" April sent him to voicemail. She swiped further and found six unread messages. She switched her phone to silent mode. "I still have like nine hours and forty-five minutes until morning. I need a shower. Can we continue this after? I'm covered in sticky stale beer and god knows what else." April lifted a hunk of hair glued in a clump.

"Sure."

April turned, eager to wash, when the chains rattled. "First, can you take these off?"

"Can I borrow your Swiss army knife?"

April sent her a puzzled look and collected one from the basketful on top of her dresser. Mathew bought her one every year for her birthday, as if she were in constant mortal danger or in need of an emergency screwdriver. He also gifted her pepper spray last year and made her promise she would take it with her always. She usually left it at home. Mathew was clearly paranoid.

April handed the tool to her roommate, and Kiko unfolded the corkscrew. She poked the tip inside the keyhole and spun the curved metal. They both listened to the clicks of the tumblers aligning. The shackles opened one after the other.

"Do I want to know how you learned to do that?" April shrugged out of the cold, heavy metal, and Kiko held them.

"It's a long story," she said. "Go get cleaned up. Do you want a nap before you go back?"

"I'm too wired. Just a shower."

While she lathered up, April thought of Sam. She could swim in his bright sea glass eyes and listen to the sexy lilt in his voice forever. But he wasn't reality. She needed to complete a mission for Kiko so Sam could fulfill his destiny, whatever that meant. But Sam appeared standoffish around her. Likely her clothing had something to do with that. And she didn't have enough time to convince him she was friend and not foe. "Can I go back earlier? I could use more time."

Kiko's high cheeks flushed. "Yes, but I recommend you dress first."

April didn't have clothing appropriate for the time, but she did have a bridesmaid dress that could pass or at least turn less heads, and she didn't care if it got ruined. Her arms would be exposed and the back dipped low, but it was a lacy pale pink with a full skirt, similar to theirs.

With their dirt roads, she stuffed her socked toes into her white sneakers and collected a canister of pepper spray and one of her many Swiss army knives from the top of her dresser. The scissors were the size of her pinky nail, but they still worked well. She took a wad of twenties from inside her top dresser drawer and folded them. Wait. Like Lloyd, they wouldn't recognize this as money, would they? It was better than nothing. The only reason she kept this bridesmaid's dress was because it had pockets—so glorious! April stuffed her necessities conveniently out of sight. She stopped in the bathroom and brought out a roll of toilet paper. "Can I bring this too?"

Kiko laughed.

"Maybe I should just pack a bag." Excitement bubbled up, as though she were packing for a rustic vacation. She hadn't taken a real vacation ever. A couple weekend trips with Levi, sure, and some with Kiko and previous friends. Otherwise she worked weekends through school, and rent was trouble enough with forty hours a week and no paid time off. That wasn't Mathew's fault.

"The less you bring, the fewer questions you will have."

April scrapped the bag idea. The toilet paper would be dirty by the time she needed it anyway. She then rummaged in the fridge and made herself a sandwich. She offered one to Kiko, who politely declined. April ate, cleaned up her dishes, and stretched out on the couch.

Her mysterious roommate stood over her and inserted something into April's pocket. "Just in case I am not available to watch you, this device is an emergency responder. You open the lid and press the button, and it will send you back immediately to this moment and location. Do not lose it."

"Why didn't you give me the trinket last time?"

Kiko's solemn features dragged her face down. "You didn't need it."

April gulped at the ominous warning. "So, how many times do I get to figure this out?"

"Two more."

April had expected a flippant answer along the lines of 'until you get it right'. "I have a limit?"

"If you haven't figured it out after three tries, then the match isn't meant to be."

"Has that ever happened before?" April didn't want to be the first to fail completely.

"A few."

Yikes. Okay, then. "I'm ready to go," she said.

Not bothering to pretend with her computer, Kiko's hand, palm forward, reached toward April's body. Kiko's face scrunched up in concentration, and the waves in April's vision returned. She closed her eyes to the blackness, ready to take on the past.

☐

Chapter 14
1852 Bridgeport, Wisconsin

One week earlier…

April returned to the same blue skies and tall grasses. At least she had sneakers on for the walk, and to save time, she'd avoid Dennis Durand and that creepy Grignon guy. April marched through the grasses and drafted a mental map of the area. Her house, which didn't exist yet, was about eight blocks southeast of the town, and her brother's clinic would be ten blocks west from there. Just being here, in real history was mind-blowing.

The clopping of hooves sounded in the distance behind her. She ducked down into the tall grasses. It was Dennis mounted on the same horse. That meant Kiko hadn't given her much extra time. She stayed low and Dennis came up near her. His horse nickered in alarm, and Dennis spun it around, looking for the source of the horse's concern. "What do you see, boy? Eh?"

April ducked lower and steadied her breathing. He was several yards away, but she realized too late horses had a great sense of smell. The horse shifted its ears and its nostrils flared. Dennis scanned the area, looking for trouble. Getting caught by him would waste time, so she waited.

After several turns, he gave up and continued his journey. April sighed in relief and when he was out of view, she set off. When she reached town, a few people hurrying about their errands took notice of her, but she marched on like she owned the place, and instead of blatant complaints about her clothing, she received disapproving looks. April pushed open the heavy door to Lloyd's bar.

The place was empty. Where was everyone?

Lloyd stood behind the bar tallying something. She walked over and leaned toward him. "Hi, Lloyd."

The tall and lean black man set a pencil down—not a basic yellow number two. It was plain, showing its natural wood. April wondered for a flash how it would do on drawing paper.

With wariness, Lloyd surveyed her up and down and asked, "Do I know you?"

So Kiko had given her more time.

"Sam told me who you were," she covered quickly.

Lloyd softened up and smiled. "What can I get for you, miss? Not to stifle my own business, but liquor isn't traditionally sold before noon."

April laughed. "Actually, I'm looking for Sam. Have you seen him?"

Lloyd picked up the pencil and pointed it out the door. "It's Tuesday. He's at Porter's."

"Right." April had no idea what day it was the last time she was here, so that reference was useless in gauging her time frame. "Where can I find Porter's?"

Lloyd lifted a brow. Before he asked questions she didn't want to answer, she added, "I'm new in town."

He smiled. "That much is obvious. The General Store. Take a right out of here, and it's a few buildings down on the left. Can't miss it."

"Thanks," April said and left.

She found The General Store easily enough, having half-remembered it from her tour with Dennis. It was tall and narrow as if the sleeping quarters were upstairs, just like Lloyd's bar. The storefront had the same long covered wooden porch that most of the businesses seemed to have. The wood siding was unpainted, but the lettering of the store name was fresh and bright.

She stepped inside and discovered a primitive convenience store. Open baskets contained dried goods in bulk with scoops for self-service. Her eyes landed on the exposed food, and all she could think of was the public's filthy hands in it, and bugs and dust. April hid her disgust, completely grateful for plastic packaging, no matter how awful it was for the environment.

An older, round man with hair that was snowy and sparse busied himself at the front counter. April cleared her throat. The man, who must've been Porter, turned around, took a sweeping look of disapproval at her, and said, "Oh dear, miss. You'll want to see Perez. He owns the clothing store up yonder."

"Thanks for the tip, but I'm looking for Sam. Lloyd said he'd be here."

Porter frowned. "Ah, yes, Tuesday." He glanced at the front door just as it opened. "Ask and you shall receive." Porter nodded toward the door, and April turned around.

Sam walked in with a dark brown suit and hat in the style of a Victorian gentleman. His brown waves were defying the brim, and April's cheeks burned. He was just as she remembered him—towering and broadly built with sea glass eyes. She melted just looking at him.

Sam froze in place, beautiful eyes wide with surprise.

Chapter 15

THE LADY STANDING NEAR Porter was stunning despite her strange dress and bare arms. Her smiling lips were bright pink, framing perfectly straight teeth. Her large blue eyes sparkled, and her tumble of brown hair reached beyond her shoulders. He wanted to brush it back and graze her skin with his touch.

She waved and approached him, confirming they were acquainted, but Sam couldn't remember where he'd seen such a woman, hardly believing he'd forgotten her. The only way to avoid making a fool of himself was to be honest. He offered his hand. "I do apologize, but I can't recall your name."

She accepted his hand, and his heart thumped wildly at her soft touch. Before he could kiss her knuckles, she shook his hand firmly like a man. How strange.

"April McCall," she said. Her smooth voice was the most intoxicating thing he'd ever heard. "I'm here on business. Do you have a moment?"

At least the lady wasn't offended by his poor memory. Sam assessed her in a new light. She had nothing in her hands to indicate her profession. Unless she was in need of horseshoes, the only reason someone would ask for him on business would be in relation to Grignon. Warily, he said, "Can you wait outside? I need a minute with my client."

April nodded and stepped out.

Sam turned to Porter and leaned on his countertop. "Good morning, Aaron."

With a grumpy jut of his chin, Porter ducked under his cash register and set a thin envelope in front of him. "There's nothing good about Tuesday mornings."

There was nothing good about any days lately.

Porter lowered his voice. "When is that bastard going to stop robbing us? He claims to be protecting us. From what? If we don't pay, he's the one we need protection from."

Porter knew Sam was just like the townsfolk, bound to rules they hated, which was why the old man traitorously asked for help. Whenever questioned, Sam tried to make light of the situation, so the town didn't tear itself apart. "Someday we will stop him," Sam said quietly. "A band of brothers together in arms, we will fight. We will be free." Sam sighed with a smile on his face. He didn't have the answers they wanted. "But I could rattle off a dozen ways we will fail. I'm not sure how many of those ways are humorous or simply pathetic. But I, for one, prefer to keep my bowels intact."

Porter shook his head. "Take his payment for the week and get out of here. I used to like seeing you, boy, but lately, you bring dread."

"I don't blame you, Aaron." Sam tipped his hat to Porter and exited, leaving the old man to silently stew.

April waited alongside his mount, picking at her fingernails, and her fingers bore no rings, not that he had any interest in her like that, but knowing she wouldn't have a husband accomplice after him was a relief. He cleared his throat. "I've got a small errand to run before discussing business. Care to join me?" He held out his hand to assist her up on the horse.

"Absolutely," she said. She accepted his hand and stood there.

"Ready?" he asked, biting back a grin of amusement.

"For what?"

Sam whistled shrilly, and the horse kneeled to the ground.

"That's a neat trick," she said.

Sam helped her seat herself and was surprised when she swung her leg over the horse's head. Frilly layers of her dress decorated the horse, amusing Sam but not the horse. How did this woman survive? "Hold on to the horn if you need to."

"I don't like horses."

"Well, you'll have to adjust, because I don't have a carriage." Sam repeated the whistle, and the horse stood up, rocking the lady. She gripped the horn, terrified. Sam stifled his laugh and mounted the horse behind her, swinging his leg over the horse's rump and settling on the saddle's low cantle. His open legs pressed up against her, while the horse walked with its head bobbing west toward his least favorite place.

Amused, he added, "Then how do you get around? Fly?"

"It's a long story," she said.

"We've got time."

April didn't respond, and he didn't want to push, so they traveled without speaking for a while. The cadence of the horse's hoof beats against the dusty dirt road would've been mesmerizing if not for their destination and the beautiful woman between his thighs. Her warmth permeated his pants, and he fought the urge to wrap his arm around her protectively. She was not Isabel.

"Are you from the city?"

"Something like that." April turned her head just enough for him to hear her, and he noticed the smooth planes of her face interrupted by dimples when she spoke. Her scent was a thrilling mix of soft flowers and fruit. She was definitely not Isabel.

"What kind of business are you in town for?"

"I've been sent to help with a problem," she said vaguely.

What would a city girl, who couldn't navigate a horse, possibly help with? Sam surveyed for trouble as they progressed, and a single rider appeared on the top of the hill up ahead. He recognized one of Grignon's mercenaries on patrol. He whispered into her ear, and her soft strands tickled his nose. "This guy is not friendly. Let me do the talking."

APRIL RELUCTANTLY RELEASED THE saddle's horn to wipe her sweaty palms on her dress. Her hands shook with anxiety, or maybe from gripping the horn too hard. Nah, definitely anxiety. She had the most handsome man imaginable sitting behind her, and she still couldn't believe this wasn't a dream. His thighs pressed against her legs, and a continuous fire crackled in her chest. That alone would be enough to make her stutter, blush, and run for cover.

The lone rider descending the hill was the second reason for the tremors. Her stomach flip-flopped when she recognized him. Dennis Durand with the subdued accent was polite to her last time, but Sam's warning sent the hairs on her arms lifting.

"Halt there," Dennis said.

Sam pulled the reins, and the horse stomped his feet, unsettled. His head rocked and he nickered. Did horses sense bad guys like dogs did?

"Good day, Dennis," Sam said. His tone was dark, and that made April even more nervous.

Dennis scrutinized Sam before turning his attention to April. The guy gave her the creeps, almost as much as Grignon had. His scowl made her wish she was back at work, safe, with Levi at the counter holding a bouquet. The daily routine didn't seem so bad now, since she was never in a position of true danger before. The only reason her butt stayed in the saddle was the security of Sam's legs behind her. He white-knuckled the reins alongside her body, protectively caging her.

"Allow us to pass. We're making a drop," Sam said. His firm voice betrayed nothing of his alarmed body language. Sam tapped a saddle bag.

Dennis tracked Sam's hands. "Carry on."

April sagged in relief.

Sam nudged the horse again, and they continued their slow walking pace. April didn't dare look over Sam's shoulder at Dennis.

"From personal experience," Sam said into her ear, sending tingles along her spine. "Don't ever mix with Dennis or his twin, Daniel. Those gents are cold and ruthless, which is why Grignon hired them."

April had already met the squirrely Grignon, but she knew nothing about him. "Who's this Grignon guy?"

Sam laughed. "How I wish I didn't know! You really aren't from here. He runs this town. Owns everyone."

"He owns the people?" April asked, disbelief in her voice.

"If each business pays him a weekly fee, he claims to offer protection from the bandits on the trade routes."

"That sounds like extortion."

"You wouldn't be wrong."

"What if someone doesn't pay?"

Sam remained quiet. She was about to repeat the question when he answered, "Then I have to deal with the delinquent store owner and the twins myself." His hands flicked the reins, and she noticed his knuckles. No longer blanched from strain, he had heavy scars and long-term swelling from misuse.

Sam wasn't a store owner, she'd figured, but he wasn't friendly with Grignon either. "What's your role in all this?"

"I collect the money."

Sam was some sort of enforcer for an extortion ring. She no longer wanted to know what he'd done to get arrested and executed. No matter how dangerous Sam could be, she still felt safe with him.

At the summit of the hill, an unmarked dirt path branched off to the right, and Sam guided them up into the dense vegetation. The path opened to an immaculate garden with moss creeping between steppingstones, sculpted hedges, and a pergola covered in climbing flowers. Standing sentry was a Victorian mansion straight from the black and white photos she saw in her history books. The color was a sunshine yellow with white trim and a wrap-around front porch. It was beautiful and absolutely not where she'd expected some villain to live.

Sam stopped the horse at the apex of the circular drive and dismounted. He helped April down; his broad hands grasped her waist.

"Wait here. I'll just be a moment." Sam retrieved a package from the saddlebags.

April took the reins and stroked the horse between his eyes. She was less afraid of him now that her feet were firmly on the ground. "What's his name?"

"Grignon," he answered, looking up at the grand windows.

"No." April smiled. "The horse. If I'm going to keep someone company, I'd at least like to know his name."

"He doesn't have one."

"I'll fix that." It would give her something to focus on.

Sam said, "I'll be right back." He walked up the steppingstones to the porch and knocked on the door. It immediately opened, and swallowed Sam.

April tickled the soft spot between the horse's nostrils. "How could you go nameless all this time? You're a big, pretty boy. I've never done veterinary care on horses. We handle dogs and cats. No offense."

The horse blinked. He wasn't much of a conversationalist, but hanging out with him distracted her from whatever was going on inside.

"Not that there's anything wrong with horses." April released his reins, and the horse lazily approached the grass for a snack. She followed and ran her hand along his shiny coat. His tail swished. "You're not so scary now. How about I name you Bucky? I like that name."

The front door reopened, and a woman with a full dress, white apron, and a matching bonnet stepped onto the porch. "Come with me, miss. Master Grignon wants to see you."

Master? What the hell kind of lord duke guy was he? She left Bucky to graze and followed the woman inside. The interior was like a mid-nineteenth-century museum, except everything was new. The vast foyer opened with a pair of curving staircases culminating at the second floor. Doorways lined both sides of the entrance. Persian rugs, shiny mahogany furniture, and large palm plants were artfully arranged. Happy chirps and clicks of budgies came from an adjoining room.

Two hulking men, wearing long sleeve shirts buttoned up and loaded shoulder harnesses, flanked the doorway on the right. Suddenly this whole extortion situation seemed far more real, and much more terrifying. April's feet froze, and she swallowed a lump caught in her throat.

One of them looked exactly like Dennis but without a scar, so that one must be Daniel. She didn't recognize the other. He was equally tall, equally muscular, but his face showed no relation. He had dark beady eyes and a hooked nose. Neither of them turned their heads to her.

"Don't be alarmed by them. They just make sure everyone stays safe. Come along, dear." The woman who invited her inside dashed between them, and April reluctantly followed with her shoulders slumped to appear smaller.

April stopped just inside the doorway out of respect. Books lined the walls, floor to ceiling, and a reading chair stood in the corner near the window.

Sam faced an expansive mahogany desk, and his hands hung casually at his sides. Grignon sat behind the desk, but upon her entering, he swung his legs off the shiny lacquered surface and stalked forward with an empty smile. He held out his hand in a strange shape. To be treated like an equal, she had to act like one, even if she trembled on the inside. April wasn't sure if he was offering her a different handshake than she knew or if he had arthritis, but she grasped his hand, twisted it to the proper position, and shook it with authority. "April McCall, sir. You must be Grignon?"

"Well then—" Grignon's lips spread into a grin. "Where did you find this girl? She is unorthodox."

Sam didn't answer, and Grignon didn't let go of her hand. Something sinister lurked within those eyes, and ice slithered down her spine and along her bare arms.

"I asked you a question, boy," Grignon said while keeping his gaze locked on April. He still didn't release her hand. She tried to jerk it away, but he squeezed tighter. There would be no equal treatment here.

April's pulse kicked into overdrive. Her legs fought between the urge to flee and the inability to move.

"She's here on business." Sam said with clipped restraint. He stepped up behind her shoulder, as if in silent challenge. His heat radiated onto her back. The reassurance helped her stay in one place.

"So, the mademoiselle is not yours then?"

That was enough. No one owned her, Grignon didn't have permission to continue touching her, and she was an adult, not a child. April yanked her hand away, and this time, she was free. She backed up a step and bumped into Sam.

Sam squeezed his eyes shut as if she'd made a mistake.

Her heart thundered in her ears.

AS MUCH AS SAM didn't want her in here, now he knew her 'business' had nothing to do with Grignon, but it wasn't much of a relief. At Grignon's interest in April, Sam's hands balled into fists, but he released them before the challenging snake noticed. Sam would not win a fistfight against Grignon and two mercenaries.

If he told Grignon that April was a random stranger, the Frenchman would claim her now. Sam couldn't stomach whatever he'd do to her, but with Daniel Durand and Rob Bertrand guarding the door, he couldn't stop him either. If he told Grignon that April was his, a target would be placed on her head, because Grignon loved useful pawns to control. That was unacceptable, too. The question was a trap.

April trembled in front of him. She rubbed her open palms on her dress. It was good she was afraid. Grignon was not a man to mess with. Sam wished he hadn't. And that was where the best idea came from. Sam had to untangle April from Grignon entirely. The only way to do that was to stake his own claim on her, get her out of this estate safely, and then make her disappear as soon as possible.

"Is she yours? I will not ask you again," Grignon repeated.

"Aye," Sam said. "The lady is mine."

April didn't react.

"Really?" Grignon circled them both like a shark, brow lifted in amusement. Everything was a game to him. "Moving on so quickly, are we?"

April was rigid from either terror or shock. As Dumas wrote in Sam's favorite book: 'For all evils there are two remedies—time and silence.' April was wise in her silence.

Grignon returned to his desk, for the moment satisfied with Sam's answer. The snake slid the day's envelope closer to himself and used a letter opener to slice through the seal. He showed a disinterested laziness at the task, which angered Sam, but he stayed silent.

Grignon counted the total right in front of him. Awkward was Sam's first thought. Afraid of what Grignon would deduce was next. Escape came rounding up third.

Sam slipped his hand in April's for reassurance. Her gentle touch tingled his hand, sending hot sensations through his body. He squeezed her hand to stop the tingles, but she squeezed tighter in return. He wanted to tease her about it, but this wasn't the place. If April could distract him while under armed guard in Grignon's personal library, Sam imagined what other distractions she was capable of.

But with their hands clasped, she was easier to protect, faster to deliver to safety. That was the truth of it, even if not all the truth.

"Is this all of it?" Grignon asked with an accusing tone.

"Aye, sir." Sam had never taken a single cent from the man. He wouldn't want his tainted cash, anyway. If Daniel and Rob weren't standing guard, he'd blast a round into the Frenchman's chest. Of course, he didn't have his gun on him. A knife would do just as well. Then he'd hunt every dollar in the house from cellar to attic and redistribute it to everyone who'd been robbed. Sam didn't care what the consequences would be. "That's every dollar."

Grignon leaned back and crossed his ankles, smashing and scattering the bills as if they were trash. He smirked and said, "What is this I hear about you organizing the business owners?"

Sam's body chilled. His reassuring private conversations, with whom he thought were his friends, had been reported to Grignon. Now Sam didn't know who to trust, and denial was all he had. "I am not aware of anything like that, sir."

"I suppose not," Grignon said. "Because we both know you're too clever for something as imbecilic as that."

Grignon's anger was well-disguised behind the calm exterior. Sam had first-hand knowledge of that, and he had no reply without angering him more. The only imbecile in the room was the one he stared at. Eventually his game would end, and Sam planned to be the one to end it.

But how?

Sam squeezed April's hand again and waited for the snake's next move. There wasn't much furniture to hide behind in the event of a shootout.

Grignon lit a cigar and inhaled deep. With a flick of his wrist, he excused Sam.

Not one to waste an opportunity, Sam whispered in April's ear, "Let's go."

He tugged April's hand, and with confidence, he rushed through the guarded library door and outside, eager to bring April to safety.

His horse was gone.

Chapter 16

"Where's Bucky?" April asked as they stood on the front porch of Grignon's estate, watching in horror as their attempt to flee was cut off at the knees. She was acutely aware Sam still held her hand, and it was reassuring, despite the circumstances.

"Who's Bucky?" Sam asked.

"Your horse."

"That's the name you picked for him?" Sam sent her a quizzical look and whistled loud and short.

Bucky appeared from out of the garden, and Sam lifted her hand in support and pressed his other hand against her thigh to help her into the saddle. April blocked out the thoughts of his hands on her, even though her treacherous body noticed.

Sam climbed up behind her and his arms reached protectively on either side of her, holding the reins. With a quick nudge, Bucky trotted down the path toward the road.

"Why not Chief, or Spitfire, or Duke or something? He's an intact specimen. He needs a manly name."

April expected some chest thumping and caveman grunts. She snorted. "If you like those names, why didn't you give him one?"

"I never named a horse before. It's just transportation."

April made a noise of feigned horror. "Not where I come from." It was hard for her to remember that horses were the equivalent of cars and not pets here, but people still named their cars out of affection. Why would this be any different?

They traveled faster on their departure, and in no time at all they hooked a left on the main road toward town. Hidden around a bend in the road and a thicket of trees, April gasped.

Sam stopped Bucky right in front of her brother's veterinary clinic. How did she miss this before? The exterior was the same, but the roof was more primitive, and the landscaping and parking lot were missing. She spotted the shiny steel plaque with 1841 engraved on its finish—the address, or was it the year of construction? Either way, it was definitely the same building. She stared in awe, and the tension in her chest released in excitement. Mathew would love to see this.

Sam dismounted and helped her down. He gave the horse a smack on the rear, sending it to graze in the yard.

"Where are we?" she asked.

Sam led her by the hand into the log cabin. "We need to talk."

Inside, the cabin was so different from what she'd expected, and she found herself browsing around like she'd walked into an open house. The registration counter and lobby were the living quarters, the exam rooms were bedrooms, but the storage closet was still a closet. The fireplace, fresh red brick, was in the same location. The original walls were exposed, making it much more rustic than the modern drywall. The windows had been replaced too, and that was good. Winters were brutal in Wisconsin. The bathroom was missing. Instead it appeared to be a closet or pantry with kitchen tools, bolts of cloth, and dried foods. On a shelf was an empty basin for water. There was no tub, no shower, no running water at all. Yikes.

"Have you never seen a house before?" a woman's voice said from behind her. Surprised, April turned to see a young woman in a plain dress, apron, and bonnet smiling at her. Her unlined skin, bright eyes, and small lips made her appear much younger than Sam, a teenager, and her nose had pale freckles. "I'm Sarah, Sam's sister. Come sit. You already made yourself at home. Would you care for tea?" She had the same accent as her brother. It was adorable on her, but not on Sam. Nope. That accent was weak-in-the-knees sexy. What in the world was April thinking? She brushed aside her ridiculous thoughts, accepted, and obliged. Sam paced in front of the fireplace in a fit of agitation.

"Is he okay?" April whispered to Sarah.

"What is 'okay'?"

Right. "Is he...fine? Well? Stable?"

Sarah glanced at her brother. "Doesn't much look like it." The girl took a sip of tea and stared at April, setting the tea plate down with a frown. "I'm more curious about you. Such scandalous clothing you've found. Your arms are exposed! This will not work at all. A lady wears an elegant dress in these parts, and I'll get you fixed right up."

"I've got money," April said, and as she dropped a stack of twenties on the table, she realized it was no good here. This wasn't a simulation. This was real, and her money was as good as kindling.

Sarah's mouth opened, and she covered it with her hand.

Sam leaned down and pushed April's money back toward her. "I've never seen money like that, but it looks like more than a single lady traveling alone should have," Sam said harshly as if accusing her of theft.

"It's mine," April said. "I earned it fairly." Now she understood why Kiko had said to bring as little as possible with her.

"Earned it how, exactly?" Sam's tone wasn't as harsh, but he was still cool toward her.

Sam and Sarah both stared at her in accusation. The need to defend herself against whatever their issue was pulsed through her. "I'd been saving a while to get away. I'm here on business, as I'd said, and I can't go back until I'm finished." She crossed her arms over her chest. And as if an extended stay explained the need for the stack of money, they both relaxed.

Sarah smiled and left the dining room table.

Sam stayed. "Tell me what your business is. and why you were looking for me."

April picked at her fingernails, uncertain how to explain enough for him to trust her, but not too much, causing him to send her away. The truth sounded insane. Did they still fear witchcraft at this point in history? She didn't want to find out.

"I know how this is going to sound, but I need you...to not get arrested," April said slowly. Even though Sam had been arrested at Lloyd's bar her first time here, this time things were different, so the arrest might happen elsewhere. Or at a different time. Or in a different way. Her foresight wasn't as useful now.

"You aren't making any sense." Sam's jaw clenched.

"I don't know how to explain without sounding crazy."

Sarah returned to the kitchen with scary amounts of fabric. Lace and fluffiness spread all around her like she carried a cloud. She set the pile down and held it up by the shoulders. "Your dress is not acceptable here. Try this on. It should fit you. It has a corset back, proper coverage up to the neck, and fashionable sleeves. If it fit me, I'd wear it."

April glanced around. There was no bathroom to change in. Okay, then. April unzipped the back of her bridesmaid dress and pulled down the straps.

Sam's face flushed bright red before he turned. April wasn't shy, but she appreciated his respect. April stepped out of he modern dress, and Sarah placed layer upon layer on her body with hooks and straps. It weighed a shocking amount for an article of clothing. Sarah laced up the back for her, and April felt like a royal princess—classy but stifled in all the layers covering her.

"What do you think, Sam?" April asked, and he turned around. He stared at the miles of fabric, and his face blanched as if he saw a ghost.

"She's lovely, isn't she? Shame it's the only dress in the house that fits. My dresses would make her look like a toddler, hem coming half up to her knees," Sarah said with a playful tone.

Without a word, Sam stomped out of the cabin and into the backyard.

"Does he hate it?" April asked.

"It's a beautiful dress. If a head-turner like you will be walking around these parts, you need a gown that's a head-turner to match. That one's Isabel's wedding dress. No finer gown in town."

"I can't wear this." April reached for the ties in the back, but it was no use.

"You have to. The menfolk in this town would never approve of what you wore here."

But this was someone's wedding dress. Where was this woman and why wasn't she here to protest?

SAM RUSHED OUTSIDE AND whistled high and short for his horse, now apparently named Bucky. The name was just as strange as the lady who sought him out. He wanted to stay and figure her out, but seeing the lush layers of taffeta and lace alive again brought back a vivid glimpse of his wedding day. Struck by the heavy guilt, Sam needed air. He couldn't show his face to the stranger or his unconscionable, wicked sister.

Sam went straight to his friend's bar, which was thankfully empty, and crashed onto a stool in front of Lloyd.

"You look like you need a drink. What happened, Sam?"

"Where do I even begin?"

"Start with why you feel the need for a pint of beer at two in the afternoon."

"I need something stronger than beer."

"You've come to the right place." Lloyd poured a finger of whiskey.

After a second drink, Sam was loose enough to talk. "It's Sarah."

Lloyd leaned against the bar, concern on his heavy brow. "What happened to Sarah?"

Sam scoffed. "Nothing. Should happen to her? I don't know. She put Isabel's wedding dress on a lady I just met. I turned around, and April's standing there, and all I see is my dead wife. I almost cried out in anguish right there in the living room. What in god's name possessed her to do that?"

"Perhaps she was trying to kick a little life back in you."

"I'm living well enough," Sam shot back.

"Not your love life."

"Hit me again," Sam said, tossing coins on the bar.

Lloyd poured the shot and slid it over to him, collecting the coins. Lloyd said, "Maybe it's time to move on. What happened to Isabel was Grignon's fault, not yours. This holding on...it's not healthy."

Sam didn't want to admit Lloyd was right, but not for the reason he thought. Sam didn't love Isabel any longer, if ever at all. He just couldn't shake the guilt. "I'm aware. One more, would you?"

"Last one," Lloyd warned.

"I'm not yet gassed. I know my limits."

Sam tossed two more coins and downed the warm amber liquid in a single swallow. His face scrunched when the fire burned a trail down his gullet, and the room spun. Lloyd knew him too good.

Chapter 17

When Sam vanished out the door, Sarah had assured April that he only needed a break, but April didn't know why, and she climbed back into her own bridesmaid dress. When a loud knocking interrupted their casual chatter, the young woman rushed to the front door. April stood to see what the fuss was about, happy to avoid questions about her zipper.

With dusk behind him, Lloyd shuffled inside holding Sam over his shoulder. The large man dropped Sam onto the couch without concern. He whispered into Sarah's ear, and her face lit up. His smile stretched. These two were close, and neither of them gave a second glance at Sam. Lloyd acknowledged April with a nod and stepped outside with Sarah following him.

April approached Sam, worried about his unconsciousness. Sleep softened the lines around his eyes. She reached down and brushed a lock of wavy hair off his forehead. A cloud of alcohol stung her nose. He was passed-out drunk. April sighed and searched for a blanket in a bedroom.

A simple full-sized bed and an end table with a gas lamp on top were along the back wall. A rug covered the floor, and the fading light through the window lit up rows and rows of books covering the side wall. The vast selection was intimidating. She ran her fingers along their tops with a smile. They weren't dusty. She opened one to admire the craftsmanship and read the title page. *The Count of Monte Cristo*. The tome was one of her favorites. No one would ever say her dad was kind, caring, or thoughtful, but he'd gifted her this book, probably as an afterthought, but she loved the tale of revenge and new love. Had Edmond put half as much effort into starting his life over rather than revenge, he would've had more time with the new love who was right there for him all along.

April gushed over the pages, the thick paper and heavy ink were new. She turned to the copyright page and saw the year of print, 1850. She was holding a literal treasure in her hands. She set it down with all the care in the world. She didn't think this was Sarah's room. It was too devoid of feminine flair. She took a blanket from the bed and brought it over to the couch. She removed his boots and tucked him in.

She watched Sam sleep and refrained from running her fingers through his hair. He seemed peaceful and happy without the weight of the world on his shoulders. She wished he could be happy while awake too. Sam collected money for an asshole boss. That wasn't much different than modern times. He used a horse instead of a car—far less parts to break down and repair. They had simple things and simple processes. Life seemed so much easier in these times. Besides the terrible clothing.

Curious about that weight, April went to the line of framed photographs displayed on the fireplace mantle. She recognized Sarah's features as a child, holding a flower and smiling. Another one showed a pair of adults looking off camera without smiling as was the custom for the day. She presumed they were the parents. The next photograph was Sam as a child on a horse. Was that Bucky? Did horses live that long?

The last was a more recent photo of Sam, standing next to a woman with Hispanic or perhaps Native features. It was difficult to determine in the grainy black-and-white photo. She was glowing with happiness, but he was stoic—not unhappy but not smiling like her. She wore a beautiful string of pearls at her throat and a lacy white head wrap. Then April saw the dress, and her stomach squeezed with an invisible punch. The beautiful lacy gown was the same one Sarah had put on her earlier.

His wife's gown.

Sam was married.

That was disappointing, but it shouldn't have bothered her since she had a boyfriend anyway. She shook the nonsense out of her head and wondered where his wife was. His bedroom didn't have anything to suggest a woman stayed there.

Sarah opened the front door with inky blackness behind her. How long had April been exploring?

"I brought the horse back. No worries." Sarah's cheeks were pink, and she had a glow about her. "I made up a room for you, whenever you're ready. Sam can stay where he is." Sarah retreated to her room for the night.

As long as Sam was inside his house, nothing bad could happen to him. April got ready for bed herself.

"We must get you new clothing today," Sarah insisted. "Your dress needs to be washed, if you catch my drift. What will you wear when the laundry's getting washed if not the gown?"

There was no way April would wear that wedding gown again, not after the look on Sam's face. But she hardly felt dirty wearing her bridesmaid dress a second day. "Can I help you with anything?" April asked to change the subject.

Sarah fluttered about in the kitchen like a dancer on a stage—bowls getting mixed, sizzling meat on a pan, steam tendrils curling up from a pot. Her skirts twirled as she spun from place to place. April was envious of Sarah's talents. They were practical, useful, and she had mastered them well.

April was okay at her job, okay at making a few basic dinners, okay at driving. At least, she'd never gotten a ticket or anything. She was the master of nothing. She didn't know where she belonged. She didn't know her purpose, and she had an aching hollowness in her chest. She was lost. At the bottom of her pity party, being waited on made her very uncomfortable.

Sam moaned from the couch where April had tucked him in last night. He sat up and tugged the blanket off with disjointed movements. His clothes and hair were disheveled, and his face was pinched in discomfort. A palm rubbed his temple.

April refrained from shaking her head at Sam's mighty ass-kick of a hangover. He'd left because of the wedding gown, but was this bender because of the gown or Grignon's missing money?

"Wake up, you big lug. Time to eat," Sarah scolded him.

April suppressed a chuckle. For a small girl she was definitely the boss of this household.

Sam dragged himself outside for a moment and then wordlessly shuffled to the pantry closet. When he came out, he was far more awake, his wavy hair was brushed, and he wore fresh clothing.

April smiled at him. Why was she smiling? She turned away and offered Sarah help again.

"If you insist, come over here. Can you make pancakes?"

"Yeah, I can," April said, finally familiar with something around here. She stood at the counter, cracking eggs and measuring flour, while Sam read the *Green Bay Intelligencer* newspaper at the table. She looked over her shoulder at him a few times like an idiot, but her idiocy was concealed by newsprint. She poured batter into hearts, snake shapes, and Mickey mouse heads, humming as she flipped the browned cakes.

Sarah laughed at her while beating eggs in a bowl. "You sure like to make pancakes."

"I guess I do." April brought the platter to the table and helped with bringing over finished eggs and orange juice.

Sam finally folded the newspaper and set it aside.

"Did you sleep comfortably on the couch?" April asked.

Sam brought his hand up and rubbed the back of his neck. "I've had worse."

"Can I get you anything?" April was trying to make conversation.

Sam lifted the platters and filled his plate, not answering her.

"There's a lot of food here," April observed, and Sarah was still making more.

Sam grunted in agreement. Hangovers sucked.

April filled her plate, and Sarah brought over the toast and butter. Sarah placed a few slices of toast on her plate and a pancake. There was so much food, there was no way they could eat it all, and April felt terrible for the waste. They didn't have a refrigerator or storage containers. "Where are you going to put all the extra?"

"Out back," Sam said through bites.

Sarah nibbled her way through breakfast while Sam plowed through it as if he hadn't eaten in days. April eagerly ate since it was the only meal she'd had since the sandwich she'd made in her own kitchen. The reminder that being here wasn't reality, just a mission, dampened her spirits.

Sarah noticed. "Something wrong with the eggs? You look like you tasted a frog."

"Everything's great," April said. Sam was aloof, and she couldn't get him to talk. How was she going to convince him to trust her, to listen to her, to save his life? This was much harder than she thought it would be. Why couldn't it have been picking daisies? "I just remembered something, that's all."

April finished her plate while the other two continued eating. Would it be polite to dive in for seconds? The eggs were fantastic, unlike any from her own kitchen or from a restaurant. The food tasted so much bolder with a stronger texture here.

April forked over two more pancakes without shame, and no one commented on her cool shapes.

Sam's head pounded with alcohol sickness. He hated drinking too much, but he'd been needing it more than usual—ever since his parents signed that contract between Jonathan Arris and Sarah. Many thoughts plagued him. If only his parents hadn't spent all their money trying to settle in America, they wouldn't have been desperate to make that deal for survival. If only Sam hadn't taken the job with Grignon for the same reason, Isabel would still be alive. If only Sam had turned his cheek to his boss's vile workings, the bastard wouldn't be a constant threat to him and his sister. Now Lloyd was facing the noose.

And there was this strange new lady in Bridgeport. He was grateful that she was wearing the original outfit. The beads dipped low on her neckline, accentuating her bosom and bare arms in a distracting way, but he didn't want others ogling her. What kind of business did she have in town, and why did she seek him out personally? Sam couldn't fathom, but first, he had to stop at Perez's for the Wednesday collection and then figure out how to get April out of town.

"What's on the agenda today?" Sam asked his sister, as his headache receded.

"I'm taking our new friend here shopping. She's in desperate need of clothing. Having one unusual outfit is a shame, it is."

Sam asked April. "And you?"

April flustered. "I guess I'm going shopping."

That wasn't the answer he'd wanted. "What about the business you're in town for? Perhaps get that settled."

"It's not that easy," April said, stuffing a bite of pancake in her mouth.

"Do you require aid? I can help you get it done sooner."

"It's not like that."

Her vagueness was frustrating, especially since she'd sought him out. "Then what's it like?"

"It's hard to explain."

Sam waited for a straight answer, but it didn't come. "Then who's your business with?"

April picked at her fingernails.

"That's enough drilling for now, Sergeant," Sarah interrupted. "Let's go, dear, Perez's opens soon."

"That's where I'm headed," Sam said. "We can go together." Sam collected the leftovers and threw them out the back door.

"What did you do that for?" April exclaimed, standing.

Sam brought the empty dishes to the kitchen. "It's for the dogs."

"You have dogs?" April glanced around with a puzzled expression.

Sam returned to the table and collected the newspaper under his arm. "The strays. Somebody needs to feed them."

"You feed homeless dogs?" April smiled at him with straight white teeth.

No matter his suspicions of her, he wanted to kiss those cute dimples. "Of course, they keep the cat population in check."

April's lips parted in surprise.

Sam dropped the newspaper on the stack by the fireplace and retreated to his bedroom to ready for the day. He was joking about the cats. They were excellent mousers, protecting their grain storage, but her reaction was amusing. His desire to kiss her was not.

Chapter 18

April grasped the horn of the saddle until her knuckles turned white. From behind her, Sarah's dainty arms held the reins. Even with Sam's hand on the halter, walking alongside. April was uncomfortable on the horse. She much preferred Bucky when her feet were on the ground.

The sun bore down extra hard this morning through the hazy sky. It was a peaceful morning, and a handful of people were out and about. Life was so much slower than she was used to. April was surprised at how quickly she'd adapted to not checking the phone in her back pocket every half hour. Without a screen to distract her, she almost felt as if she were living more. Things hadn't been all rainbows and unicorns since she'd arrived, but she had to admit the danger added to the excitement. April would be perfectly content to never see Grignon's face again, however.

April wasn't a lucky person.

Between bursts of nerves when Bucky made a sudden move or a swish of the tail or a snort, April daydreamed about Sam, and her eyes roamed his broad shoulders. He was within arm's reach, but she didn't dare touch him. He was married, and she needed to knock those thoughts away. They led to nothing good.

On the edge of town sat a squat brick building with Couture Clothing in cursive font above the front door. An extra wide windowpane sat to the right of the entrance with a pair of mannequins in the window advertising billowy dresses en vogue.

Sam tied up Bucky while his sister dragged her inside. Sarah was relentless and apparently enjoyed shopping.

A tall, broad Hispanic man with a black broom of a mustache greeted them as they entered. A petite woman, who was a spitting image of him except for the mustache, flitted around the store adding new merchandise or straightening things out of line. She came right over to them with a beaming smile of friendliness. "Good morning, Sarah."

"Hi, Marisol. I've got a lady here who needs help."

Marisol assessed her with a keen eye and said, "Clearly. Come this way."

April should've been offended, but she wasn't. The energetic woman led them to a small selection of basic dresses in navy, bronze, and ruby. Marisol chose a ruby one and handed it to April. "After my mother's accident, she couldn't sew any longer, so I started making these dresses for her. She explained how easily my design could fit a range of bodies, and she encouraged me to put them in Daddy's shop. Try this one. I can alter it if the fit isn't right for you, but I suspect it'll fit like a dream."

April took it from her outstretched hands, and Marisol led her to a place to change. On her way through the shelves of fabrics and spools of thread, April stole a glance at Sam. He was unusually pasty with a bead of sweat on his furrowed brow while talking to the shop owner.

Behind a dressing screen, April slipped into the skirt, and fastened the hook and eye closures at the waist. She unbuttoned the top and put it on and refastened it from belly button to throat. Sleeves were a little short, but she figured the billowy design was meant to be that way. April stepped out, and both girls smiled and clapped. April's face heated from the attention.

"Much better," Marisol said.

April caught Sam's glance on a careful spin. The corner of his mouth quirked up in a smile, and guilt stabbed at her. What was she doing? She stopped twirling and smoothed the fabric. "Where are the pockets?" There was no way April would wear a dress if she didn't have pockets.

The two girls exchanged a glance, and then Sarah showed her the access through the material by her hip. A strange location, but it worked.

"I'll take this one," April said, satisfied.

"Excellent," Marisol said and then returned to the racks.

April ducked behind the screen to switch back into her clothes when another dress flopped over the top. "This one next, please."

Begrudgingly, April shrugged into the next one, fastening the row of hooks and eyes of a bronze dress with cream sleeves and details. Other than color, it appeared identical, reaching from throat to toes with a smooth cream collar and a row of cream buttons. It even fit the same.

She poked her head out and showed an arm to display the color while stealing a glance at Sam. His face was flush with anger, and the shop owner had his arms crossed over his chest in defiance. That didn't look good. April wanted to leave before something bad happened—like an arrest. With no time to change back, she stuffed her modern things into this dress's pockets. "I'm all set. I've got two now. We should go."

Marisol said, "Are you sure? A lady should always have four dresses. You never know when you'll need a clean one."

April stood firm. "Two's enough for now."

"You'll need a bonnet, parasol, shoes, apron, and undergarments."

"I'm all set, thanks."

Marisol nodded, and April collected her bridesmaid dress. Sarah led her to the counter where Sam and the owner were still disagreeing about something. Time to put on a brave face and interrupt two angry men. April cleared her throat and waited for the large shop owner to acknowledge her. "I'll take these two dresses, please." April indicated the bronze one she wore and the ruby one in her arms.

The owner uncrossed his arms and his face flipped like a switch from angry to cordial. It amused her. Proper customer service extended back centuries. He said, "Twenty-five dollars, miss."

April blinked at the low price. "Each?"

The man's mustache shifted. She couldn't tell if he was smiling or not.

"Total, miss."

April dug in her new pocket for the wad of twenties when she remembered Sam and Sarah's reaction to her money. But she didn't have anything else. Reluctantly, she set a pair of twenties on the counter. He took her bills and flipped them over in his hands, studying them. He quirked an eyebrow at Sam, and Sam nodded with a frown. April wondered what their secret conversation meant.

SAM DREADED HAVING TO make this collection in particular. After the women dashed off to choose clothing for April, Sam approached his former father-in-law, Ralf Perez, with his handlebar mustache resting over a frown.

"Good day, Ralf."

"What are you doing with her?" The tension in his voice was thick. Ralf gestured toward April, who was out of earshot.

"She's a woman under my protection." Until he could get her out of town.

"And?" Ralf pressed.

"And nothing. She is just under my protection. Do you have the payment ready?"

Ralf didn't move. He cast a suspicious glance at April and stared Sam down. "I want you to leave and never return."

"Not possible and you know it."

"Look, you never should've gotten mixed up in all this, but it's time to walk away."

Ralf blamed him for Isabel's death, and seeing April likely hurt Ralf tremendously. But Ralf only wanting to help Sam for his own selfish gain hurt him in return. "You're only telling me to leave because I'm here for your money, otherwise you wouldn't care at all."

"That's not true, and you know it," Ralf's stern whisper flushed his face red.

"Envelope please," Sam said.

"No." Ralf Perez folded his arms over his broad chest, like a bull ready to charge.

"This isn't personal, Ralf. You of all people should understand that. What will it take to finish this now?" Sam asked.

Ralf grunted in frustration; his face was red as cherry coals. After everything that had happened, Sam didn't hate the man. Everyone grieved in their own way, but Sam was sure furious with him now. Ralf understood the rules, and Sam didn't want to dole out the punishment required of him. And not just because Ralf Perez was a large man.

Sam glanced over his shoulder again, not wanting the girls to hear. The bronze dress on April was breathtaking, and as she approached, Sam simmered down. He didn't need her knowing more than she should. He still didn't know who she was, and he didn't need her getting wrapped up in his problems.

"I'll take these two dresses, please," April said.

Ralf uncrossed his arms and brightened for his customer. "Twenty-five dollars, miss."

As Ralf inspected the money Sam had previously determined to be of foreign origin, his ex-father-in-law quirked a brow at Sam.

Ralf was suspicious too, but to spare the lady embarrassment, he silently expected Sam to cover the cost. Sam didn't have any coin to spare, but he'd figure it out.

Sam nodded to finish the purchase and close this deal.

Ralf rang up the purchase in the register. It chimed, and he arranged the bills in the stack and gave her genuine change. The large man shut the drawer, without giving up Grignon's payment.

"Sarah, take April outside. I'll be with you in a minute," Sam said while keeping a stern eye on Ralf.

A frightened Sarah took a puzzled April by the arm and dragged her outside to the waiting horse.

Sam curved his fingers at the man, urging him away from the counter. Ralf, knowing what happened when an owner refused payment, walked to the back of the shop without a fuss. Sam followed him out the back door.

The sun baked the dry ground, grasshoppers rattled their wings in the distance, and dust stifled the air. Sam ran a hand over his forehead, wiping away sweat. A breeze would be nice or even some rain that appeared to be on vacation. Sam wished for a vacation, especially as of late. He loosened the neck of his shirt, and Ralf rolled up his sleeves.

Sam was conflicted. He hated Grignon's policy, but if he didn't fight, the fight would come to him. A wee knuckle therapy with his former father-in-law might help him tremendously right now, after all that he'd lost.

Chapter 19

April picked at her fingernails, trying to make even tears with trembling hands. She only did it when she was nervous, and as of late, there weren't any fresh nails left to pick. Sarah's arms crossed over her chest, and she paced back and forth in front of Bucky. What was taking Sam so long in there? And why did Sam ask them to wait out front?

Sarah cleared her throat, alerting her to a pair of menacing men in trousers, long-sleeved shirts, and vests. The first one, with the scar, was Dennis. The second one she remembered from the library—all black beady eyes and a long, hooked nose. Both of Grignon's men gave her the creeps.

"Sam here?" Dennis asked.

April couldn't deny it. She huddled close to Bucky. "Yeah."

Sarah said nothing but kept near the horse too.

Dennis entered the store with Hooked Nose on his heels as if they were on a mission. No sounds came from inside.

"What do you suppose is going on?" April asked, hoping for reassurance.

"Nothing good. When you see them, nothing good."

April had a sinking lump in the pit of her stomach. What felt like forever passed under the blistering sun before the two men exited the store. April saw they were clean, unmarked, and calm. Perhaps they'd just had a polite discussion. When they were safely away, April said, "Stay here."

April charged in to ask the owner what happened, but she didn't find him. "Sam?"

Marisol popped her head out from a side door and pointed to the back. That was definitely bad news. April marched through the back door and stopped short. Her hand reflexively lifted to cover her gaping mouth, and her breath caught in her throat. April ran back through the store to gather Sarah for the rescue mission. "I need your help."

She pulled Sarah through the shop to the back exit and the girl gasped. Sam was an unconscious bloody pulp discarded like garbage. Not too many steps away, the shop owner sat leaning against the brick, also out cold. His face was bloody and swollen.

The fight hadn't ended well for either of them.

"Is he alive?" Sarah asked.

April took a few deep breaths to calm her stomach. What would Mathew do if this were an emergency case? She pressed fingertips along Sam's throat, feeling for a pulse. It was strong and steady, and she sighed in relief. She lifted an eyelid to see its reaction to light. The pupil constricted. That was good news. She pressed an ear against his chest for strained breathing sounds, but it sounded normal—from what she could hear.

"He's alive," April confirmed.

Lastly, she made a fist and rubbed against his sternum to wake him.

Sam shifted and moaned, fingers twitched in pain.

That was excellent.

"What are you doing?" Sarah asked with curiosity.

"A sternal rub helps wake unconscious people. I'm trying to make sure he's not paralyzed." April stopped at Sarah's expression. "What?"

"Are you a physician?"

Ignoring that, April said, "We need to get him out of here now. No cops. Help me lift." April lifted Sam from under his arms, and

Sarah picked up his feet. His head flopped forward to his chest, and the two of them carried him through the back door and out front to Bucky. They both huffed in exertion and set him carefully back down. To get him on the horse...

April remembered the shrill whistle. "Can you do the whistle? The one where the horse kneels?"

Sarah smiled and gave the whistle her best shot.

It didn't work.

Sarah tried it again, and the horse rocked in lazy movements as it folded down.

April happily exclaimed. Since she wasn't strong enough to keep him upright on the horse, April flopped him over the back of the saddle, face down, silently apologizing for her less-than-gentle maneuvers. His arms and legs dangled over the sides of Bucky. She had Sarah guide the horse since Bucky would be more familiar with her, and April stabilized Sam since she was taller and had better leverage. None of her logical explanations had anything to do with the fact that she wanted to touch Sam and stay close to him—nope, nothing at all.

"Those were Grignon's men. Somehow I get the feeling all of this damage was from them," April said as they slowly made their way back to the cabin. Sam bounced under Bucky's footsteps. He moaned as consciousness fought to return, which was a great sign.

"Aye. Usually Sam just pops them a good one in the nose, and they call a truce and pay up extra the next week. This is not normal."

"Usually?" April repeated. "This happens frequently?"

"When an owner refuses payment, then Sam must make them pay, so to speak. But this is the first time Grignon's guards interfered."

The dangerous man who controlled the town was increasing his threat. April's mere existence was making everyone's lives worse. According to Kiko, if she didn't interfere at all, Sam and another good man, whoever he was, would be killed. With a press of a button, April could disappear from this place, and the increasing threat would leave with her. She had no guarantee of that outcome though. She couldn't just listen to the tale from Kiko, and live with those consequences. No matter what came her way, she would stay and fight to save Sam.

When they reached the cabin, Sarah repeated the kneeling command, and they two-handed Sam inside and back onto the couch. He had a deep laceration on his face from knuckles, maybe even brass knuckles. "Do you have a doctor around here?"

"He's up delivering Mrs. Smith's baby. I can send a telegraph requesting his assistance."

"That'll take too long. Can you get a bowl of clean water, some towels? He's got a gash here that needs stitches. Do you have a needle and thread? Gloves, forceps. Lidocaine?"

Sarah stared at her.

"He's bleeding. I need to close the wound," April said with mild agitation.

Sarah snapped to attention and collected supplies from around the house.

April unbuttoned Sam's shirt, exposing his chest. Her heart thumped wildly inside her ribcage. She inhaled a deep breath and blew it out to steady herself. Several bruises on his smooth and taut chest already formed purple splotches. There were no protruding bones or stab wounds. She determined it was an extra gory fistfight resulting in a knockout. He didn't display the symptoms of a concussion, but he'd been out a while. She buttoned his shirt back up.

Sarah set down a basin of water and a towel. She disappeared and returned with a needle and thread. "This is all I have. I don't know what the other things are you need. You can try Martin, the chemist, down the road." Sarah had a confidence under her roof that April admired, but here, with Sam injured, she froze.

April surprised herself by taking charge. "Take a dry towel and apply pressure to his gash there. Okay? I'll be right back."

There was no way anyone could convince her to take the horse, and she was grateful to be wearing her white sneakers. April bolted to the chemist, a half mile toward town. Fabric bunched between her legs. She gripped as much material as she could to keep it out of her way while her legs kept pumping. How did the women function while wearing these clothes?

Her pulse was maxed, and her breath strained while she blurred toward town. The buildings were all labeled, and she had no trouble discerning the lettering for Bridgeport Chemist on a tall narrow building, just beyond Porter's.

She entered, sweating and pulsing with adrenaline. Using her forearm, she wiped away beads of sweat from her forehead. She found the clerk, and he stared at her in alarm. He was a teenager with curly blond hair sprouting around his cap. His apron was stitched in cursive with the name Ross.

Logical assumption here, April said, "Ross, I need gauze, antibiotic ointment, lidocaine, suture thread—nylon if you have it." She didn't want to use cotton thread if she could avoid it. "A pair of scissors, a needle driver, and forceps. Hand soap and gloves." She took a deep breath. "I think that's it." April waited for the clerk to move, to do something, but he just stared at her. Crap. She wished she had the internet to search for information before opening her mouth and getting into trouble. How much of her list wasn't even invented yet? "I'll take whatever you have. I'm in a hurry."

He still stood there. She was about to poke him to be sure he was real when he finally started moving. Ross placed a dismal number of her requested items on the counter: a spool of cotton thread—she sighed—a bar of soap, and a pair of scissors.

"Bandages? Honey?" April pressed.

He set a roll of cotton next to the frustratingly small pile and said, "Porter's for honey."

April growled in annoyance and asked, "How much?" She yanked out her wad of cash again and freed another twenty.

"One seventy-five."

April gaped at him in disbelief. The cost of living was so low, she would be comfortable here with the cash she brought for a long time...if they accepted it. She slipped out change she'd received from Couture Clothing.

The boy relaxed when he saw her payment. He made change, and April gave her thanks. She didn't bring a basket with her, so she stuffed her pockets full and sprinted next door to Porter's with her arms loaded.

Porter greeted her with a friendly smile, and then he saw the look on her face. "What's the matter, dear, can I get you anything?" He noticed the supplies in her arms. His brows knitted in concern.

"Honey."

"Coming right up." Porter retrieved a bottle off the shelf. "Anything else?"

"No."

"You don't look well."

"It's not me you need to worry about. How much?"

April paid the nickel, and Porter tucked the honey into her full arms. She ran off before the old man could ask more questions. Sam was bleeding, and she didn't want to lose time.

She sprinted out of Porter's and within seconds various voices closed in around her.

"It's her! That weird one."

"Is she stealing?"

"Thief!"

Who were they talking about? They continued spouting off angry accusations, but April kept running, minding her own business. The scissors fumbled out of her armful of supplies and tumbled to the dirt road. She skidded to a halt and picked them up. April took a moment to catch her breath. Dusk approached, and the air chilled her sweaty skin, sending a shiver up her body.

An alarming noise spun her head around. Faces peered out of windows. Townsfolk poured out of buildings, and three men on horseback galloped toward her, circling like hungry sharks. Her vision blurred over them. The people closed in. The chants swirled through her ears like the incessant moan of a spook.

"What's going on? What are you doing?" she begged.

A familiar tinny voice reached across the chanting and hoof beats, but she couldn't see him. "Hello, there. Looks like you've been causing trouble."

The horses stopped circling, and their newly created wall blocked her escape. Hooves stomped and nostrils snorted. She recognized all three riders—Dennis Durand, Daniel, his scar-free twin, and Hooked Nose. All Grignon's men. April fought the urge to vomit. The horses nickered and bobbed their heads, awaiting their next commands.

April spun to face the townsfolk. Released from the belly of the crowd, a short man with black hair and dark eyes approached. He was the spitting image of the large man from Couture Clothing, less the broom mustache.

"I didn't do anything," April pleaded. Her pulse raced and tears threatened.

The short man smiled and tapped his chin with his fingertip. "Everyone knows you've been stealing. I recommend you confess to all these witnesses." He swung his arm in an arc behind him and the crowd pressed close. "Punishments are more lenient then."

"I didn't steal anything." April panted, fighting back pure panic. "Please let me go!

The crowd murmured. And the shouts began.

"Look at her shoes!"

"Her hair is not right," shouted another voice lost in the sea of the crowd.

"Not a real lady."

"Thief!"

"She doesn't belong here. Causing trouble—that's all."

"Thief!"

"Whore finally covered up!"

The last one was a punch to the chest. They were throwing personal insults at her, and they didn't even know her. Tears of humiliation sprung forth as she cried again, "I'm only trying to help. Please. Sam needs my help. I just want to help."

She dropped the bottle of honey, and with her arm free, she swiped the tears. April collapsed to her knees on the dirt road to collect the bottle. A new wave of sobs hit.

The yelling brought her back to her parents' fights. They had screamed nonsensical things at each other, trapping April in the middle. She had been powerless to stop them as a child, and moreso as a teen. She had folded over, hands clamped over her ears, chest wracked with sobs. April had begged for them to stop yelling, and they had yelled back that it was her fault. It was always her fault. Mathew had hid on the staircase, eyes rimmed in red, hands fiercely gripping the spindles. After Mom had stormed out like she did so many nights, Dad would drink in front of the TV, and when enough alcohol pulsed through his veins, he came upstairs to her bedroom for punishment. The sound of a leather strap sliding from belt loops made her stomach convulse and paralyzed her with fear even now.

"Dirty whore and cheat!"

The chants brought her back. They clearly wanted her arrested for her supposed crimes. Then she would be at the mercy of Grignon. Kiko had told her Sam was executed after his arrest. She would not be safe in a cell, and never seeing Mathew again sent her into hysterics.

She dropped all her purchases and did the only thing she could think of—her fingers pinched a stack of change from Ross and the clothing shop. She held it up. "I didn't steal. Here. Take it!"

With a sneer, the short man snatched the money, inspected it, and stuffed it into his pocket with a smirk. Still no one budged. Who was he, and why did he seem to hate her? The crowd murmured, and a few yelled more unwarranted insults. The wall of horses stayed put. How was she going to get out of this?

A booming shout behind the crowd silenced everyone. Heads turned, including Grignon's men.

"Let her go," the voice ordered.

The crowd parted, and a head loomed tall above the masses. Lloyd! "She's not a thief. She's with Sam."

Protective and wonderful Lloyd had come to her rescue. With a quiet respect, the townsfolk watched Lloyd approach.

The three horsemen whispered among themselves and dissipated. Without their enforcers, the crowd dispersed and the instigating short man spit by her feet and disappeared into the crowd.

Lloyd reached her without further resistance. "Did they hurt you?"

April sniffled. "I'm fine. Thank you. Thank you so much." She bent down to collect her supplies. Lloyd kneeled and helped her. "I don't know what would've happened if you didn't save me there."

Lloyd chuckled. "You're safe in my hands and equally safe in Sam's. He's a good man. He's just had a rough go of it lately. Everyone's been on edge, but some people like to take their issues too far."

They both stood, and April asked, "How can I repay you?"

Lloyd's smile was warm. "Take care of Sam."

April flushed. It was obvious Lloyd cared for him.

He added, "Come with me, and I'll get you a ride."

"No. I prefer to run, and I really need to go. They hurt Sam."

Lloyd's smile disappeared. "Go. Quickly now. No one will stop you."

"Thank you, Lloyd."

Her legs were jelly from humiliation. Finally getting her breathing under control, April secured her supplies in her arms and ran. She would stop for no one now.

Chapter 20

APRIL SET HER SUPPLIES down next to the couch. Sarah was sponge-bathing Sam's face, trying to control the blood flow, but it just kept drizzling down his cheek.

"No!" April yelled, and Sarah recoiled. April checked herself. "Sorry, no water on the wound. Dry pressure. Just let me handle it, okay?"

Sarah backed up and watched her work.

April blotted the streaming cut dry and inspected it. Fresh blood oozed out immediately, and she pressed a towel on the wound and turned her head away, covering her mouth with the crook of her elbow to settle her stomach.

"Is something wrong?" Sarah asked.

"Just give me a minute."

"Is it the blood?"

April's stomach squeezed. "Here. Take over. Quick!"

Sarah resumed towel duty, and April ran outside, sick against a tree. She would need more stomach strength to get through this. It was just cells and water and platelets. No big deal. Everyone had some. April exhaled a few more deep breaths. But blood meant someone—a stranger, a cute puppy, or Sam for instance—could be dying. Get a grip! It was nothing but a gash. A deep, fat spewing, blood pumping gash...

She remembered when Dad hit Mom. That one night in particular, he'd had too much to drink as usual. There was blood all over her chest and forehead. April's screams pierced the air, and

Dad had silenced her quickly. After Dad drove off, April had tried to stop the bleeding, but it just kept coming, and Mom wouldn't wake up. April's tears had blocked her vision, her feet slipped in droplets speckling the floor. She'd found a hand towel and covered the gash on Mom's forehead. Strong arms had pulled her away while she sobbed. Men had carried Mom off on a stretcher.

April heaved onto the grass again and leaned against the tree. Sam needed help. He could get an infection, and with no antibiotics, that was a big deal. She regained control of her empty stomach and returned to the scene with shaking hands.

"Shit, I should've asked at Porter's. Do you have any whiskey or any alcohol over seventy proof?"

Sarah hesitated. "We do, but—"

"I need it now. I have to disinfect the wound as much as possible. Triple antibiotic ointment isn't available for another hundred years, so this has to do."

Sarah tilted her head in confusion. "But it's Sam's private stash. I don't think…"

"I'm sure he'll get over it." April filled a second basin with fresh water from the hand pump outside and washed her hands. Then she took over pressing the towel.

Sarah fished in a cabinet near the fireplace and brought a glass bottle of unlabeled brown liquid over. "Are you sure you need this?"

The concern and hesitation were plain, but April would just replace it. This was more important. April uncorked the bottle and took a whiff. She coughed and her eyes watered. It smelled like kerosene. "This will do. Thanks."

Reminding herself of Mathew's surgical suite and the routine process for treating wounds, which she'd done tons of times with the same old shaking hands and upset stomach, April tapped Sam on his unmarked cheek. Pouring bourbon over his open wound was not something she wanted to do while he was awake. She didn't want to do it while he was asleep either, but it was only the necessity of the situation allowing her to hurt him. He didn't move or make a sound.

"I'm sorry. This will sting." April apologized anyway, giving her a witness in case Sam asked Sarah about what happened later. April poured the liquid over his cheek, careful not to splash any near his eyes, and he flinched. She kept pouring until she was satisfied. His shirt was drenched. She would take care of that after.

April then poured more bourbon onto the needle and worked it down the thread. With a grimace and a light grip on the scissors, she poked the sewing needle through the edge of his seeping skin and tugged the thread taut. The scissors couldn't cut the needle, so it was the best grip she would get.

She continued poking and pulling and knotting off until she'd made a neat row of sutures on his cheek. It was a shame to mar his handsome face with a thin line and little dots of scars, but the alternative would've been worse. Leaving it gaping, if it stopped bleeding on its own and if it didn't get infected and kill him, would've left him with a wide jagged pink scar. Once more for good measure, she poured bourbon over the closed wound and pressed a rectangle of the cotton from the spool over it.

"Can you get him a clean shirt and pants?"

Sarah retrieved clothes while April removed his boots. The man would end up with brain damage for how often he got knocked around. Wait, no. The first knocking with a mug never ended up happening, and neither did anything that would've triggered the police to be there that night. She had a fresh reset. Then again, his knuckles showed he did in fact get knocked around frequently, or at least he did the knocking.

April used the scissors and cut the soaked and damaged shirt off. She sponge-bathed his smooth chest to rid him of the stickiness, admiring his bare chest, and a flutter of warmth ran through her core. Sarah helped her carefully put a new shirt over his head.

April's cheeks were roasting hot the whole time. She hoped his sister didn't notice.

After Sarah lifted his hips in bursts of strength and April tugged the wet trousers, they managed to remove them, but they scrapped the idea of putting on clean ones. April brought over a blanket instead.

"I'm really sorry for yelling at you," April said. "I was just startled at seeing the wrong wound care, and the people outside were stopping me from getting here. I was so worried he would be worse, or awake before getting sutured. I'm just really sorry."

"No, you're right. I wanted to clean his face, make it go away, and I didn't listen. My apologies." Sarah sighed. "What did you mean about something not available for a hundred years?"

Oops.

After the mob outside, she would have to be more careful or they would hang her for being a witch—did they still do that?—or for being just plain crazy. No one trusted her enough to believe her. "Nothing..." April chuckled awkwardly. "Just, you know, silly frustration."

"I see," Sarah said with little confidence. "Well, I'm off to bed. What a day! Will you be all right?"

"Yeah. Thank you. I'm just a little wired from everything. I'll be off to bed shortly."

They both said their good nights, and April, alone but for an unconscious Sam Hartley, sat on the floor and leaned against the couch. Her ears focused on his breathing rhythm. Smooth and steady. She dropped her face into her hands, and her body shook with the receding adrenaline now that the emergency was over. She'd thought this time was calm and peaceful. Not quite. How do these people live like this every day?

SAM AWOKE TO A bright wall of pain and blinding morning light. His whole upper body ached like he'd spent the night on a pile of rocks. The last thing he remembered was paying a visit to Ralf Perez, and now he was in different clothes, half naked at that, and on his couch yet again. He turned his head to find a mostly empty bottle of his best bourbon, and his eyebrows lifted in surprise. Starting now, he vowed to be more careful with his drinking. Strange enough, Sam didn't have the usual headache or nausea from getting gassed. He leaned forward and almost dropped his feet onto April. She slept on the floor in front of the couch, curled up as if cold. She was such a strange but fascinating lady.

He rubbed his eyes, and a pain seared the left side. Sam carefully planted his feet and walked to the pantry for the mirror. He was surprised to find a slip of cotton with a streak of brown blood stuck to his upper cheek. His eyes were both bruised, one was purple. He had bruises along his arms, and a sore spot on his ribs. He remembered punishing Perez, who fought back well, but as they circled during the fight—blackness. A void. No memory.

In the kitchen, he brushed his teeth in the washbasin that Sarah had filled, and April stirred from the floor. Her hair was disheveled, her face smeared in dirt. Something had happened to her as well. Anger surged at the thought of someone harming her. He would find out what happened and make it right.

"Good day," Sam said to April.

"Oh, hey. How's the gash feeling? Is it hot?"

"Just sore."

"Great." Her voice sounded strained.

April bundled his blanket and set it on the couch. She sat up and her face fell into her hands. Sam sat next to her and fought the urge to rub her back in comfort. "What happened yesterday?"

"A lot," she mumbled through her hands.

"Can we start with Perez's?"

"Sure," April said, lifting her head. She looked so much worse up close—puffy, red eyes and dirt streaked down her face. "You and Perez went to the back of the store. Two of Grignon's men followed not long after, and when Sarah and I found you, you were knocked out and bleeding. Perez wasn't in much better shape."

Sam took inventory of the damage to his head and sure enough, found a tender spot square in the back. He flinched. "Did you see which men?"

"Dennis and the other one—I don't know his name. He's tall with black beady eyes and a long, hooked nose."

"Rob Bertrand." Sam growled the name. He balled his hands. He was so close to snapping on Grignon. Sam didn't know how to stop him while ensuring everyone's safety. His chest burned with rage and...desire. Sam wanted her, and he wanted her safe.

"Do you have any cotton swabs?" she asked. "I would like to remove the gauze from your face and inspect the stitches."

"I don't know what swabs are." She always said such strange things.

April pressed her lips together, and her eyes glassed over. She looked like she was on the verge of falling apart herself.

"What happened to you?" he asked. His hand found its own way onto her knee. She looked at it with wide eyes, and he snapped it back. "Apologies."

"A lot of things," she said and released a deep breath. "Sarah and I brought you home. You were unconscious. I gathered supplies from the chemist and ran over to Porter's for honey." She paused as if trying hard to form the words while blocking the mental images—a familiar difficulty. "I guess the crowd thought my arms full while running meant I was a thief. They chased me and yelled at me. Three of Grignon's men circled me on their horses." She let out a small sob.

Sam heated with fury but checked himself, so he didn't scare her. He took her hands in his and stroked them with his thumbs.

She continued, "Lloyd broke up the crowd, and Grignon's men left. I came here as fast as possible and tended your wound. Sarah and I changed out your clothes. Sorry about your bourbon. I needed it for disinfectant. I promise to replace it."

He understood enough of what she said. Grignon's men were ready to enact a citizen's arrest on the spot over false allegations. Grignon needed to be stopped as soon as possible, and Sam needed April to leave for her own safety. But...he didn't want her to go. Her kindness and vulnerability surprised him. He wanted to caress her skin, the softness of her lips, the curve of her bosom. Heat rushed through him, and he shifted his position on the couch so she wouldn't see.

"I feel like a freeloader around here," April said. "Is there something I can do to earn my keep? Or, is there a hotel around? I don't want to intrude any more than I already have."

He touched the gauze covering his stitches and couldn't imagine how such a sweet, beautiful, caring woman had just fallen into his lap. "That's unnecessary. You can stay here. Besides, Astor House is half a day's journey across the river, and I don't know how anyone affords a night there. Besides, crossing the bridge safely is another matter."

She smiled. "Thanks. I really wish I could do something though, you know, to help."

Sam drank in her face. There was definitely something she could help with. Her gaze lingered on his lips, and he took that as a sign. "I'm sure Sarah would appreciate help in the garden." He leaned closer to her.

"That sounds nice," she said, eyes still on his lips.

The quickening of her breaths puffed against his face. His heart pounded in his chest with anticipation, heat bloomed in his groin, and he shifted position again. He wanted her, all of her, right now. The wait to taste her was giving him the biggest ache of his life.

SAM LEANED IN SO close the heat of his body warmed her skin. The roar of blood flowing through her veins throbbed at her core. His hot breath puffed against her lips, and she licked them as her mouth dried out like cotton. She fought her hands from reaching for his neck. So close and he would be hers. The air crackled with tension between them. She shifted her weight on the couch and something in her back pocket poked her hip.

The pepper spray and the Swiss army knife both grabbed into her flesh. What was she doing? Last she knew Sam was married! Where was Isabel anyway? Traveling to family?

April leaned back and forced herself to stand, fingers fidgeting. She'd almost kissed a married man, and she refused to get between him and Isabel. What was he doing? That was too close. Her thoughts bounced back and forth as Sam looked at her, pained. She just couldn't. "Maybe I should get that hotel room."

"It's too far away. I insist you stay."

April nodded and stepped into the pantry for a towel to clean up. She wanted to stay. She didn't deny her crush, but she had adult responsibilities she couldn't ignore. When she came back out, Sarah was a flurry in the kitchen, and Sam sat at the table with the day's newspaper.

April centered herself and stood over Sam. "Mind if I check the sutures?"

Sam folded the paper and set it down. He studied her while she dragged a chair over and sat in front of him. Heat flushed her face under his gaze. She peeled back the rectangle of cotton, careful not to tear any scabbing, and watched him for any signs of discomfort. He must've been hurting. Her nerves tingled where her fingertips brushed his skin. The cotton tugged on the ragged and raw flesh. He winced, and her wayward fingers caressed down his soft five o'clock shadow she released her touch.

April glanced at his smooth pink lips. "Sorry," she said, vowing to pay more attention while she continued to tug away the fabric.

With the wound clear of the bandage, she cleaned the skin by dabbing a corner of a damp towel on his cut until it was softened enough to wipe away the moistened blood.

The edges were pink with anger but not inflamed. She touched near the wound with her fingertip. It wasn't hot. Likely there would be no infection. She smiled.

"Is that smile of yours a good sign?"

"It should heal well. You'll have a scar, though. Sorry about that."

He seized her hand from his face and held it tight. "It wasn't your fault. No need to apologize."

She cast her eyes down, cheeks roaring with heat like an idiot. Sorry was her defense mechanism, the only word that diffused a situation whenever she screwed up. "Just habit. Can I check the back of your head?"

He released her hand and turned in his chair. Part of her wanted to be sure there was no open skin on his scalp, but another part of her wanted an excuse to touch him. She carefully slid her hands through his long brown locks, relishing the soft waves floating through her fingers. Heat rushed from her chest down low. His scalp, at the occipital bone, showed a raised contusion consistent with a blunt force injury. "They sucker punched you?"

"I don't understand the question."

Right. "They fought dirty?"

"Ralf Perez and I took a few hits each, nothing major. Next thing I knew I woke up here."

She glanced at his knuckles. They were puffy and scarred, but it was mostly old damage. There was no way Sam had done all that damage to Perez.

"Dennis and Rob did all this?" she asked in disbelief.

"Appears that way."

"You're safe now," she said with warmth.

He shot her a crooked smile. Her stomach rumbled with hunger, which differed from the type of hunger she wanted to satiate. But under the circumstances, her stomach won. She felt guilty that Sarah had been doing all the work again. Did Sam ever help her? April strolled over to his sister.

"Here's the ingredients for pancakes, since I know you're so thrilled to make them," Sarah said.

April measured and mixed batter and poured, but this time when she caught a glance at Sam, he was watching her rather than reading the paper.

Sarah made scrambled eggs and bacon. The sizzle on the cast iron pan sounded heavenly and smelled even better. If she ate like this every day, she'd gain a mountain of weight.

"I was wondering if you needed any help in the garden," April said. "I need to keep busy."

"Sure," Sarah said, delighted. "Picking weeds and harvesting is a daily job. I'll be thankful for it. You can borrow one of my aprons, since you insisted on not buying one."

Oops. "Oh, thank you." April smiled and poured shapes onto the pan.

Chapter 21

THE BACKYARD WAS MOSTLY rows of vegetable beds surrounded by fencing, likely to keep deer out. Bucky was their yard machine, nibbling away at the tallest grasses within his reach. Sarah kneeled on her apron and dug into the dirt with her bare hands. and April copied her. The young girl looked so innocent in her thick cotton bonnet, plain dress, and dirty apron.

April didn't have a green thumb at all, but the job description included pulling weeds. She could handle that. It seemed silly to wear a beautiful ruby dress while digging in the garden, but Sarah insisted. Instinct made her move delicately to avoid ruining the material.

"If you don't mind me asking," April said. "Where are your parents?"

Sarah cut cabbage and stacked it into her basket. "They've both passed."

"Oh, I'm sorry."

Sarah looked at her strangely. "Why do you ask?"

"Neither of you mentioned them, and pardon me for saying you seem young."

Sarah scowled. "Seventeen is not young. I'm to be married in a few weeks, right after my eighteenth birthday, to Mr. Jonathan Arris."

April smiled at the good news. "What's he like?"

"He's tall, of good breeding. A landowner about half a day's travel across the bridge," she said as if reciting his online dating profile.

"Is he funny, sweet, kind?"

"I don't know," she said, "I only met him briefly once." Sarah brushed off a radish, inspected it, and placed it into her basket.

"What? Like an arranged marriage?" April couldn't imagine, but she knew they still existed back home in some cultures.

"We have a contract."

"Pardon me for being frank, but do you want to marry him?" April yanked a pair of weeds, shook the dirt ball out of the roots, and tossed them into her pile. She looked at Sarah since the girl hadn't answered.

"There is another I would marry but it's not to be." Sarah gazed at the horizon of farm fields as if visualizing a dream of running away with her mysterious man.

"Contracts can be broken. You only need both parties to agree. Usually there's a clause somewhere in the fine print," April suggested.

Sarah refocused. "How is it you know so much about so many things, but have no clue how to ride a horse or tend a garden?"

April laughed. "It's a long story."

"Well, this garden's not maintaining itself, and the afternoon is young."

"I'm more of an indoor girl." April flattened her weed pile down.

"An indoor girl that wears clothes like a strange man, who can run like lightening, stitch wounds like a physician, and knows contracts? Sounds like a fascinating story."

April snagged small weeds by the root base and pulled. Her wrists were sore already and she wished she had a tool. How much could she tell the girl without scaring her? April didn't need anyone else turning on her like the townsfolk had. "Some of it's the fashion where I'm from. Some is schooling."

"I've never heard of wound care and law in the same school."

"I changed majors a few times."

"So you're a physician and a lawyer?"

April laughed. "No. Not even close."

"You seem mighty smart to me."

"I didn't finish college," April said. "I couldn't decide what to do with my life, so I majored in whatever people told me was best, and I did it to make them happy. I still don't know what I want to do when I grow up."

"Grow up?" Sarah's face pinched. "You're already grown. I don't understand."

"Where I come from you can do almost anything, as long as you can pay. Even people in their sixties take classes for enrichment or late-stage career changes."

"Sure sounds nicer than here." Sarah sighed and tucked a stray lock of golden-brown hair back under her bonnet.

"What do you mean? Besides a lot of manual labor, it's not so bad." April took her stack of weeds in a bundle and carried them off to the edge of the woods. She brushed her hands free of loose debris, and the sides of her index fingers were raw. She returned to Sarah.

"There's a lot of things here that aren't good," the girl said solemnly.

"Like what?" April had her share of complaints, but the girl's tone piqued her interest.

"Not being able to do what you want, where you want, with whom you want for starters."

April smiled. Sarah sounded like the teenager she was.

Sarah continued, "Then having to watch out for armed men who think you deserve to die, just for trying to live. It's too late for farmer Joseph Van Cleeve. All he wanted to do was bring his extra food to market without paying Grignon's men half a month's income. Now his widow is struggling to survive."

"Jesus."

Sarah kept her eyes on the dirt, working hard in the blistering sun. "Jesus got nothing to do with it."

Sam stopped by Lloyd's bar on his way to Thursday's collection. It was a scorching afternoon, and Sam wished once again it would rain. Even clouds would be a welcome reprieve from the angry sun. Several other people were here, some farther down the bar, others at tables. No privacy. Sam sat at the bar, and Lloyd appeared from the backroom of the building. "Nice shiner you got there. April said you were in trouble last night."

"And I heard you stopped an angry mob. Thank you. I don't know how bad this was." Sam pointed to his stitches. "But I imagine it'd be much worse if she didn't clean it up."

Lloyd leaned over to inspect the stitches. "Good work there."

"Aye," Sam said with admiration. "It is."

Lloyd lifted a mug and filled it with beer. "On the house."

Sam smiled and took a few gulps.

"You know," Lloyd said, "she's a fine woman."

Sam shook his head. "I know what you're thinking, but no. She's here on business, and then I need her to flee."

"Did Grignon make a pass?"

"Aye."

Lloyd shook his head. "That man will stop at nothing to get what he wants from everyone. You know that more than anyone. If Grignon has his hooks in her, it's only a matter of time now."

Sam swallowed down a few more gulps. "That's what I was afraid of."

Lloyd paused as if an idea sprung to him. "Why not though?" he asked, wheels turning.

"Why not what?" Sam asked.

"I've seen the way you look at her. April's gazing at you the same way. Why not go for it? Is it because of Isabel?"

Sam finished his mug. He knew how Lloyd would react to the truth, but he couldn't lie to his friend. "She rejected my advances."

Lloyd barked laughter and exclaimed, "You! Sam Hartley rejected by a woman? Impossible!"

Sam cracked a smile. "I know. Absurd right?"

"She's the smartest woman I've ever met."

Sam agreed with a smile and let the quip pass. "Thank you for the drink, Lloyd."

"If you need advice on any other aspect of catching that woman, my door is open."

Sam smiled and turned away.

Lloyd called after him, "Pick some flowers. Women like flowers."

Sam gestured his acknowledgement and left.

When he reached David Schneider's Feed Mill, he tied up the horse—he couldn't bear to call it Bucky—and stepped inside. There were a few customers around, baskets full of goods. He found David helping a customer. He waited until the old slender man saw him, and then Sam smiled apologetically.

David frowned and walked to his register.

Sam followed.

"Here to buy anything this week or just rob me?" David said with bitterness.

"Sorry sir, just my orders. Fifteen percent as required."

David opened the register and counted out an amount for him. He stuffed the money into an envelope and handed it to Sam. "Take it, and get out of my sight."

"I don't have a choice here, David," Sam placated.

"Yes, you do, son."

Sam tucked the envelope into his trouser pocket. These people didn't know half of what was going on.

"Getting mixed up in his business was a bad move. I think you know that." David paused. "Staying in it is worse."

"I didn't ask for advice," Sam said on a defeated breath and left.

He untied the horse and trotted back to his house. Grignon's delivery would wait. Sam needed to think, so he sought his workshop around back. The whole town hated what he did, but he didn't see a way out even if they thought there was. Easy to say when it wasn't your arse on the line or your sister's.

He threw open the barn doors and stood staring into the darkness with the bright sun behind him, casting a shadow like a beast over his work.

April spun and dropped a piece onto the dirt floor. When it hit the table leg, it made a loud clang.

Sam stiffened. The lady, beautiful in her red dress, was in his smithing shop. He found himself surprised that he didn't scream at her to leave his place of pain, and that the pain wasn't on the forefront of his thoughts. Instead he fought the desire to close the door behind him and ravage her right here. His pulse pounded and heat rushed through him, culminating where he didn't want her to see.

But his visit with David made the violation of his private space anger him. Why had she been looking for him?

APRIL QUICKLY RETRIEVED THE sculpture off the floor and replaced it on the table. Anger lurked on Sam's face. She screwed up. "I'm sorry. I just...I didn't mean to touch it. It's so beautiful though. Your dad's?"

"What are you doing in here?" His broad shoulders bunched as he prowled closer.

She swallowed a sticky lump in her throat. "I was looking for something," she said. "For the garden." April held out her raw, dirty hands as if that explained it. "A small hand tiller or pliers. I'm not used to gardening."

Sam kept coming closer without a word, and April backed toward the walk-in door, breath quickening, dirt-caked hands trembling. She hadn't seen him like this before—seething. She didn't belong in here. She'd invaded his space, and he was raging mad. Why didn't Sarah warn her to stay out?

Sam reached a long thick arm behind her and closed the door, trapping her inside and against his chest. Her breath hitched. April wanted to duck under his arm and dash for the large bay door, but in this restrictive dress, she would faceplant and he would still capture her.

Eyes ablaze, Sam grabbed her wrists.

April gasped and twisted her hands out of his grip, but it was like trying to slide out of those iron shackles—useless. Didn't stop her from trying though.

He lifted them up closer and inspected them. "You don't have calluses."

April's fear vaporized, replaced with confusion. "No. Why?"

Sam glared at her as if secrets to the universe were written on the backs of her retinas. She broke the gaze. This unexpected anger terrified her. A curl of the fist, a slam of the door, the menacing silence—she knew where that always led, and she'd already escaped it once.

Sam released one of her wrists and picked up a tool, placing it in her palm.

A hand tiller.

"Thanks," she croaked out.

But Sam didn't let go of her other wrist. He just kept staring at her, but his anger was gone, and his touch softened. Sam's chest brushed up against hers. Standing this close to him, his labored breathing was nothing more than...attraction. He said gruffly, "All you had to do was ask."

"You're not mad?"

His face flickered with confusion. "Of course not. Although some days I wonder..."

The rage had been clear to her. Maybe he misunderstood. "I mean angry?"

"Not at you. I wasn't expecting anyone in here. Everything about you surprises me, and I haven't felt that in a long time."

The fiery gaze in his eyes as he focused on her lips was clear. She knew what he wanted, and she wanted it too. Heat raced through her veins, lighting up her nerves like a string of lights, sending a pulse-pounding throb down low.

April dropped the tiller with a clang and reached her hand up to the nape of his neck. She brought his lips to hers. Large protective arms wrapped around her, pressing her against him, and April's need and desire took over. She'd never felt more alive as she wove her fingers into his locks and pulled on his neck, forcing his lips to stay on hers. Sam clearly had his flaws, and they had so much to discuss, but April couldn't get enough of him. Her heart soared.

Sam moved her against the wall, and his hard erection pressed against her lower belly. The pounding of her heart became deafening.

A feminine gasp came from behind them, and Sam released her immediately, taking all the heat and pleasure with him. No, she begged, don't stop now.

Sarah stood in the open bay door, mouth gaped like a fish. "I heard a strange noise, but I see all is well." She smiled and ducked back out.

April flushed with embarrassment and covered her broad grin with her hand.

"You'd think she'd knock first." He adjusted himself and grinned at April, lips puffed and pink. His breathing slowed back to normal. "I knew you'd come around."

April shoved him back. "Arrogance is not attractive."

"I didn't mean that. Only that I see something between us, and you were bound to realize it too. I didn't want to regret not kissing you." He sheepishly ran a hand through his long wavy locks. And it was sexy as hell.

But April needed to change the subject. "What is this place?"

"My shop."

"Yours?" April asked in surprise.

"It's a long story."

April laughed at having her line repeated to her. "The lettuce won't be disappointed to share dirt space for another day."

Sam laughed, a deep, resonant melody. The kind of voice that belonged to rugged men of the forest, who drank all day while working and sweating hard, and it made her weak in the knees. "I was a blacksmith, an apprentice as a child, and a master as I learned. I inherited this shop." There was a sadness in his tone. Sam wandered slowly around the shop, inspecting his pieces while he spoke. "Then I met a lady."

"The woman in the dress, the one Sarah put on me?" April prompted.

"Isabel was to be my wife, but blacksmithing wasn't good enough. I needed to make something better of myself to be worthy of her hand. I accepted a job at Grignon's bank, and shortly after, my parents and Isabel's reached an accord. We were wed."

April silently urged him to continue.

"Grignon saw something else in me. I had a way with the townsfolk, and he needed someone to do a special job."

"The one you do now, collecting from the businesses?"

"I refused. I wanted no part of it." Sam removed a piece off the wall and turned it over in his hands. His body stiffened with anger. "And she was murdered for my defiance."

April gasped.

Sam hurled the piece against the wall with frightening force. It tumbled and clanged, ringing other pieces and echoed through the barn. "Let's get out of here," he said.

April followed him to the house where he gathered a blanket and packed a basket of food. She watched his hands work quickly. Despite the terrible circumstances, April realized Sam was single. And if he was packing a private meal for the two of them, perhaps she could spill the beans about his fate.

Chapter 22

APRIL AND SAM RODE Bucky in comfortable silence while the horse navigated the primitive roads east through town. Sam's thighs pressed against her legs again, and she bit her lower lip to cover the smile. They hooked a left, turning north on the road between Lloyd's and the feed mill.

"Where are we going?" she asked.

"It's a surprise," he whispered into her ear, sending a shiver down her spine.

After a short while, a clearing appeared, and near the center was a wood stage with a taller platform and a podium. "What's that?"

"Common Square. It used to be for festivals, dances, and weddings. Lately, it's only been used for hangings. Grignon added trapdoors to the platform."

April swallowed a lump in her throat. At the far end of Common Square, there was a narrow path leading into the woods. Bucky climbed up a vast hill over rocks and exposed tree roots.

April brushed away overhanging branches as Sam maneuvered the horse through thick undergrowth. The woods cleared to a grassy hilltop. April craned her neck to take in the area, and she lit up with recognition. Sam stopped them with a tug on the reins, and he helped April down by grasping her around the waist. The feel of his hands on her never got old.

April headed to the edge of the hilltop, drawn by the familiarity. The view was breathtaking. Three small villages hugged the Fox River about three miles apart, and in the coming decades, they would merge and grow to become her city in the present day. She saw where the interstate highway would eventually be, but for now it was all trees. The massive interstate bridge over the river didn't exist yet either. Steamboats bobbed in the bay and logs floated down river to the lumber mill. Fort Howard's menacing walls kept watch over the water. A pair of men patrolled the roads, probably Grignon's men, and a farmer, with a trailer of hay pulled by a set of horses, was heading west.

History was alive.

Sam laid out a blanket on the grass and set a picnic basket on it. He came up behind her, his heat giving away his presence, and her back warmed. "Nice view?" His words blew warm air over her ear. She shuddered.

"Beautiful," she said.

"Aye, it is, isn't it?" She had a feeling he wasn't talking about the villages and the bay. She blushed. His fingers snaked through hers and brought her to the blanket. "Sit, have a sandwich. It's not gourmet, but I didn't have enough time to properly fix a spread."

"A sandwich is great." April joined him and dove in with a generous bite. "Thank you. It's delicious. Your accent, you weren't born here," April said, fishing for information.

"Ahh," Sam laughed. "My parents brought us over from Ireland when we were wee kids. Da worked on the Erie canal, and after its completion, he settled us here. Bridgeport, you notice, has quite a mix of people. You got the Perezes from the west coast, Grignon is from France or perhaps French Canada, he hadn't specified, and I didn't have the care nor the ear to ask which. Lloyd is from the south. His parents escaped slavery and brought him up here. Fine people. Rest their souls. Not sure about the rest of the citizens, but they seem to blend in better, if that's a good term for it."

His story was fascinating, just like her standing right here in history. "This is Overlook Hill."

"It has a name?"

"Yeah. Where I'm from, this is where the teenagers go to make out." She laughed. "They always tell their parents they're going to the other friend's house for a sleepover. Then they come up here for the night, crossing their fingers neither parent calls the other. They text occasionally to check in. Not that I have personal experience with it or anything..." April had in fact been one of those teens.

"Text?" Sam asked.

"It's a city thing."

"What is a make out and sleepover?"

April coughed. "Another city thing."

"Did you do those things?"

"My parents rarely knew where I was. Mom worked twelves overnight as a nurse. Dad worked at the plant, and after his shifts, he'd drink himself to sleep in front of the...fireplace. When he woke up in the middle of the night, he'd look for us, and we'd better be home or he'd take it out on us."

"Us?"

"My brother Matty and I."

"The veterinarian?"

"That's the one."

"What does 'take it out on us' mean?" Sam asked.

"His belt." April shuddered. The sound of leather slipping out of belt loops made her shiver, even a decade since the last time he'd raised it to her bare ass. Luckily, she didn't have to be anywhere near him anymore. "He took his anger out on me, mostly. Even if I didn't do anything wrong. So sometimes I would justify his actions." April lifted her sleeve and showed Sam the long-since faded jagged mark on her upper arm. She'd gotten that one because she'd turned at the last second to protect her ability to sit.

"Your scars," Sam concluded.

April nodded, fighting tears from forming. She had many more hideous marks from her father.

"Why didn't anyone stop him?" Sam asked through clenched teeth.

April took a bite. "Mom was busy, but she chose to turn a cheek. When she interfered once, Dad made sure she'd regret it. My brother also tried twice. The first time he mouthed off to him and received a sock to the gut he'll never forget. The second time he ended up in the hospital for a week. That's when I begged Matty not to intervene. He wasn't happy about it, but I didn't want to lose the only person who stood on my side."

"I'm sorry he did that to you. There's no excuse for it. I'd have laid him out flat after the first swing."

April believed him, and it was comforting to know he would've protected her.

"Where you're from sounds terrible. Around these parts, men don't hit ladies or children. There are a few exceptions running around, but if you avoid them, it's mostly safe. You're mighty kind after putting up with all you did."

"I knew I couldn't stop him, so for Matty's sake, I tried to keep calm and wait for the pain to end. I didn't always succeed."

Sam's molars ground, flickering his jaw muscles in a protective fury. April appreciated the sentiment, but his reaction troubled her. She was here for a mission, and then she had to leave. "What did you mean when you told Grignon I was 'yours'?"

Sam closed his eyes. "Grignon takes whatever he's interested in. The bank he now owns. The town he controls by extortion. He owns me by holding people I care about hostage. Then he met you. If I didn't declare to him that I owned you, he would've taken you."

"Taken me for what?"

Sam's brow crinkled at the thought. "Whatever he wants; however he wants it."

April recoiled. "What about the police?"

"He owns the sheriff."

April scoffed. "You can't own the sheriff."

"With enough money and guns you can own anyone," Sam said.

So if Grignon wanted Sam arrested, no matter what he'd done or didn't do, Sam would be cuffed and executed. "And everyone allows him to do this?"

Sam's anger flared as if she hit a sore spot. "No one allows him to do anything, but no one has stopped him yet."

The whole town was under Grignon's thumb. Maybe all three towns or more? She didn't know how far his reach extended, but the only way to truly prevent Sam's arrest was to stop Grignon. The question was how?

The sun shifted its position, and April needed to find a bathroom—which seemed impossible. She'd take an outhouse, but she wasn't rustic enough to use a tree and a leaf, and she would be mortified if Sam insisted. "We should get back."

"Are you sure? We aren't finished yet."

"I need to go now."

A sadness filled his features, but Sam nodded. "I understand."

SAM WAS SAD AND withdrawn as he dropped her off at the cabin and remained on the horse.

"Aren't you coming inside?" she asked.

"I have a drop at Grignon's to complete."

April didn't want him anywhere near that monster. Her hand touched Bucky. "Don't go."

"I must or terrible things happen," Sam said. "When I get back, I'll assist you however you need."

April wasn't sure what that meant, but Sam turned away and set off into the growing orange of the evening sky.

April used the facilities and washed up. She needed a drink, and Sam's bourbon was as good as any other. April poured a glass and sat on the couch. After the initial burn from the fumes, it wasn't half bad.

"You're trying your luck with Sam's best bourbon." Sarah said, coming inside.

"After I dumped half of it down his body, I already told him I'll replace it."

The fiery drink barreled into her empty stomach like a soaring cannonball. It helped calm her nerves. It was time to tell Sam the truth about what she knew so they could make a plan to save his life.

Sarah washed her hands in the basin. "Now's your chance. I need to gather some ingredients for dinner, care to join me?"

April swallowed her glass dry and stood up, eager to spread the buzz through her limbs. She had switched to her bronze dress and made sure her modern items were in their proper pockets. And seeing as she refused to buy any other shoes, her not-so-white sneakers were still cocooning her feet, hidden beneath layers of linen. "Count me in."

They both walked the dirt road to town. Sarah's arm hooked around April's, while the other arm carried an empty basket.

"I caught you and Sam."

"I saw." April winced.

"For a while I didn't think he would get over Isabel." Their skirts fluttered around their legs in rhythm to their steps. "I thought her death would kill him, but I see the way he looks at you. He never looked at her like that."

April's chest bloomed with heat, and a smile curved the corners of her mouth. She remembered the throbbing tingle of her lips on his, and then she quickly dashed those thoughts away. April didn't mean to lead him on. And now when she left, she'd break his heart again. This whole time travel mission thing was unfair. As soon as Sam got back, she was telling him everything.

April and Sarah neared two women talking outside the bank, and as they approached, the townies gave April an appraisal. The shorter one said in a cheerful voice, "Good afternoon, ladies. Fine weather today."

Sarah returned the greeting, and April nodded with a smile as they walked by. Was their approval simply because Sarah was with her, or did Lloyd's speech have that much impact?

"Where do I get a bottle of bourbon, Sam's favorite?" April asked.

"Lloyd would sell you a whole bottle. We can stop there last."

They reached Porter's, and Sarah tasked her with collecting eggs and flour. April browsed the store and found them simply enough. It wasn't like a grocery store with twenty different options for peanut butter and twelve kinds of mustard. April's stomach growled at the idea of a juicy hamburger fresh off the grill. Soon, she'd return home.

April waited at the register for Sarah to finish up, and Porter greeted her. "I hear things got testy the other night with the townsfolk and Grignon's men on patrol. Are you holding up all right?"

"I'm just fine."

"Sam too?"

"We survived. Thanks."

"Good to hear. He's a good boy. I had the pleasure of working with his parents, bless their souls, when he was just a child. Good people—the lot of them."

She smiled and Sarah came up. Porter gave them the total and Sarah paid, guilt wracking April.

With the basket full, they headed for Stanton's Spirits to replace Sam's favorite bottle. A man and woman were walking toward them with arms linked. Just before they passed, the man said, "Looking well this afternoon, ladies."

"Why are they being nice all of a sudden?" April asked.

"If they're yelling or spitting at you, be concerned, but as long as they're pleasant, you rank among them. I'm not sure I'd describe them as nice. That depends on who and where you are, if you don't mind my frankness."

At least April didn't have to worry they would gang up, hog-tie her, and toss her onto Grignon's doorstep. That was an improvement.

"See him over there?" Sarah whispered.

April followed her finger across the road. Leaning against the wall of Bridgeport Chemist was a short Hispanic man with sharp black eyes and a soft jawline. The failing light cast an eerie shadow across his face, but it was him! He was the one riling up the townspeople and accusing her of theft. Perhaps it was a simple mistake, but the way he stared creeped her out.

Sarah said, "That one you have to watch out for."

"Why?"

"That's Jaime Perez, Isabel's brother."

April never stole but that Jaime guy wouldn't listen to reason. What did he have against her? It was not like April would replace Isabel. With an ugly glare in return, April moved with Sarah into a packed Stanton's Spirits.

The young woman brought April straight to the bar where customers filled the space almost entirely elbow-to-elbow. And the tables had many customers mingling around. Sarah flagged down Lloyd, who turned his head and suppressed a smile. "Evening, my lady."

"Evening, good sir. I need your finest bourbon—Sam's favorite. It met an unfortunate end."

"As the lady wishes." Lloyd moved down the bar and into a back room.

Sarah smiled like a star-struck teenager.

He came back quickly carrying a bottle identical to the one she emptied between Sam's injuries and her afternoon glass. He held it out as if it were a fancy bottle of wine.

"Thank you," Sarah said.

"That'll be ten, please."

April dug out her remaining ten bucks from when she'd broke her twenty on the dresses, and Ralf was kind enough to give her local change. She paid and cradled the bottle. They turned to leave, but Jaime glowered at April from the corner by the door. April shivered, holding on tighter to the small girl. Was he following them too?

Her footsteps fell faster on their way back to Sarah and Sam's cabin, and she couldn't stop herself from looking behind her. Now she wasn't so sure his accusation of theft was an innocent mistake.

Chapter 23

April opened her eyes, confused to see her own darkened ceiling reflecting a soft glow from the streetlights outside the window. She was lying on the same old fluffy couch in her own house. It had all been a dream. Kiko's wacky story, time traveling to 1852, Sam and Sarah. Especially that creepy Jaime Perez. He must've been her subconsciousness's projection of her dad. And that horrific Grignon guy. What a ride that was! She felt refreshed, energized, but was she relieved or disappointed it was over?

Levi came in the front door, carrying take out to the kitchen table. The trailing scent bore straight through her nose to her stomach, which growled with a furious need for the tangy sweet and sour chicken. She joined him at the table, and he unpacked the cartons from the plastic bag. April used her perfectly American plastic fork to take a bite of the chicken and moaned its deliciousness. Her stomach would hate her later, but her tongue was in heaven.

"Why aren't you dressed?" Levi asked with a strange tone, and his dark eyes bore into her.

"For what?" April wore jeans and a T-shirt, nothing out of the ordinary.

He sighed. "I suppose you don't want to stain your wedding gown. Eat up and get dressed." He checked his watch. "We're leaving in twenty minutes."

"Hold on. Did you say wedding gown?"

Levi's frustrated eyes rolled toward her as if she were a child. "It's our wedding day. Was your bachelorette party that intense last night? I will have a talk with Kiko about that."

In a flash of bright light, she found herself the center of attention on a carpeted stage, holding a bouquet of pink, purple, and white flowers. An organ played traditional church music, while a chapel full of people stared at her. White flowers and green ivy dangled on either side of the aisle. She didn't recognize anyone. Not even Matty attended.

"What is going on?" she whispered to herself, stomach twisting with bile.

Sounds of the priest behind her swirled into her head. Was he reading vows? This couldn't be real. Someone in the audience sneezed, and a hand seized hers. She turned and Levi's face sneered, as if irritated she wasn't paying attention. He said, "With this ring, I thee wed—" He pulled her finger out from her fist and stuffed the ring up past her knuckle.

"No," she whispered. "No, I can't." She pulled her hand back, refusing, but his grip was like a vice.

"—and with it, I bestow upon thee all the treasures of my mind, heart, and hands," Levi continued.

April had to stop this now. She wouldn't let herself be controlled by Levi for the rest of her life. No Florida, no matching BMWs, no pile of kids...with Levi. A fiery rage burned within, and April's strength broke free of the confines her father had forced it into all those years ago. Over the priest's droning, April shouted, "Levi!"

The vows stopped. The audience gasped, cell phone cameras flashed, and a loud banging on the chapel doors echoed through the chamber. No one else turned toward the sound. Was it only in her head? The doors crashed open. Her dad stood in the frame, a menacing, bald, and beer-bellied man filled with fury that oozed from the very pores of his skin.

"Go away!" April screamed.

April wrenched her hand free from Levi's grip and shoved him back. Her dad's pounding footsteps thundered toward her. She took a step back in horror, and the black hole had finally come to the rescue, swallowing her up.

"April, what's going on. Are you all right?" It was Sam's voice.

Warm relief washed over her, and her panicked breaths began to slow. It was a dream. No, it was a nightmare. Sticky sweat covered her body.

April shifted in her bed and found darkness. She lit the gas lamp on the table by the quilts, sat up, and called, "I'm fine. I'm awake."

"Come out for breakfast," Sam called back through the door, his voice less steady than usual.

He'd missed dinner. At least he'd come home last night.

That nightmare was so real. April wanted a stiff drink. Bourbon was acceptable before nine in the morning, right?

After a full belly and a proper goodbye, then Sam could escort her safely away from this nightmare. But the full belly didn't have to come from anywhere ordinary. He sat by her bedroom door, knee bouncing and rattling the handful of wildflowers in his fist. Hopefully she liked them, otherwise he would kick the shite out of Lloyd for embarrassing him. Back in Da's time, marriages were arranged contracts, and love was for kids, who had no one planning their futures. Sam had already tried a contract, and now he wanted something more. He wasn't going to think about how dreadfully short it would last. A petal shook out of the bouquet, and finally April's door opened. He rose to his feet.

April rubbed her eyes, but what she wore—or lack thereof, made Sam's face flush hot, and he spun to give her privacy. How could she show him that much skin? It wasn't proper. Sam was curious what kind of city she'd come from.

April yawned behind him, and then she cleared her throat. "Is everything okay?" she asked.

"Um, well…" Sam stuttered. "I…I just came over to…" April stepped around to face him and he turned again.

"What's the matter? Is it your cheek? Give me a look."

With his back turned to her he said, "No. I insist. It's just that you're…"

"Oh shit. Just give me a minute." Her door closed behind her. She popped back out while fastening the last few buttons on the front of her dress. "I'm sorry about that."

Feeling far more comfortable, Sam brought the flowers forward. "These are for you."

"Thank you." April accepted the flowers from him and inhaled their scent. "They're beautiful."

"It's only natural to bring beautiful flowers to a beautiful woman."

Her face turned bright red, and she smiled.

Thank you, Lloyd, Sam thought. His best friend hadn't let him down, and Sam wouldn't have to kick the shite out of him. In all honesty, he didn't think he would win against the larger man, and Sam would take that admission to his grave. Lloyd didn't need more reasons to tease him.

April brought the flowers to the kitchen and scooped water into a vase. She placed them in it, arranging them with a few shuffles. Then her soft footsteps came back and stopped in front of him, inside his personal space. Not knowing what she would do gave him a rush.

Fingertips prodded his cheek, and he jerked back at the touch. It was tender, but nothing he hadn't dealt with before. That wasn't why he jerked away. His body sparked with heat at her tickling touch. He wanted her fingers all over his body.

"It looks good," she said. "In a few more days I can remove the stitches."

Sam smelled her bare scent, and it stoked his fire. He couldn't stop it. He wanted to jump out of his skin whenever she was around.

April cupped his forearm and lifted the sleeve of his shirt. Her touch burned a trail across his skin. Against his wishes, his erection woke up screaming. The damn thing had terrible timing lately.

"Listen, after breakfast—" April started.

"Actually," Sam interrupted. "About that. I wanted to ask would you care to dine out for breakfast?"

"That's sounds fun," April said, brightening. "Sarah too?"

His sister just stepped out of her room, sleepy and yawning, as if the word 'breakfast' were a beacon. "Sarah what?"

Sam said to April, loud enough for his sister's ears, "Sarah can make her own breakfast, and extra for the dogs, aye? April and I are going to Max's."

"You two have fun," Sarah said.

April had an easiness about her, a confidence. Unorthodox, as Grignon had said, for sure. Fascinating as hell and beautiful as a field of wild blue phlox swaying in a summer breeze. He was going to make this date count.

IT WAS ONLY BREAKFAST, and depending on how busy it was, she could speak privately with Sam. April mulled over her strategy while they strode into the diner. She'd never had to explain something as wild as what Kiko had sent her here for.

The diner was just as April expected—retro and rustic. A raised brick fireplace behind the counter was the grill, sizzling sausage over an open flame. The walls were a pale stone. Windows bathed the tables in the warm morning sunlight. A pair of elderly customers were reading the newspaper and sipping from mugs. Sam held a chair out for her. She sat, and he pushed her in. It was foreign to be waited on by someone else, treated like something special. She enjoyed the attention and care.

They browsed the menus. A woman in a plain gray dress and stained white apron came by and offered drinks. April asked for a water; Sam a coffee. The waitress smiled and left, and Sam said, "You say you're from the city. But I see soft smooth hands, a scandalous dress, strange shoes, unfamiliarity with horses, and Sarah told me about your interest in doctoring and legal business. You have no traveling companions. Which city fits all these pieces together?"

"Oh," April said, strategy thrown right out the window. She wanted to be careful about giving him the whole truth. There were ears around. "My traveling companions abandoned me."

"Your brother abandoned you?"

"My brother didn't go with me."

"Why didn't he insist?"

Because Mathew didn't know she'd left. Because he was a modern man who believed women were equals. Because he was in a different century. And she didn't need a babysitter to go anywhere. "Mathew and I don't have that kind of relationship."

"That's a shame. I wouldn't trade my relationship with my sister for anything. She can get under my skin frequently, but she's a good kid."

April smiled. "I can tell. You never said what happened to your parents."

"Mam passed from the fever, knowing I was a blacksmith apprentice and happy as a young man could be. Da struggled, and I acted out. My sister wasn't always so agreeable either." He chuckled. "After things settled, Da secured marital agreements for me and Sarah. Then Da followed Mam not long after. His official cause was the fever too, but I think he just loved Mam too much. After making sure the kids would be cared for, he was free to be with her again."

"That's so sad and yet sweet." His vulnerability talking about his parents' love for each other melted her.

"So, it's been Sarah and I until she reaches the age of her contract here in a couple weeks. Then she will be wed. As for my contract..."

"Isabel."

"Aye."

"Are there any repercussions? What about her family?"

"Ralf Perez blames me for her death and hates what I do. Ironically, I do my job because of him."

Their personal conversation at Couture Clothing made more sense now—as did their anger. "He's the one you needed to impress?"

"Aye. So he would approve the contract between me and his daughter."

"It must be difficult to pretend things are normal with her death hanging over everyone's heads."

Sam looked at her with a pained expression.

She cast her eyes down. "I'm sorry."

"Stop saying you're sorry. You have nothing to be sorry for."

The waitress brought their drinks, and Sam sipped the smooth coffee while April downed her water like a parched camel. The waitress took their orders and retrieved the menus from the table.

"How's the water?" Sam asked with a curve of his lips.

She glanced at the empty glass and licked her lips. "The water doesn't taste very good around here, I've noticed."

"Aye. That's why Lloyd's bar does so well. It's either burn your throat and forget about it, or choke down metallic shite water."

April cringed and laughed at the same time. He was so wonderful. She had to tell him. No more delays. "Sam, there's something I need to tell you."

Sam smile fell, but he waited.

"I...I'm not from around here." How did she spit this out? Why was it so hard?

"I already figured that out," Sam said.

"Where I came from is hard to believe, but I was sent here on business to—" April cut off. Over Sam's shoulder was Jaime Perez, the man following her and Sarah yesterday. The troublemaker riling up the townspeople and accusing her of theft. Now he stared at her with a grim determination.

"What is it?" Sam's shoulders bunched with tension and his hand slipped below the table.

"Jaime Perez is here," she whispered.

"You two met?"

"Not exactly."

Sam turned around and smiled. "Jaime! Great to see you, come over here."

Jaime sauntered over with his usual smirk.

Sam said, "Jaime, this is April McCall and April, this is Jaime Perez, officially."

April reluctantly allowed Jaime to take her hand as a gentleman and kiss her knuckles. She wanted to punch him in the nose. And the moment his touch released, she snapped her hand back.

"Pleasure to meet you, miss. I've heard much about you."

She wanted to accuse him right back of being an inconsiderate jackass, but she refrained for Sam's sake.

"April is staying with Sarah and I until her business in town is complete," Sam explained.

"Is that so?" Jaime said, still watching her. Creepy bastard. Finally, he shifted his attention to Sam and said, "So, you and Father had a lick of trouble the other day."

The waitress returned with their orders, and April waited until Sam took a bite before digging in herself.

"Aye, how is Ralf?"

"The same as you, I'd wager. Broken more in ego than bones."

"And Marisol? They must have frightened her," Sam added.

"She's shaken, but you know Grignon's men. They do that to everyone."

No kidding, April thought.

"I had been meaning to stop by the shop. I'm glad all is well."

Jaime fixed his gaze on April's plate while she forked up bites and chewed. "Until later," he said and tipped his hat.

April took another generous bite, and Sam quickly cleared half his plate.

He sipped his coffee and said, "What does a veterinary assistant do? That's your business here?"

April forked a few bites of her eggs and hash browns, scooting them into ketchup.

"I update patient records and assist in surgery, but I have a weak stomach for blood."

"Why do you dress wounds if blood makes you ill?"

April scooted eggs around her plate as if searching for the answer under them.

"I didn't mean to pry," Sam added.

"I wasn't sure how to answer. I guess because Matty needed me, and it's as simple as that. Tell me about your blacksmith shop. From what I gather, those pieces hanging weren't for any practical purposes."

"I used to make tools and horseshoes on commission, like my master taught me. Although I took pride in my necessary work, I felt a desire to do more. As a hobby, I experimented."

"The pieces are stunning."

"Thank you kindly," Sam said, his voice breaking with humility. "Do you practice art?"

"I used to," April said and finished her last bite. She took a drink of her refilled glass, and Sam finished his coffee. "I lost the passion for it."

"What kind?"

"I draw portraits. Graphite on eighty-pound paper."

"I'd like to see your work, you know, from one artist to another," Sam said.

"I'd like that too." Her face warmed. Why did he have to be so damned perfect?

Chapter 24

Outside of Max's diner, Sam offered his arm just like his sister had. April accepted it, guilt stabbing her in the chest, and they strolled along the dirt road. She didn't want to lose his trust or the way he looked at her when she smiled, but she needed to tell him now. The words just wouldn't come out.

April spotted Jaime leaning against a tree between the buildings. She tugged on Sam's arm to get his attention.

"What is it?" he asked softly.

There was one truth April was giving him now. "Remember when I told you about the mob accusing me of theft?"

"I will never forget."

"My accuser is staring at us. Over there." She nodded toward the tree.

"Jaime? You must be joking. He's been struggling with his grief, but he's harmless."

"Then there's a side to him he doesn't show you."

"I'll show you." Sam redirected their path toward him. Alarm bells clanged inside her head, and her stomach quivered with its full load of eggs and strange ketchup.

"Jaime, who are you waiting for?" Sam asked.

Jaime straightened and ignored the question. He pointed at April. "What is she then? Your new fiancée?"

"What?" Sam asked, his body tensing.

April had suspected something bothered him. Jaime had been stalking and sabotaging her. But this was a surprise.

"We're not engaged," Sam said. "I told you she's in town for business, and she is staying with Sarah and I until it is complete."

"That's what you tell yourself, but this isn't right."

Sam must've seen something in Jaime's eye, a twitch, a change in posture. Sam released her hand from his arm and whispered in her ear, "Stay here. Don't get close."

Sam's fists clenched just as Jaime came in swinging. Sam dodged the right hook. "What are you doing? Jaime, stop this."

He didn't. Swing after swing came flying by.

April stepped back, covering her mouth with her hands, and she tripped on her skirts, falling flat on her butt.

Sam dodged and parried so many swings, he must've finally lost patience. Sam clocked Jaime square in the jaw, sending the man stumbling back. "I told you to stop already. What has gotten into you?"

A small crowd gathered outside of nearby stores. They watched and whispered. A couple children were laughing. April stood up and dusted herself off. She had a large patch of dirt out of reach on the back of her dress. Perhaps it would've been a good idea to get a few more dresses. Staying clean in these barbaric times was impossible. She shook the dirt from her hair and wished for a hot shower.

The men circled as if they were boxers, forearms up in defense, feet shifting position as they turned. She tried to catch Sam's glance, but he was lost to the fight. She had to admit he was skilled, hardly taking any damage. Her mind's eye flashed back to him as a bloody pulp at the back of Perez's store. She realized when he was a mess, he'd been outmanned, hit with a cheap shot, and in a very serious fight. She shivered and hoped to never see that kind of carnage on him again.

The contrast between these fighters was clear. Sam appeared to be holding back, so he didn't hurt the smaller man. April wanted

Jaime to take a hard knock to the head, just so he would leave her alone.

With the crowd watching, April worried someone would send for the sheriff. Her body tensed with concern as her eyes scanned for anyone scurrying off with a purpose.

With Jaime's back to her, he swung low, right toward Sam's liver. Sam stepped to the side and used the smaller man's momentum against him, slamming a right hook into his jaw with a crunch.

April winced on his behalf, and Jaime flew back, smashing her to the dirt and gravel. A flash of white blinded her vision when her head struck. A ringing in her ears blotted out all other sound, and she gasped for air with the wind knocked out of her. A hundred and fifty pounds of unconscious man squeezed her chest. Her vision narrowed.

When her sight and hearing returned, Sam was rubbing her cheek with his thumb, brows knitted in worry. "April. Wake up. Please wake up."

April blinked and her head swam. The world spun before her, and Sam helped her stand. She wobbled, but he stabilized her. "I'm so sorry. That should never have happened. It was my fault for losing awareness of the situation. I don't know what got into him."

How much time had passed? April searched for trouble. She didn't see a sheriff or anyone in the crowd causing a stirring. Jaime laid in the dirt, face up, looking swollen but peaceful. She crouched next to him, and Sam helped so she didn't fall over.

April felt his pulse at his wrist. "He's alive. Let's go."

Sam helped her walk, but she kept stumbling as if she were drunk. He picked her up in his arms, and she rested her head against his chest, listening to his strong heartbeat, and feeling safe. April smiled, and he carried her all the way home. To his house. Home to his house. Not her home because that would be inappropriate.

When they pushed through the door, April was finally functional. She fetched her medical supplies and treated Sam's knuckles. They were bloody and swollen stiff. Perhaps it was the knock to the head or perhaps because the damage wasn't lethal, but seeing the blood didn't bother her. She carried on through the motions of tending his wounds like it was old hat. The only thing bubbling inside her was his hot gaze on her face while she worked.

SAM STUDIED HER AS she dressed his knuckles. They'd been damaged so many times, swinging fists didn't even hurt anymore. He watched her hands tremble with the aftereffects of being knocked silly.

"You were right about Jaime. I don't know what's gotten into the man."

April touched her nose and winced. "It's not bloody, right?" She seemed so fragile and scared. He wanted to cocoon her from all the dangers and all the stupidity.

"No. Maybe a bit crooked."

She gasped, and he laughed. "I'm just kidding with you. It's still a cute nose, just as it was before."

Barking turned Sam's head to the back door, and he remembered he'd asked Sarah to leave extra breakfast for the dogs. He found the bowl and carried it to the back door.

"Come with me," he told April.

"They sound excited out there," she said. "They didn't find a cat, did they?"

"No. I was teasing." Sam stepped outside and was swallowed by a pack of hungry, filthy mutts. They jumped up at him and barked, tails wagging. Sam laughed and sprinkled the food around, so they each had a chance to eat. He kneeled at the smallest one.

"This one's Doug. He's a special guy." Sam's smile was broad as he roughed up his ears and babbled at him like he had to his sister when she was a newborn. He couldn't help it. Some weird urge made him treat the mutt like a wee person, and he didn't care if April thought he was foolish. Doug smiled his big doggy smile and licked him. Sam gave him a palmful of breakfast just for himself.

April kneeled beside him. "I love your accent."

Sam stared at her, and April's beautiful eyes widened. "I mean...I...I didn't mean to say that out loud." Raw need shot through him, and he loved the way her face burned with embarrassment. She added, "What did he do?"

"What?" Sam asked, lost in another one of her city references, perhaps.

"To be special." She scratched Doug in all his favorite places. His leg mimicked her scratches, but he missed his own mark.

"After Isabel was gone, Doug came to my back door every morning, whimpering until I opened it and gave him food."

"That's standard doggy behavior," she said.

"He gave me kisses before he'd take the food. The homeless dog with no guarantees for a meal, who also was the smallest and last dog to eat if there was enough food, lifted my spirits before tending his own needs."

April tumbled with the little guy, playing puppy style, and Sam's heart melted to a puddle. She smiled at Sam, and it was then he realized he was lost to her.

"He's very cute despite his scruffiness," April said.

The pack of dogs rushed off to their next stop, and Doug gave goodbye licks to April before joining them.

Sam rested his hands on his hips, offended. "What about me, you filthy mutt?"

April laughed. "I guess he traded teams."

"He's a traitor, is what."

"Can I give that a try?" she asked and nodded at his wood pile.

"You want to split wood?" Sam asked. No lady had ever asked to split wood. They'd only done it begrudgingly out of necessity. Besides, it was a man's job and not a fun one at that.

"I've never done it before. I want to try."

Curiously, Sam led her over to the stump, set a log on top, and retrieved his ax from the barn. He passed it to her and waited, hiding his amused smile with a scratch of his nose.

She held her hands close together and arched her back incorrectly, so Sam stopped her before she hurt herself. "Like this." He slipped her hands apart and mocked a few swings with her, his body pressed over hers. "Now you try it."

He stood off to the side, silently chuckling. She took a big swing, and the ax bounced off the side of the log, knocking it over. He laughed.

"It's harder than I thought." She bent over and retrieved the log, set it up just as he had, and prepared for another swing.

"Keep the blade straight," Sam reminded her.

She made contact with the log this time, and the ax pierced the wood. She jiggled the stuck axe, which did nothing but make him laugh more. Then she put a foot on the log and yanked hard. She tumbled backward with the ax flying off, and that's where he stopped her. Sam collected the wayward ax and helped her up. Being the gentleman he was, he needed to instruct the lady on proper axing technique.

SAM REMOVED HIS SHIRT, and April sucked in a breath at seeing his sculpted, muscular bare chest. Sam sent her a hot gaze, but she didn't care that he knew.

"Watch this," he said. "You know, for educational purposes."

"Oh, absolutely. I'm focused. Completely paying attention." April smiled. That was entirely why she'd asked—for the view. It was true she'd never split logs before, but if she tried, masculine ego would dictate he'd show her how to do it properly. Bonus points for showing a gleaming bare chest while doing it.

Sam set the log up and swung down hard. The muscles in his back shifted position throughout the arc and shook upon impact. He split the log in two pieces on a single strike. April stared at his biceps, and her heart skipped too many beats.

"Wow," she said with a hint of surprise, wonder, and a bit of huskiness.

He smiled. "Would the lady require another demonstration?"

"Yes, please."

He was flirting, and that was perfectly fine with her.

Did she feel bad about it? No. Did that make her a bad person? She didn't think so. She was human after all. There was energy between them, a connection, something she hadn't ever experienced before. She would enjoy it while it lasted, because it had to end. April had to go back to her brother with her magic trinket from Kiko. It wasn't even up for debate. If he weren't giving her a demonstration right now, she'd be daydreaming of a shower instead of Sam's glistening muscles.

Probably.

But she'd never been happier, and right now she wasn't ready to give that up.

Sam retrieved the smaller piece of log and fought with it to keep it standing. He swore at it under his breath, and she laughed. He lifted the ax for another blow. A single arc sent two hunks flying again. He grabbed them and tossed them onto his neat stack.

"It's easy. You just need practice." He winked.

"I'm practicing my management skills. You're doing just fine."

Sam's intoxicating laugh rolled through her, and he returned the ax to the barn. He picked up his shirt, but he didn't put it back on. Sam hooked an arm at her to follow and they strolled inside.

Chapter 25

Sam accepted a sandwich from Sarah's offering. His sister and April worked together in the kitchen, laughing and telling stories, and his home felt warmer, less empty. He smiled. He didn't want her to leave, but he couldn't be the reason for holding her up.

"April, can we talk now?"

April's jolly time instantly stopped. She nervously looked at Sarah and back. "Are you sure you want to do this now?"

No. "Grignon is interested in you. He will strike. It's not a matter of 'if' but 'when.'"

April sat next to Sam. "What are you saying?"

"The best course of action is for you to complete whatever business you have in town, and leave." Just saying the words hurt so much it hurt to breathe.

April stared at him, lips pulled tight. She nodded. "I've been working on it. When I'm finished, I promise I'll go."

Oh, that was easy. Sam finished his sandwich and stood. "Glad to hear it. I'm off for today's collection and drop. Have a good morning, ladies."

Sarah waved her hand at him in disinterested dismissal.

April smiled softly, but there was sadness there. Sam couldn't face her like this.

Sam mounted his horse, he daresay Bucky, and set off to the chemist. The morning sun beat on the back of his neck and he wished once more for rain. The wells would run out soon at this pace. It had been the longest stretch of drought he'd ever known.

Farmers were getting concerned. Sam didn't want to think about what that meant for crops this winter.

He entered the front door just as the clerk unlocked it.

"Good morning, Ross," Sam said.

Ross was an amazing young gent. He sensed people like none other. Sam liked him even more since Sarah had praised him. His sister had that way with figuring out who was straight and who was conniving. She seemed to have taken well to April, which pleased him.

"Hideyho, Sam. Here for the week's payment?"

"Is the boss around?"

"Nah. Just me today. Martin's wife is sick. They think the baby might be in trouble. So, Dr. Frank is camped up there, keepin' an eye on her," the clerk said. "But he left an envelope for you." Ross rummaged around behind the counter, lifted a metal box, and unlocked it with a key from another shelf. He handed the envelope to Sam and smiled. "Can I get you anything else while you're here?"

"Aye. I'm looking for stationery and pencils. The best you've got. It's a gift for a lady."

"No problem. Come with me." Ross stopped and took a second glance at him and pointed to his own cheek. "Say, that's a mighty nice line there. Little Jaime sure got ya good, eh?"

Sam touched his cheek with a smile. He didn't remember the hit to the back of the head, nor April's fine work with a needle, but he remembered her caring eyes while she'd cleaned his repaired skin. "No, this was Grignon's men. Caught me by surprise."

"That makes more sense then. I haven't seen you lose a fight yet. Well, it looks clean. Still the handsome devil you always were, no worries. Was it that April lady who did you up good? Mighty fine job she did, I tell you."

Sam's chest bloomed with pride. "She did."

"We've got a few different sizes of paper here. Is there a particular one you're looking for?"

"I don't know," Sam said. "Portrait size?"

Ross nodded and handed him sixteen by twenty inch paper in a stack tied with twine.

"What sort of pencils?" Ross asked.

"Artist kind," Sam answered, completely out of his league. "Graph-something?"

"We've got five different grades of graphite. Which one?"

"All of them?"

Ross smiled and handed him a fistful of dainty black sticks.

Sam balanced them in his arms. "Do you have something to sharpen the tips?"

"I've got just the thing." Ross added a bell-shaped instrument to his pile, and Sam followed the clerk back to the register. "Anything else then?"

Sam said, "Can you gift wrap? Something nice."

"Ahh," Ross exaggerated with understanding. "I've got just the thing for the lady."

"Thank you kindly." It appeared Ross thought highly of April too. But this conversation was stirring things that needed to stay quiet. Business, business, business. Then April returned back home, to Chicago, she'd said. Although she seemed confused when she'd stated it.

Everyone Sam met that dealt with April on some level seemed to speak highly of her. He couldn't fathom the townspeople chasing her and accusing her of theft, or that Jaime had instigated it. He believed her story, but it just didn't add up.

Sam secured the package tied with flowers in his saddlebag. He pictured her beaming face when she saw his gift, and his palms were sweaty. He wiped them on his trousers and mounted up for the trek to Grignon's estate.

Sam needed to switch mindsets from choosing the perfect gift for a beautiful lady to handing over confiscated cash under force like a slave. Having to see Grignon nearly every day made his blood boil.

The mental about-face showed Sam how different life could be without the bastard on his mind.

Chapter 26

APRIL HAD A RAGING headache. She assumed it was from Jaime slamming her to the rocky dirt. She rubbed the back of her head but didn't find any lumps. She didn't have any memory lapses either. Maybe it was too much sun and not enough water. April wished she had some ibuprofen. She swung her feet off the bed, and a beautifully wrapped gift sat on the end table. That hadn't been there when she'd fallen asleep last night. Someone sneaked into her room.

April pulled the twine loose and found the edges of the brown paper wrap. She slipped her finger inside and unfolded it. She smiled. Oh, Sam. The tears rushed forth. A stacked pad of paper with a set of drawing pencils on top awaited her fingers. He'd even included a strange bell-shaped object she figured was a pencil sharpener. It was so thoughtful.

April wiped her face dry and slid out a sheet, laying it flat on the table and setting aside the extra. She selected a lighter grade pencil. For her to create a portrait, she needed a reference photograph.

She brought her materials to the kitchen table and moved to the fireplace. The rest of the house was quiet, and the dawn sun radiated warm rays throughout the kitchen. Perhaps the siblings were sleeping or already gone for the morning. She found the photo of Sam with Isabel. He was looking off camera and not smiling, but she could work with it.

She sketched for what felt like minutes when Sarah came inside from the garden. April promised herself to spend all day tomorrow out there to make up for slacking today.

"Oh, very nice. Artists all around these parts," Sarah said as she carried a basket of greens to the kitchen.

April's fingers were sliding and smoothing, taken over by force. She hadn't been inspired in years. The urge to create seized her, and soon a familiar face took shape. Before she realized, it was complete. April signed her name, but she didn't know the date. She found the stack of newspapers by the fireplace and the most recent one sat on top. *Green Bay Intelligencer*, May 12, 1852. Scrawling the date on made it official, and she held it up to inspect her work. Her stomach growled as she realized the day was half gone.

Sarah loomed over her shoulder, "That's beautiful. You do stunning work."

"Thank you."

April returned the photograph to the mantle and placed the drawing in her room, satisfied with how it turned out.

Sam came home and hung his hat on the coat hook.

"How was your day?" April asked.

"So far, less than agreeable, as my growling stomach will demonstrate, but breakfast yesterday was the best I ever had."

"I heard that!" Sarah shouted over her shoulder, taking insult to her cooking.

"You must have low standards," April said, knowing he was talking about the quality of his date.

"You must learn to accept a compliment," he countered with a spicy intensity in his eye.

April's chest warmed, and she smiled.

Sarah prepped sandwiches for lunch, and April remembered the girl had breakfast alone yesterday, so she decided to make it up to her. "Sarah, take tonight off. Sam and I will cook."

Sarah froze and Sam laughed as if the concept were the most ridiculous thing he'd heard.

"What's so funny?" April asked.

"Men don't cook," Sam said with amusement.

"What about Max?" April countered.

"What about him?"

"Surely a restaurant owner can cook. He's a man, right?"

"Aye, but that's different."

"How so?"

"It's a business." Sam shrugged.

April understood his viewpoints were the standard of this time, but she wanted to be treated as an equal, not a possession to be used as Grignon saw her, so she asserted herself with that box of strength she'd busted open. "That means nothing. You have two hands. I have two hands. You are no better than I, just because you have a penis."

Sarah turned red and covered a smile.

Sam's mouth dropped open. "What bloody devil gave you a crazy idea like that?"

"Are you telling me you don't have a penis?" April taunted.

Sarah barked laughter.

Sam stood up, anger flaring.

Regardless of understanding his societal beliefs, April hated it. Being treated less than for no reason but gender-identifying organs was insulting, and after she'd spent so many years being told what to do and how to do it by men—namely Dad and Levi, and sometimes Mathew—she was done.

"Your accusation is an outrage," Sam said with a bit more anger than April was comfortable with. "I'm not one to play tit for tat, but a strange city girl, in town for business she won't disclose, wearing a scandalous dress... What could that possibly mean about you?"

He was right to be suspicious, and rather than escalate, giving him the truth would set him far more straight. "And yet, I'm here for *you*."

Sam didn't answer. His jaw clenched with shifting muscles. Underneath that seething anger, he was embarrassed.

April added calmly, "Where I'm from, your views on men and women's places in society are antiquated and unacceptable. I will not be treated as a second-class citizen." She glared, waiting for him to double-down or apologize.

Sam's jaw worked hard and he knew a headache was coming. She'd thrown his insult back at him so simply yet effectively. It was impressive, but humiliating. When he'd put the confusing pieces of her puzzle together, none of it made sense. She'd told him she was a veterinary assistant working for her brother. Magically this brother was nowhere to be found, and a veterinary assistant didn't exist.

He'd never met someone with such a fiery spirit, and it happened to be both infuriating and exhilarating. Sam's views weren't antiquated. What a foolish assertion that was. Men worked and provided. Women tended and cared. That was the way it always was and always would be.

Everyone he knew would attest to that.

But...if lifting a ladle meant he could spent more time with her before she left, licking batter off her fingers was more appealing than fighting. Besides, he needed to know why she'd sought him out, and if she was angry, she wouldn't open up. Swallowing back his pride, he asked, "What's on the menu then?"

Sarah's jaw dropped, and the knife in her hand stilled, dripping with tomato juice.

"What's available?" April asked with a smug smile that slowly softened.

"Every cut of pig. The vegetables out in the garden. What else do you want?"

"Seasonings? Bread?" April asked.

"We don't have many herbs. The drought this year has been unfavorable," Sarah said, assembling the layers for the sandwiches and carrying the tall stacks to the table. "If you're going to the store, mind you buy some flour and sugar? I'm getting low."

Sam devoured his meal, and April wasn't far behind.

Sarah dumped her leftovers outside for the dogs.

When cleanup was finished, April, bursting with excitement, took Sam by the hand, ceding already worth it. She said, "Let's go."

Outside, April whistled shrilly, copying Sam's command for the horse to kneel. Sam popped his brows in surprise. It would explain how she'd gotten him home after Perez's, but the horse didn't respond.

"Sarah was able to do it," April said. "I'll keep practicing."

Sam called the horse over and he helped her up. In front of him, April resumed her deathly squeeze on the horn—and Sam framed her as he took the reins. The horse nickered when Sam gave him a wee jab.

"The horse can sense your unease. If you relax, you'll both be better in tune. Do you want to steer?"

April hesitated, but she placed her hands on the reins.

Sam wrapped her soft fingers in his own hands. They fit perfectly inside his. He whispered in her ear, "I'm right behind you. I won't let you fall."

April nodded and her arms pulled the reins tight as a safety line.

Sam gently corrected her. "Hold them loose, so the horse is ready for your orders. Tug one way or the other to turn, and pull both to slow or stop. Easy." He released her hands and gripped her waist, enjoying the undulation of her middle as she struggled to hold herself steady.

"Do you need to hold so tightly?" she asked.

Sam smiled from behind her ear. "Just in case the old stallion decides he doesn't like ladies taking control."

April snorted. "I'm sure I won't be able to fix his antiquated views."

"Some men secretly like ladies to take control." Sam spoke right into her ear, his breath blowing down her neck. He wanted to kiss that exposed skin.

April murmured and tilted her head, inviting him.

To do such a thing in public was highly inappropriate, and he didn't want to spin the rumor mill while riding through town, but he gleamed with masculine delight when she moaned.

They reached the front door to Porter's General Store and Sam waited on the horse.

April swung a leg over and slid down the side like a seasoned rider. She landed on the road and her dress billowed up like flower petals. April raised an eyebrow at him. "When you're ready."

Sam needed a few minutes to regain his composure, his face burning with his body reacting to her. When he was soft enough, he dismounted and tied up the horse, Bucky. The name sounded weird in his head. Perhaps he could get used to it. He took April's arm in his, and they entered the store together.

She measured out seasonings, sugar, and flour as his sister requested. It was fun to watch her. She seemed excited about the selection, which was puzzling. April smelled the bundle of parsley as if it were roses, and she handed him potatoes. He could watch her for hours while she stacked his arms full.

"There. That's everything I can find," she said.

Sam carried his armful to the counter, and he paid. April didn't object. She looked away, embarrassed or ashamed, he couldn't tell.

Porter wrapped their purchases. "All set, you two. Have a great afternoon."

With their arms linked together, they exited the store and turned right into Jaime Perez. His eye wasn't swollen anymore, but it was still yellowish with healing.

April gasped.

Sam tensed and pushed April behind him. He didn't want her to get hurt again. "Good day, Jaime. Feeling better I see."

Jaime said, "I wasn't thinking straight, Sammy, and I want to explain, but I'd rather we do this without her here." Jaime gestured at April.

Sam held firm. "Say what you need to say."

"If you insist." Jaime shrugged and stuffed his hands in his pockets. "What do you think you're doing replacing Issy? Was my sister really nothing to you? Did her death not matter to you?"

Sam and Jaime had gone in circles with this numerous times, but never had Jaime been so blatant about it. Not since April arrived. Jaime had no right to use Sam's feelings or lack thereof as an accusation. "You're out of place on this. Back off."

"She was my sister, and you just threw her away like trash." Jaime spat at Sam's boots. "It should've been you."

That stung. All this time Jaime had commiserated with him, Sam had no idea his brother-in-law's true feelings. But clearly, the young man didn't know the whole truth. Sam stated with a tone of warning, "You know nothing of what you speak. Leave us be."

"I won't, until you explain. And her..." Jaime flicked his head in April's direction and narrowed his eyes at her. "How could you?"

"How could I what?" April quirked a brow in confusion, and she glanced around nervously. "Sam, we should get moving."

Sam had no idea what Jaime was accusing April of now, but he was curious. "What are you talking about?"

Jaime spat by her feet next, and he said to her, "I haven't forgotten Greenleaf, you whore. You can change your hair, but that doesn't fool me."

Sam didn't know what their relationship had been or what happened in Greenleaf, a small town a day's ride south of here, but April appeared afraid. Knowing Jaime's state of mind lately, Sam gave April the benefit of the doubt, and that was one too many insults for Sam to brush off. Sam's fist connected with Jaime's nose. No one insulted his lady, his family, and no one told him how to lead his own life.

April picked up the food that had fallen out of the bag.

Jaime bent at the waist and held his nose, blood flowing out of his cupped hands. He shook the blood off his hands and onto the road.

April tugged at Sam's arm.

Jaime covered his face again to catch the bleeding. He deserved worse.

"Pinch your nose and tip your head back," April said. Sam gave her a quizzical look, and she shrugged.

"My life is none of your business," Sam said to Jaime. "Do you understand, or do I need to explain it further?'

Jaime straightened just enough so the blood wouldn't ruin his shirt. He spoke through bloody hands, "This isn't over yet." He walked away, taking his weak threat with him.

Sam turned to April. "Are you all right?"

She nodded and then smiled as if she weren't convincing enough. "We need to get out of here."

"Agreed," Sam said.

They mounted the Bucky horse, and April took the reins.

April tilted her head back and asked, "Are you worried Jaime will go to the sheriff?"

Sam asked, "Why would he?"

"Well, battery is generally frowned upon."

Sam chuckled. "You say the strangest things."

"You're not at all concerned the sheriff will come knocking on your door?"

"What is it with you and the sheriff?" Sam asked.

"I just don't want to see you get in trouble. That's all."

Trouble? Sam was already in more trouble than he knew how to navigate. But April wasn't going to be involved any more than Grignon's interest, so the less she knew, the safer she was. "Don't worry about me, April."

He gripped her waist all the way home.

A PAN OF PORK loin sizzled on the wood burning range, and steam rolled through the kitchen that evening. April set out the garden ingredients and tried to think of a pork sauce recipe off the top of her head. Typically, she'd just dump a jar of gravy on the meat and call it good, but that was ahead of its time. Some of the simplest things she'd taken for granted weren't even invented yet. It was hard to wrap her brain around it.

April had collected fresh basil, onion and garlic straight from the garden she helped tend, and potatoes, tomatoes, and carrots from the store. With whole fresh ingredients, this would be the best roast ever. April's usual dinner included browsing the Internet on her phone, while microwaving a frozen dinner if she was by herself, and takeout if she were sharing with Levi, Kiko, or Mathew. Not that she couldn't cook, but a fancy meal for one wasn't worth the effort.

And never had she cooked alongside anyone she had the hots for, and she could totally get used to this.

Sam stood next to her, and she handed him a tomato and the paring knife. He slowly made wobbly cuts. He obviously never assisted in the kitchen before, and respect flooded through her at his willingness to try.

"It's not an ax, but I think you can do this." April stepped inside his arms, placing her hands over his and steadying the knife, helping him make smooth cuts. His warm body cocooned hers as they worked together. She could stay in his arms all day, nestled against his chest. His warm breath puffed through her hair and she tilted her head back in desire.

A hot sting slashed across her finger. Oops. A thin line of blood seeped on her index finger. She laughed. "It's not good to get distracted around knives."

"Who's getting distracted here? I'm paying attention." Sam's warm amusement sent her heart fluttering. "But I think you should take your top off. Show me how it's done right."

April turned and playfully slapped him on the arm.

Sarah giggled, sitting at the table, no doubt thoroughly entertained. "No one's getting naked while I'm here."

Heat tore up April's cheeks. She peeled potatoes while Sam slowly chopped the rest of the vegetables. Out of the corner of her eye, she caught Sam watching her, and he quickly averted his gaze. A secret smile played on her lips while she measured the seasonings for the roast. When Sam's vegetable pile was sufficiently large enough to impede his chopping, she reached toward him. "Let me empty your load."

And, her cheeks burned.

Sam waved his invitation. She picked up the cutting board and tossed the vegetables into the rapid boil. When she replaced the board in front of him, a smokey gaze heated Sam's eyes. Did he understand her innuendo? April wasn't brave enough to ask.

"You're doing great so far," she said.

"I've got a great teacher."

"Your sample size is insufficient."

Sam cocked his head. "I've had plenty of teachers, so I trust my judgement. You should too."

April turned away from him, hiding from the compliment.

Needing the minced garlic, she captured Sam's chopping board and caught him staring at her again. This time, she slid over to his side and bumped his hip with hers. He stepped off balance and gave her a competitive smile.

"I'll be needing this next," she said and leaned over to take the butter. April spread the butter across the surface of the bread and licked her fingers a little more sensually than necessary.

Sam stalked closer. "That must be some fine butter."

April removed her fingers from her mouth, and he placed them between his lips. April sucked in a breath as he licked her fingertips. Heat rolled through her body, and he slowly cleaned every bit of butter off and withdrew her fingers while holding her hot gaze. She pinched her legs to make the sudden throbbing go away. His sister watched!

"It is good, but I need another demonstration." He pressed his lips to her fingertips in a kiss and smiled.

"Oh, your kitchen skills are...pretty hot," she said playfully. "I mean good. You're a natural."

Sam winked.

Sarah made a gagging noise, and Sam and April chuckled.

With dinner almost ready, Sam set the table. He set a plate and fork in front of Sarah, and she said, "You know, I never thought I'd see a day like this. I wonder what Mam would say. Do you think we could take turns making dinner? Sounds mighty nice to me."

April caught Sam's knowing eye. He smiled, and she returned it. She would like to make dinner with Sam again, and she hoped she would get to, because at any moment their fun could end. April didn't want to think about it, but soon he would trust her enough to listen to her tale of impending doom.

April brought over the salad bowl while Sam carved up the roast. They sat to eat, and before April lifted her first forkful, Sam grasped her hand.

And then his sister's.

"I'm feeling mighty thankful at the moment," he said. "How about we all share thanks?"

April set her fork down and clasped hands with Sarah, reminding her of a Thanksgiving meal.

Sam said, "I'm thankful for delicious food and great company."

Sarah took her turn next, smiling at Sam. "I'm thankful for open minds, and I have you to thank for that, April."

April shared a glance with Sam. "I'm thankful for wonderful people, happy memories, and fresh food."

April had never experienced a real family dinner where everyone was attentive and happy. Dad always ate on the couch, Mom on the run or while still cooking—if she cooked at all. April and Mathew took turns heating leftovers or fighting over the microwave.

April felt peaceful, as though she really belonged. Knowing this fairy tale was temporary squeezed her chest.

If April was to prevent Sam's arrest, how long was she expected to play bodyguard before the main event? Or was April's small gestures enough to prevent a series of potential arrests? Kiko didn't expect her to stay... Did she?

Chapter 27

After making his collection at Lloyd's, Sam dismounted at Grignon's estate and knocked. The first floor windows were open, and the curtains drifted at the edges in a game with the soft breeze.

The housekeeper opened the door for him, and after all this time, he'd never learned her name, but since it wasn't proper to address her by name, he followed her into Grignon's library as usual. Today it was guarded by Daniel Durand and Joe Pool. He hadn't seen Joe around lately. The strangely quiet man was short and lean with a long narrow face and flat nose, but Sam knew better than to let the small stature fool him. Joe was light-footed and quick with a blade. Sam had seen him in action and never wanted to be on the receiving end of it.

Upon entering the library, the Frenchman waited at his vast desk.

"Here are your payments." Onto the desk, Sam dropped two thin envelopes and Lloyd's thick one. "And none of it is missing," Sam said and clenched his jaw, dreading whatever else swirled in that serpentine brain of his.

Grignon arched a brow. "You sound so sure. Do you guarantee it?"

"I only guarantee the amount given to me is the amount you receive. Nothing more."

Grignon chuckled. It made Sam want to knock his face off. Every time he saw that French bastard's mug, he saw the face of his murdered wife. Indentured to him with almost daily visits was the equivalent of hell. How could he stop this arsehole without risking his sister?

Or April.

She had nestled right into his heart, but he was afraid that he wasn't strong enough to keep both the most important ladies in his life safe. He'd failed once already.

"We're done then. Good day." Grignon brushed him off.

Sam turned to leave, but Daniel and Joe approached with arms crossing their chests.

Sam swallowed, his tongue suddenly cottony. "What more do you want?"

They stopped just in front of him, too close for comfort.

Grignon spun on his chair. "The payments from Stanton's Spirits are always more robust than the other shops. Why do you suppose that is?"

"Perhaps he's the most successful," Sam retorted, annoyed. That wasn't a matter he controlled.

"Observant, I see. That matches what I assume too—not at all that shopkeepers are banding together to short their payments on purpose."

Sam stiffened. He didn't organize the businesses. Sure, he told tales of breaking free, but he wasn't responsible for anything they were doing. He didn't even know the amounts he was supposed to collect besides a percentage. "I know nothing about it."

The two imposing men stepped aside for him to leave.

Sam scuttled out of there swiftly, not eager to be inconvenienced again. He reached his horse and through the open window, a word chilled him to the marrow. He listened closer while slowly and quietly mounting up, pretending not to hear.

"...in three days. I want him arrested and brought to the jail. Spread the story if the townsfolk question what happened. If they interfere, they join him as accomplices. His legs will dangle in the air at Common Square by the end of the week," Grignon said.

Sam shivered. They were going to hang someone, but who and why?

"What of his bar then?" Daniel asked. "Do we leave it empty or do we need to guard it before your declaration speech?"

Lloyd.

They were going after Lloyd. But why? Grignon had just asked Sam about the success of the business. If it were the most profitable, wouldn't he rather keep it under his thumb? The banded group of businesses should be of more concern.

Sam's horse nickered, giving away his nearby position. He nudged the horse to a casual walk, so as not to alarm them. He risked a glance over his shoulder and found an unnatural stirring in the curtains.

GABRIEL GRIGNON HAD SAID in three days his mercenaries were coming to hang Lloyd. They'd be sneaky about it, coming in the night like they had with farmer Joseph Van Cleeve. Sam wouldn't let that happen. No way in hell.

Sam pushed through the front door of his cabin, thoughts a jumbled mess, but one thing was clear, Sam needed April's affairs cleared, so they could leave.

"What's the matter with you?" Sarah asked, perturbed.

Ignoring his sister, Sam marched straight to April. His hands grasped her upper arms, startling her. "Time's up. What is this business you have in town?"

April asked, "What? How do you know it's up? What happened?"

"Whatever your business is, you need to finish it now. What is it so we can help?" Sam glanced at his sister, and Sarah eagerly nodded.

April caught Sarah's eye and faced Sam. She inhaled deep as if preparing herself for something, and she said, "Can I trust you to believe me?"

The urgency surging through him mixed with curiosity. "Of course I'll believe you. Tell me. It's important we get this sorted now."

"You should sit down." April waited.

With growing frustration, Sam did. Sarah joined him.

"Grignon has plans for you, and they aren't good."

Sam's brow darkened. Grignon's personal spy made a fool of him. He stood and said sharply, "What plans?"

Sarah tugged at his arm, urging him back onto the couch. Sam brushed her off.

April met his gaze with despair. "He intends to kill you."

Sam wasn't surprised, but hearing it put to words still shocked him. "How do you know this?"

"I overheard they will arrest you, and while in jail, you'll be executed." Her voice was small and scared.

"They planned to come after me all this time, but haven't enforced it yet? What does this have to do with your business in town?"

"That is my business," April said carefully. "I'm here to save your life."

Sarah gasped and pressed a fist to her chest.

Sam stepped back as if struck. This was not hard to believe at all. "You're certain?"

"Yes."

"Well, that bastard is going to be doubly disappointed. Pack your things. We go on the morrow."

"What?" April said.

"Go where? I'm not going anywhere," Sarah said, standing.

"I'm done with this tyranny. I'll buy a wagon and fetch Lloyd while you pack, and we're gone on the morrow. Sarah, you know where the crates are. I'll be back."

"No," April said, and Sam paused at the desperation in her voice. "She said two...two good men would die. I don't know yet who the other is. We can't leave the other man to die." Her face paled.

Sam's heart squeezed. Who was 'she'? "I know who the other man is. Start packing."

Sam already lost his wife to that bastard and had been living as a slave. He wasn't going to lose Sarah or Lloyd...or April. They were all going, even if April didn't join them. She'd always said she was leaving after her business was complete. Now it was time. Sam ran back out the door to convince his best friend to walk away from his whole life on Sam's word.

THE DREADED END WAS back in motion. All her efforts so far had been for nothing. April's heart broke at the thought of what loomed ahead. Sam was right—they needed to leave town, but she didn't want him out there alone—with advanced warning or not.

"Do you think he was serious?" Sarah asked as they stood in Sam's panicked wake.

"Definitely."

"You believe this then?"

April nodded. "Completely."

Sarah turned on her. "Why do you think Sam will be killed? What does Lloyd have to do with it?" The suspicion darkened her voice.

"There's no time to explain," April said. "We need to do as he says."

"I am not leaving my home until I get answers."

What could April tell her that wouldn't anger or confuse her more? The stubborn girl needed to listen for once. "I was told that Gabriel Grignon would kill Sam, and that he was innocent of whatever he was charged with. That's what I'm here for. To prevent it."

"What took you so long to say anything?"

"If I told Sam straight up, he wouldn't have believed me, just as you aren't right now, and you know that. We need to pack. Where are the crates?"

Sarah's shrewd eyes drilled into her. April braced herself for a big question. If April could be convincing enough, here and now, they had a chance of getting away from Grignon. But if she failed, Sarah would stop Sam from leaving by simply staying put. It wouldn't just be mission failure then. It would be the loss of people she cared about very much.

Sarah folded her arms over her chest. "Who told you Grignon would kill Sam, and why didn't *they* stop him?"

Yeah, that would be the one, April thought, and paced the kitchen and living room. The truth would come out eventually, but when someone was already on the fence about giving their trust, a crazy idea would tip them onto the wrong side. She needed to try another one of those not-quite-a-lie ideas.

"Someone already tried and failed. I'm here to try again." April didn't need to tell Sarah the previous failure was herself.

Sarah paled. "Oh. Oh, dear. Someone already died trying to stop Grignon from killing Sam?"

April allowed the assumption to take hold. It helped with the true gravity of the situation.

Sarah's fists bunched in a rage. "Then you're the bravest woman I've ever met for filling those shoes. Grignon is a monster. He has his hands in everyone's pockets, and his whims bring murders. Sooner or later someone will stop him. I sure hope it's you."

April was not taking on Grignon by herself. Her mission was to keep him from getting arrested so he'd live, because he was destined for greater things, whatever that meant. The best way to keep him from getting arrested was to leave. "We can stop him when we're safely away."

Sarah scowled, unconvinced.

April added, "When someone stops Grignon, we'll come back. I mean, someone has to feed the dogs, right?" April smiled.

Sarah smiled in return. "I suppose you're right. I've got some crates in the barn. Follow me."

April exhaled a deep breath, grateful she was on the right track, when the front door banged open on its hinges a second time. Sam wouldn't have done that twice, nor would he be back so soon.

When April turned around, she gasped. Daniel and Dennis Durand. They didn't exactly bring a bottle of wine or flowers.

Sarah unleashed the hidden fury within that tiny package. "Get your dirty boots out of my house. I didn't invite you. Be gone with you."

The armed twins marched inside, undeterred.

April needed to buy some time. "Are you looking for Sam? He's out back. I can get him for you."

The broad men kept coming like a garbage compactor squeezing the air out of the room.

April shivered with fear, her chest tight while she backed up one slow step at a time. She didn't know what they were planning, but it was nothing good. She placed her hands in her dress pockets, ready to defend herself.

"Sarah, come over here," April said. She couldn't help Sarah if the girl just stood there waiting to get bowled over.

"I told you to be gone! Trespassers! I'm sending for the sheriff. I'm warning you!" Sarah crossed to the kitchen and grabbed a frying pan.

April would've been proud if she weren't terrified.

Before she pried her pepper spray out of her dress pockets, Dennis with the scar picked April up, and he tossed her like a toy into Sarah's bedroom. April landed with a bounce on the mattress. The door slammed shut and wood scraped the floor on the other side. The knob rattled.

April fumbled off the bed and ran to the door. They'd wedged it shut.

Sarah screamed and kept screaming as the men carried her away. The clang of the pan hitting the floor made April scream until her voice was hoarse.

Chapter 28

Sam launched himself off the horse and ran into Stanton's Spirits in desperation to save his best friend, but Lloyd wasn't at the bar. Sam skimmed over the faces, but a tall colored man was nowhere in sight. He dared not shout for the man and turn unwanted eyes his way. With the business owners organizing behind his back, it was clear they didn't trust him. Sweat formed on his brow and the palms of his hands.

Sam had never been more scared in his life. What Grignon said, he did. If anyone was ignorant enough to brush off his threats—well, they didn't live to tell the tale.

Sam ducked into the back room and found Lloyd sitting on a pine crate, marking on paper. Another crate rested at his feet with glass bottles poking out of packaging rags. Sam breathed a sigh of relief through the pounding in his ears. "Lloyd!"

The bar owner swiveled his head away from his paperwork. One glance at Sam's face, and Lloyd's smile vanished. "What's the matter, Sam?" Lloyd set down his work and stood. He stretched his back as if he'd been sitting for a while. The larger man placed a comforting hand on Sam's shoulder, who teetered on the edge of hysteria. "You look like you've had a fright."

"No." Sam panted, his brain scrambled with thoughts—images of Grignon's guards marching into the bar, Lloyd protesting the injustice, and a flash of his friend's face void of life.

"Take a deep breath and tell me."

"There's no time to explain," Sam said. "But I need you to pack your essentials."

Lloyd tilted his head. "Slow down. What's going on?"

"We have to leave on the morrow. It's Grignon." Sam's breathing evened and he rubbed his palms on his pants.

"What did he do this time?" Lloyd's voice darkened.

"You'll be arrested and hanged."

Lloyd's darkness switched to fear. "Are you certain?"

"I heard him with my own ears. He ordered his men to arrest you, fabricate a story, and arrest anyone who's helping you. We have to go tonight."

"You're serious."

Sam didn't answer, so the request would carry more weight.

"Jesus." Lloyd ran a hand over his trimmed hair. "Did he say why? What did I do?"

"Aye, Lloyd. I sat there and played twenty questions with him. He answered everything and thanked me for my thoroughness," Sam said dryly.

"All right. All right."

"Go upstairs. Pack what you need quickly. The girls are already packing right now."

Sam spun for the door, ready for his next errand.

"Where are you going?"

"Farmer Ted has wagons. I'm going to buy one, but if he doesn't have one for me, I'll beg or borrow one of his own."

Lloyd nodded and glanced at his crates, determining his next move.

Sam jogged through the crowd to the front door and heard a blood curdling lady's scream. It came from down the road. His cabin. He felt like he'd been stabbed in the gut.

It was Sarah's scream.

And he was too late.

Sam jabbed the horse with his heel and the animal sprinted straight home. He leaped from the mount as it came to a trot and ran through the open front door. He found everything in order but both girls were gone. After a silent but frantic inspection, a quiet clatter from Sarah's bedroom caught his attention. He sighed in relief. Sarah wasn't known for fits of fright, but every so often, something jolted the poor girl like a ghastly spirit.

A chair was wedged under the doorknob. That was odd. He kicked the chair out of the way and the door swung open. April tumbled onto his boot.

Sam's fury exploded. He grabbed Grignon's spy by the arms and lifted her until her toes swung free. "Where is she? Where is my sister!" His grip was crushing, but he couldn't release April. Tears sprung forth under her lids and her chin trembled. He shook her to get an answer. "Where is she, dammit? Tell me something!"

Her bright blue eyes were red from sobs, her lips parted but no words came out. Sam's arms burned from strain, but still he shook her again. He must know what happened. "Where?"

April's eyes moved to the front door.

Sam released her, but her feet didn't catch. She tumbled to the floor in a heap of linen. He marched to the kitchen and retrieved the long, narrow paring knife—the same one they chopped vegetables with only last night. He returned to her, still on the floor, and pointed the tip toward her chest. The contrast from that sexy moment to this one rattled in the back of his mind, but he refused to stand by and watch the rest of his life unravel. He didn't know who to trust any longer.

"Talk now. Tell me everything. Who are you? What have you done?"

She stared at the knife in true horror. She hadn't seen the things Grignon would do when he was in a mood. That was horror.

"Tell me now or so help me..." The knife glinted in the sun shining through the window.

A quiet sob escaped her lips. She hadn't moved from her pitiful pile on the floor. She was a brilliant spy, a perfect actor, resolute to complete her mission for Grignon, come what may. And she twisted him right up, and he ate from her palms. The betrayal crushed him, but his blind trust and open heart angered him.

Sam needed answers, but threatening her life wasn't going to make her talk. Just because her act was convincing didn't mean Grignon didn't own her too. And when Grignon asked about Sam's ownership of her, he must've been bursting for joy at sending in his most effective spy. Maybe April needed help escaping him too.

The pounding in his veins muddled his thoughts. He dropped the knife with a clatter, and April flinched back in fright.

Sam bent over and took her hand to help her up. She wrenched from his grip, complete and total terror on her face. She looked at him like he was a monster. What had he done?

TEARS BLURRED HER VISION. April didn't know he was capable of this. While trying to earn his trust so he'd believe her unbelievable tale, she'd betrayed it instead. All the pieces were moving fast. She'd failed again, but now there would be no third try. What was worse—a mediocre life with a nice guy who didn't know her, Mathew's criticism, and her parent's hate? Or Sam? Sweet, caring, loving Sam and his wonderful spitfire of a sister? Sam, who now wanted to kill her for his sister's kidnapping and April's presumed involvement.

For being incapable of choosing, she would have neither.

April curled up on the floor in a pile of impractical dress, sobbing, with the man she cared for most blaming his sister's loss on her. She didn't know what to say. If she told him the truth—that she was from the future—he would assume she lied and push harder. With the look in his eye, she wouldn't doubt he would've killed her if she said the wrong thing. He was terrifying when he was angry. Now she understood why Grignon wanted him. He was sweet when he needed to be, but utterly terrifying when he felt like it.

Fear of a loved one was familiar to her, that was her whole childhood. The foreign feeling was her being capable but unable to defend herself. As a grown woman, here on the floor, she was no better than when she was a child wailing while Daddy stalked close, unbuckling his belt. She had an excuse then. What was her excuse now?

April held her breath as Sam casually retrieved the knife off the floor. Frustration worked his jaw, but his posture was relaxed—controlled. He ran his forearm across his forehead and blew out a breath, silently deciding what to do next. He squatted in front of her, pointing the knife at the floor. He said with a scowl, "People are going to die. There is no time."

No kidding. "What do you want to know?"

"Who are you? Who do you work for?"

She wiped her face clean and leaned her head against the wall, defeated. She'd give him the truth. She had nothing more to lose. "April McCall. I work for my brother, Matty, at his veterinary—"

"Lie. Try again." Sam rose to his full height, fury radiating off him, knife flickering under the afternoon window light, hanging at his side.

"It's the truth, I swear. Please, Sam."

"Wrong answer."

"I don't know what else to say. On Overlook Hill and in Max's diner, I told you the truth. You know me." Her voice cracked.

Sam chewed over her words. "You're not leaving this house until this is cleared up. Until Sarah is home."

"I can't help you if I'm a prisoner. We can both go get her together." Despite April's failure, she still wanted to fight. Sam was still breathing, and that meant there was a sliver, a flicker, of hope.

Sam's face twisted with her words. "You're willing to deliberately disobey Grignon for my sister?"

"I told you, that's what I'm here for—to save your life, and if saving your life means finding your sister, I'll do whatever it takes. Even if that means we storm his mansion and search every room until we find her."

Sam raked a hand through his wavy hair. "If he catches you, he'll kill you."

April had Kiko's magic trinket, and that put a little brave into her step. "I'm aware of his tendencies for murder."

"You would never suggest something so obtuse if you knew him." Sam gazed at her as if trying to figure her out. "Tell me the truth—are you a spy for Grignon?"

That was the funniest thing she'd heard in a while. "Never in a million years would I go anywhere near that asshole voluntarily. He's a creep and a homicidal psycho with an overinflated ego Freud would love to dissect."

The corner of Sam's lips lifted briefly as if he believed her, but the sadness returned. "If you don't work for him, then how do you propose we get Sarah back? The estate is crawling with guards, and I hate to admit, but on my best day I can't take them all on. For a moment I hoped you knew a secret entrance."

Her courage returned. "We need help. Who do you trust?"

"Lloyd, but since he's a target, I don't want him anywhere near that building. We don't know Sarah's in there, but since that estate is his fortress, if Sarah's alive, I'd bet my life that's where she is. If you're prepared to do this, we go now. The longer we wait, the more time passes for Sarah to say something wrong and for Grignon to have a change of mind." Sam moved to the kitchen. "Can you handle a gun?"

April's stomach quivered. She'd been brave while making plans, but actually having to go was terrifying. "Never touched one."

"I thought not. Pack a few knives in your dress. It's better than nothing." Sam set out a couple choice blades for her. "I'm packing my gun, but I want the ax, just in case." Sam moved through the back door, but he stopped short. His hands went up in the air in surrender.

"What is it?" April asked.

Sam backed up into the house at gunpoint by Dennis Durand.

April gasped.

"This is your only warning," Dennis said calmly. "If you want your sister to remain alive, you will stay away."

Sarah was alive! And from the sound of it, Grignon intended to keep her that way.

"What about my daily drops?" Sam asked. It was a good question, but it also fished to confirm if she was at the estate.

"Continue as previously ordered."

That wasn't the response April expected. If Grignon had Sarah hidden away at the estate, he wouldn't want Sam getting too close. Was she not there? Where else would Grignon hold her?

"And if I don't?" Sam asked.

"Then you and the colored man will be hanged together." Dennis smiled. "Don't look so surprised. We know you were listening."

Two good men would die. Damnit! April had to keep Sam away from his sister to keep them both alive. That wasn't going to be easy.

Sam's jaw tensed and he glared with absolute hatred at the twin.

"Do you understand?" Dennis added. "The boss doesn't want me to put a hole in you today, but if you won't listen, I have carte blanche."

"Understood," Sam confirmed.

Dennis nodded and walked out.

When the door closed behind him, the wind in the room went with him. April asked, "What do we do now?"

Sam picked up one of Sarah's vases and hurled it at the wall.

April flinched.

"The bastard loves to torture people."

"You think he's going to torture Sarah?" April asked in disbelief.

"Me."

"What do you mean?" April asked.

"I haven't told you what happened to Isabel." Sam fell onto the couch.

April joined him. She thought she'd heard the whole story.

Sam teared up. "Isabel wasn't just murdered right here by the fireplace," he said, voice catching.

April's eyes shifted to the spot in front of them while she waited, listening silently. Her heart squeezed at his pain. She hated to see him hurting so much.

He brushed his eyes with his forearm. "They made me watch, and now I have the constant worry they're doing that to Sarah. I can't stop the images, and that's how the bastard operates. But I know deep down they aren't, because if they intended to harm her, they would make me watch again."

April's chest clenched. She couldn't imagine the depths of his pain. The pure evil in what Grignon had done to Isabel, to Sam, to break this wonderful man, sent her veins pounding. "I'm so sorry. Words don't even come close to easing that pain," she said with sincerity. "All this because you didn't want to work for him anymore?"

"He tends to overreact."

No kidding.

"And now I have to underreact. Going about the day-to-day with these thoughts while that snake rolls in his glee is...torture."

Chapter 29

IT HAD ALREADY BEEN an exhausting afternoon when a familiar tinny voice said, "Knock, knock."

April wanted to leap out of her skin.

Jaime Perez leaned against the door jam with a smirk on his face and hands in his pockets.

April and Sam both stood.

"You're not welcome here. That should've been obvious," Sam said.

Jaime stepped inside anyway and glanced around. Why wouldn't he leave them alone?

"Not much changes, does it? Oh, wait." He looked straight at April. "I was hoping, dearest Sammy, you would've had a chat with her and decided my warnings were to be heeded."

"Last time you tried, it didn't end well for you. Just leave," Sam said.

Jaime laughed. It sounded wrong, twisted. Listening to her gut, April rummaged in her dress pockets, locating her Swiss army knife and pepper spray.

Jaime wandered into the kitchen and sat his menacing ass on top of the dining room table.

"Since she won't, then I'll have to give you the truth," Jaime said.

Sam glanced over his shoulder at her, and a flicker of confusion crossed his features. April's heart sank. She couldn't lose his trust again.

"I know enough," Sam said, but it was a lie. He didn't know the most important thing about her, but at least he was still on her team.

Jaime smiled. "That means no. I know who she is. I've been trying to get you away from her for your own good. But you can be so block-headed sometimes, my brother."

"We are not brothers," Sam said firmly.

"No, I suppose not anymore."

"Why don't you make your case and be gone? We're busy here."

Jaime slipped off the table and crossed his arms. "I remember Greenleaf, and I'm never going to forget it."

April's face scrunched in confusion. She had no idea what he was talking about. Sam waited for April's reply, but she shrugged her shoulders.

"What exactly happened in Greenleaf?" Sam asked Jaime.

The crazy man prowled toward them. Sam tensed in front of her, knuckles blanching.

April slid her folding knife out of her pocket and opened the tiny blade. It wasn't much, but it would still hold someone away at least for a moment. She tapped Sam on the forearm so he would take it. He ignored her. She took the handle of the knife and touched it to his fist, but he wouldn't acknowledge that either.

Jaime's eyes darted to her hands. He pointed and yelled, "She's going to stab you!"

Everything happened in a quick blur. Sam spun on his heels to face her, trusting Jaime for some dumbass reason. And his eyes darkened at the tiny utility blade in her hand.

Jaime pressed a kitchen knife to the front of Sam's throat.

Sam's hands opened and lifted in surrender.

"You are so stupid sometimes," Jaime said. "I don't care what Grignon says."

Sam froze, eyes wide in surprise. April had tried so hard to keep him from getting arrested so a 'third party' wouldn't execute him.

And now, perhaps Jaime had been the 'third party' the entire time. This was not how it was going to end. This stupid weasel wasn't going to end Sam like this.

April stepped forward and lied through her teeth, "I remember Greenleaf."

Both Jaime and Sam stared at her in confusion.

"Let Sam go free, and we can talk about it," April demanded, flashing the tiny folding knife in a taunt.

Jaime cackled.

While it distracted him, April scrunched up her face and then stared at Sam. He nodded that he'd gotten the message. Gripping the pepper spray behind her back, she waited until Jaime calmed enough to look at her.

April stretched out her hand with her finger on the button of the canister. "Close them now!" she yelled, and not knowing the accuracy, April was liberal with the stream of burning liquid.

Jaime dropped the knife and he folded over, eyes pinched shut. Within seconds, he coughed and swore quite creatively.

April grabbed Sam by the arm and rushed him outside. She inspected his face for any overspray, but it appeared she missed him entirely. Jaime sounded like a dying cat screeching in the fires of hell. Served him right.

"What the hell is that stuff?" Sam asked, brow furrowing.

She wagged the canister with a smug smile. "Pepper spray. It hurts like a bitch, and he won't be able to see for a while, but there's no permanent damage."

Sam's face became unreadable as he studied her. "After you sprayed my brother and admitted to whatever happened in Greenleaf, you will tell me who you are. Your clothes, shoes, funny money, strange weapons, weird things you say—explain it all, and I'm warning you, my patience is very short right now."

She thought he wasn't his brother. How the tables had turned so suddenly. April had twenty minutes, thirty tops, before Jaime was functional again. Sam needed to know the whole truth, so he could make up his mind about whose side he was on. "I'm really from here," she insisted.

He waited.

"I'm from this town...only in the future."

A flash of confusion passed over his anger. It was disbelief.

She continued, "The pink dress and shoes are styles of my time. The money I had was real, and only one paycheck's worth, not enough for a month's rent even. I never rode a horse before, but I drive a car. Cars"—she laughed, on the verge of hysterics—"that don't exist yet for another few decades. And I do work at the veterinary clinic." She waved her arms at his cabin. "It's here. In my time, your home is Matty's veterinary clinic. Over there"—she pointed at the living room window—"is the reception desk where I spend most of my time. That fireplace is still there, but I painted it white. The pantry was upgraded to a bathroom with flushing toilets, automatic faucets, and paper towel dispensers. The bedrooms are exam rooms. Matty added a surgical suite onto the building, and he paved the front here for a parking lot. But it's all here. It still stands."

Sam was silent for a while, murder in his eyes, and he was capable of it.

She waited, her stomach in knots. If Kiko could see this, would she return April home before he killed her? She blinked back tears.

"What about Greenleaf?"

"Jaime held a knife to your throat. I lied to distract him. I don't know anything about Greenleaf."

"How...?" Sam's voice caught. He sounded strained, upset, confused, a whole ball of a mess. "How did you get here if that's the truth?"

She was relieved that he considered her insane story. "The real answer is I don't know. Someone I lived with for over a year turned out to be capable of time travel in order to 'match people'. Her words." April even used air quotes. "She sent me here to save you. To stop Grignon from killing you because, she said, and I quote 'Sam is destined for greater things.'"

Sam's anger drained. He whispered, "Are you human?"

April smiled. "One hundred percent."

He was so close to believing her. April dug in her pocket and retrieved a twenty-dollar bill. "Here. The final proof you need." She opened the bill, face up.

"Your funny money. I've seen it."

She pressed her fingertip near the year. "Look closer. Check the year it was printed."

Sam squinted at the tiny numbers. "Two thousand seventeen. That's the year you're from?"

"This is an older bill. I'm from a hundred and seventy years into the future, give or take. Mental math isn't my strong suit."

Sam leaned against the front of his house, sliding down until his butt landed on the grass. Jaime was still choking, gagging, and moaning inside. A few swears permeated the air between pleads for water.

Sam's hand ran through his hair. Then he froze. "If you know how this ends, what happens to my sister?"

"That I don't know. I really wish I did. I was only told two good men would die, and you were one of them."

"Lloyd's the other," Sam finished.

He'd said he knew who the other was, but Lloyd? "You're certain?"

"I heard it with my own ears."

April didn't know whether to be relieved to know the other target or more terrified because it was Lloyd.

Jaime Perez crawled his way out of Sam's house, meeting April and Sam on the front lawn. His watery eyes were swollen shut, face beet red with pepper burn.

Sam stood up and April joined him. They watched him writhe in pain on the grass, coughing and covering his face. She should probably get him some water to rinse with, but she really didn't want to.

"How long until that wears off?"

"Not long enough."

APRIL'S HEAD POUNDED, JAIME raged in pain on the lawn, and Sam's trust was precarious at best. She wanted to go back to cooking dinner and having her fingers in his mouth. Instead, a pack of hoof beats turned her attention to the trees at the bend, revealing another nightmare—Gabriel Grignon, flanked by the twins, Dennis and Daniel Durand.

At least it wasn't the sheriff, but at this point, April believed Grignon was the bigger threat.

Sam sighed next to her. "Now what?"

"Nothing good."

Grignon stopped his horse on the front lawn, frowning at Jaime's writhing mess. "What happened?" Grignon demanded.

The calm menace coming from the twins gave her gooseflesh.

"He attacked us, so we incapacitated him," April said, speaking for Sam. She wanted to keep Grignon's direct attention off Sam.

"Mademoiselle, I was not speaking to you, but since Sam hasn't found his tongue, will he survive it?" Grignon asked her.

"Physically he'll be fine," April said.

"Collect him, boys. I want him back at the estate."

Sam stepped in front of Jaime, chin tipped up. "No."

Grignon grinned, and April's blood chilled. The smile was worse, she realized, because it meant he had a plan to his advantage. And why in the world would Sam protect Jaime? The psycho put a knife to his throat only minutes ago.

"Trade for Sarah."

Grignon laughed. "Honorable attempt, Sam." He gestured a swirl above his head and said to his men, "Boys, take him."

Dennis and Daniel dismounted and stalked over to Jaime.

"Back off," Sam warned and shifted into a defensive position, but his hands were empty and the twins were armed.

April shook the canister behind her back, judging the remaining quantity. She had enough left for the twins if they stood close together, but not enough to include Grignon.

Jaime climbed to his feet, hunched over, and blinked. He ran to one of the twin's horses.

April's stomach eased. They got what they came for and now they would leave.

Instead, the two burly men continued advancing. Sam's arms came up to protect his face, fists bunched for action. The men didn't engage. They just kept coming like Death itself—unfazed, inevitable, an unstoppable power. She feared they would drop him quick with a Colt round or a knife to the throat and not think twice about it.

Not on her watch.

April waited for them to get within range, and she held out the canister. They ignored her even as she depressed the trigger, firing a stream of pepper juice over both their faces. They instantly stopped and faced her. Their eyes pinched shut.

Now knowing the effects of her modern pepper spray, Sam backed up.

Within seconds, Daniel dropped to his knees, gasping. Dennis pressed his eyes with his thumbs and coughed as if being choked. Sam put his arm protectively in front of April, urging her back, and Grignon turned his terrible gaze on her.

Jaime had climbed into the saddle, having regained all his senses but perhaps full eyesight. He shouted, "I'll get you for Greenleaf, you whore!"

Jaime wasn't crazy. He wasn't making up some secret for attention. He truly believed April had something to do with whatever that was. Knowing nothing scared her more than just thinking he was crazy.

"That was a mistake, boy," Grignon said through gritted teeth.

Trembling from head to toe, April watched Grignon's hands, worried he'd put a bullet in Sam's chest for the inconvenience. Grignon simply waved to his men telling them to get it together and move out. It would be a while.

Sam climbed Bucky and held out his arm to lift April up. She accepted his assist and hopped up in front.

Grignon scowled in pure rage as Sam and April galloped away toward town. They'd just pissed off Grignon even more, and April couldn't see a peaceful solution here. The situation was escalating out of control, and April was over her head.

Escaping at Stanton's Spirits, a few dozen people were milling about and drinking, playing cards, and dancing. At least she could count on safety in numbers.

Sam brought her to the bar where Lloyd filled a mug from the tap. "Pair of beers, my friend," Sam said.

Lloyd poured out two mugs and set it before them. Sam dropped coins on the bar.

"I'm packed," Lloyd said with his voice low. "Are we going soon?"

Sam sighed. "It's too late."

Lloyd laughed. "Preposterous. This place is too decrepit to be heaven and not terrible enough for hell. I'd wager we're both alive, and since we're in my bar, we are both free, in a manner of speaking. It's not too late to leave."

"Sarah's been kidnapped, and Grignon won't negotiate."

Lloyd dropped a mug. It shattered on the floor planks. Pain twisted his features for only a flash. He leaned forward on the bar. "You're certain?"

"Aye. If I don't leave her be, Grignon is coming after both of us, but I have a feeling he's going to regardless. I can't leave Sarah behind, but it's foolish to stay."

"I've already left my home because of old white folk telling me what they own. I'm not doing it again. And if they come around, they'll get a shotgun to the face. So, what's the new plan?" Lloyd asked.

Sarah was keeping these two in town at risk of being killed, so April needed to remove that variable. Kiko didn't say Sarah would die too.

"We go get her," April said. "With the two of you and my special weapon together, nothing can stop us. The twins are down for the count and Jaime is still a mess." April shook her canister. There was possibly enough for one more spray if she aimed just right.

"What happened to Jaime?" Lloyd asked.

Sam took a long drag off his mug. "He broke into the wrong house."

"I sprayed him with a solution that burns the eyes, nose, and lungs for a while," April added. "He's barely functional right now, and right now is our best shot. That leaves Grignon how many men, two more? How many are inside his house?"

"No, April," Sam said. "Why do you think those men obey Grignon? He was a competent soldier and he beat enough of them to convince the others. Tell Lloyd how long those effects last."

"One or two hours before they're in fighting condition."

"It's been a half hour already," Sam said, "By the time we prepare and get there, they'll be recovered. The risk is too high."

"Sam's right," Lloyd said. "Grignon is the worst kind of news. There's nothing we can do without coordinating a town-wide attack."

April refused to believe that one man could rule a whole town. "Then we leave," she said. "Everyone else can fend for themselves, but you two will be safe."

Lloyd said, "We must fight. There is no alternative. I will not sit here, dishing up mugs of the finest liquors in the state, and pay the man who is going to kill me, all the while he's got Sarah."

"I can't leave either," Sam said. "I can't go, knowing she might think of me, terrified in Grignon's cell, awaiting whatever fate he has for her. I just can't. I know it's not logical, but I can't," Sam said.

"Any ideas on how we can pull this off?" Lloyd asked.

Sam finished his mug. "The declaration speech."

Sam had April and Lloyd's full attention. "I heard the men say Grignon is giving a speech soon. You need a town-wide coordinated attack? That's the best time."

April didn't want to dampen his spirits, but she also didn't want him to make a fatal mistake. She couldn't lose him. "The speech might not happen as you heard it. I've been here before, trying to fix things. The first time you overheard the threat outside Porter's, but this time it was at the estate. He could come through that door any second—"

"We have work to do," Sam said, brushing her warning off. "Lloyd, keep your eye out. We should be safe for a few days. Grignon has to get his men back in shape and figure out his next step."

April hoped that was true, but she feared it wasn't.

Chapter 30

After three of Grignon's men were sprayed on his front lawn, Sam stepped through his gaping front door on high alert. He collected a knife from the kitchen and inspected each room, ready for anyone lurking.

The house was empty. Sam waved April inside, and as soon as she came in, she went to the kitchen. "I'm making sandwiches. We need our strength for what's to come."

"What's it like?" Sam asked, turning to face the woman from the future who'd traveled through time to save his arse.

"What's what like?" April approached and retrieved the knife from Sam. He handed it over without a thought.

"The future."

April laughed. Oh, how he missed that laugh.

April returned to the kitchen and sliced tomatoes. "In a word—convenient, which is both good and bad. Problems you could never imagine are rampant, but the problems you have are nonexistent."

"Intriguing. Give me an example."

April pushed the blade down. "Well, take food for example. Here you have to grow it, tend it, and hope for the best with weather, bugs, and animals. Then you spend an inordinate amount of time preparing it. In the future, you drive to the store, collect what you want, swipe a card for payment, come home and place a cardboard box in a different box, press a few buttons and in five to seven minutes—a hot steaming meal. It doesn't taste the best, but it's convenient."

Sam grimaced. "That doesn't sound very delicious or very convenient."

April laughed. "It's easier than it sounds. Even worse, those foods are adding to people's waistlines. Companies release healthy versions to combat the problem for a premium, doctors prescribe pills to work faster, and exercise programs in every form imaginable promise easy weight loss."

"Do they work?" Sam was curious about the future, fascinated at how terrible it sounded. She stacked the sliced vegetables and spread them onto slices of bread.

"Generally no. Everybody wants fast, fast, fast—immediate results and no effort. The truth is it takes effort. A lot of effort. There is no magic pill, but they keep trying them anyway, afraid to give up hope, because a meal from a box is faster and easier than this." April spread her hands over her work. "And I'm guilty of it too, but on a lighter note, we have faster travel. Distances that take you days, take us hours. In my time, the average person owns a car to get around, and only the wealthy have horses."

April was a strong, spirited, independent woman, unlike anyone he'd ever met before. She was kind, wicked smart, and she drove a car—whatever that was. Sam laughed. "I find it hard to believe you're just average."

"After all I've told you, that's the hard-to-believe part?"

She brought plates of sandwiches to the table, and they ate in comfortable silence. A small buzz from Lloyd's beer finally calmed his nerves.

Sam watched April while she cleaned up the table and tossed the leftovers out back for the dogs. At the basin, she washed the dishes and teased him with her small body movements and a flirty wink.

Unable to resist, Sam stalked up behind her. He swept her hair off her throat, and he nibbled and kissed the skin, and she tipped her head with a soft moan. The fire in his groin ignited. Her movements became jerky as she struggled to wash the plates. He slid his hands down her back and massaged up her soft belly to her supple bosom.

She still washed.

Sam leaned over and kissed along her jawline. He tipped her chin toward him, seeking her mouth. Her panting breaths heaved her magnificent chest. At last, she dropped the dishes and spun to him.

Success!

Sam smiled, and a need burned in her gorgeous eyes. His hips pinned her against the counter as his lips took control of hers. They breathed hard, the lust, desire, and pulling need taking over.

April wrapped her arms around his neck, holding him in position. He burned with the need to satisfy her.

She hopped up onto the counter and wrapped her legs around him with a wicked smile.

Sam accepted the permission and carried her into the bedroom. He laid her down carefully and loomed overhead, drinking in the sight of her on his bed. He lifted the mountains of fabric to explore those delicious legs of hers.

April's breath hitched while his hands slipped all the way up onto her arse, and he frowned as his fingers found a curious and strange rigidness. He shifted the fabric.

"Wait," she protested.

"What is this?" He pushed the fabric out of the way and gasped. On the peach of her skin, dozens or more white scars crisscrossed her perfect arse. His heart ached for her pain—her torture. "This is what your father did?"

Tears shone in her eyes and she nodded.

Anger flared through his chest, and energy—rage, surge through him. "I will not lie to you. If I meet the man, I'll kill him."

She sniffled and smiled sadly.

"April, I can see plain as day what you survived, and it never should've happened, but you don't need to hide from me. I don't see imperfections. I see reminders of the beautiful lady you've become, the spitfire who told me my penis doesn't make me better than her."

April chuckled.

"You're beautiful to me, just as you are. The only thing that matters to me now is if it hurts."

April's lips lifted. "It's half numb all the time from nerve damage. Only my self-esteem hurts."

"I may not have the healing abilities you have with a needle and thread, but I plan to help you with your self-esteem." His skin glistened with the heat of his need.

April sniffled and smiled. He took her mouth and tasted the saltiness of her tears. He never wanted her to be in pain again. He would pleasure her all evening just to make her forget. His hands reached for the hooks to free her body from the confines of the dress.

"Wait," April said. "Wait," she repeated when Sam didn't stop quick enough.

He backed up to see what the matter was. "What's wrong?" he asked with gentle concern.

She was still troubled. Anxiety and worry filled her.

"Is something else bothering you?" Sam asked. "Tell me. Let me help."

April scooted back from him and sat up, sliding the strap of her dress back into place. "Can I ask you something?"

He sat facing her on the mattress and held her hand. "Anything."

"Do you still love her?"

A blast of cold air shriveled his erection quicker than a retreating line of troops from gunfire. And just as painful too. Sam winced at the reminder, and then he sighed. He ran his hand through his wavy hair. He should've suspected she'd worry.

"Do you want the truth?" he asked, uncertain how to navigate this.

Her voice was hoarse. "Yeah, yeah I do."

If he told her the truth, she probably wouldn't believe him, but if he lied, she would leave. He would try the truth and work his way through it because he didn't want her to go. "I do not."

She searched his face, and the pain on her vulnerable features showed she wasn't convinced.

"I..." Sam trailed off, uncertain how to explain. "Since my parents had financial troubles from the immigration and failed to recover before Mam passed, Da wanted to be certain my sister and I could survive after he was gone. I've told you how he quickly made arrangements for Sarah and I. Me to the daughter of the booming clothing business owner, and my sister to a farm boy, Johnathan Arris, from the next town over. Isabel and I were married only a few months before Grignon changed my life."

"You don't love her?" she asked as if still processing his answer.

"I never did."

April looked at him with accusation, so he continued to explain. "Isabel was beautiful, I won't lie, but we weren't a great match." Sam chuckled. "She hated my art. She didn't understand anything that wasn't practical."

"But her family makes beautiful dresses?" April asked in disbelief.

"Her family brought in fabrics, and Marisol learned to tailor, but Marisol is not her sister Isabel."

"I see."

April was withdrawn, conflicted. Sam had the feeling there was something she wasn't telling him.

"Are you in love?" Sam asked, now fearing what her answer would be. He never asked her if she were engaged or even married. He took foolish liberties even when he knew she would leave after finishing her business. Unwisely, he hoped she would stay, but how could he even consider asking, when she had her own life in the future?

Chapter 31

APRIL WAS RELIEVED THAT he wasn't repulsed by her scars. Not many men could accept a disfigured woman, and Sam's acceptance was more important to her than any of the previous men in her life. He understood the scars made her stronger. But just like she was concerned over Sam's feelings for his wife, he was concerned for hers. She'd never given him any reason to suspect she had anyone else.

Was she in love?

She had been dating Levi for six months. The man was everything she wanted on paper—offering a home, a family, and the stability she craved—and most of all he wanted to marry her. But he didn't care about her interests, didn't show any respect for what she wanted in life, didn't listen to her viewpoints. Could she be content in a marriage like that?

Then she met Sam Hartley. He burned a fire in her like never before. Sam made her whole, as if everything from her past didn't matter. He was strong, passionate, considerate, and honorable. But Sam wasn't reality. This was a temporary dream. Once Sam was safe from Grignon, Kiko would return her back home to Mathew, her job...and Levi.

Tears welled under her eyelids, and she blinked them back. Even knowing what she'd have to give up—the brother she loved more than anything—April didn't want to return. Because there was someone else she loved.

"Yes," she answered Sam.

She loved...Sam.

The tears turned to sobs, because the man she loved she couldn't have. Sam tilted her against his chest and held her, strong and secure.

"That's not normally a question that causes such grief."

She chuckled through her sobs and rubbed her face on her dress like an uncivilized cretin. "I have a confession to make," she said, straightening. April needed to tell him and get it off her chest. Then they could be together for however long they had.

Sam stiffened next to her.

"When I was little, I did everything possible to make my parents happy," April said. "They fought incessantly whenever they had a mind to be in the same room together. On the rare occasion either of them smiled, it was when I did something good at school or around the house. So, I put all my energy into making them smile so the fights would stop. I only wanted the four of us to be a normal, happy family. Dinners together. Telling stories, playing games, even watching TV."

"TV?" Sam interrupted.

April ignored it. "But it never happened. They still divorced, and they hated each other's guts, with good reason."

"That wasn't your fault," Sam said. "You cannot change who people are. It sounds like your parents weren't right for each other."

"I know that now. It took many years for me to get to that point, since they both made it no secret that it was my fault they divorced. Matty always told me to the contrary, but what does a kid know? He was four years older than me. so I didn't listen to him. That's why I floundered through college, switching majors to please my parents, then Matty, and then there was Levi. Everything I did was to make others happy, to keep the peace."

Sam shifted back. He looked like the wind was ripped from him. "Levi is your husband, the man you love?"

April's brows lifted. She hadn't mentioned him before, so that was a leap. "How do you know of him?"

"In your room, you called out his name and whimpered for him."

"I did?" April asked, astonished.

Sam stood up, disgusted, and anger formed on his brow. "Unwilling to leave a woman on the streets, I excused a lot of things, risking my own respect in this town, but I cannot allow a married woman under my roof. How could you come in here, playing the whore, when another man is waiting for you?" Sam held up his hand before a word could escape her lips. "Spare us both dignity and propriety, and please leave."

A wave of pain rolled over her, and April's tears washed down her cheeks. She scrambled out of bed and turned to see if he regretted his hurtful words, but he stood there, resolute, a stubborn Neanderthal of anger. There was no use arguing with him. Men in her time with plenty of education on the matter hardly changed their ways, how could she expect Sam to in just weeks?

Regardless of who she shared her bed with, April had plenty of dignity, and that meant she wasn't going to beg him to see her side. He didn't deserve her explanation. April gathered her bridesmaid dress in a ball and ran away from the pain of his demeaning words, but she couldn't stop her feet. April stumbled through the front door, arms full, and ran out into the cool spring night.

She didn't know where to go, or what to do, but running was the only thing that cleared her head right now. April's lungs were on fire. While she ran, her tears turned to anger. Who was he to throw himself at her again and again, when she'd had reason to believe he was still married, and then later still in love with his deceased wife?

Hypocritical jerk.

April slowed to a walk with her dress bundled in her arms, the only possession she had, the only proof she existed in this town. At this time of night, the businesses were closed—dark windows and locked doors. The night air mixed with her sweat, sending a chill down her spine. The moon cast just enough light to see large objects. There was no one around, and the sadness threatened to return.

The safest places were inside Lloyd's, which was closed, or in the tall grasses where her rented house would exist in the future. But there was no protection from any of Grignon's men patrollling.

April could press the button on the magic trinket and go home, but no matter how much Sam hurt her, she couldn't disappear without saying goodbye. She couldn't turn her head on Sarah and whatever was happening with the girl. She couldn't abandon Lloyd, knowing he was going to be hanged. She couldn't fail Kiko.

Except...there was no school project on the line. Hmmm. Either way, she couldn't quit on her friend. Kiko picked her for a reason, and April was done being a quitter.

That left one safe place.

April marched up the dark wooded trail until her legs ached, tripping and stubbing her toes several times, wishing for the flashlight feature of her cell phone, and subsequently wishing she'd brought the damned thing in the first place.

With the help of adrenaline and numbness, she reached the summit of Overlook Hill and took a few deep breaths. This distance must've taken her an hour or more, and April was exhausted.

April's heart pounded as she gazed off into the horizon. To the north, the eerie blue moonlight lit up the soft waves of the bay, and where the villages were, she saw only a handful of flickering lanterns of travelers. Probably some trying to outsmart Grignon. Good luck to them, they would need it.

As the night chill reached her bones, she laid her bridesmaid dress out as a makeshift sleeping bag against the upcoming morning dew and nestled the layers of skirts around her. It wasn't much, but any extra warmth was welcome and needed.

Tall grasses whispered. Twigs snapped. An owl hooted. She kept her fingers crossed the mosquitoes wouldn't find her. The worst night sleep in the world was always ten times worse by the incessant buzzing of a bug trying to suck her blood. April's body trembled with the crash of adrenaline and tickling empty air. Her hollow chest ached with the miserable loneliness that followed rejection.

After a while, a chill settled into her marrow, and April rubbed her arms for warmth. The grass was hard under her hips and shoulders. Frustrated sleep hadn't come, she would never, ever take for granted a memory foam mattress. Or tap water. Or flushing toilets. Or a hot shower caressing the soreness from her aching muscles. Tears sprung under her closed eyelids. Sleep wouldn't come.

She missed home.

April fumbled through the layers of her fabric and found the magic trinket Kiko had given her. Her hands trembled while she held it close to her nose to see it. With a press of the button, this would be over. She could go home to Levi—gentle, if inconsiderate, Levi and his crappy music. Leftover Chinese in a box sounded like three-Michelin-star gourmet right now. She missed fast food. She wanted cheese curds—beer battered or squeaky fresh—she wasn't picky. She missed Mathew and his annoying speeches, and she would take them all if it meant she could get a hug.

April's finger hovered just over the button. Pushing it would be easy. Then she'd be back home. Just a push.

A sniffle broke through the silence. If she were lucky, wolves would eat her and then she wouldn't have to choose.

April gave the flippant thought actual consideration since the risk was real, and she had nothing better to do. Visualizing that series of events was...gruesome, and not at all something she'd truly wish for. April put the trinket back into the hidden pockets of her dress, and sat up, listening.

A nearby rustling snapped her wide awake, and she craned her neck to follow the noise. Under the moonlight, only a few general shapes took form. The rustling got closer. It was too noisy to be a person sneaking up on her, or if it was a person sneaking, they sucked at it. Still, having no defense but a partially drained pepper spray canister, she froze in position and hoped whoever or whatever it was left her alone.

And then a snort echoed above the grass—a non-human terrifying snort. April held her breath and sat stock-still, while her pulse roared in her ears. She chanted in her head, please don't be a wolf, please don't be a wolf.

A warm lick slid up her cheek. April screamed and scrambled back, tangled in layers of fabric. Paws landed on her chest, knocking her back. April recognized his wagging tail and smiling doggy face. He licked her again.

"Jesus, Doug. Give me a heart attack, would you?" April smiled and hugged the dog. "I'm so glad you're here. You have no idea. I don't have any food, but could you stay with me tonight?"

She laid back down onto her dress, and Doug curled around her middle, keeping her warm. She wrapped an arm around him, and a content chuff came from the wonderful mutt. Sleep dragged them both down.

When he'd looked at April, he was ashamed, and he couldn't begin to think straight until he was alone in his house. How could she keep something like that from him? Sam shook his head. It wasn't the crazy claims of being from the future that did him in. No, it was because she was married.

He'd felt many things when Isabel was captured, tortured, and murdered in front of him by the fireplace. But he didn't love her. Still, the guilt had burdened him ever since.

Now he'd nearly laid with a married woman, and the guilt for his actions was overwhelming. It wasn't just guilt weighing him down.

It was the breaking of his heart, and it was his fault he'd let her in so deeply.

He loved a married woman, and now he had to somehow untangle those wonderful feelings from his selfish head. The best place to start—Sam marched over to his bourbon stash. Instead of the partial bottle that he'd been nursing for months to make it last, Sam discovered a full, brand new bottle. Where had this come from? Sarah had no money for it, neither did Sam. Even his kindest friend Lloyd wouldn't gift this much. Sam cursed again.

April.

She'd bought him a new bottle like she said she would, after she'd used it to doctor his wound. His fingers sought the suture line on his cheek. It wasn't tender anymore. What kind of married woman would go through all that effort to care for him, provide for him, protect him, and save his sorry arse?

A widow, perhaps, which was why she'd cried when she said she was in love.

He hadn't even given her a chance to finish her story, because he was embarrassed and hurt. And April had fled into the night, alone, with Grignon's men out there. He'd invited April to stay with him, to protect her, and he failed her, but it wasn't too late.

Sam returned the bottle to its hiding place and ran outside. He couldn't see her. He listened for footsteps or crying, but heard nothing. It wasn't safe for him to call after her. Anyone overhearing—especially Grignon's men on patrol—would act on the opportunity at once. With only a sliver of moonlight to guide her, the most logical move would be to stick around the house.

Sam moved swiftly around the perimeter, checking shadows and around trees. He whispered her name, but no reply came back.

Sam headed to the workshop and opened the door with squeaking hinges. The moonlight cast a paltry beam for him to see. "April?" he whispered. "Are you in here? Please come out." He stepped over tools and ducked under hanging art pieces. He made a loop inside, calling her.

She wasn't here either.

He skimmed along the gardens, but he found nothing but a startled rabbit. April had to be out here somewhere. Sam whistled for his mount. It took three tries before the horse decided to make an appearance.

If Sam charged around, he'd gather unwanted attention. He needed to be quiet, stealthy, and he needed to be able to hear. Sam mounted up and tapped the horse into a slow walk. He made a circle of each building in the area, checking front and back doors, looking for any ajar. He searched for open windows, or signs of her pink dress. When he trusted no one else was around, he whispered her name, but it only carried on the breeze.

It almost felt like she'd vanished.

Surely if Grignon was responsible, April would've screamed bloody murder to wake the town.

What if he believed she was from the future? What if he upset her so much she'd left? Not his house, not even his town, but what if…she returned to the future…to her home? Sam didn't know what he would do if he could never see her again.

He turned in place, trying to figure out where she'd go. Thankfully, Common Square was empty. No one was dying tonight. And just beyond it…the trail.

Sam jabbed the horse into a gallop, and slowed at the trailhead. Bucky stomped one leg in front of the other as they climbed the rough path to Overlook Hill. He pushed branches out of his face as they passed through the overgrown brush. At the grassy clearing at the top, Sam shielded the brilliant oranges and pinks of the coming dawn from his eyes to see what lay hidden in the grasses.

Near the edge of the hill, where April had admired the view, something disturbed the grass. Sam launched himself off the horse and ran toward a familiar bundle of clothing, heart pounding in his ears, worry tearing through him, relief on the verge of washing over him. The fabric shifted, and a furry mutt's tail wagged.

"Doug!" Sam rushed to the fabrics, where April slept, instantly checking her for injuries. He shook her shoulder. "April? April, wake up. Please, wake up."

April moaned.

Doug sat up, tail wagging. Sam pet him. "Thank you for protecting her, Doug. You're a good boy."

"April?"

A very drowsy, shivering woman sat up, appropriately disheveled considering the circumstances, and she rubbed her eyes. "Sam?"

"I'll take you home."

He scooped her up off the ground and set her on Bucky. He leaned down to scratch the mutt in his favorite spot, and his big doggy grin left his tongue lolling out the side of his mouth. "You're the best dog a man could ask for. I owe you a big one. Come along for breakfast."

Sam mounted up behind her and grasped the reins. She snuggled into him for warmth, and she smelled like mangy mutt, the scent of his best dog protecting the woman he loved—because Sam had failed her. He was going to make everything up to her. Sam grinned, feeling like he struck gold right alongside those lucky bastards in California. He knew she still had to go home, but he was just grateful for a chance to make things right.

And maybe, just maybe, she could stay.

Chapter 32

April remembered swaying on a horse, shivering with cold, warm softness holding her in place, and warm breath on the top of her head. Regardless of Sam rescuing her from being miserably cold and alone, she wasn't forgiving him. April reawakened on Sam's couch, a blanket draped over her, but the aches of the hard ground were still there. She sat up and stretched to ease the pains, and her feet landed on unusually soft flooring. She must've dropped blankets during the night.

The floor mumbled, and she leaned over in surprise. Sam slept at the foot of the couch, just as she had when she worried for his recovery. Why was he there? April touched her face, inspected her arms. Nothing hurt other than what she'd expected from sleeping on the rock solid ground.

April stepped over him, placed her warm bundle on top of him, and cleaned herself up in her guest bedroom. When she returned the wash basin to the pantry to start breakfast, Sam was already in the kitchen. She let her smug smile fly. Oh, he knew he screwed up. Served him right for making her sleep outside all night in the cold. He still wasn't forgiven, but she was famished.

April stepped up alongside him and asked, "Need some help?"

He paused from cracking eggs. "I'll handle the food. The morning paper is there if you'd like."

April could get used to this. She took a seat at the table and lifted today's newspaper. But she'd never get used to seeing that year, 1852. It was easy to pretend this town was a tiny, socially backward blip on the modern radar. Perhaps too isolated or restricted from modern technology, like that town in West Virginia with the monster-sized satellite. That didn't explain the lack of cars, but Mackinac Island didn't have any either. April really was back in time, and Sam in the kitchen was a big deal for him.

April still wanted to kill Hitler, but since keeping Sam alive was so damned hard, she'd settle for trusting Kiko's refusal.

Sam scooted eggs around the cast iron pan and flipped some toast, scrambling carefully, and shaking a burned finger here and there.

April avoided laughing. She didn't want him to know how much she enjoyed this. She glanced at the headlines. A few mentioned Gabriel Grignon. He was smiling and shaking hands with someone, accepting an award. A headline read, 'Grignon Approves City Loan to Construct Library'. She almost couldn't hate the guy. Almost.

With a towel over his broad shoulder, Sam brought over her plate and set it in front of her. She set the newspaper aside and waited for him to join her before shoveling food in her face. Purely out of politeness, she was still a lady after all—not that manners had anything to do with her bedroom activities.

Sam sat across from her, fork hovering over the steaming plate. He cleared his throat. "April, I'm so sorry about last night. I overreacted, and I wasn't thinking or I was thinking too much. I didn't mean what I said, and it never should've happened."

"You said terrible things about me. You can't take them back."

"I was impatient and rude. I should've given you a chance to defend yourself or explain. The truth is..." He trailed off, recollecting his thoughts. Yeah, he was definitely sorry, and April almost hated to see him squirm so much. Almost. "The truth is...I was jealous of Levi." Sam gave her a pointed look, and April's heart fluttered.

"Regardless of your marital status, I treated you terribly, and I'm sorry. Please tell me how I can make it up to you, and if you could stop Levi from hunting me down, I would appreciate it."

April remained cool. "You don't."

Sam's chin quivered for just a moment, and his hand flashed to his face in a quick swipe. "I'm so sorry," he said, voice gravelly.

There was nothing he could do to take those words out of her head, but she believed he meant his heartfelt apology. "Breakfast is a good start."

He looked up at her and smiled. "I promise I'll never do that again."

"Call me a whore?" she asked for clarification.

"Send you away."

"Just so you know, calling me names is forbidden as well, and I'm not a whore."

Sam nodded. "Consider it added to the list."

April finished her plate and dug her Swiss army knife out of her pocket. She scooted her chair right next to him and picked out the micro scissors.

"What are you doing?" Sam said. For all he knew, her folding knife was simply a knife.

"Sit still and you won't get hurt." April demonstrated the scissor action. "Those sutures need to come out. Hold still." She snipped the first one just below the knot and slipped it out through his flesh. It came out smoothly. "Did that feel okay?"

"A wee bit weird, but didn't hurt."

"Nine more to go. Hold still."

Her face so close to his, April snipped and tugged all of them, deliberately taking her time. Sam's hot gaze locked on her as she worked. Sam wasn't moving, but she brushed her fingers against his cheek and jaw to 'hold' him steady. His short beard was soft, as she'd hoped. April bit her lip to hold back her smile. Heat rolled through her.

April slipped the last suture free. "All done." She admired the barely perceptible scar line and tiny pink dots. "Looking good too," she said.

"Thanks. You're good looking yourself."

They locked gazes. He knew he was hot, but she didn't want to compliment him. "I meant your scar."

"And I meant you," he whispered.

April rose to her feet. "Why are you doing this? Just last night you accused me of being married, and now you're trying to seduce me again. I don't understand."

Sam stood. "Are you married?"

April had a feeling she knew where this was headed, but for the sake of open communication and less secrets, she said plainly, "No, I'm not, and I never was."

Relief passed over Sam's handsome face. He reached out for her arms, but she stepped back. "I want you, April McCall. I don't have much experience with women, and everything you've taught me has been incredible and yet confusing. I don't know the right way to do things with you. I'm trying, and I'll keep trying every day. I don't want to mess this up."

"Mess what up?" she asked, only to get him to say it. She wanted to hear it from his lips.

"I want us to be together. I care about you so very much. I don't want to lose you again."

AFTER POURING HIS HEART out to her, Sam ached to hear her response, but her withdrawn face didn't give him hope.

"Sam, I can't say what you want to hear."

Knowing his love was unrequited hurt more than anything he could recall. She punched a hole in his chest, and tore out his heart, but she didn't do it on purpose. Her answer was kind and gentle, and he appreciated the truth. They had no future. "Are you leaving then?"

April frowned. "I'm here on a mission to keep you and Lloyd alive, and I can't let Kiko down. We need to stop Grignon."

A brave woman like April wouldn't come waltzing into his life twice, but once Grignon was finished, she'd go home. Sam had time, and time meant hope. "I don't want you risking your life for me, but if you insist on staying until then, I hope I can change your mind."

"Sam—" April started.

He held out a hand. "No more talk about this. We have Grignon between us, a brutal man with a small army. We have a couple days—as you said—to change this game in our favor. I'm going to make my rounds to the local businesses. Someone has been spying on my goings on with the owners, and I need to ferret out who's behind it."

"It's got to be Jaime," April said. "He seems to pop up everywhere like he's following you."

Sam stared at her in disbelief, until he remembered how eagerly the weasel ran to Grignon for safety. "I think you're right. Shite."

"The good news is the business owners are on your side then."

"Possibly not Ralf Perez," Sam said. "He claims to think of me as his son still, but I truthfully doubt it."

"So what do we have on our side?" April asked. "You have a gun, some knives. Lloyd is strong, and I assume he has weapons," April said, strategizing. She was just so perfect, but Sam needed to focus.

"You have that spray canister. That's a surprisingly effective little thing," Sam said. He didn't want her anywhere near Grignon, but he wanted her to have something for defense.

"It won't help much. There's only one more use left, if that. Then it's a paper weight."

"Can you get more?"

April finally cracked a smile. "They aren't invented yet, and they're hard to find even in my time."

"Do you have any other interesting weapons?"

"Afraid not," she said.

For peace of mind, Sam would teach her a few things—what he should've done for Isabel. What he should've forced his stubborn sister to agree to. Both their fates may have been different if he had, and Sam wouldn't make that mistake a third time. Sam crooked his arm at her and leaned into a defensive stance.

"What are you doing?" April asked.

"Hit me," he said.

"Excuse me?" The shock on her face made Sam laugh.

"I'm going to teach you a few simple moves just in case you need them."

"What do you mean 'in case I need them'? We're not storming the castle. We're getting the townspeople to uprise against him during the speech."

"Isabel couldn't defend herself, and Sarah refused my teachings."

April considered the gravity behind that statement.

Sam gestured for her to hit him. "You won't hurt me. Go ahead."

April exhaled deeply, and just when Sam was about to insist, she reeled back for a punch to the face. Sam lifted his arm to parry. In a flash of a second, she changed trajectory and socked him in the gut. Sam blew out his breath and folded.

"Are you okay?" she asked. There was amusement in her voice, and Sam would've laughed in surprise if he could. Instead he held up a finger to wait, and slowly regained his breath.

"Can't say I expected that. That's the last time I underestimate you."

April wore a smug smile, and he loved the challenge.

"Try again," he said.

"Are you sure?" April asked, teasing.

Sam grinned. "Hit me."

April drew back in a defensive stance, mirroring him. Her footwork was good. She had some training. Sam's chest expanded with respect. She wasn't making the first move, so he did, careful not to hurt her. He swung at her face, carefully controlled.

She ducked and spun, kicking the side of his leg. A sharp stab of pain lanced his knee. He babied the leg and hopped a bit. "Do you have a brick for a foot?"

"Sorry." She laughed playfully. "Matty insisted I take a few lessons. He was always paranoid about my personal safety, especially after Dad... You know. Where do you think the Swiss army knife came from? I get one every year like clockwork. Do you want to try something else?"

Sam smiled and rubbed his leg. With an unintended hint of seduction in his tone, he said, "Aye."

Sam dove at her, grabbing her around the chest and twisting, so they both fell with her on top of him. Then he rolled them both until she was under him. Sam cradled her head and stroked her hair away from her eyes. Both of them panted, and it wasn't just exertion.

"Are you going to ask me to free myself from your grip, because you won't like it," April said.

He chuckled, excited for her to try. "Go ahead."

April smiled deviously and wrenched her hips up in the air while smacking his elbows down, causing him to drop his full body weight on her. He continued chuckling while they struggled. She grunted and tried to roll him over, but she couldn't.

April broke out in a laugh.

"Nice try, love."

"Love?" April asked, face flushed bright red.

Sam had to cover. He didn't want to scare her off. "Just like you, love is beautiful and caring but aggravating sometimes. And you pack one hell of a punch."

April smiled, and he kissed her once on the lips.

She lifted her brows in surprise, but the heat in her gaze on his lips told him what he wanted to know.

She wanted him too.

As heat roared through his body, and the desire to take her now pounded in his ears, he lifted her up off the floor and carried her to the bedroom.

SAM CARRIED HER TO his bed. It smelled like him, a masculine pine and leather mix. She closed her eyes and inhaled the scent, memorizing it. Sam loomed over her and untucked his shirt. She climbed up to her knees and took over. She lifted the fabric, sliding her palms over his chest, exposing miles of sweet sexy ridges that flickered and glistened when he'd swung the ax. Now she'd get to finally feel what his body could do. The shirt fell to the floor, and April drank him in.

"Like what you see?" he asked.

"You know I do."

Sam grinned and took her lips. While she kissed the man who cared very much about what she wanted and how she wanted to be treated, Sam's hands unfastened her dress. He wanted her to be protected, to be respected, and she'd never felt more safe in her life.

April's lips danced with his, and she stroked his scruffy jawline with her thumb. His swift fingers worked at the layers on her body, unwrapping her like candy.

She wanted to be eaten.

Preferably with a clean-shaven face, but she wasn't picky right now.

And the kinks in his beliefs? He was actively trying to fix them...for her. She'd never felt more loved in her life.

With a little assistance, Sam finished tugging the fabric off her, and now it was her turn. While she unbuttoned his trousers, his fiery gaze drank her in, and she was rewarded with a firm erection straining behind his underpants, broad thighs, and thick calves. Who needed the gym when Sam's entire life kept him in amazing shape? He was gorgeous, almost criminally hot.

"Are you sure you want to do this?" Sam asked.

Kneeling in front of him, April grabbed his cock in her fist. "Don't ask me that again."

Sam smiled. "I'll add that to the list."

April chuckled, and Sam's lips found hers. With one arm, he lifted her against him and he laid them onto the bed. He caged her, holding his weight with ease. A calloused hand traced along her body, and a shiver of nerves hardened her nipples.

"Like a magic button," he said.

April laughed, and his mouth found her breast.

She stopped laughing.

Sam moved down her body, kissing gently and stroking her bare skin, and April's breathing deepened with regular gasps of surprise.

Not very experienced? Like hell.

His mouth found her clit, and a pair of thick fingers carefully, slowly made their way up inside.

April squeezed the bedding in her fists.

He stroked and thrusted, tongue and fingers sending her up the hill, awaiting an explosion she'd desperately wanted since she'd first seen him in the bar—a gorgeous, ruggedly handsome gunslinger cowboy, who looked at her like she was the only person in the room. He was perfect, exactly what she'd dreamed her dream man to be.

She didn't expect him to be so much better.

April's panting shallowed. Her muscles tensed. She lifted her hips to meet his licks, waiting, ready, about to reach that cliff.

Sam didn't stop. He was a machine of perfect stamina and he kept charging until she crashed over. April held her breath as the waves of release rippled through her. Sam slowed with her, and followed her as she lowered her hips. He wiped his mouth on her thigh and rested his chin on her lower belly.

April smiled back. "Are you waiting for an invitation?" She crooked her finger at him.

Sam leaned over her and captured her mouth, his erection pressing against her thigh. She gripped it with her hands and stroked. Sam shuddered under her touch, and she loved the power to control his pleasure.

April shoved him over and climbed on top. With her splayed hands on his strong abs, she seated herself over him slowly.

Sam closed his eyes and tilted his head back with a moan. April bit her lower lip and moved over him. Sam gripped her hips and assisted, directing her speed as he needed. His intense eyes met her gaze. April leaned forward, hands resting on his pecs, thumbs teasing his nipples.

Sam's breaths quickened and his gaze flashed to her bouncing breasts. He pressed her hips harder, faster, as his own climax neared, and at once he sucked in a breath and held still. April felt the pulsing within as he filled her up. Nothing would ever be the same. Sam would always have a piece of her heart now, and it was both wonderful and scary.

April rested on his slick chest. Sam kissed her forehead as their breathing evened out.

"I'm supposed to say something profound, aren't I? Like, you were perfect."

April smiled and made circles with her finger on his chest, listening to his heartbeat. "Enjoy the peace."

Sam kissed her head and they cuddled.

When the cool air chilled the sweat on her body, April shivered. Sam rubbed her back and shifted out from under her. April covered herself in his sheet while Sam's sexy ass slipped into his underwear.

"I'll be right back. Don't go anywhere," he said with a playful tone.

April smiled, drowsily satisfied. Through the bedroom door, she watched him go to the fireplace and open a small creaking drawer hidden under the mantle. One that shouldn't have been there. It creaked again as he closed it and he returned, holding a small box in his hand. He sat on the bed next to her, and she scooted to a seated position, covering herself with the sheet.

"What's that?" she asked.

He opened the box to reveal a stunning string of familiar pearls, a set she'd seen in the photograph of Sam with Isabel. "This is for you. I don't have much, so I hope you like it."

"That's Isabel's necklace," she said simply, trying not to feel hurt.

"This was my mother's first," he said. "It was her most treasured possession, the necklace she wore to all social events, so she would feel like she belonged. Isabel wore it for a photograph. I want you to have it."

"Why?" April asked, heart swelling with his words.

"Because I think it would be beautiful on you." He removed the string of pearls from the box. "Do I need any other reason?"

She wanted a reminder of Sam, and she didn't want to hurt him by rejecting the meaningful gift. April lifted her hair, and Sam fastened the pearls around her throat. Her fingers glided across their surfaces. They were beautiful, and they meant a lot to Sam. She would treasure them just as his mother did.

Chapter 33

With a loose plan under his belt to save his sister and the town from the tyrant ruling them all, Sam stopped at Aaron Porter's for the collection, energized and excited. The store was unfortunately busy, and he found the old man working the register for a pair of teenage customers. Sam lined up behind them, and he smiled and nodded at them in politeness. They whispered to each other, and as soon as Porter passed them their change, the girls scooted away, as if a pair of mice had spotted a lurking cat. Strange.

When Porter noticed Sam, the smile left his jolly face.

Sam urged the customer behind him to go next, and with the line cleared, Sam approached the register.

"Sam," Porter said. "I wish I could say it's nice to see you, but that wouldn't be true."

"No offense taken. Is the payment ready for delivery?"

"You seem unusually chipper today." Porter ducked under the counter and slid the thin envelope over. Sam tucked it safely into his breast pocket.

Porter was one of Sam's most trusted confidants. If April's assumption about Jaime was correct, Sam could still trust Porter. "Can I ask you something?"

A pair of young women in bonnets whispered behind Sam. He stepped aside to allow them to complete their purchases, but his business wasn't finished yet. Standing off to the side, the women secretly glimpsed at him, and Sam couldn't make heads or tails of their entertainment. As they left the store, they glanced at him once more. Did he have something on his face? Sam swiped at his mouth and checked his hand.

Privacy restored, Sam kept his voice low. "Grignon suspects the business owners are colluding to short him. Do you know anything about that?"

Porter glanced away, perhaps in guilt, and then he cleared his throat. "I don't know what you're talking about, son. It would be best if you didn't ask questions about that."

That would be a yes, but Porter wouldn't give him any more information. They were trying to salvage their money at a direct risk to Sam's life. The gravity of their secret actions sunk in, and the friendships he thought he had...twisted. "I understand." But he didn't. Not at all.

Porter said, "Now, the real question you need to concern yourself with is—who is that new girl in town that's been staying with you? Talk's been all over town, and I have to say, it hasn't been good."

Another wave of unease rolled through him. "What has the gossip mill been churning lately?"

"Oh...you know." Porter hesitated. "Just the usual."

"Apparently not, since you brought it up."

The old man skimmed his store for wayward ears. Sam mirrored him to verify for himself. "The word is this girl is working for Grignon undercover, you see? Now, everyone here knows you and they trust you. Some might even like you, but I can't imagine why." Porter said that with a chuckle. "Anyway, this strange girl with her funny money—everything weird started when she showed up. I don't believe in coincidences, my friend. I just want you to be aware is all."

Sam bristled. "She doesn't work for him."

"Are you sure about that?"

"Grignon has Sarah. This has gone on long enough. Can I count on your support at the speech?"

Porter's solemn face told him what he needed to know. "I'm sorry for your loss again, Sam."

Sam spun on his heels and left, seething from the town's ignorance. He mounted Bucky and tore off for Grignon's estate to make the drop. With Grignon having interest in April, and then a calm fury at her disabling his men, Sam could imagine Grignon was moving his chess pieces against her now...instead of for her.

Sam dismounted in front of the grand entrance and further unease settled over him like a suffocating blanket. The estate, a beautiful sentry on the outside, reeked of suffering and death on the inside. Every ounce of his being fought to make the daily drops when all he wanted was to burn the place down.

The only reason he delivered Grignon's payments was to find out if Sarah was here. Would he be able to control himself if he heard her cries for help?

Sam closed the distance to the front door while scrutinizing the windows for any signs of his sister—a wave of a hand, a note jammed in a sill, a stirring of curtains, but he found nothing. The house was eerily still. The housekeeper opened the door without a greeting, and Sam entered without a word.

As usual, Sam followed her into the library while craning his neck and listening for any suspicious sounds. His heart thundered in his chest, making his mission futile. Dennis and Daniel stood guard, fully alert but with red-rimmed eyes from April's spray. The men had an array of weapons displayed on their solid bodies. More than usual, in fact. He nodded to acknowledge their presence and ease their imposing stance, but they didn't even blink. A swirl of anger settled into his belly as he wished for a private moment with Dennis. Someday he'd avenge Isabel.

Sam's hands itched for a weapon when he saw Grignon's vulnerable position at the window, fingers laced behind his back—the very same fingers Sam visualized doing horrible things to his sister. Sam briefly considered ambushing him from behind, stabbing him quickly and quietly, and then searching for Sarah, but the twins would put him down before he made five paces, and if she wasn't here, then Sam would never find her. He inhaled a ragged deep breath and tossed the envelope onto the bastard's desk. The envelope slid across the lacquered surface and teetered at the edge.

Grignon finally spoke, his voice softer than Sam expected. "I suppose you have some questions for me."

The gentle tone threw Sam off. He understood Grignon well, or at least he thought he did. This was new. Sam swallowed a lump and took the opportunity. "Where's Sarah?"

Grignon sighed and turned around. Sorrow replaced his usual scowl and confidence. It surprised Sam, but he didn't flinch. Grignon walked over to his desk, used a finger to push the envelope away from the edge, and then sat down. "She's safe."

Sam exhaled and his hands shook. He wiped the perspiration on his trousers. His heart squeezed as the words sunk in. There was hope, but he didn't break his stoic stance.

"I'm not surprised you made a collection for me. Your attempt to seek her out is plain, but I respect it, even if I warned you to stay away."

"Where is she?" Sam demanded. Sam spun on his heels to project louder through the house. "Sarah!" he shouted. "Sarah!"

No answer.

"Don't bother. She's not here," Grignon said. "This is what's going to happen. You will carry on with your services for me and forget your sister."

Sam didn't believe Grignon. Something changed in him, but the snake still held all the cards, and by agreeing, he'd have more chances to find her here, and more opportunities to organize the business owners—to his plan. "I won't forget her."

Grignon sighed. "I figured as much. Go."

Sam headed back home at a gallop with hope tugging at his heart. He could do this. He'd find Grignon's vulnerability and strike when Sam had assembled his team.

APRIL WIPED HER SWEATY brow with dirt-caked hands, feeling like an ant under the magnifying glass of the summer's sun. The plants were wilting. Retrieving buckets of water from the well was on her to-do list. She plucked away at the weeds that seemed to pop up any time she turned her back. The little devils were mocking her.

She harvested a few more pea pods and realized at that moment she'd essentially replaced Sarah. Cooking, cleaning, garden tending, caring for Sam. It felt wrong, bizarre even, to have taken the wonderful girl's place instead of helping by her side. In the meantime, someone needed to do the work, since Sam was gone most of the day, slowly enacting the plan. It killed her that he was gone, unprotected, but worrying was like a rocking horse—it was something to do but didn't change anything.

The sound of hoofbeats had her standing for a break and a stretch of her lower back. April brushed off her hands and brought the basket of vegetables inside to freshen up. Sam carried a mix of emotions on his face. He paced the living quarters.

"What is it? What happened?" April caught his arm and guided him to the couch.

"Sarah's alive, as he'd said."

"That's great news!"

"But Grignon said she's not at the estate. We could search forever and never find her."

"I'm so sorry, Sam. Hopefully wherever she is, she's happy," April said to comfort him, but she didn't believe that to be true.

"I don't want to think about how he's treating her. I couldn't live with it."

"Now what?" April asked.

"He said he wants me to continue to work for him as if nothing ever happened. I don't know if he's lowering my defenses, but I'm not taking a chance. We're leaving tonight. Lloyd's already packed. I'm going to tell him we leave at nightfall."

Sam moved to the door, and April followed him as if she couldn't bear to part with him. He said, "There are wooden crates in the back of the workshop. Pack up the essentials."

April nodded with butterflies fluttering in her belly. Sam left, and she closed the door behind him and sighed. She was scared. Deep-down, stomach-churning, hair-raising terrified.

But so long as she had her magic trinket, she wouldn't quit.

SAM ENTERED LLOYD'S BAR cautiously. He watched the townspeople more closely, judging their glances and stares, their whispers and laughs. What would his parents think of all this? Left a country of war, famine, and filthy urban conditions to start a new life here, only to find out the town conspired against them, and now they had to leave with only a fraction of the Hartleys left.

Lloyd was sweeping the floors when Sam found him. The friendly smile dropped off as Sam leaned in close. "Lloyd, do you know anything about the owners organizing against Grignon?"

Lloyd's brows popped, and Sam knew the answer with that reaction. Lloyd hid nothing from him. "No. They left me out of whatever they're planning. I'm not surprised though."

"What do you mean? You're the most loved business in town. Who could survive these times without your amazing beer?"

"Stop being such a kiss-ass."

"The only arse I'll be kissing is my own, if we survive this mess. With Jaime in Grignon's pocket, I don't trust his father. Porter was a bust, but he confirmed they're deliberately withholding payments from Grignon. I'd consider them on our side, except—"

"By shorting Grignon, they're putting a target on your back," Lloyd finished.

"And the whole town suspects April is spying for him, which she's not. I trust her fully. The only thing keeping us here is Sarah, but Grignon said my sister isn't at the estate."

"You believe he tells the truth?"

"There was something off about him today, something unusually genuine and sullen. I believe him, and when I called for her, I received no response."

"So what's the new plan?" Lloyd asked.

"We're leaving tonight for Astor. We need to be armed to cross the bridge. Do you have space in your wagon?"

"I don't. It's completely full, and I have to pack my personal effects yet."

Sam needed to requisition a wagon for the short journey. "That's where I'm headed next, and after we settle, we'll begin the search for Sarah."

Lloyd studied his face for a minute, and Sam stared back with warmth, grateful for his friend's trust and mutual love for Sam's sister. Lloyd was like a brother to him. "That sounds like a plan. I knew you could figure out something. I just wished it involved me keeping my bar."

"Grignon wouldn't have allowed it either way."

"No, I suppose not."

SAM HAD ONE PROBLEM before he could leave. A wagon costed money, and his money was at the bank—Grignon's bank. Sam returned home, finding April packing as he'd requested. The beautiful and radiant April, so brave and kind. Watching her carefully pack his things—kitchenware, so far—left him beaming with affection.

An idea came to him. "April, can you pretend to be my bride for a wee bit?"

April gaped. "What? Why?"

"I can't trust the townspeople, and I need an excuse to withdraw funds from the bank without the tellers tipping off Grignon. A wedding to the woman I've been seeing for weeks isn't suspicious. All you have to do is pretend you're over the moon with me. Can you do that?"

"I'll do my best, but I'm no actress." April snorted.

They entered the bank, and the teller acknowledged Sam with an overabundant smile. "Hi ya, Sam. What can I do ya for?" Despite being annoyingly nice, Mark was firmly tucked in Grignon's pocket.

"Mark," Sam said as a way of greeting while April hugged his side. "Withdrawal please."

"How much today?"

"All of it. We're getting married." Sam smiled wide, and April impressed him with a display of over-the-top affection, clutching his arm, kissing his cheek, and smiling the way newlyweds did. For a fleeting moment, he wished it were true.

"Well, congratulations are in order. Allow me to go make an announcement." Mark spun for the offices.

Sam stopped him. "We need to put our deposits down today. Just the cash, please. We'll come back for the big announcement after."

"Oh, all right. So eager, are we?" Mark winked and wrote up a ticket before removing the funds from a drawer. He counted the bills in front of him and when he finished, Sam scooped up the stack and rushed April away. "Thanks, Mark!" he called behind him.

Behind Common Square was the horse ranch where Farmer Ted made wagons. To his luck, Ted had one available. Using every penny of his life's savings, Sam scooped it up and attached it to Bucky.

He and April made it home as quickly as they could without turning heads. Dusk was setting in. Bucky dragged the large wagon while carrying two riders, and Sam wondered if a second horse would've been wise, but they didn't have time or money. "Grignon will get wind of this soon. He'll know something is up. Let's load up."

It was backbreaking to choose and pack everything with haste and carry the crates onto the wagon. The two of them, exhausted and sweaty, crashed on the couch. They'd left the bottle of bourbon out in case they needed it before leaving.

"What about the dogs?" April asked.

Sam gulped down a shot's worth. "They've been getting on for years before me. After I go, they'll make do without me again. If not, the poor wretches will follow us."

Satisfied, April asked, "How long until we get Lloyd?"

"At nightfall, he'll come. So, an hour, maybe. What were you thinking?" Sam slyly inspected April's heaving slick bosom and thought they definitely had time.

"I need to run to the store for something quick. Is that all right?"

"Bucky's tied up and ready to go. I need time to disconnect the hitch."

"Bucky!" April said with excitement and grasped his arms. "You finally called him Bucky. No, no, don't untie him. I'll run. That's why I wear my sneakers." She lifted her dress to show off her previously-white-but-now-dirty running shoes.

"You're not going alone. The townsfolk believe you work for Grignon, so they won't bother you, but it's not safe," Sam said.

"This is something I need to do by myself. I'll be careful. Besides, I pack one hell of a punch." April smiled, repeating his admiration for her.

Sam sighed. He hated the idea, but she was stronger than he'd given her credit for. "If anyone stops you, use those skills of yours." Sam heated, remembering her body under his.

April said, "I'll be right back."

"And I'll be here finishing up." When she returned, all his attention would be on her until Lloyd arrived, but in the meantime, he didn't want to forget anything.

APRIL MOVED SWIFTLY THROUGH the fading dusk toward the general store. She'd made one mistake, but she wouldn't do it again. Condoms were necessary even in this century. Her body hummed with excitement for when she returned to Sam's bed, wishing this wasn't necessary. There were only a couple people milling around town outside. And a few at Lloyd's. April swung into the general store, her face hot and chest heaving from exercise. She quickly found Porter.

"Hello, Miss April, what can I get you this evening?"

April kept her voice low, awkwardly asking a man for birth control. "Do you have condoms?"

Porter spoke softly, "We don't carry any articles of immoral use here. I'm sorry miss, but we don't support obscenity in these parts, and I suggest you be careful who you ask for such things."

April scrunched her face, frustrated once again with this time and not comfortable taking risks again. She wanted to explore Sam without worry.

"But you can try Martin's, the chemist."

"Thank you," she said and stepped out into the dark of night.

April calmly walked on the side of the road toward Bridgeport Chemist. When was her last period? She counted and recounted on her fingers, failing to pinpoint a date in all the confusion with differing times, when the sound of clomping horse hooves interrupted her thoughts.

A surprising strength hoisted her up in the air, feet dangling. April gasped and opened her mouth to scream, but a foul smelling vice-like hand clamped over her lips, muffling her. She pushed against his fingers to bite him, but she couldn't.

The shrouded stranger calmly and silently positioned her onto the horse and pinned her. April wriggled and scooted and shoved to get free but couldn't budge him.

"Don't move or you'll never see light again." It was a deep voice with a familiar accent—Dennis Durand or his twin.

A chill trembled her spine and the hairs lifted on her arms. With his size and strength, she would never get away from him, and if she managed to launch herself off the horse, Dennis packed a lot of heat.

April needed to wait for the right moment, somewhere dark with dense woods, and then she had a shot of escaping. The journey felt like forever, and the cool of the night sparked many more chills. She just wanted to be home, warm and safe by Sam's fireplace. Sam's home.

Instead, Dennis brought her to Grignon's vast estate.

"Don't make a peep, little chicken," Dennis hissed in her ear as he helped her down. He never released her wrist even after her feet hit the dirt. He dragged her inside Grignon's estate. Screaming would be a waste of energy. From this location, no one would hear except those already in the house.

He brought her to the library, where the door was guarded by two more men. Both she recognized—Rob Bertrand, and the other was Dennis's scar-free twin, Daniel. They nodded their heads as Dennis pushed her inside.

Grignon's nose was buried in paperwork on his desk, and he looked up at her in complete surprise. Her appearance wasn't planned, and that had to be to her benefit.

"Good evening, mademoiselle. What a pleasure seeing you here." He leaned back in his chair.

"What do you want with me?" April asked.

Grignon rose and walked around the imposing desk to stand before her. The Frenchman was only a few inches taller than her, but still terrifying. She shuddered at the thought of what ran through his mind.

A sharp pain pierced her cheek, and her head twisted. Tears welled in her eyes at the humiliating slap. April touched the hot wound.

Grignon smiled. "You will speak only when asked."

She nodded, unable to find her tongue.

Grignon hooked his finger at the hall behind her, and the twins entered. "Take her up to my room."

April's stomach flip-flopped as they dragged her up the stairs. Her feet stumbled, and she would've fallen, but the burly hands held her in the air as they climbed. This couldn't be anything good, and Sam wouldn't even know she was missing yet.

Chapter 34

SAM PACKED A PHOTO of him and his sister. They weren't likely to ever return, and he didn't want to leave it behind, even if it taxed Bucky further. The minutes ticked by, but April still hadn't returned from her mystery errand in the dark. Worry filled his gut. He stepped out into the inky darkness, and his eyes adjusted to the bluish cast of the moon. Something didn't feel right. Sam disconnected Bucky from the wagon. He patted the horse on the snout and said, "I think something's wrong. Help me out here, my friend."

He trotted toward town, searching for any sign of April, and the longer he came up empty, the more frantic his searching. Sam made the same loop as before, calling out April's name in a strained whisper. She'd said she'd be back. April didn't leave.

They took her.

Sam raced back to Lloyd's. He checked himself at the door so he wouldn't gather too much attention. Fear trembled his hands.

Inside, Lloyd smiled at his customers as if they were friends, but Sam knew better. Underneath the surface Lloyd must be seething, awaiting the moment he'd close the bar for good and flee.

Lloyd whispered, "Are we set?"

"We aren't going."

Lloyd tipped his head in disbelief. "Would you make up that blasted mind of yours?"

He had.

Lloyd searched Sam's face, and he lowered his voice. "What happened?"

"April's been taken."

Lloyd ran his hand over his short curly hair. Then his face scrunched in anger and resolve. "We'll get her back. Sarah and April. We get them both back."

"I have nothing left to lose," Sam said. "Can you leave the bar?"

Lloyd glanced at his four customers. "They won't notice I'm gone, but if they figure it out, worst they can do is steal my cash and drink all the booze." Lloyd shrugged. "Considering what I face, that would be considered a win in my book."

"Arm yourself and meet me at my house."

Lloyd nodded.

Sam rushed back to his cabin and hopped into the wagon parked out front. He shuffled through the crates and found what he sought. He checked the safety on his loaded flintlock and tucked it into the waistband of his trousers. Around his waist, he strapped a utility belt with double knife pouches and filled them.

Horse hooves clomped nearby. He ducked down beneath the rail of the wagon and waited.

Lloyd arrived.

Sam leaped over the rail. "We're storming the castle. This is going to get ugly."

"Are you sure they're at the estate?"

"No, but it's a logical place to start, and if they aren't there, we can send Grignon a clear message."

Sam and Lloyd prepared for the fight of their lives. The women depended on them. The town needed them. And Sam couldn't live with himself any longer if he didn't fight.

ON THE SECOND FLOOR of Grignon's estate, April was locked in a small, musty room with a fireplace crackling. There was a wooden table and four chairs tucked under it, and no windows. She didn't know what awaited her, but this room with soundproofing and no escape reminded her of an interrogation room. They'd trapped her, like a mouse in a maze with no exit and no prize at the end. When she tried to swallow, her tongue scraped against her throat. She searched for something, anything she could defend herself with.

She wasn't going to risk getting nailed with overspray, so the pepper spray was out of the question. By the fireplace was a vertical holder of pokers. She moved across the room for them, but stopped as the heavy oak door creaked open. She rubbed her sweaty palms down her dress. A quiet whimper escaped her lips.

Grignon walked in, unaccompanied, with a smile on his face that strangely seemed genuinely friendly. To save herself from another slap, she waited for him to speak. Grignon closed the door behind himself and strode over to the fireplace, staring at the dancing flames, his hands resting in his pockets.

Pulse pounding, April didn't lower her defenses.

Finally Grignon faced her. He gestured toward the table. "Mademoiselle April, sit down. Let's have a word."

With shaking hands, she obeyed, and Grignon sat opposite her. He folded his hands together on top of the table and wrinkled his nose to adjust his glasses.

"I know what the town says of me, and since you are an outsider yourself, you must understand my position. I arrived here five years ago and opened my bank, only to realize commerce of this quaint town suffered great losses from bandits on the roads." April wondered if that were really true. "For mutual benefit, I hired several strong men, and the town has been safe and prosperous and growing since. I don't see why anyone would be upset with that."

April took a chance in breaking her silence. Her voice quavered only slightly. "When the people are not free, safety is a mirage."

He chuckled, a cold abrupt sound. "Without my efforts, the town reverts to the days of raids, rapes, and murders. If they prefer that uncivilized behavior, they're free to leave."

But what he did to Isabel made him a hypocrite. April's hand gripped the magic trinket in her dress pocket, and bravery loosened her tongue. "What are you planning to do with Sam and Lloyd?"

His cool demeanor failed him as his brows rose in surprise. Then he squinted in suspicion. "These are business matters that don't concern a woman."

Anger flared up April's chest, heating her face. "Sam and Lloyd concern me, and I won't accept anything but a straight answer."

His lips pressed thin with restraint, but after a moment, a wicked smile appeared, and that was even more terrifying. "Hanging. Both of them."

April gasped, and she blinked back tears in the dim firelight. "Why?" It was the only word her lips uttered without her voice betraying her.

"A little business, a little personal." His casualness with their lives made her want to scream.

"Common Square?" she asked.

"I knew you understand my position. Everyone will see what happens when you disobey me."

No longer would Sam be arrested and executed in his cell by some mysterious third-party, presumed to be Jaime. Now it would be a public hanging, a warning, to maintain his fear and control. April wanted to vomit, but trapped in this room with the only man who could change all this, April had one tool in her box. "Can we make a trade?"

Grignon chuckled. "You want to hang yourself instead of them? You are full of surprises."

"No. Of course not. I have a lot of money. I'll buy their lives." April held back her grimace at the wording, but she'd do whatever it took to save them. She reached into her pocket hidden in her dress and fished the wad of twenties out. If he didn't look too close...

Grignon waved away her stack. "That won't be necessary. Do you think I want money?"

April tucked her bills away. "You own the bank and you make everyone pay for your protection. Why would anyone assume differently?"

"You're a young child. I don't expect you to understand the ways of the world just yet."

"I'm not a child." April's temples pounded.

"Oh?" Grignon said with a piqued interest that frightened her even more. He stood and loomed over her before walking to the door. He put his hand on the knob and said, "I'm sending in a visitor for you. Do be careful with that mouth of yours."

Grignon left the suffocating room, and April rose at once. There had to be a way out of the room for ventilation, maybe. There were fire codes back in these days, right? She pawed at the books, searching for an anomaly. She found a hard piece of metal in a corner, disguised as a book.

The door creaked back open behind her, and she spun, trying to hide what she was doing, and her stomach sank when she recognized the black curly hair and dark eyes.

Jaime Perez.

Her hands trembled, and her eyes searched with increasing panic for a way out. He closed the door behind him and leaned against it as if expecting her to run.

"Have a seat," he said politely.

"I've had enough sitting."

He smiled. "I see Grignon was right." He sauntered over to her with dark, dead eyes. "Your mouth needs a lesson."

When he got close enough, April pushed his chest and scrambled behind the table, keeping the wood between them. "Stay away from me."

"That's exactly what I won't be doing."

She shifted from one side to the other as he attempted to move closer. It was only a few seconds before his patience ran out. Jaime lifted a chair and threw it at her. She ducked, and it crashed against the bookshelf wall, raining books on her head.

He stepped around the table, and she sidled against the wall toward the corner, away from Jaime and away from the open fire—where the pokers rested. She was paralyzed, cowering in the corner.

A sinister smirk crossed his face as he unbuckled his belt. The nightmare sound of leather sliding through loops sliced up her spine. She slid down to the floor, curled in fear, and now it wasn't Jaime's smirk before her. She only saw her father. April was twelve years old again, staring at his tomato red face scrunched in anger. She shook her head and squeezed her eyes closed. "No, no, no, no, please no. This can't be happening. No. Oh, god no. Please."

A sob escaped her lips, and she defensively covered her head with her arms.

A chuckle penetrated her defensive cocoon, the familiar chuckle of enjoyment. The belt made a snapping sound as her father prepared for whipping. His baritone voice spit words, shaming her scars and calling her a whore. April's vision became watery.

"After you meet my belt here," a tinny voice poked through her nightmare, "you'll be ready for lessons. Then just when you think it's all over, we have Greenleaf to settle."

Chapter 35

APRIL CAME TO, NOT knowing how much time had passed. She shifted ever so slightly, but her ass screamed with a searing pain that held her down. Surprisingly. She'd thought she was fully numbed. Her ears rang with an endless pealing of bells, drowning out sound. She forced her whimper to stay deep, blinking and willing her eyes to focus. April laid on the floor of a bedchamber. Two gas lamps were lit near a table and chairs, just like the other room she was in, but this one had a fluffy queen-sized bed. Voices floated above her, an angry woman's voice. She craned her neck and stared as people came into focus.

Gabriel Grignon.

And he was taking a verbal lashing...from... April blinked and squinted. Sarah?

The small girl leaned forward as her lips formed rapid words. Grignon's shoulders slumped as he accepted the scolding. He grasped Sarah on the upper arm, and the girl yanked free from his grip. She pointed a finger at him in anger and then at April on the floor. April willed the buzzing out of her ears, waiting for sound to register into words.

"I... responsible..." the bastard's voice said, defeated. "It... safety. Trust..."

"What is...?" Sarah said. The words finally took shape. "April didn't do anything to you. There is no reason for this. Don't touch me! I don't want to see your face right now. Leave. Leave us now!" April was surprised Sarah commanded Grignon, and even more surprised he obeyed. He didn't call for his guards. He didn't hit her. He didn't show any sign of anger at all. Grignon almost looked...ashamed.

When the door closed behind him, Sarah kneeled on the floor by her head. April watched the girl tuck away stray hairs from her own face and wipe betraying tears. April understood the terrible shape she was in as his prisoner.

"Untie me?" April squeaked out.

"You're not tied," Sarah said and sniffled. "Can you move at all?"

April's pulse raced with panic. They'd pinned her hands underneath her body. She focused all her energy into wriggling her fingers, but they were numb. Sarah helped dislodge her arms, and they stung and throbbed with sleep. She stiffly wriggled her fingers again, fighting through the pain, and this time they moved. After the pain subsided, she pushed herself to a seated position with Sarah helping her. Her ass immediately howled in pain, and she hefted herself onto her side.

Sarah gasped.

"What is it?" April asked.

"There's a lot of blood on your petticoat. I need to see what happened." Sarah batted at the layers of linen, and April stopped her with a quick hand.

"Best you don't see that. Help me up?" April twisted into a kneel and dragged her feet under her. She wobbled and then gained her balance with Sarah's support.

April remembered what happened. Jaime Perez and his belt, again and again. Covered in scar tissue, she resisted his strikes until a snarl of fury pierced her ears, and white pain struck her face before blackness had taken her down.

April reached for her mouth, finding her jaw tender and a seeping gash on her lower lip. She'd never felt so violated and humiliated in her life. They needed to get out of there before

Grignon returned or Jaime showed up again. April shuddered. "How do we get out of here?"

Sarah retreated to a rocking chair by a crackling fire. She put her hand on her lower belly and admired it. "I'm not leaving. If you go through that door, take a right. At the bottom of the steps you'll be out."

"What do you mean you aren't leaving? He's holding you hostage. He kidnapped you!"

"He did, but I'm not leaving."

April kneeled by her chair, unable to sit. The girl's bashful eyes cast aside. April said, "What has he done?"

A sob broke through her lips, and April held her hand. When Sarah regained her composure, she explained. "Grignon promised to take care of me, so I can't leave."

"Take care of you? Sam takes care of you."

"No. You don't understand. I can't go back."

"If you want me to leave you in the wolf's den, I'll need more convincing than that."

Sarah sniffled. "I can't go! I can't marry Jonathan Arris. I can't be with..." Her bold declaration sputtered off.

"With who?"

"It is not proper for a white woman to be with a colored man. No one will accept it. I must stay here. I've humiliated myself and my family enough."

April remembered Sarah's fits of giggles and her extra trips to the bar. "Lloyd."

Sarah nodded.

"You love him?"

She nodded again and a warm smile crossed her face.

"Then go to him. The townspeople think I'm some loony whore. It doesn't matter what they think. Sam protects me, and Lloyd will protect you. I've seen how he looks at you."

"That's not all." She patted her lower belly.

"I'm going to play dunce here. Lloyd's?" The girl nodded again, and tears glistened in her eyes. April asked, "What does Grignon have to do with it?"

"He will take care of me and the baby—if it's white."

That noble declaration didn't sit well with April. "Grignon doesn't come across as the kind of guy who cares about others."

"He loves me."

If Grignon loved Sarah and wanted her baby, why had he kidnapped her in such a dramatic way? Why didn't he just propose to her? It didn't really matter. If she won't go home now, April couldn't make her. April witnessed the power Sarah held over Grignon. The girl would be safe.

"I have to go now," April said.

Sarah pointed to the door and collected a needlepoint, tugging thread in and out of the grid. April hobbled toward the door and cracked it.

"April?"

"Hmmm?" she replied while peeking out the door.

"Do be careful. They don't want you to go."

April stuck her head out of the doorway first as a precaution. It was clear. She shut the door behind her, took a right, and then ran down the hall and down the stairs. Just as she was about to open the front door, it flew in at her, striking her in the head. She pinwheeled backward onto the hard floor. A whimper escaped her lips at the second white flash of pain in so many hours. Sprawled on the floor, she rubbed her forehead. A flintlock pistol pointed at her head.

"APRIL!" SAM SHOUTED IN happiness and scooped her up into his arms. "I'm so sorry. Are you hurt? Of course, you are. I'm getting you out of here."

April passed out in his arms. Sam carried her out to Bucky, settling her in the saddle and leaning her forward against the horse's mane for stability. The damage to her face showed how much pain she'd suffered, but she was safe now. He swiped at his tears of relief.

Thundering hooves drew up behind him.

"Lloyd, any sign of...?" Sam trailed off as something seemed wrong. He retrieved his pistol and knife and turned to find Dennis and Daniel stopped in front of him, mounted on horses. Without hesitation, Sam aimed and squeezed the trigger at Daniel's gut. The quiet twin covered his wound with a shocked hand and tilted to the side, falling onto the dirt.

Dennis jumped down with his pistol drawn, a knife in his other hand, face scrunched with fury about to be unleashed.

Sam kept his back to his horse and April, slowly drawing Dennis away from them, weapon drawn. He'd wanted this chance for a long time, but he wouldn't bother asking the scarred rapist why he'd done it. Grignon had ordered it. Whether Dennis enjoyed it or not was irrelevant.

If he shot Dennis, the larger man could easily return fire on him or April. He was at a standstill. "Dennis, she's hurt terribly. I need to get her out of here. Can we call a truce and resume this another time?"

Daniel moaned from the ground as if in protest.

Dennis snarled. "You killed my brother."

"He's very much alive," Sam countered. For the moment.

"I'm going to kill your girlfriend." Dennis's pistol swung over to April, helplessly exposed and resting on Bucky. Sam dove for Dennis's meaty arm and pushed it away as the trigger fired.

Sam regained his footing and punched his knife upward into the man's chest. Dennis held Sam's gaze with calm understanding. It was over. They stood chest to chest, and Sam relaxed his grip on the fatal weapon.

"For Isabel," Sam said. "And far less than you deserve."

A cough brought up a trickle of blood from Dennis's mouth. His voice was wet. "When we meet again, it will be a fair fight."

"You don't know what fair is."

"True." The corner of his devious mouth curved. Dennis's knife-wielding hand arced through the air, aimed at Sam's throat.

Sam abandoned his knife, still plunged into Dennis's chest, and dodged the swing.

Dennis grunted. He removed Sam's knife and lifted them both, intending to dual-wield. In seconds, Dennis fell to the ground like a bag of sand. His face relaxed as the light left his already dead eyes. Sam resisted the urge to spit on his body. He kicked dirt on him, though. The bastard deserved that much.

"Sam!" Lloyd's rough voice floated over.

"Lloyd, where are you?"

Sam collected his discarded knife and found Lloyd on his knees in the grass. Sam's stomach sank in worry and his hands shook. Sam grasped his friend's arm and lifted him to his feet. "Are you all right?"

"I was better a minute ago. Next time watch where the asshole is aiming."

Sam chuckled in relief. A sense of humor ruled out dying. He hoped anyway. "Where did he get you?"

"Lower leg. It's not worrisome, but I can't put weight on it."

Sam helped Lloyd climb Dennis's horse. That arsehole won't be needing it anymore. After Lloyd was secured and ready to ride home, Sam launched himself up onto Bucky and leaned April against his chest.

"Both twins?" Lloyd said, assessing the corpses on the ground.

"They won't be causing any more trouble."

"Good. How are you doing?"

Sam didn't have time to think about it. But only one word came to mind. "Relieved. I'm glad I can put all that behind me."

"Terrible thing he did to your—"

"Aye," Sam interrupted. "I'm glad I can put all that behind me," he repeated and shot Lloyd a warning glare.

"Understood. Now what?"

Sam spurred Bucky to walk home carefully, and April moaned. Sam held her tight, stroking her hair. "We have some wounds to address. After we recover, we're hunting down Sarah."

"I've got my own to deal with. I'll see you later." Lloyd spurred off at a faster pace, headed for home.

Sam continued at their slower pace to keep the ride as comfortable for April as possible. Her soft murmurs worried him, and he felt terrible. Some of her pain was his own fault for smashing in the front door. He would do whatever it took to make it up to her.

Again.

Chapter 36

April didn't want to wake up and face the reality of last night, but eventually the piercing pain broke through the pile of cozy blankets. She awoke in Sam's house, her pounding head and throbbing lip secondary to the pain on her chewed ass cheeks. Sam peered over her, concern knitting his brows. She tried to sit up, to stand up, but with a gentle press to her chest, she gave up. Her whole body weight pressed against her wounds.

"Good morning. How are you feeling?" Sam asked.

"I've been better," she said, not wanting to worry him further.

"I cleaned up what I could, but I don't know what else to do. I think you're going to have scarring here." His thumb brushed near her lip. "Drink some water. I'll help you hold it." Sam held a glass near her lips.

April drank it down. "I need to roll over. My backside hurts."

Sam helped her turn onto her belly, and the shifting of her dress showed streaks of red in places it didn't belong. Sam frowned. "May I?" he asked permission to inspect more wounds.

"Tell me it looks better than it feels."

Sam lifted and rolled the layers of linen away from her backside, and a fresh sting from cool air exposure streaked up through her skin. She sucked in a breath and held it. Sam gently peeled stuck layers from her skin and inspected her. He blinked. His voice betrayed his composure, "It's bad."

"What does it look like? Red, purple, or greenish black?"

He balled his hands and released them. "Red, brown and lots of pink angry lines."

"I can deal with that. Would you mind washing the wounds?"

Sam retrieved the wash basin and a clean cloth. He stopped with the cloth dangling in the air, staring at her mutilated flesh.

"Now's not the time to be prudish. It needs to be cleaned or it'll get infected."

"Aye." He gulped. Sam sponge bathed her butt, dripping the water and patting it clean, until only smooth skin marred by gaping cuts and fresh red lines remained. "These wounds need stitches. I don't know how to do it, and I'm guessing you can't do it yourself."

She chuckled and winced from the pain. "Any bourbon left?"

Sam collected the bottle, opened it, and leaned it over her mangled flesh, hesitating.

April darted out a hand to stop him. "Me first."

Sam passed her the bottle, and she slammed down several generous gulps of the burning liquid before returning it to him. She fisted her hands into the couch cushions and took a few deep breaths. "Go ahead," she ground out through gritted teeth.

Liquid hit her skin, worse than the burns of the leather belt snapping against her flesh. April stifled a scream, but some escaped anyway. Her body trembled.

He stopped.

"Keep going. It has to be disinfected."

Sam poured again, and she saw her pain reflected in his face. He was forcing himself to continue.

April squeezed her eyes closed, the facial cuts throbbing under the strain.

Sam set the bottle down and retrieved the supplies she'd bought for his cheek wound. He delicately threaded the needle, and it impressed her. "How did you learn to do that?"

Sam smiled. "Sarah likes needlepoint. I may have watched once. Don't tell her."

Sarah.

April needed to tell him, but she'd wait until he finished sewing her ass. "It's like needlepoint. Use those scissors there for grip. Grasp the needle and poke it through about a quarter inch from the open edge. Curve it to about a quarter inch on the other side and pull the two sides together. Tie a knot, cut, repeat. If too much blood wells up to see, pat it clear."

Sam nodded, but his face turned a few shades of green. Funny, that was her not so long ago. Now talking about it was like nothing, doing it didn't seem to bother her either, and like her spirit, her stomach seemed to have strengthened. A sharp spearing pain told her that Sam had begun work on her exposed wounds.

She grasped the bottle of liquid painkiller and took a few more swallows. Sam stitched her through two waves of endorphins that temporarily eased the pain. Her whole body trembled with exhaustion. Time ticked by and she was getting concerned. "Almost..." She grunted through the next poke. "Done?"

"Just one more and I think you'll be set.

"How many stitches? Just curious."

"Fifty-seven. And starting fifty-eight. Your thread spool here is almost gone. Want to talk about it?"

"I can pick up more later."

"Not that."

"Then no, I don't."

Sam finished the last suture, and he cut the ends with the scissors. How was she going to sit for the next two weeks? He helped her stand and remove the soiled garment. She stood before him, half naked, and he looked her over clinically as if assessing more damage. Warmth bloomed in her chest with his caring attention. He returned to her with her pink dress. April's blood ran cold. "Why this?"

He helped her into her bridesmaid dress. "I thought this would be more comfortable against your skin."

"Right," she said, suspicious of his intentions. She dressed with his assistance, doubting the comfort of her 'scandalous' dress, and now she felt foreign. April picked up her stained dress and shifted her pocket contents—namely the cash, magic trinket, and Swiss army knife. The pepper spray was about useless. She dropped the ruined dress back to the floor.

Sam stood before her, staring at her lips. He frowned. "I want to kiss you, but I don't want to hurt you."

She wobbled from the bourbon and fading endorphins, making her dizzy and unstable. "I need to tell you something, but I think you should sit."

He sat down on the couch, and she duck-walked over to the table and folded over it, so her butt was free from additional pain and her face was level with his. "Sarah was there."

Sam jumped to his feet. "You stay here. I'm going to get her before it's too late for her to marry Arris."

"Why would it be too late?"

"She's getting too old to be single. If I can't close this deal with Arris, she'll be single forever, and she'll need to find a job or enter an asylum for mental illness."

Irritation flared through her exhaustion. "If she's too old to be single as a teenager, how old do you think I am?"

Sam spun to face her. He searched her with a look that meant he was afraid to answer, but he did anyway. "Twenty?"

"I'm twenty-five. Where I come from, people of all ages, even in their seventies and nineties have gotten married, or mostly, remarried. Losing that contract doesn't make her disposable, and it's insulting to think so. There's nothing wrong with getting a job. I have one back home. And being single is not an illness. Some might even say it's smart. You can add that to your list too."

Sam didn't say anything for a while. He just stared at her, and his face changed as if she were a stranger to him.

April didn't like it. Something wasn't right. "What?"

"Things here are different than what you're used to. Society isn't going to change because you say so. I have to get her."

"No," April said.

Sam crossed to the front door, ignoring her request.

April added, "Sarah's there voluntarily. She won't leave."

Anger reddened his face. "That's preposterous. He's keeping her prisoner."

"You don't understand."

Sam checked his weapons in his belt.

April needed to stop him now before he got himself killed. "She's pregnant."

Sam froze with a pistol in his hand.

"She's carrying Lloyd's child. They're in love, but Grignon is protecting her from the townspeople and from her contract. He's going to take care of it."

Sam dropped back onto the couch and put his face in his hands, pale, defeated. "Why?"

"Grignon loves her."

"Does Lloyd know? He mustn't. He would've told me. Why didn't they tell me they wanted to be together?"

April attempted a shrug while leaning over the table, but she felt like a flopping fish. "Sarah told me it was because of the townspeople's views...of Lloyd. Because he's—"

"Colored," Sam finished.

It was ridiculous that this was even an issue in the first place, but April just got a stinging reminder of the time she was in. Besides, there were backwards people in her current year who still believed the same.

Sam rose and paced around the living room while April lay helplessly. She was worried he would do something stupid.

SAM MADE FISTS, RELAXED them, ran his hands through his hair, grunted in frustration, only to return to making fists again. He didn't know how to fix the problem. His sister and Lloyd loved each other and had a baby on the way, which was wonderful. He wanted to be an uncle. But they couldn't be together. He was afraid of what awaited both Sarah and Lloyd if the truth escaped. Grignon, that rotten bastard, loved his sister, which was a horrific thought. And April here was strong, brave, courteous in the face of pure pain, and yet with her wounds closed, there was no guarantee she'd live through it.

The world was unjust.

Sam needed to tell Lloyd. Plus, he'd been shot and likely needed tending as well. Lloyd knew as much about doctoring as Sam did, which was nil.

"I'll be right back. I'm going to get Lloyd," Sam announced as he ended his pacing. April started to protest, but he reassured her, "I'm bringing him here. They shot him last night."

"What? Oh no!"

Sam mounted Bucky, loaded with weapons, and galloped to Lloyd's bar, dismounting in a quick leap. The establishment was closed to business at this hour, so he took the back steps two at a time to the second floor quarters and pounded on the door. "Lloyd! It's me. I'm coming in."

Lloyd didn't respond, so Sam jiggled the knob, found it locked, and smashed in the door with a swift kick. The place was neat and clean, mostly packed. In the kitchen Sam found blood—a lot of blood—and Lloyd draped over the lip of a washbasin, unconscious. Sam carefully stepped around the slippery pool and woke him. "Lloyd!"

His friend shifted with grogginess.

Sam took a thin towel and tied it tight around his leg wound. "Let's get you out of here. Come on up. There you go."

Sam helped Lloyd hobble down the stairs and up on the horse, hoping April could help.

He burst through the front door, and April gasped when she saw them. She still leaned over the table. "Bring him here."

Sam helped Lloyd sit at the kitchen table and propped his leg up by April's face. She grimaced. "Bring my supplies."

Sam brought her a handful of items and placed them within reach. Then he filled the wash basin with clean water from the hand pump. While April untied the towel, Sam retrieved his bottle of bourbon. He had Lloyd drink plenty to prepare him, but the man was barely conscious as it was

April removed the make-shift bandage, and the gunshot wound was still seeping blood.

"I have to get the bullet out to close it. Scissors." She held out her hand and Sam placed them in her palm. "This is going to hurt a lot, Lloyd. Bite down on something and hold tight."

Sam pressed a clean towel between his teeth. His friend's eyelids fluttered, teetering on consciousness. April used the closed scissors to probe the hole and Lloyd, even in his delirious state, clenched with pain.

"The bullet entered just to the left of his shin, where there isn't much muscle damage, and I don't see bone splinters." April popped out the round, and it thumped to the table, a fresh stream of blood following. She poured more liquor onto it, and Lloyd's body turned limp.

April stitched him up as quickly as possible, fingers slipping in the blood, sweat forming on her forehead. By the time she finished, she looked like she'd killed him. Blood splattered all over the table, dripping onto the floor, covering her shirt, hands, and face. The scent of coppery blood, of death, hung like a cloud in the house. But finally, the job was finished, and the bleeding stopped.

"He needs to keep that leg up in the air. He lost a lot of blood. When he comes to, give him plenty of water, no more alcohol," April said, words tinged with exhaustion and defeat. "There's nothing more I can do." She stood, and her face twisted with horror at her pink dress.

"I'll get that cleaned," Sam said. He moved Lloyd to the couch and shifted his body to prop his leg up on the armrest.

April took a few steps toward her patient but winced and folded herself back over the table.

"I'm sure he'll be fine." Sam walked around April, and red stripes soaked through her dress. "But you're not." He sighed in defeat. She needed to go home to get proper care. Their medical capabilities weren't good enough now.

Sam's chest constricted at his thoughts. He'd dressed her in her pink dress after seeing the wounds, because he'd feared it would come to this. "April," he said and sat on the chair by her face. He folded her hand in his. "I need you to go home."

She smiled. "I am home, silly."

His stomach fluttered in guilt, and his shoulders felt so much heavier suddenly. "No." He paused and remembered their argument. She wasn't married, but she was in love. "I mean your real home...with Levi."

"What are you saying?"

"I..." Sam trailed off. It would be selfish of him to keep her here. She had a life. She belonged there. He'd hoped to change her mind about leaving, but she had to go anyway. "You need more medical care than I can do for you. Your stitches are bleeding. Levi needs you. Your brother needs you."

Her face showed the hurt from his words. Her split lip quavered, and she blinked. It cut him up inside.

"That is my decision to make. I'm staying..." her voice broke. "I..." A sob escaped her lips.

Sam held back his own tears.

"I can't leave you. I can't." April set her face down on the table and sobbed.

The pearl necklace was still around her throat, and he cast his eyes down. It killed him to see her hurting so much. The easiest way for her was to make her angry. He didn't want to lie to her, but if she stayed, she would die here. "The truth is, that pearl necklace is filled with horrible memories, and since you were leaving, you could take it with you. Conveniently, both my problems were solved at once. The time has come. I want you to leave."

She cried. "I know you don't mean that."

He crossed his arms with his jaw set and didn't answer. A piece of him shattered.

How could he want her to leave? Like Sarah, was she tainted by Grignon now—a non-marriable wench?

Sam couldn't mean what he said about his mother's necklace...unless it wasn't his mother's.

Or was he upset about the mess she'd made of his life? Lloyd was shot and his sister was gone.

Perhaps it was all three, and all of it was her fault.

Sam finally said, "I needed you to save Lloyd, just as you prophesized. Job done, now you go."

"What about you? It was two good men."

Sam wouldn't look at her. She followed his gaze to Lloyd, passed out on the couch. April sniffled and wiped her nose on the back of her hand.

He didn't answer.

"Just like that?" she asked in disbelief, a curl of anger forming in the pit of her stomach.

He seemed like he didn't care, but he wouldn't meet her eyes.

April stood and winced. Her knees wobbled, and her butt was fiery hot beneath her blood-soaked pink dress. April previously had wounds just like these, but this was much worse. Perhaps he was only saying these terrible things to convince her she needed real help. She couldn't leave him though. A piece of her belonged here, and she refused to abandon what had become hers. With quavering resolve she said, "Make me."

They exchanged glances. Pain lurked behind his eyes. Sam stood and opened the front door, whistling for Bucky. He returned and scooped her up into his arms. His chest was warm, his heart pounded like mad, but he was back to refusing eye contact. She was in immeasurable pain—pain that bourbon couldn't fix.

Gently but firmly, he hoisted her up onto the horse, leaning her forward onto Bucky's nape so her stitches didn't contact the saddle. April sobbed—from injury and heartbreak. April was supposed to marry Levi, but she was sent here on a mission for Kiko to give her time to process, and what did April stupidly do? Fell for the man she was supposed to save from execution. If Kiko intended Sam to be April's 'match'—well, Kiko was wrong, and April was done doing favors for friends.

April smeared her tears into Bucky's rough mane.

Sam closed the front door and mounted behind her. "Where do you come in from?" he asked coldly.

She pointed to the tall grassy area southeast of town, and the horse walked slowly along the route. Sam's hands held her hips steady, but they weren't comforting. Her raw flesh screamed with each shifting step of the horse.

April reminisced about each business as they passed by. Porter's General Store—he had always been nice to her even if many others weren't. Grignon's bank was where they'd pretended to be newly engaged. Ironically, that was a happy place for her, even if it was fake. Max's restaurant—the food was wonderful, and she'd had the best date ever. Ross at Bridgeport Chemist was pleasant.

Perez's Couture Clothing and Marisol. Marisol was sweet to her, helping instead of judging.

Then she thought of Jaime Perez. April shuddered. Perhaps it was good she was leaving after all. She didn't know how she would handle ever seeing him again. His face would be etched on her eyelids every night.

Townspeople saw her crying with Sam, and they stepped out to watch, concern on their faces. Did they care or was this more gossip fodder? It didn't matter anymore.

They reached the grassy area. "Stop here." Her voice was small.

Sam hopped down and gently lifted her by the hips until her feet planted on solid ground. Now her tears were more of the physical pain than emotional. Sam still wouldn't look at her.

April slid her fingers along the sticky pearls at her throat. His eyes tracked her movements and glanced away.

She wouldn't stay where she wasn't wanted—humiliated and broken. Besides, she had her brother to return to, and Mathew gave her strength. And April still had her dignity.

April turned away from Sam without another word, without a kiss or a hug or even a goodbye. It was easier that way, she supposed. She trudged through the tall grasses to a safe area from her living room. Pain slashed her like a fresh whip with every shift of movement, and her knees threatened to fail her. She found the little magic trinket in her pocket, opened the cover, and didn't hesitate to press the red button.

Chapter 37
Present Day, Green Bay, Wisconsin

THE AIR WAS COOL, the streets quiet, and streetlights flickered off one by one as dawn broke over the city. April teetered on the front curb, lost her balance, and fell onto her hip on the concrete. Her teeth clacked with the impact, and her breath ripped from her lungs. Her wounds were much worse than she realized. The emergency room was inevitable. April rose carefully and climbed the steps into her house.

"Kiko?" April asked. After doing her roommate a big fat favor, she could at least offer her a ride.

But she wasn't home. As usual.

April's phone sat on the end table where she'd left it, and she scrolled through her contacts and pressed send.

She wasn't calling an ambulance. Not with her insurance.

"Hello?" The familiar peppy voice made her heart skip with comfort. She'd missed Mathew so much.

"I need a ride to the ER. It's not too early, I hope?"

"Of course not. Be right there."

April hung up and waddled to the bathroom so grateful and relieved to see a clean flushing toilet. Plumbing was a marvelous miracle, and one she'd never take for granted again. She washed her hands and face in the sink and her mouth dropped open at her appearance in the mirror. She looked like she'd spent several months roughing it in the backwoods and then slaughtered someone before falling down a mountain.

April stepped into her closet and changed out of the dress stained in her and Lloyd's blood. She shimmied into comfortable sweatpants and almost felt clean. Shower would have to wait.

She collected her purse and placed Kiko's magic trinket inside it for safekeeping.

A knock at the door sent April moving as fast as possible. She opened it wide, and Mathew assessed her critically. "What happened? Do I need to take you to the police station after?"

"No. Nothing like that. It was an accident, really." April didn't want to think of the pain she'd manage during the car ride to the hospital, but she reminded herself that in this century there were painkillers. Good ones.

Her big brother helped her down the stairs with her arm slung over his shoulder, and she limped as little as possible. He helped her into the passenger seat, and she winced and cried out. Mathew's panicked gasp and flailing hands had her comforting him. "It's just a wound. I'm going to be fine, really."

A look of skepticism passed over his features, but worry kicked him into action. He closed her door, and sunk into the driver's seat, quickly buckling in next to her. "I want to say, 'Just like old times, hey?' but it just doesn't feel right."

"Yet, you said it anyway."

"You've spent too much time in the ER. I should've invested in the company that makes saline bags. Could've had a bigger nest egg in my measly SEP IRA by now."

"At least you have something," April said. "My employer doesn't offer a retirement account, and it's my insurance causing me to call my boss instead of an ambulance." April's pain justified the dig.

Mathew's cheeks pinked, and he said, "It's not feasible with only two employees. Sorry."

"Yeah, well, you can buy me ramen noodles when we're in our eighties."

"No way. My little sis will not be clinging to my shirttails for the next sixty years. I love you, kid, but eventually I will kick you out of the nest."

April had grown years in just the last few weeks. As much as she didn't need Mathew's help, she still wanted to know he'd be there for her. He was her only family. "Is that a promise?"

A smile popped onto his lips. "Nah. I'll always help you out, but I won't be wiping your ass. You'll have to cover that yourself."

"Deal."

Mathew took a corner, and April noticed the street name. She shouted in recognition, "Grignon!"

"What?"

"Nothing. Uh, the answer to a Jeopardy question that was bugging me." She knew the name sounded familiar. What did he do to earn a street name? April remembered the newspaper article where he'd funded a library. That was probably it.

April smiled through the searing pain on her backside and woke her phone screen. Levi's messages still waited. She checked the current date on her home screen. She had only left for eight hours. April blew out a breath.

"Everything okay over there?" Mathew asked.

"Yeah. Just Levi." April pressed on the messenger icon, and her vision turned wavy all on its own while she read them.

 "I'm sorry for putting you on the spot."
 "I take all the blame."
 "Please forgive me for being a moron."
 "You looked great tonight."
 "We can wait if you need more time."
 "I love you."

She covered her mouth with her hand. Levi still wanted her, but she'd call him later. First, she needed to fabricate a believable story for what Jaime had done to her.

Mathew pulled the car into the patient unloading area and a stretcher came out with two medics. Mathew helped her out of the car, and she told them she needed to be face down. They saw her rear end and exchanged surprised glances. She must've bled through her sweatpants. Obliging her request, they lowered the back rest flat.

"Sorry about your seat," she said to Mathew as they wheeled her inside, knowing his cloth interior would be stained as well.

"Don't worry about it. I'm going to park the car, and I'll be waiting for you like usual," Mathew said.

Behind a curtain, the medics cut away her sweatpants with scissors. One medic even whistled his surprise. It hurts like hell. Let's take a bit longer to push the morphine, shall we? April thought.

"Where did you have this done?" the first medic asked.

"I needed a field dressing. He wasn't trained, and I talked him through it," April said.

"It's not pretty but not too bad either. Unfortunately, we have to do it over. This thread isn't ideal."

They started an IV line on her inner elbow and hung a bag of antibiotics. The first medic pushed a syringe of morphine into her line, and within moments, the pain drifted off. She floated on the edge of an abyss, marveling at the view, but unable to enjoy it. Cold liquid drizzled over her butt, scissors snipped, and the medics continued to manipulate her tissue. She was painlessly poked and tugged as they properly stitched up her broken ass.

She laughed.

The first medic asked, "Everything all right over there?"

The second one said to the first, "Side effects."

The first medic nodded.

They covered her with gauze and surgical tape, securing it around each thigh and her hips.

The second medic said to April, "Still doing okay?"

She felt like she was wearing an ass corset. She laughed again.

"I'll take that as a 'yes,'" he continued. "Go easy on the backside for a few days, okay? In two weeks, you can come back to have them removed."

The first medic said, "We're all done. When your bag's complete you can go. I'm sending in someone for you to talk to."

April nodded in understanding.

Moments later a woman in scrubs approached. "I don't mean to be intrusive, but your wounds are suspicious." She glanced at April's rear end, her lip, and then her eye. "Would you like a rape kit performed? I would ask you a series of questions and then do a thorough examination."

"No. Nothing like that happened, and I was awake the entire time."

"That's your choice. I do need to ask you a few questions. All your answers are confidential. This conversation won't be discussed with your significant other, nor any family member, without your consent. Okay?"

April's loopiness didn't care what the nurse said, as long as the morphine held out. She nodded.

"Many people experience problems in intimate relationships that can cause health problems. So we ask all patients: Are you in a relationship with someone who has hurt you today?"

April shook her head.

The nurse frowned. "Do you know who did this to you?"

April shook her head again. No use being honest here.

"I'm concerned about how you got these injuries. Do you mind if I photograph them?"

"No, thanks."

"Would you like us to call the police for you?"

"That's not necessary." April didn't know she'd get the option. So far, pleading the fifth worked in her favor.

The nurse looked disappointed, and April understood why. But she didn't want to waste resources or lose her privacy on the invasive examination and photographing with no recourse against a man who died over a hundred years ago.

Shortly thereafter she was discharged with a pamphlet about a crisis hotline, and with a script for pain pills in hand, she found Mathew in the waiting room. She was grateful to see him, although it brought back old memories she didn't care to have. Mathew used to wait for her after her trips to the ER as a kid. Still, having someone who cared made her feel a little stronger. She hobbled into his arms, and he squeezed her.

His arms weren't Sam's. Tears sprung to her eyes when she realized she wanted Sam's arms more than Mathew's.

"Thank you," she whispered into his ear.

"How about we make this the last trip, okay?" He released her and wiped her tears with his thumbs. Mathew drove them in silence to the pharmacy. The morphine made the ride better this time.

Mathew broke the silence. "Can I ask you something?"

April was still happy-buzzed, so she smiled and said, "Sure, Matty, dude. What's ticking in your mind?"

"Did Levi hurt you?"

"What?" April's knee-jerk reaction startled Mathew.

"I won't tell anyone. Just level with me."

"No." April sobered quickly with Jaime's snarling face floating in her view. "He didn't. Levi wouldn't harm a fly. A mosquito—absolutely—but not a fly. I don't want to talk about it."

"Did you visit Dad?"

April's eyes widened like saucers. The imagery of Dad's face melding over Jaime's while he whipped her made her stomach twist. She held her breath and watched the road.

"You'll tell me when you're ready though? I can't stand that someone did this to you."

"I'll tell you everything when I'm ready, I swear." If she avoided coming forward with the story, Mathew would continue asking. What the hell was she going to tell him? Maybe she could have Kiko explain everything, and then April could just drop Jaime's name meaninglessly.

He shot her a sad smile, and they stopped at the twenty-four-hour pharmacy for pain pills and returned to her house. They said their goodbyes, and April crashed on her soft bed. She'd missed her comfortable bed so much, and the drugs gave her a wonderful sleep. Without them, she would've been awake for hours.

BY LATE MORNING, APRIL'S butchered body was thankful for the rest, but she wasn't chancing her luck. A quick swallow downed the prescribed pain pills on schedule. It was deadline time for Levi. She thought she knew exactly what she would tell him. But now, being back home grounded in reality, it wasn't so clear.

Levi replied to her text, saying he'd be there in an hour. Her stomach quavered with nerves, and her heart rattled faster as each minute ticked by. She kept checking her phone to see if he sent another message, hoping he would delay the inevitable conversation.

No messages.

It was strange Kiko didn't come home today, but after what April just survived, not much seemed weird anymore. She doused her sugar pile with a cup of fresh brewed coffee for that pick-me-up she needed. A deep swallow sparked pain in her lip. "Oh, no!"

April set down her mug and dashed to the bathroom to attempt a makeup application convincing enough that he wouldn't see her purple eye or split lip. A thick wool skirt and the pain pills would have to do for her new ass stripes.

If she ever got a chance to get revenge on Jaime, she'd enjoy every second, assuming someone held him down for her. She didn't want to go toe-to-toe with him directly. He'd win.

A swipe of lipstick matched the angry red of the vertical line on her lip. The doorbell rang as she pressed her lips against a square of toilet paper and tossed it into the bowl. She answered the door with a nervous smile.

Levi stood in his usual suit, but his smile was forced, and his hands were restless. She hadn't seen him like this before, and it made her heart break. Did he even get any sleep? She broke his heart last night by turning down his proposal twice, but it felt so long ago for her.

She waved him in, and there was a cordial distance between them, an invisible void.

Levi sat on the couch and fidgeted like it were a first date. But he already knew every inch of her skin, he'd strewn his clothes on her floors, and they'd shared Chinese at her kitchen table. It was as if he were a stranger here.

"Coffee? Water?" she offered.

"Water would be great." His knee bounced.

She took a deep breath and hoped the pain pills allowed her to pretend to be normal. She slowly sat next to him, feeling a small sting, and handed off the glass.

"Thank you," he said, took a sip, and set it on the coffee table. "Where did you get that?" He pointed at her pearl necklace. She forgot she still wore it. It felt so natural to have it on.

The truth would be crazy, and that was not a conversation for today. "It was my mother's. I just found it."

An awkward silence followed. This was the moment. The actual, one-and-only moment. What she told Levi now would decide her future forever. "I—" they both said at the same time. Then they both smiled.

"You first," Levi said.

The still air suffocated her. She wanted to get up and pace, but she didn't want to alarm him—or stress her stitches. Why couldn't she just answer him and get it over with? She was terrified—that Levi wouldn't accept her answer.

"Let's take a walk," she said and grabbed her purse.

Levi stood. "Sounds like a great idea."

She wasn't the only one feeling stifled. They walked down the street, very slowly. Both kept their hands to themselves. It was a full block before either said anything. April decided she wanted food. Any delay was better than facing the inevitable. There was only one man for her, and she knew which, as Kiko said, he was The One. But there was still a problem. "Hungry?" she asked.

"Sure."

They walked down the sidewalk to a small sub shop. He held the door open, and she thanked him. Why was she acting like this was their first date too? The awkwardness was so thick she could cut it with a knife, throw it against the wall, and watch it drag slime down to the floor.

The fresh baked bread and chocolate chip cookies made her stomach growl. An elderly couple ate in comfortable peace, as if they'd done this hundreds of times and knew everything there was to know about each other and had no reason to talk. They smiled and chewed. April envied their tranquility.

She and Levi both ordered, and she let Levi pay, swallowing back the guilt. Levi collected the bags of sandwiches.

April sat at the table farthest from the other guests and winced from the breakthrough pain. Hopefully she wouldn't bleed through the thick wool. Levi passed her whichever sandwich was hers, and she bit into the crispy yet zippy sandwich. She blocked a satisfying moan from escaping her lips. April missed this.

"You aren't acting normally. Can we talk about this?" Levi asked.

April didn't answer. She didn't want to talk; she wanted to eat. Bite after bite, she polished off her sandwich in record time.

"We need to talk about last night," he pressed.

A jolt of nerves disrupted her digestion, but she kept calm. "Sure. No better place," April said with a hint of sarcasm, which Levi didn't pick up on. He never did.

"I saw you got my messages. I figured out you don't like Purely Plaid, and I'm sorry for making you go so many times. I just really like my two favorite things together. I see now that I should savor them separately. So I will never ask you to see one of their concerts again."

April's pulse pounded in her ears. She struggled to process his words. Her mind raced with all the 'what if's and 'should I's.

"So, with that settled, I would like to ask—Would you marry me at some point in the future, under your own terms, with the wedding of your own dreams?" He slipped the velvety black box out of his sport coat and opened it again.

April expected just about anything, but certainly not that. She stood up in a panic, unable to breathe. She shook her hands in front of her, trying to clear her head. Levi looked at her with reserved happiness. He genuinely wanted to marry her.

"We still didn't discuss our future," April said.

"Yeah, we did." He closed the box and set it on his knee. "Four kids, we live in my house, and we move to Florida eventually. Remember, in the car last night?"

"No. You told me what you wanted, and you didn't wait to hear what I wanted."

Levi's smile faded. "Fair enough. We'll hash it out right here. Sit."
"I'd rather stand."
Levi stood to match her. "How many kids do you want?"

"I…" April had never thought about it, but four sounded terrifying. "I don't know."

"Where do you want to live? I don't want to live in your rental house. I'm not big on roommates, so, my house. Agreed?"

She had been to his house many times. It was sterile white with glass and metal accents, clean and fresh. It wasn't bad or anything, but it also never seemed like home.

"How about we buy a different house together?" April suggested.

"That's ridiculous. Why would I spend all that money on closing costs and agents' fees and moving expenses when I already have a nice home we can share?"

Why didn't she see all this before?

Levi added, "And that leaves Florida. We have to go there after I get a few years of experience. I mean, my extended family is there, and they can help with the kids."

April's vision sparkled. He wanted her to move across the country to people she'd never met to help with kids she didn't have and away from the only family she had. "I can't, Levi. I just can't." It was a lot easier to say than she thought it would be. She loved Sam. He was the only one for her, even if she couldn't have him. She'd rather be alone than settle. Both she and Levi deserved that.

"You're sure?" he asked.

April nodded and gave it one last fair chance. If they could fix their disagreements, that was a different story. "How about we do couple's counseling?"

Levi waved a dismissive hand. "I don't need therapy. How could you even suggest that?" He stuffed the box back into his sport coat and placed a hand on her shoulder in kindness. "I wish you well then." He left the sub shop and walked with purpose back to his car parked down the block.

April gave him a fair opportunity to compromise, but he refused, and April didn't regret it. She slurped down his remaining drink, thoughts drifting to Sam. She saved him and Lloyd, but yet, they were still dead now. If she ported back in time to where he was at this moment, was he working in the blacksmith shop? Kidnapping Sarah back? Traveling the countryside with Lloyd? Thinking about her? Tears welled in her eyes at the thought that he'd forgotten her already, and she tossed her and Levi's garbage into the trash.

She gave Levi a few more moments' head start before venturing back home at a slow waddle.

Chapter 38

MATHEW STOPPED BY HER house with cheesecake, a chocolate bar, and a bag of greasy fast food. All the best things in the world—that were edible, anyway. "Thank you so much. You are a lifesaver. Why hasn't some woman stolen you already?"

He passed her the goods with a prideful smile, and she chowed down on the hamburger and fries first.

"How's your ass?"

She snorted. Somehow, she didn't think she'd ever live down the ass jokes, once the seriousness of it had passed.

"Better with drugs," she admitted, and bit off another generous mouthful. Mathew studied her, and she cleared her throat in discomfort. "What?"

"I thought you'd be more upset."

"Starving. Upset later," April said between bites.

"Did you talk to Levi yet?"

"It's over," April said. She took another bite as Mathew watched her, trying to read her. "I turned him down."

"Not that it's any of my business, but can I ask why?"

"He just wasn't the one, I guess. It didn't feel right."

April finished the bag of grease and cracked the plastic lid on the cheesecake. She stabbed her fork right into it and licked it clean. She groaned in ecstasy. "This is so good."

"I'm glad you chose what you wanted." Mathew paused. "I just want you to be happy. That's all."

April bit off another mouthful and said, "It was my choice, and I made it." She hoped he would drop the subject. She didn't want to talk about turning down the life she could've had—even if it was mediocre. She swallowed. "And you'll be pleased to learn I'm going to re-enroll in nursing." Inspired by Sam and Lloyd's injuries. April waited for her big brother to praise her.

He didn't.

"You shouldn't pick something just because Mom did it, or because I suggested it, or because Levi said you should. I want you to pick something you want, okay? That's all. Don't you get it? I want you to do what makes you happy."

Nursing would be practical, and now that she could handle blood, there were no barriers for her to finish. Is nursing what she wanted to do? Not really, but it meant a steady paycheck and she could handle it now. She'd rather open a portrait studio and sell art, but everyone knew how great of a life that would be. Plus, she didn't have the capital and didn't want to be saddled with debt for a chance at a dream job. Instead she said, "It makes me happy, and I can do it."

"The problem is if you will."

Ouch. That was enough for her today. "Thanks for the food, Matty, but I would like some time alone. I have a shift tomorrow and all that."

Mathew stood, displeased. He wasn't her parent; he couldn't tell her what to do. April would make her own decisions for her own life, starting with finishing nursing school while opening an online art studio—a nice blend of paycheck and happiness. The plans had perked her up. She smiled. "I'll be fine. Don't worry about me."

"I do worry, and that's what worries me."

She laughed.

His seriousness faded, and he laughed too. "I'll head out then. Watching you pig out is gross, anyway. See you tomorrow."

"See ya." She waved with her fork in hand and smiled with a mouthful.

Mathew let himself out.

She had plans that fooled him, and tomorrow she would smile for the public.

But it wasn't what she really wanted.

Eventually, she'd stop dwelling on what she couldn't have.

Chapter 39
1852 Bridgeport, Wisconsin

SAM UNLOADED THE CRATES from the wagon and slowly unpacked—trying to return his life back to normal—as normal as could be with Sarah gone. The house felt empty. His heart felt empty. Sam had sent April away for her own good, and he felt like a selfish arsehole for regretting it, but keeping her wasn't possible.

The one person he loved most, his sister, was in the hands of her own choosing, and the only woman he'd ever truly been in love with, was in love with someone named Levi. *That lucky bastard better appreciate her.* If Grignon wanted revenge for the twins, Sam and Lloyd could take a stand here, and if they fell, someone else could clean up the mess. Sam had nothing left to fight for. In the meantime, he needed clothes and kitchenware.

Sarah had managed all the domestic chores, as was a woman's duty—or so he was raised to believe. As he replaced the pots and pans in the cabinets, he was grateful April had taught him to cook, even if only a few things. Because with both women gone, he had to fend for himself. Even if he hadn't thought of it before, he was relieved he didn't require a wife immediately to care for the homestead. If Sam couldn't have April, he was better off alone. He'd never be a great husband to anyone else. He'd always be settling and no woman deserved that.

Except for empty crates and packaging materials, his house looked just as it had before. But everywhere he looked, memories of April squeezed his heart.

Sam dropped onto his couch and chugged a few deep swallows of his bourbon, but it didn't help. Sam placed it back on the shelf, just in case new injuries needed—what had she called it?—disinfecting?

Nostalgia forced his feet to the mantle where he viewed his photographs—his sister, his parents. He saw the wedding photo of him and Isabel. The one where she was wearing his mother's necklace. He was an arsehole for saying terrible things about it. That was his favorite necklace, reminding him of the toughest and most stubborn woman he'd known—his mother. He hoped April kept it.

That photo he wrapped in the crinkled newspaper and gently placed in the empty crate. That part of his life was over.

When he finished packing away the memories of Isabel and brought the remaining crates out to the workshop, the sky was fiery orange with approaching dusk. Sam sank into the couch cushions and stared at the wall, wondering what he could've done differently. His father used to say, 'Never dwell on the past; no one can change it. Just learn from your mistakes and try to make them right.'

Sam couldn't save her from Jaime's wrath, and from those injuries and Lloyd's, April's pink dress had been destroyed.

She would never see it.

She would never wear it.

He would have one made, anyway, even if he had to sell the wagon to pay for it.

Sam rode straight to Couture Clothing, cautious of Ralf who thankfully wasn't here, and found Marisol sifting through bolts of cloth. She straightened upon seeing him and stepped back as he approached as if afraid of him. "Marisol," Sam said with hurt in his voice. "Are you all right?"

"I..." The girl's voice trembled. "I thought you'd be upset with me."

"Where would you get an idea like that?"

"I heard what Jaime had done. I'm sorry. I'm so sorry about it. I don't know what's gotten into him. He's like a different person, and I don't know him anymore."

"I'm not here for him. Do you remember April's strange pink dress she wore with the open back?"

"I recall."

"Can you make a duplicate?"

"From memory?" she asked, astonished.

"Aye?" Sam replied, not having thought of the complexity of the request.

"I can probably get close. No guarantees though."

"Thank you so much. I'll be back for it in a few days."

"I'll see what I can do. No promises."

"Farewell until then," Sam said, and gave her a kiss on the cheek. She gave him a crooked smile, and Sam returned home.

With that settled, he entered April's room. He hadn't been in here since she left. He hadn't been strong enough to face it, but now he feared she was nothing but a figment of his imagination. He needed to know she was real.

On the wrinkly duvet, he found the paper and pencils he'd gifted her. She hadn't taken them with, because he hadn't given her time to pack. Touching something of hers made her seem real, as if he hadn't imagined she'd disappeared from the grassy field with his own eyes. It didn't seem possible, but it was. April was from the future.

On the end table, he found a drawing and picked it up. He ignited the gas lamp to inspect it. His hands shook when he saw the image in front of him.

She'd drawn him.

She'd captured all the detail of his face so well, it was as if he was smiling in front of a mirror. She'd even included the scar left behind by her sutures. His hand touched his face, sliding along the scar while he smiled. He may have lost his chance with April, but he could at least apologize to her, tell her the truth, and then he could sleep soundly. It wouldn't help his pain, but he could live with that. Sam's tears spilled down his cheeks.

He flipped the drawing over. In her own pencil, he wrote her a note. He folded it into a small square and tucked it inside the hidden drawer of the fireplace mantle—his secret hiding place for things he wanted to remain private. Sam rubbed his face with open hands to clear away the running tears of his sobs.

Satisfied with his confession, he stepped out back and fired up the forge of his blacksmith shop.

Chapter 40
Present Day, Green Bay, Wisconsin

APRIL SWUNG THROUGH THE drive-thru, bought a steaming cup of coffee, and parked at work—Sam's cabin, currently Mathew's clinic. She inhaled deep and held it until she couldn't any longer. She could do this. Yep, she could. April's shaky legs carried her inside. The familiar antiseptic lingering in the air and the modern aesthetic helped. She set down her stuff on the communal reception desk and logged into the computer system. She scrolled through the day's appointments, and it would be busy enough to keep her mind off the breakup with Levi, but that wasn't what tormented her. It seemed so long since she'd been here, but it had only been a couple days of the present time, weeks in her past time. No matter how therapeutic the movies made watching soap operas while eating whatever the hell bonbons were, going to work would be easier than staying home alone. Baby steps.

Except her eyes drifted to the fireplace, where Sam kept his precious pearl necklace, the one April couldn't take off—because it was pretty and fit her right. She would not think about him, or she'd start bawling right here at work. And no, she wouldn't look at where the couch had been, or the kitchen table, or the pantry closet. The exam room door—her guest bedroom—swung wide, startling her. Mathew appeared, a distraction with perfect timing today.

"Good morning. You seem to be in a great mood, considering how your ass has been," Mathew said.

"Pain pills. How are you?" April sipped her hot cup of coffee.

"I'm fine, but I'd be better if I knew what happened to you. In the end, it's not my business, but I worry. I don't want that to happen again, but I feel like you're covering for someone, protecting someone who doesn't deserve it."

"It was a misunderstanding. I promise I'll never see him again." Which was one of many benefits to being home again. She was safe.

"Right," Mathew said, not entirely satisfied. He leaned over and placed a hand on her shoulder. "If you need to talk, you can come to me. You know that, right? Even if it was your heart rather than your ass. You can come to me."

"I know," she said. Mathew would always be there for her, but she couldn't explain what happened or where her heart was.

Becca opened the front door and waddled in with a pained smile. A hand supported the bottom of her belly. April admired her roundness, and for a flash of a second, she wished it were hers. That stupid desire was impossible. She smiled for Becca and greeted her co-worker.

Becca blew out a long sigh as she sat and placed a hand protectively on the top of the mound. "Ready to start the day?" she asked.

"Yeah," April said. "How's the little one doing?"

Becca tried to take a deep breath. "Squeezing everything in my body—including my lungs and bladder, tipping me off balance, and hurting everything from the neck down. At least I'm not getting kicked anymore, but that happens near the end—lack of space. Would you mind taking the surgery case this morning? My back is killing me." Her face pinched in discomfort, but a maternal glow of misery—in the best way—radiated off her.

"Surgery?" April double checked her screen, and read the details. "Cat, tumor, send sample for biopsy. I can handle that one. No problem," she said without hesitating, confident in her stomach's new strength. April got up and entered the surgical suite to find Mathew already scrubbing in.

April collected the patient from the holding room and brought it in before prepping herself. Mathew gassed it down to sleep, and April shaved the affected area according to the x-rays.

Mathew calmly worked, minding his business, but she knew what he was thinking, and the truth was threatening to explode out of her. Who else could she talk to about her wild adventures and heartbreak? Kiko was away, and April had no one else.

"It was a guy," she said at last.

Mathew flashed her a look but didn't dare interrupt.

"He was punishing me for something someone else did—for what? I have no idea. He used his belt like Dad used to, but I won't ever see him again. It's not possible."

"I'm not telling you what to do," Mathew said, "but cooperating with police to have him prosecuted is the right thing to do, even if it's hard to face him."

April shook her head, amusement quirked her lips thinking of Jaime's reaction to being sent to the future. Now that would be entertaining, shortly before she ran him over with her car. Hmmm, she thought, maybe she'd borrow her brother's SUV for more oomph. "That's not possible."

Mathew made the first incision and he lifted an eyebrow. "Is he a ghost?"

"Something like that." A smile parted her mouth. He was already dead. Long ago dead.

Just like Sam.

Logically, Sam had to be dead, but picturing it, and not even knowing how it happened, made her stomach twist. Grignon had still been at large. Regardless of Sam's insistence he and Lloyd were fine, April had failed her mission. Maybe that was why Kiko was gone.

Kiko was fixing April's mess.

April's stomach flipped in warning. She was so stupid for not telling him she loved him. Instead, she'd let him upset her and she left. If only she would've told him, they could be making sandwiches or weeding the garden right now. But she would've never seen Mathew again. Her brother wouldn't never known what happened to her—a missing person, an unsolved case forever.

Would Kiko have explained it to him?

April blew out a deep breath.

"How's your stomach?" Mathew asked.

"It's fine. I'll be fine." Better than it used to be. She helped Mathew along, passing instruments. Shortly thereafter, Mathew pinched a golf-ball-sized lump between forceps and set it on the tray, and he sewed up the hole in the cat. With more precision and expertise than Sam had sewed her split ass cheeks.

Tears threatened to spill over. She blinked them back. With contaminated hands, she couldn't wipe them free.

Finished up, April returned the furball to the holding room to let it sleep off the anesthesia. Mathew balled up and trashed his paper gown, and April copied.

While Mathew documented the surgery and tumor, April cleaned the suite, but before she could leave for the reception desk, Mathew stopped her with both hands on her upper arms. He leaned down into her face, completely serious. "I want you to quit."

April's eyes grew wide. "What?"

Mathew waved his hand around, indicating the clinic in general. "I know this was never for you. I've appreciated all your help these years, even though you never liked it. I've been selfish, and for that, I'm sorry. I want you to go find yourself. If Levi isn't for you, then figure out what or who makes you happy."

April teared up. He was right, and he was finally letting her go in a way that didn't induce a stubborn rebuttal. Levi wasn't for her. The clinic wasn't for her either.

Sam was.

Sam wasn't here.

April nodded and said, "What about my position? And Becca will be out soon."

"Just like you to worry." He chuckled. "I've got it covered. That's what temporary staffing is for. Go. I'll send out your final check. If you need extra, I can send you some cash until you figure yourself out."

April smiled at his generosity. "That won't be necessary."

"The offer stands." He smiled.

April pushed through the door and returned to Becca's side, debating what to do next, not quite ready to walk away from Sam's cabin. Did she really want to enroll in nursing school? There were lots of majors she hadn't crossed off her list, and there were tests available to decide what her personality and preferences aligned with. Business school, perhaps. Right, for a business she could never afford to start.

She tapped her pencil on the desk and a customer arrived. April checked in the gangly Great Dane, confirmed the information of his owner, and then watched the dog sway as it led his person to the waiting area, in front of the fireplace.

The fireplace in which Sam had a hidden drawer.

Today was the last day she would see it. April stood up and walked around the desk, the painted mantle pulling her like a vortex. She reached under the wood, searching for the indentation of a secret drawer she'd painted over. Nimble fingers found it, and her heart raced with anticipation. It was here, but it wouldn't budge.

April brought a pen over from her desk and kneeled beside the clean, unused fireplace, stabbing upward at the wood, ignoring curious looks from the customers. She fished out the edges of the drawer with her pen and tugged on the dent. It shifted. With the desperation of a treasure hunter opening a chest, she grasped the edges and pulled with her entire body weight. It creaked open like a hundred-year-old window painted shut. She stood and looked inside. Her breath caught in her lungs. The necklace box was no longer there. Her fingers ran along the string of pearls at her throat.

A folded piece of paper sat in its place.

She lifted it out with extreme care. Her hands trembled as she unfolded the ancient paper. Her temples pounded, and her heart constricted. She knew what it was before she saw it.

Her drawing of Sam—Sam's beautiful smiling face, yellowed with time, covered with dust. Her finger touched his cheek where the sutures were, and April's chin quavered.

Becca called over to her, but April ignored her.

April saw her rough lines, made hastily in a spurt of inspiration. Fingerprints were in the graphite. Sam's. April dashed away tears, fighting back sobs. She flipped it over and dropped into a waiting room chair to read the delicate cursive.

Dearest April,

You are the brilliance that shines upon my heart. You are the light that guides me by day, and the warmth that cocoons me in comfort at night—an encompassing feeling I'd never had before and will never have again. I hope Levi makes you feel even a fraction of how I feel for you.

As Alexandre Dumas wrote in my favorite book—'I have always had more dread of a pen, a bottle of ink, and a sheet of paper than of a sword or pistol,' I am no longer afraid of what evils are headed my way, but I am afraid of what my words have done. If you can find strength in your heart to forgive me one last time, I may finally rest.

Always yours,
Samuel Hartley

April blinked back tears. She refolded the delicate, aged paper and placed it in her back pocket. She needed to find Kiko.

Chapter 41
1852 Bridgeport, Wisconsin

THE MID-DAY SUN DOUBLED the heat from the forge in the workshop. Sam set down the hammer and used tongs to move the glowing twist of iron to a cooling area. Inspiration had hit him swiftly and unexpectedly. For the first time in almost a year, he felt like himself again. His shirt clung to his sweaty skin, and he lifted a forearm to wipe his glistening face, but he scratched himself with gritty soot. Time for a break and a wash. Sam stepped inside his house and pulled greedy swallows of cool water.

Hooves thundered by, and shouts of excitement rang through his windows.

Sam opened the front door and caught a woman walking by with a basket. "What's going on?" he asked.

"Grignon's giving a speech at the Square. Everyone's going."

Sam nodded his thanks, and she continued on her way. *Everyone* was going? Of course, Grignon would be there. Could it be so simple as that? Sam dashed back inside and cleaned up quickly. He mounted Bucky and took a chance.

At the front door of Grignon's estate, he knocked and waited, and knocked again. The front door opened, and a wave of nausea flowed through him. He was an imbecile. Sam should've enjoyed his freedom while it lasted, rather than walk into the angry bastard's own home.

The housekeeper popped her head out. "What are you doing here, Sam?"

That wasn't her normal greeting, which gave him hope. "I've come to see Sarah. Is she here?"

The housekeeper craned her neck for witnesses and then nodded. She flicked her head back, indicating he follow. He did. Sam closed the door behind him and trailed the housekeeper. She brought him up the stairs and down the hall.

In front of a nondescript door, she stopped and whispered, "There's only me and the scullery maid here right now. Do what you must, but please keep the volume down. If anyone finds out I helped you..." she trailed off with gentle warmth in her tone. "You've always been a good boy, Sam. You don't deserve any of this. None of you do." She gave him a sad smile.

"I understand. And I thank you kindly, ma'am."

"Millie. Call me Millie when Grignon's people aren't around."

Sam smiled. "Thank you kindly, Millie."

She touched his arm and left him be. Sam waited until she was out of earshot before knocking. "Sarah?"

He heard shuffling, and the knob turned. Sam laid eyes on his sister for the first time in days. He grabbed her in a bear hug and tears of relief pricked his lids. She was alive—Grignon hadn't lied about that. Sam had finally saved her.

He studied her. She looked clean but sad. The bubbly bossy sister was gone. In her place was—defeat, resignation, fear? He didn't know, but he had time to make it right. "Let's go before everyone comes back."

"I'm glad to see you well, my brother, but as I told April, I'm not leaving. Grignon will take care of me."

The sound of her name shot pain through his chest. Sam said, "I know about the baby. I know about Lloyd. We can fix this ourselves. Come with me."

His sister gasped in surprise. "April told?"

"Aye. She did it to stop me from barreling in here on a suicide mission to get you."

"And yet here you are."

"The house is empty except for Millie, who helped me, and a maid. Grignon's speech at the Square is starting soon. Now's our chance." Sam yanked his sister's wrist, but she resisted.

"I'm not going. Grignon will hunt me down if I leave."

Join the list, Sam thought. "The declaration speech is when Grignon planned to hang Lloyd. We have to go now!"

"Why didn't you say that in the first place?" Sarah's face dropped in fear. She lifted her skirts and ran out the door, dragging Sam behind her. □

Chapter 42
Present Day, Green Bay, Wisconsin

April ran to her desk with tears streaming down her face, collected all her belongings, and logged out of her computer.

Worry knitted Becca's brow. "Is everything okay?"

April smiled and sniffled. "I hope it will be." Arms full, she ran through the parking lot and sped the mile back to her house. She took the porch steps two at a time, ignoring her stitches rubbing against her jeans, and barged through the front door.

Kiko stood in the living room, arms loose at her sides, staring straight at her, as if expecting April's entrance that second.

April wheeled for a moment, catching her breath, and dropped all her things on the chair. "How did you...?" she trailed off in confusion and rubbed her eyes clear. "Never mind. Can I go back?" April said, thinking of Sam.

"You've used two round trips. You have one left. I can send you, but be warned, if you come back once again, you can never return."

"Understood. And like last time, you can send me *when* I need to be? I don't want Sam to forget me this time," April said.

"Correct. I have time at my fingertips." Kiko lifted her hand and shimmied her fingers.

April sighed in relief. Her biggest fear was Sam forgetting who she was or only thinking of her as a dream.

"Will you be here when I need you?" April asked.

Kiko smiled. "I'm always here when you need me. Do you want to go now?"

April paused, looked around, and said, "I need to tidy up a few loose ends. I'll need a couple hours, if that's okay."

Her strange roommate nodded, and excitement bubbled in April as she headed to her bedroom. First, she emptied out things from her purse she would never need again—credit cards, driver's license, insurance cards—things that would prove difficult to explain. In their place, she packed a handful of Mathew's useful Swiss army knives from over the years and her last canister of pepper spray. She slid one knife into her back pocket, just in case, next to the magic trinket. April packed a photo album and her phone. It wouldn't last long, and there was no way to charge it, but she wanted it anyway for the week or so it would light up. She wished she would've printed out all the rest of the photos.

April peeled a sheet of artist paper and wrote a note to Mathew.

Hey big brother,

Thanks for the kick in the pants. My ass is still sore, but at least I finally got the message. I'm leaving to find the man I love. Wish me luck. Also, I accept your offer to quit. Maybe Kiko will fill in until you can find a temp. Thank you for all your help and support over the years. You are my only family, and I love you. I hope you find your own happiness as well.

Forever your sis,
Meatball

P.S. Spend this wisely. Don't let it expire, or I'll haunt you.

She folded her goodbye note in half, tenting it on top of her dresser. April collected the remains of her cash savings and set it under her note, and she added a handwritten check for the balance in her bank account—a final parting gift to help with all his bills. Then she stacked the identifying cards with it. He could shred them at the clinic.

Next, April gathered a backpack full of clothes—undergarments, jeans, T-shirts. All the comforts of home. The next bag was filled with art supplies. She stuffed her pain pills in a zippered front pouch. "Kiko, I need to make a run to the store. Can I?"

Kiko smiled and nodded. She had the patience of a saint while April scrambled to settle her needs and prepare.

April made a stop at the drug store for a slew of supplies, and at the department store, her cheeks burned as the cashier checked out her thirty packs of socks and underwear, silently judging. Finally, April loaded up the car with bags of fast-food.

When she returned home, she packed the third bag full of wound care supplies and set out a spread on the kitchen table worthy of a starving college student. All the favorites she would miss—ramen noodles, deep fried French fries, chicken strips, a pizza, and donuts. She would feel sick afterward, but it would be worth it for the memories. She invited Kiko to join her, and they ate together like the old roommates they were.

"How did you get your job?" April asked, tossing a fry into her mouth.

"That's a long story," Kiko said and selected a donut with filling.

"You've got all the time in the world, right?"

Kiko chuckled. "True. But not all of it is for mortal ears. Understand?"

"You're a mortal," April dryly pointed out.

"I was, but this job comes with a certain longevity. Prior to that, I was in love with an amazing guy, Kiyoshi Takai. We had the sappy love-story type of relationship, and we were young and dumb, but I have no regrets." Kiko swallowed a bite of donut. "These things are great. Anyway, just as everything was picture perfect, someone we thought was a friend fought Yoshi over me, and my husband was murdered. There was nothing I could do."

"I'm so sorry." April touched Kiko's hand in comfort.

Kiko smiled with years of sadness. "I had a great friend to lean on, until one day a man arrived, needing help. He had a job for me, and that it would heal me in time. The man was Chaos himself, in the flesh. He had a new opening in his ranks for a Love Curator. I accepted his offer, having nothing to lose. The job was real, and it's what I've been doing since."

"For how long?" April asked.

"Almost a hundred years."

April stared. Her barely drinking age roommate was *that* old. "You look good for your age."

Kiko laughed.

"Did you heal? As the job promised, I mean," April asked.

"I suppose time heals all wounds, but the scars are a reminder of those we lost. It's Order's way of making sure we remember love is fragile and painful. He wants us to avoid repeating that pain. Someday I might have that choice again, but until then, I'm here to make sure you find your happiness and to piss off my boss's brother."

April laughed. They'd made a decent dent in the buffet and packed away the leftovers. "Do you want me to take out the garbage before I go?"

Kiko smiled. "I'll take care of everything here. Don't worry."

April hefted all her bags onto her shoulders, ready to leave.

"Are you sure you want to wear that?" Kiko asked.

April checked herself over. Mathew had given her a pass on wearing scrubs at work because of her injuries, so she wore jeans, snuggly holding her stitches, and a blouse. She'd washed her white sneakers. They still weren't white. "I don't have another bridesmaid dress. My little black dresses would bring worse attention than this."

Kiko nodded. "Do you want to say anything to Mathew?"

"I left him a note and a bunch of cash on my dresser. Can you see that he gets it?"

"Yes."

April fished out her keys to the house and her car. She passed it to Kiko. Her roommate's eyes watered—from the goodbye or from what she could see?

"How far can you see in time?" April asked, surprised her voice didn't break.

"Only as far as necessary. Have a seat when you're ready. The trip can be disorienting."

April counted her bags, checked her pockets, and sat down carefully for the queasy ride with a stomach full of grease.

"I wish you well," Kiko said. She leaned down and gave her old roommate a hug.

April snorted at the closing of the biggest chapter of her life and patted her friend's back. She closed her eyes, and her eyelids showed her Sam. Her heart swelled with love.

Chapter 43
1852 Bridgeport, Wisconsin

APRIL FOUND HERSELF IN the grassy field again, the summer's sun blazing. She shifted her bags up her shoulders and began the trek to Sam's house. She kept a close watch on the road, uncertain about the route schedule for Grignon's men. Dennis and Daniel were presumably both dead, but she didn't know how many others, besides Rob Bertrand, he had at his disposal. She shuddered at the word disposal.

April cut south behind the back of the stores to draw the least attention possible until she could find Sam and get another of Marisol's dresses.

Doug sniffed around, and she smiled at him. As if on cue, the mutt loped over, and she gave him scratches behind the ear, and he licked her hand in greeting. He tilted his head, twitched an ear, and pranced off with a purpose.

April kept moving. Her feet were hot, and perspiration slicked her chest and forehead. Finally, his home was in sight. Tension in her neck released, her heart blossomed in renewed hope at seeing Sam, and with a surge of new energy, she picked up the pace.

The knob was unlocked. April swung the door wide and announced, "Sam!"

She rushed into his bedroom. "Sam!"

Then she checked the pantry. Empty. The whole house was empty. She dropped her bags on the couch and rushed out to his workshop, thrilled at the possibility that he'd rekindled his passion.

She entered the walk-in door but found it dark. He wasn't in there either.

Bucky was gone, and the wagon too.

Something wasn't right. She hadn't seen a single person on her entire trip across town. She had been avoiding people, but still. She returned to Sam's house. His stuff was all here. He'd unpacked. He hadn't left. April stepped out front and scanned down the road toward town. Nothing and no one.

Horse hooves clopped along the road to her left, and she smiled and turned, shielding her face against the blinding sun.

It wasn't Sam.

She didn't recognize this man at all. He had a lean, narrow face and a flat nose. He wore a wide-brimmed hat and a long-sleeved shirt.

"Hi, there," she said. "Do you know where Sam is—the man who lives here?"

The stranger smiled, leaned over, and offered his hand. "Sure do. Come on up, and I'll take you to him."

"Thank you!" April climbed in front of him, careful to lean her weight off her stitches without appearing more strange than she already was.

He spurred his horse, and they galloped toward town and turned north, toward Common Square. Her stomach sunk so low she was frightened for her bowels. What day was it?

Grignon stood at the podium on the raised stage next to a platform and spoke through a megaphone. The whole town appeared to be present, and every set of eyes watched him. A pair of hangman's nooses hung above the platform just to his left. A scream built inside her.

Sam and Lloyd.

Kiko could've given her more time or a warning. She clambered off the horse and opened her mouth wide to scream for Sam. A salty, smelly hand clamped over her mouth, her arms pinched to her sides, and she found her feet being dragged out from under her. Out of sight of the crowd, the helpful stranger dragged her around to the back of the platform.

Lloyd was here, tied and gagged. His eyes popped wide when he saw her. She tried to scream through the meaty hand, but couldn't. Another man bound her wrists behind her, painfully pressuring her shoulders. April's muffled noises were drowned out by Grignon's booming speech.

April dragged desperate breaths in through her nose. Her pulse raced, and her vision speckled. She couldn't believe what was happening. Every yank of her wrists struck blinding pain through her shoulders. The hand constricting her mouth squeezed her jaw but uncovered her lips. Before she could drag in a breath, a gag filled her mouth.

Flat Nose released her, leaving Rob Bertrand to stand guard with a pair of revolvers pointed at her and Lloyd. She looked at Lloyd for any information or help, but his face displayed resignation to their fate. How could he give up so quickly?

April wriggled her wrists in their bindings, careful to keep her torso still. They were tight. Every twist ground the rope tighter into her flesh. She needed to get out of here quick. There were two captives, and on the stage overhead, there were two nooses. She shivered.

April still had her emergency trinket in her pocket, but if she used it, she could never return, never see Sam again.

She didn't know if Sam was alive, but she had to believe Kiko wasn't that cruel.

April needed a plan. Nimble fingers reached for her back pocket and found her Swiss army knife. Sudden luck helped her focus. She opened the folding utility knife and began sawing at her rope bindings in small imperceptible motions. This would take forever.

Lloyd saw what she was doing, but she couldn't read his expression. She kept sawing until Rob grabbed her by the arm and said, "You're up first. Step forward and up the stairs. No shoving, no pushing. Keep your hands to yourselves and no one gets hurt...prematurely."

April slipped the open knife into her back pocket so as she passed, he wouldn't confiscate it. With April in the lead and Lloyd behind her, they took the creaky stairs. She stopped at the top of the platform with the whole town looking at her. Hundreds of pairs of eyes stared. Sweat broke out on her palms and her pulse quickened with anxiety.

So similar yet so different from Levi's very public proposal. At least Purely Plaid's audience didn't want her dead. She didn't trust which way the townspeople would lean with Grignon directly pressuring them. Would any of them have the guts to speak for her?

Sam would. If Sam were still alive.

A few gasps of surprise and whispers came from the townspeople, but no one objected. Her heart sank. The only fight left in her was finding Sam.

Flat Nose grabbed her upper arm and led her to the hinged square just below the swaying noose. He stopped her and whispered, his voice icy cool against her ear, "Don't move. You can save yourself if you just wait."

Fat chance.

Flat Nose slipped the noose over her head and collected Lloyd. He repeated the process next to her, but she couldn't hear what he said to him. All the while, the crowd remained silent. Lloyd had never harmed anyone. Spineless bastards.

Grignon continued his speech, "...and it is with a heavy heart that Monsieur Lloyd Stanton is charged with armed burglary for breaking into my home. At such a time when criminals no longer feel the sinful urges of crime, then we will live in peaceful harmony. To drive this point home, Lloyd Stanton's sentence is death by hanging, and to cover the fine owed, his bar, Stanton's Spirits, will be confiscated. To all you fine people of Bridgeport, it is my promise to you that I will always do my best to keep you safe from harm and ensure prosperity continues to grow."

The crowd clapped slowly, as if it were the expected action and not necessarily an approval.

Killing a man and stealing his way of living and legacy wasn't right. Even if Lloyd was guilty for trying to rescue Sarah, April didn't hold it against him. And no one in the town cared enough to stand up for him?

Oh right, April thought dryly, because a black man in love with a white girl was a sin, and if the townspeople knew she was pregnant, they'd probably clap at Lloyd's hanging body. April was going to need a lot of time to compromise on some of their societal values, but it wasn't going to be this one. April slipped the knife back out of her pocket and continued sawing along the remaining thin rope.

One man shouted from the center of the crowd, "What did the woman do?" It was Porter. Even though he given her grief about condoms, she wanted to give him a hug.

"Oh, *oui*," Grignon said calmly, as if discussing the week's price of beef. "Mademoiselle April has been condemned to death by hanging as well, for the crime of treason."

The crowd gasped at the same time April froze in shock. What?

"But what did she do?" Porter repeated.

A dark cloud passed over Grignon's features. He was not amused. "That is private information between her and Jaime Perez. They both will have to live with their actions for the rest of their lives, however short hers will be."

April shuddered at the sound of his name. She kept sawing, her fingers going numb from the angle, her wrists on fire.

She met Porter's gaze. He seemed apologetic for not trying harder.

The final rope gave way. April slipped her hands apart but kept them behind her. She tucked the folding knife back into her pocket and then leaned back just slightly for the least resistance when slipping the noose off. She would only have seconds to act.

"And with that, any final words?" Grignon asked the crowd.

As if on cue, Flat Nose, who'd captured and brought her here, stepped up to a large lever. Rob Bertrand stood next to Grignon, hands clasped in front of himself as if he were a gentleman.

Time was up.

Lloyd had saved her from the townspeople when they accused her of theft and chanted at her like an outcast. There was no way on this earth she would let him die.

April reached a hand around her neck, slipped the noose up and over her head, and dashed two steps over to Lloyd.

There were shouts of alarm from the crowd, and Grignon spat fire. April gripped Lloyd's noose and slipped it up over his chin, but she was too late. The floor gave out under their feet, and she fell to the hard-packed dirt. Her stitches screamed in agony.

Lloyd dangled, his feet kicking in the air, looking for purchase. She didn't have time to cry at the sight. April stood, grasped his feet, and placed them on her shoulders. She took his weight, and Lloyd was a large man. He wriggled. There were more shouts all around, and then the full weight of Lloyd Stanton crashed on top of her.

SAM GALLOPED THROUGH TOWN with Sarah grasping his waist and turned left for Common Square. Angry shouts sunk his heart. Sam spurred Bucky to go faster. The angry crowd packed together, yelling and throwing things toward the stage. Grignon stood behind the podium with Joe and Rob guarding him. Where was

Lloyd? The noose, both nooses, were empty. Why were two set up?

Sam circled behind the crowd to the back of the platform and found a pile of bodies writhing. He jumped down and helped Lloyd up. He took out his knife and sliced his friend's hands free. "What happened?"

Lloyd wiped tears from his eyes. He nodded at the woman on the dirt. "She saved my life. God damnit, Sam. She saved me."

"Lloyd?" Sarah slid down off the horse and ran to Lloyd. She publicly hugged him, not that anyone could see back here.

Lloyd hesitated, eying Sam with guilt and shame. Sam smiled and nodded. He was happy for his best friend and sister. Sarah and Lloyd embraced like a pair of teenage lovers, and it was comforting to know his sister was happy.

Lloyd's incapacitated savior was flattened to the dirt. Sam's heart skipped a few beats at the feminine form in outrageous clothing. "April?" He sunk to his knees and rolled her over. He inspected her for blood, cuts, holes, damage of any kind. He cut the gag from her mouth. "What happened to her?"

Lloyd pulled away from Sarah long enough to say, "I landed on her. She's breathing. I think I just knocked her out is all. I think she'll be fine when she wakes up."

Sam lifted her and set her on Bucky, leaning her face against the horse as he'd done when she was severely wounded by Jaime. He had no idea if she was healed, but he wasn't taking chances. Sam had something to finish before bringing her home to safety.

From Bucky's saddlebags, Sam tossed a sheathed knife and a pistol to Lloyd and took a set for himself. "Sarah, stay with April. Lloyd, come with me." They climbed to the platform and found the three men huddled together, trying to dissuade the crowd's hostilities.

"You get Joe," Sam said. "I'll take Rob. Save Grignon for last."

Lloyd nodded, and they aimed their revolvers. The crowd silenced, and Grignon turned to see what the abrupt change was about. The Frenchman's brow sunk in fury. His face reddened to a radish. The two guards shifted stances to reach for their weapons.

"Halt right there. I'm only telling you once," Sam warned.

Both men stopped and placed their hands up in surrender. Grignon moved his hands and eyes down toward the podium. The smirk on the guards' faces was enough.

Sam said, "Lloyd."

They both fired, and Rob and Joe collapsed, clutching their legs with their faces screwed up in pain. Seeing defeat inevitable, Grignon's hands lifted in surrender, and his face dropped in panic.

The crowd cheered.

Over the deafening roar, Sam said, "Set up the noose for Grignon. This ends now."

"You got it." Lloyd eagerly shoved the lever, resetting the trap doors in the platform's floor. He reset one noose and flipped the other off the banister. The crowd's cheers slowly turned to chanting. Sam couldn't make out the sound until a few beats later.

They were chanting, "Freedom."

Sam shook his gun to tell Grignon to move. The Frenchman sidled away from the podium and walked toward the noose, sweat on his brow and hands trembling. Sam would only give him the same treatment he planned for Lloyd and April.

Lloyd placed the noose over Grignon's head and whispered in the Frenchman's ear. Grignon blanched. Lloyd unsheathed the knife Sam had given him. He knew what Lloyd planned to do, and Sam wasn't going to stop him. Not after everything Grignon had done to their town.

To Isabel.

To Sarah.

To April.

To Lloyd.

To all the business owners held in extortion.

Grignon deserved worse.

Lloyd buried the knife into Grignon's side. The blood wouldn't be obvious right away, and he wouldn't die from it quickly. That was the noose's job. Grignon buckled over in pain but was stopped by the short length of rope. Grignon righted himself, face contorted in pain, balmy skin white with fear. Lloyd discreetly cleaned the knife on the inside of Grignon's sport coat and tucked it out of view. Lloyd whispered into Grignon's ear again and stepped aside.

Sam turned to the crowd and tucked away his pistol. "By the power of citizen's arrest, the town of Bridgeport hereby charges Gabriel Grignon with murder, rape, kidnapping, extortion, and theft. The punishment of hanging to be carried out immediately. I was his slave for the last several months. He murdered Isabel. He kidnapped my sister and held her prisoner. He held all of you in fear from the day he arrived. Does anyone object?" Sam waited as the crowd murmured to itself.

"My sister visited him and never returned!" a voice shouted from the crowd.

"Joseph Van Cleeve," another victim's name was shouted, and others murmured their agreement.

"Brandon O'Connell."

"Martha Johnson."

"Ashley McRigger." Different voices shouted names in memoriam. Sobs came from the audience.

Raspy gasps came from over his shoulder, just loud enough to hear. Grignon said, "We had a mutually beneficial arrangement. I wanted everyone safe, but I had to be paid, and I was keeping Sarah Hartley under my protection."

Sam stalked over to the bastard and whispered to him, "Don't ever say her name again. There is nothing you could say that would ever justify your actions. You are through here."

The Frenchman blubbered, "Please let me go. I'm sorry. I didn't mean any of this."

Sam addressed the crowd, "I heard no objections!"

Grignon continued blubbering, and bright red trailed down his side.

Sam spoke to Lloyd. "Do you want the honors, or should I?"

"If we tally up the wrongs, you deserve the honors, but should you pass on the opportunity, I will gladly do it myself." Lloyd smiled.

Just in case the townspeople had a change of heart afterward, Sam walked over to the lever to protect Lloyd from judgment. He said to Grignon, "This is for Sarah, for Lloyd, for April, but mostly for Isabel. Rot in hell."

Sam pulled the lever, and Grignon's eyes bulged as the trap door dropped from under him. His feet dangled in the air, and his body swayed as he fought for purchase. Grignon's face changed to a shade of purple. Sam's need for closure blocked everything else, and he watched in silence. This memory would help ease the one where Sam was bound, gagged, and held at knife point by Daniel, as Dennis raped Isabel, and Grignon sliced her throat. She'd bled out in his living room by the fireplace.

This man was a monster, and it ended now.

The crowd cheering at the dying man pulled Sam from his focus. Lloyd stood next to him, watching just as he was. Lloyd's arm wrapped around his shoulder.

At last Grignon's feet stopped kicking and his bloodshot eyes rolled up into his skull.

Sam said, "Wait ten minutes and cut him down. We're done here."

The townspeople calmed down. The show was over, and they dispersed. Ross took the stage to volunteer for body disposal. He was a weird man.

Porter stepped up to the lip of the stage. 'Sam, I want to say thanks. Thank you for stopping him. I knew you could do it, kid."

Porter smiled, and Sam's chest puffed with the praise. He was conflicted with murdering a man and being held on a pedestal about it. But for now, he would take Porter's kindness and pick up the shattered pieces of their lives.

"I couldn't have done it without Lloyd. So, I only get half the credit," Sam said to him.

Lloyd gave his shoulder a squeeze, and they left the stage to find their women.

Chapter 44

APRIL DROWSILY WOKE TO find herself swaying on Bucky with Sarah behind her. Her head swam like she hadn't slept in days—a lightness and throbbing she could do without. Breakthrough pain stung her butt. None of that mattered—only the man leading Bucky, wearing a large straw hat blocking his whole head, brown trousers, and a long sleeve shirt. That was not Lloyd or Sam.

April turned around, and Sarah placed her index finger over her lips to shush her before April said anything. She whispered over her shoulder anyway, "What's going on?"

"Stay quiet or he will kill us."

She glimpsed black mussed hair from the man leading Bucky. Still no recognition. She shook her head and rubbed her face. After Lloyd's weight literally crashed down on her shoulders, she was woozy and stunned. "Where's Sam?"

Sarah shrugged.

The man turned to inspect his captives. April's stomach flipped, and she fought bile from rising.

Jaime Perez.

Like hell she would stay silent. As if reading her thoughts, Sarah whispered, "Don't say anything. He has a gun in his pocket."

Bucky walked with a calm laziness, and Jaime without concern. He was either arrogant or cunning, but April was no match for him, especially not while stunned. She gripped the saddle's horn until her knuckles were white with fury.

Thunder clapped overhead, startling her, and threatening clouds rolled closer. Rain would be a relief from the dusty heat.

Jaime stopped the horse at Couture Clothing and said, "Nice to see you awake. This would be no fun otherwise. Now get inside and don't say a word."

His smile curdled April's blood, and her backside throbbed in ghost pain—or maybe the pain pills were wearing off. Either way, her ass hurt.

As Jaime watched with a smirk, April slipped down and helped Sarah. She gripped the girl's hand as they walked inside. Jaime moved Bucky out of sight. She thought fast. "Marisol! Marisol, are you in here?"

No response.

"We can't stay here," April said. "I've already been through his fun, and it's not worth repeating."

Sarah said, "If we try to run for it, he'll shoot us in the back. What good would that do? Everyone's at Grignon's speech. No one will hear us either."

"Then we take a stand. Two of us against him." April searched around the register for any weapons. There was nothing obvious. Footsteps approached, and she scurried away from the counter. April slipped her pocketknife out, unfolded the small blade, and slipped it back into her pocket, ready for use.

Jaime stepped inside with his gun drawn. "Smart of you to stay still." He waved the gun to have April and Sarah walk toward the back of the store. April led them and searched for anything usable. Coat hangers wouldn't help much. She wasn't strong enough to wield a coat rack. Most clothing items were folded on shelves, anyway. There was nothing of use in the store. Perhaps that was why Jaime chose his family's business to bring them to. April stopped at the back of the store. There was a storage closet.

Sarah gasped, and a second later, a cold circular hunk of metal pressed against the back of April's neck. She only needed one guess for what that was.

"Closet now. Both of you."

Sarah entered first, and April followed. April's breathing was erratic, and her hands shook. Jaime reached in and slammed the door shut. The lock clicked into place. April held Sarah in complete darkness.

And they waited.

"What do you think he wants with us?" Sarah asked.

Torture. Maim. Kill. The usual trio for sociopaths. That thought wouldn't help Sarah any. "I think he's mad at Sam," she answered truthfully. Every time she met Jaime, he was always itching for a fight over Isabel. He'd accused April of replacing her, which was ludicrous, but sometimes those suffering from grief were immune to logic. She pitied him but hated him more.

"What did my moronic brother do now?"

April smiled in the inky darkness and ticked off all the possibilities: He'd let April live at his house, which was surely not appropriate for the time. He'd taught her how to ride a horse. He'd brought her gifts. He'd rescued her from Grignon's house, after she already got outside. He'd faked being engaged to her to withdraw money to escape. And he fell in love with her—that much she discerned by his letter written on her own drawing. "Nothing wrong or illegal, as far as I can tell."

"That figures. You must be guilty by association, and I'm just collateral damage, I'd wager." Sarah's observation was keen.

"I think you're right," April said, releasing her. "I don't know about you, but I don't feel like being Jaime's toy today. My ass isn't done healing from the last meeting we had."

April's blind hands searched the closet. She found shelves with bottles—not helpful. A broom made a loud clack against the wall. Both women gasped, froze, and listened for any creaking of footsteps on the wooden floor outside the door. April heard nothing, so she assumed Jaime wasn't close. April's fingers found a cold metal snow shovel. That'd do. She leaned it by the door and continued to feel around. She tripped on some buckets on the floor. After the clattering died down, dread seeped into her bones as footsteps approached. Jaime returned.

A hand turned the knob, but it didn't open. "April, Sarah?"

It was Sam.

Relief made April's knees buckle. Her chest warmed. "Sam! We're in here. It's locked from your side. Jaime has a key," April shouted through the door.

Another set of footsteps approached, and Sam's hand left the knob. The door muffled a gunshot. April flinched and checked the door for holes and patted herself for leaks. There weren't any. "Sam!" she shouted, dread seeping into her bones, palm slapping the door.

April slipped out her Swiss army knife. She folded the knife in and started tugging various instruments for the corkscrew. She remembered Kiko opening her shackles. She slipped the tip in the knob's slot and realized it was an old-fashioned knob—skeleton key style. Similar, if not the same, as the shackles. It shouldn't be too difficult.

She pressed the metal twist in and turned until she heard a click. She tried the knob. Nothing. A shuffling sound—feet shifting and grunts—was on the other side of the door. She pulled the metal twist out just a little and turned for another click. One more try, and the knob opened.

April pushed through the door and found Sam and Jaime in a fist fight, the pair circling with hate snarling their faces. She felt a bit smug seeing Jaime's face bloodier than Sam's.

Sarah shot out of the closet, stepped close to the circling men with her finger pointing at them, scolding like a mother would. Sam's arrival apparently brought her confidence back. "You two be done with this. No sense in you both being knocked down. I don't need more blood around. I've seen enough these days."

They continued to circle with snarls on their faces. Jaime took a swing and missed.

"I said be done with it!"

Jaime broke the circle and gave Sarah a vicious kick to the head. The girl spun from the force, and her skirts fluttered around her as she plummeted to the floor. April ran to Sarah and helped her sit up.

Sam grabbed Jaime's arm and spun him back to engage, redirecting him away from Sarah.

The girl pressed a hand to her temple, and April tipped the girl's chin up to assess her. "Look at me." She inspected the girl's pupils. "How many?" April waved two fingers in front of her face.

"Uh, two, I think."

She smiled. "You'll be okay. I don't know about those two, though."

Sam and Jaime circled and took turns swinging at each other. Sam had the upper hand with his size and strength. Was Sam holding back because he still cared for his ex-brother-in-law? Sam slammed the smaller man in the jaw, spinning him on his heels, and Jaime dropped like a bag of sand.

Guess not.

Sam rushed to their side and kneeled. Sam stared at her in disbelief. "You're here. You're really here. I watched you leave." Sam's palm cupped her cheek in amazement, but after a beat, his face scrunched in pain. Sam arched his back, falling forward.

April caught him and used her body and arm to hold him upright, but he was incapacitated. April's pulse roared, her chest constricted in debilitating worry, but she exhaled and counted to five to calm herself. Panicking wouldn't help anyone. April caught a glimpse of Sarah, who scooted away with her hand protecting her belly. April's straining arm still held Sam upright while she dug in her pocket for the folding knife. Then she dug deeper still for the confidence to face her mutilator.

Over Sam's shoulder she pointed the blade at Jaime, finding strength rather than fear, and she snarled. "Back off or you'll regret it."

Jaime laughed. "What are you going to do with that?"

Her offense melted, and she looked at her knife—currently a corkscrew. Great. Sam deliriously reached behind him as if trying to find a wound. She turned him and set him down gently, unsure of his condition. She'd told herself she would enjoy her revenge, that the devil himself wasn't walking away again, and she fought to keep images of her dad from her mind. April needed to focus on Jaime. Her sweaty hands trembled. She could do this.

April stepped back in a circle to lead him away from the siblings, while she folded the corkscrew and dug for the knife. Jaime followed her. She found the small blade and took her offensive stance again.

Jaime laughed once more. "That's not much better."

While Jaime was distracted, April dove at him, knife prepared for a full body slam. She made contact in his abdomen, the small blade sheathed fully. He arched in pain and shoved her away, and April crashed into a rack of Marisol's dresses, tangling herself in layers of skirting. She fought to free herself before Jaime could go after Sam in his weakened condition.

April climbed to her feet, and Jaime stared at her with those dark, dead eyes of her nightmares and that smirk. This was beyond a punishment. He was enjoying it. "I left you a few marks. I think it's time to finish what we started." Jaime unbuckled his belt and slipped it free.

Sam limped toward Jaime's back.

April's betraying eyes widened, alerting Jaime, whose smile slid off, and he dodged a strike on time. Jaime slashed at Sam with the belt. Sam grunted and stumbled.

April cried out, "Leave him alone. Jaime, stop it." She didn't know what to say to get through to him, to take his attention away from Sam. How would she go on if Sam died here, after everything they'd survived? All she had was taunting. "Jaime, you disgusting, pathetic excuse for a man, come over here and get me. You're weak!"

One of those words worked. His head snapped back to her, and he snarled all over again. "I suppose I'm overdue in teaching this whore some manners."

She held out the knife as if to repeat her move and slowly retreated out the front door. She wanted him to follow to increase the distance from Sam and Sarah.

Jaime cackled as he followed, but the grating noise petered to a small grunt of pain. The wound in his abdomen was seeping blood. At least she'd done that much. He stumbled backward and clutched the wound.

April taunted again with a shake of her injured ass. "Come and get it, asshole."

His face curled into a snarl, and he marched toward her on a renewed mission. April finally got him outside, and if only for a moment, the Hartleys were safe.

Jaime kept coming, rage blinding him to reason, but she never could overpower him. Her last hope was to punch him in the wound. She didn't have the strength to hit hard enough to affect him otherwise.

The crackle of thunder brought a downpour of rain. Droplets splashed her face.

Jaime stepped within range, and she ducked his grasp and punched him in the wound. He grunted and backhanded her swiftly, sending her tumbling over and landing in the rocky mud. New pain speared up her spine and through her backside. She couldn't move, couldn't flee.

He stalked up to her, limping and angry, and he didn't wait for her to stand for a fair fight. He crouched at her side and reeled back a fist for another strike.

All at once, Jaime tipped over sideways. Sam's foot circled around as he finished his kick. Sam limped over to Jaime's still body. He unsheathed his large knife and positioned it over the small man's chest for the kill.

"Wait," April said.

Sam paused. Rain poured through his hair and dripped off his nose. His shirt was soaked, and patches of red turned pink from dilution. Jaime was incapacitated and under control. She could get her revenge, but after all the daydreams of this moment, now that it was here, it didn't seem fun. There was no enjoyment in participating or watching Sam do the deed. "Are you sure you want to do that?"

Sam looked her straight in the eye. Under him was the pathetic squirming body of his ex-brother-in-law, who clearly hadn't processed his sister's death appropriately. Murdering another as payback wouldn't help anyone move on from the loss of a loved one any easier. Jaime was caught in a blind rage. He needed time.

Sam bowed his head and re-sheathed the knife. He stood up slowly and held out his hand to April. "If I kill him," he said, "I'm no better than Grignon. When he heals, I'll pay him a visit about your wounds. A few times. Until he gets the hint."

Lloyd showed up with his mount. Sarah dashed through the front door. They embraced again as if they hadn't just seen each other a few hours ago. Sam smiled at them in approval. Lloyd helped Sarah up onto the horse, and then he said, "I'm taking her to my place. Will you two be all right?"

Sam stepped over to his friend. "I'm happy for you both. Get out of here and stay out of trouble."

Lloyd and Sarah smiled like smitten lovers while the rain soaked them through. With a nod at April, Lloyd spurred his horse toward the bar. Sam whistled for Bucky to kneel, and he and April both mounted. "Let's get out of here."

Sam's warm arms wrapped around her, embracing her as if afraid she would vanish in the blink of an eye.

Again.

Chapter 45

April kneeled by Sam, who was stretched out on the couch. Energy pulsed between them, but she kept her inspection of him professional. She needed to be sure he hadn't sustained any mortal injuries. He stared at her with a drunken smile, while she opened the slash in his trousers and cleaned and stitched a gash on his thigh. He'd have a black eye in the morning. A small cut on his forehead didn't need stitching, but she cleaned that as well. His eyes followed her as she inspected everything in sight, and he never winced despite the pain he must be in. She held back the urge to blurt out everything that had happened.

"I need you to take your shirt off now," April said clinically.

Sam laughed. "I like when you're direct." He winced as he pulled the fabric over his head.

Her eyes opened wide. He was covered in bruises and small cuts as if the punches had included brass knuckles. "You look like tenderized steak."

"That's a new one."

"I need to see your back, where Jaime got you."

Sam sat up, and she stood behind him, pressing fingers gently at various points and asking if different areas were painful. "Does this hurt?"

"Not anymore."

He had a line of circular bruises near his spine. They broke through the skin, but weren't deep punctures. Puzzled, April asked, "What did he get you with?"

"Brass knuckles."

Ah. That little snake never played fair. "You'll be sore for a long time, but you'll live. I'll wash off your cuts."

April tracked his gaze in her periphery while she stroked his skin with cleansing water. Her face flushed and her body roared with heat. He did look like tenderized steak. and just as yummy too. April moved to sit behind him, and she dipped the cloth and wrung out the excess, carefully patting and stroking his back with it, taking extra time to enjoy the rigid muscles under her fingertips.

"So," Sam said, and he cleared his throat, "I saw you brought bags. Plan on staying?"

"If that's all right with you. I'd like to." She dipped the cloth again and his muscles shifted under his skin.

"What happened with Levi?"

"We broke up."

"And how do you feel about that?" Sam was fishing.

She finished his back and pressed her fingers to his chest, gently leaning him back down. She took in the sight of his bare skin—smooth and contoured with rigid muscles. She shuddered, dipped the cloth, and washed his chest. His nipples peaked with the cool of the water. She washed them attentively. Sam moaned just a little under her touch.

April smiled. Kiko had said her job was to match people, and the dummy that April was, finally figured it out. She was sent to Sam for more than just saving his life. "I'm where I'm meant to be." Her hand stilled. "You asked me once if I was in love, and I cried when I told you I was. The tears weren't for what I'd left behind, but for what I wanted and couldn't have. I love you, Sam."

Sam leaned forward and captured her face with his hands. He brought her lips within inches of his. "Say that again." His voice was hoarse, and his breath tickled her face.

She knew what was to come. "It's you I love, Sam. It always was."

He kissed her with a passion she could've only dreamed about, and within moments, and despite his injuries and soreness, Sam lifted her and carried her to his bed. He kissed her all the way over and all the way down, pausing only when a loud thump had him sucking in a breath. "Ow."

He'd kicked the table with his leg.

April chuckled against his lips. "I'll have to inspect that."

He grinned and kissed her again. "That sounds like fun."

April's body turned on in places she didn't know existed, and she finally felt at home.

They rested, tangled in the sheets, breath pumping, and wide smiles on their faces. Sam stood up in his glorious birthday suit, and April drank in his shape. He strolled to the kitchen with the slightest limp and came back with his hands behind his back. She bit her lip taking in his chest gleaming with sweat, thick thighs, and a perfect erection ready for round two. He brought one hand forward and crawled over, plopping his weight on top of her. He brought his other hand forward, and it held a small box.

"What is your middle name?"

April laughed. "That's a strange question. Elizabeth."

Sam smiled. "That was my mam's name." April didn't know what to say to that, so she waited. Sam cleared his throat purposefully. "April Elizabeth McCall, you are impossibly strong, incredibly caring, very considerate, gorgeous, and you've saved my life more times than I can count. I wouldn't be here if it weren't for you, and I don't want to be here without you, even if that means I have to cook you dinner every night while you read the paper."

April chuckled through her trembles.

Sam opened the box to reveal a gold ring engraved with laurel leaves, antique in style, but breathtaking. A round diamond was surrounded by a cluster of smaller ones, all sparkling under the sunlight through the small bedroom window. April held her breath in anticipation.

"I love you, April. Will you—"

"Yes!" she blurted, unable to wait another moment. It was perfect. Sam was perfect. Her pulse raced with excitement. She didn't want to be with anyone else but Sam. April wrapped her arms around him and squeezed. "A million times, yes."

"—marry me?" Sam finished through a beaming smile. He placed the ring on her finger, and April pulled him back down and covered them with the sheets. It felt right. She never felt surer of anything in her life, and his proposal was just perfect.

THE NEXT MORNING APRIL awoke smiling with the best soreness. She walked like a cowboy, but it didn't matter. She and Sam made eggs and toast together, nudging each other with their hips, licking fingers when the butter slipped too far, and flirting their way through breakfast.

The ring on her finger felt perfect. She unpacked her bags and put on her own bra and underwear. Sam watched her with interest. "What?" she asked and slipped into a T-shirt and a pair of jeans.

"Your clothing is very odd, but I have to admit I like it very much."

"It's only until Marisol can make me a new set of dresses, but I'm keeping my bras."

Sam chuckled. "I have something for you." He padded into his bedroom and returned with a large flat box and a beaming smile on his face.

"What's this?"

"Just open it."

She lifted the lid off the box and a pink dress gleamed at her. It was similar to her bridesmaid dress, but a little more modest, the color off a little, and the materials from what was available. It had pockets. "Where did you get this?"

"I had it made for you."

"From memory?"

"Aye," Sam said. "Mine and Marisol's."

"Wow."

"Do you like it?"

April's eyes watered. His thoughtfulness was overwhelming. "I love it. Thank you so much." She removed her T-shirt and jeans and shimmied into the dress. Sam helped her tie the back. It felt softer than the commercially made polyester she was used to. She hugged herself and stepped into Sam's arms. He squeezed her tight and kissed the top of her head.

A scratching at the door turned both their heads. "What's that?" April asked.

Sam prowled to the front door with a knife in his hand. Grignon was gone, but they didn't stick around to find out if any of his guards survived.

Sam opened the front door cautiously. When he looked down, a nose stuffed its way inside.

"Doug!" April shouted.

The mutt jogged over and gave her licks and kisses.

"Traitor," Sam said to his wagging tail.

April laughed. "I guess he stays with us now."

"He's just figured out where the freshest food is."

April stood up after giving Doug a rigorous welcome, doggy style, and wrapped her arms around Sam. She kissed him until her lips tingled. Reluctantly, she freed herself and popped a pain pill for her sutures. She didn't tell him she hoped it would help with her soreness from last night.

"So now what?" April asked. She didn't have a job. Gardening and cooking would only go so far.

"Well, you could undress again. I like to watch that part."

"No, I mean, do you have a job anymore? What kind of job can I do here? We didn't figure all this stuff out before."

Sam scratched his stubble. She wanted to slide her fingers through it herself, but she forced herself to focus. How were they going to make money to live?

"I'll reopen the shop. I need a hand though," Sam said.

April smiled. "I've got a semester of experience in accounting. I can tackle the books." After all, accounting in 1852 couldn't be nearly as extensive as the present day.

"Great. I'd like to expand too. Instead of just tools, repairs, and horseshoes, I'd like to add art pieces."

"I think that's a great idea. This is going to be so much better than Artstreet."

April and Sam strolled out to the workshop and opened the big bay door, light pouring in like a dam exploding on a river. April coughed with the dust. Doug nosed around the shop and sneezed regularly.

Then she saw it, and its beauty stole her breath. An iron sculpture, similar to the dancing lady but almost life-size. The curves of the metal and twists of the ends were magnificent. "It's stunning."

"I was inspired," he said, "by you."

"That needs to be seen. Put it out front, like a business sign. It'll draw crowds."

"It's not a monument or anything. It's just a hunk of metal I bent."

"Don't be so modest."

April cleaned for days and helped Sam build a nice addition to the front of the shop. Most of that help was in the form of holding this, handing that, finding that other thing, and bringing a glass of water, but she loved it. They had an office and another space for the gallery which opened more space for Sam's workshop. After a couple weeks, the whole place was ready for business. April made advertising fliers to pass around Bridgeport and for the towns over—Astor and Navarino.

Their first customers were Sarah and Lloyd. Sarah's belly was showing now. April noticed she spent a lot of time rubbing it, just like Becca had. April watched her with new interest. April's belly stirred and her clit throbbed.

Lloyd wrapped his arm around Sarah's shoulders protectively. "Thank you for everything, April, and Sam too. We never would've had our little family without you," Lloyd patted Sarah's belly too.

"Don't mention it," April said, dismissing the compliments. "We only did what we could, and not everyone would agree with you." Like Grignon, Jaime, the twins, and Joe and Rob.

"Without Grignon taking his cut, we could pay off my contract with Jonathan Arris," Sarah said. "We're getting married at the courthouse in Navarino next week. We're leaving for the journey this afternoon."

"Congratulations!" April said and hugged her. She was thrilled for the two of them.

Sarah glanced at her hand, and April tucked it under the counter. She had removed the ring any time she was cleaning to protect it, despite Sam's objections, and they hadn't told anyone yet. She didn't know how Sarah would react.

"Sam proposed, I take it," Sarah said. "That was Nana's ring. It's a real stunner."

April admired the jewel and agreed. "It's beautiful."

"Can we browse Sam's art? We have a space above the fireplace that needs a feminine touch," Sarah said. Lloyd smiled in support.

April showed them through the door to the gallery, and Sarah gasped. Lloyd grunted in surprise. Rows and rows of black glistening sculptures, some freestanding, some wall mount, all beautiful and twisted curves.

Lloyd selected one, but Sarah shook her head. She selected another and Lloyd nodded. They paid for their piece and left, holding hands.

April smiled as they walked away. They were so happy, as was she.

Sam came through the door from the shop and saw them leaving. He was sweaty and covered with streaks of dirt. Her chest flashed in heat, and the throbbing returned. He was so damned sexy.

"How are they doing?" Sam asked.

"Great. Really great. They bought a piece for Lloyd's fireplace."

"Aye, there was definitely something missing there." Sam chuckled.

"Say, do you think we can call it an early lunch? I'm a bit hungry."

Sam smiled mischievously. They kissed, grasping each other with a passion she'd only read about. April shuffled them both toward the front door, while continuing their kissing, and flipped the open sign to closed.

Sam picked her up and brought her into the gallery and closed the door. He pressed her against it and loosened his belt buckle. April lifted her pink dress layers. Now she understood why dresses were so popular. He dropped his pants, displaying an ever-impressive erection, and Sam claimed her body against the door. Gripping her hips, he steadily thrusted. April kissed his neck and ear, and her fingers climbed up his shirt for his nipples. Sam moaned in pleasure and moved faster.

April arched in ecstasy. "Sam..." she said between pants and thrusts. "Let's get married now. We can tag along with Lloyd and Sarah."

Sam said, "The sooner the better. I can't wait to make babies with you."

His thrusts sped up until he collapsed against her in satisfaction, sweaty and panting. Sam gave her light kisses along her chest and neck, jawline to her lips. Now was the time. She was sure.

She held his face in both her hands and stared him in the eyes. "We already did."

She intertwined her fingers with his and brought his hand down to her lower belly, still too early to show.

The lines of Sam's face eased for the first time since he passed out on his couch. He was relaxed and happy, and Sam shouted with excitement. He immediately kissed her hungrily, ready for another round. She laughed, throbbing in all the right places but still ready for more.

Epilogue
Four weeks earlier...

JAIME PEREZ COUGHED WHEN the wind found his lungs again. His body felt like a butchered cow. He rolled onto his side so that the rain wouldn't drown him, and he winced with pain. Townspeople were leaving him, whispering and staring. Anger boiled in his gut. Sam had showed him mercy, so Jaime would let his brother-in-law live in peace, but he would not give that same blessing to April.

After what she'd done to him in Greenleaf, he wouldn't let her get away so easily, or at all. Jaime would've accomplished his revenge had Dennis not interrupted him in Grignon's study. He could still feel the slick of her blood on his leather belt. He wanted more.

A pair of hands reached under his arms and hoisted him skyward. His head flopped forward in its weakened state.

"Jaime, can ya stand?" He heard Joe Pool's voice, and his glazed eyes sought him out. Jaime's body never hurt so much in his life.

"Joe," Jaime confirmed. He swung his eyes to his companion. "Rob. What happened?"

"April messed ya up good, eh?" Joe chuckled.

Jaime's veins pounded in a rage. He hoped no one saw him lose. "No," Jaime said through gritted teeth. "What happened with the crowd?"

"Grignon's dead," Joe said.

"And the twins too," Rob finished. "Now what?"

Jaime smiled. "Looks like there's a job opening, and I happen to be in need. Will you agree to work for me?"

Rob and Joe exchanged glances, and Rob shrugged.

"We will," Joe agreed. "What'll we 'gon do first, boss?"

Jaime's smile darkened. He needed to settle Greenleaf, but first, he would gain control of Bridgeport and Astor. Grignon had never bothered with the towns over the bridge, but that was where the old man went wrong.

"Let's introduce ourselves to the staff at Grignon's estate. New residents are moving in."

DEAR READER,

Find out Jaime's fate in Mathew McCall and Verity Arris's story **Hours to Arrive (Matchmaker in Time Book 2)!**

As an indie author, I'm thrilled you decided to share your time with me, exploring the crazy worlds residing in my head and keeping me up at night. Your reviews are very important to me, so if you enjoyed this book, please consider leaving some stars for April and Sam's story, **Seconds to Act (Matchmaker in Time Book 1).**

Don't forget Kiko's backstory in **Minutes to Live (Matchmaker in Time Book 0.5).**

If you found any typos or errors, I blame my cat. Rat her out at: support@stephanieflynn.com.

Thank you for your support!

Also By Stephanie Flynn

Find my catalog at StephanieFlynn.com

Immortal Protector series

0.5 Vampire's Distraction

1 Vampire's Deception

2 Vampire's Secret

3 Vampire's Promise

3.5 Elf Bound

4 Vampire's Demand

Immortal Protector Side Tales

Deer Holiday

Love Claws

Depths of the Heart

Matchmaker in Time series

0.5 Minutes to Live

1 Seconds to Act

2 Hours to Arrive

3 Days to Hide
4 Years to Savor

Pirates in Time series
1 Pirate's Prize
2 Pirate's Treasure
3 Pirate's Plunder

Time Travel Romance Shorts
Fateful Time
One Crazy Time

If you like your urban fantasy without the romance, too, check out Stephanie Flynn's other name, Marie Flynn!

About Stephanie Flynn

Stephanie Flynn writes action-packed paranormal romance filled with adventure, suspense, and danger. She lives in Michigan, USA, with her husband and kids, and she spends her writing time surrounded by a herd of normal cats who bat everything off her desk, including her coffee. Check out her website for more books: StephanieFlynn.com